Praise for *The Batter's Box*

"Andy Kutler has the eyes and ears of combat soldiers and the heart of those who love them. The horror, courage, and camaraderie of battle rivals the grit of *Once an Eagle*, while the poignant authenticity of Will Jamison's struggles with his hidden wounds highlight that, for many, the impact of war lingers far past the last shots of battle. *The Batter's Box* is a superb work of historical fiction that carries important lessons for today."

—William E. Rapp, Major General, U.S. Army (Ret.),
Former Commandant, U.S. Army War College

"*The Batter's Box* is historical fiction but emotionally real. Anyone who has experienced or led soldiers in combat understands the untellable horrors, traumatic sensory overload, and emotional depravity of war. Andy Kutler weaves baseball, combat, and the deep relationship between an emotionally scarred couple to show how even when dreams may change, the human spirit has the capacity to rebound."

—Mark Hertling, Lieutenant General, U.S. Army (Ret.),
Former Commander, U.S. Army Europe and Seventh Army

"Regardless of what it is called throughout history—shell shock, battle fatigue or post-traumatic stress disorder—it continues to be an issue that is not discussed or treated as openly as it should be. *The Batter's Box* shows that while this is not a new phenomenon, it is one that must be addressed openly and with compassion if we are truly to fulfill President Lincoln's promise to care for those 'who shall have borne the battle' and their families."

—Richard M. Lake, Major General, U.S. Marine Corps (Ret.),
Former Director of Intelligence, USMC

"Historical fiction, if it reflects careful scholarship, is a powerful tool in the hands of a gifted writer, and can deepen our understanding of real events and people. Andy Kutler's *The Batter's Box* offers an impressive addition to World War II literature, bringing fresh attention to the adjustment struggle faced by so many returning war veterans. Kutler's depiction of one of the more heroic small-unit engagements in U.S. Army history is both compelling and long overdue."

—Gordon H. "Nick" Mueller, President & CEO Emeritus,
The National WWII Museum

"We remember World War II as 'the Good War,' when right and wrong seemed so clear. We won, they lost, and our guys came home as heroes. But as gifted author Andy Kutler tells us in *The Batter's Box*, mortal combat is anything but good, heroism comes with a horrific price, and some of the most tragic wounds don't bleed—and don't go away. If you want to know what really happened at Bastogne in the terrible winter of 1944, read this powerful, haunting book."

—Daniel P. Bolger, Lieutenant General, U.S. Army (Ret.)
Author of *Our Year of War: Two Brothers, Vietnam, and a Nation Divided*

"A creative, compelling, and profound piece of historical fiction, you won't be able to put this book down."

—Tim Kurkjian, Senior Analyst/Writer, ESPN

"*The Batter's Box* is a riveting read. It is a love story and a war story and a novel with far more truth than fiction. I'm a psychiatrist specializing in treating men and women with post-traumatic stress disorder. If you love someone with that invisible wound, read this book. If you are curious and concerned about the condition, read this book. Most survivors of profound trauma lack a language to convey their life stories because those stories include the unspeakable. When the hero of this compelling novel speaks, we listen, we learn and we are transformed. If you are currently struggling with the impact of major trauma, reading passages here may be disturbing and 'triggering.' But I believe it is worth the risk because this book affirms your reality and your dignity."

—Frank M. Ochberg, MD, Former Associate Director,
National Institute of Mental Health

"Enjoy gripping tales of World War II? Heroic sports sagas well told? Or just a fine novel full of engaging characters? *The Batter's Box* gives readers all three and more. I enjoyed every page I read of this epic story. Highly recommended!"

—Ralph Peters, award-winning author of *Cain at Gettysburg*

"*The Batter's Box* is a thoughtful and imaginative look at a conveniently hidden part of our history—the psychic wounds carried by The Greatest Generation. The battle scenes are a taut mix of fear, tension and chaos."

—Ed Ruggero, author of *The First Men In:*
U.S. Paratroopers and the Fight to Save D-Day

THE
BATTER'S BOX

by Andy Kutler

WARRIORS PUBLISHING GROUP
NORTH HILLS, CALIFORNIA

THE BATTER'S BOX

A Warriors Publishing Group book/published
by arrangement with the author

PRINTING HISTORY
Warriors Publishing Group edition/March 2019

Warriors Publishing Group
16129 Tupper Street
North Hills, California 91343

Library of Congress Control Number: 2019900026
ISBN 978-1-944353-21-6

10 9 8 7 6 5 4 3 2 1

PUBLISHER'S NOTE

For my father

What better gifts to
pass on to a son than a
love of baseball and
a passion for history.

Kay couldn't have scripted the timing better. She heard the distant crunch of tires easing to a stop in the gravel parking lot just as she finished her final chapter.

That was the only positive. As she lowered the book into her lap and heard the quiet thud of a car door slamming, she questioned for the hundredth time the wisdom of agreeing to meet with this man. The truth shall make you free, went the storied Bible verse, one that Kay reminded herself of a week ago when the man first called. Now, she had her doubts.

It was a brisk mid-week morning, and though the skies were overcast, the forecast was for dry weather, an anomaly for the Pacific Northwest on the brink of springtime. She sat before an array of youth baseball fields, each as pristine and well-groomed as any major league stadium in the country, nestled among some of the most prized real estate in Portland. At least by Kay. Her folding camp chair was perched on the crest of a hill that ran parallel to the third base line of the main playing field. It gave her a commanding view of the entire venue, a rambling outdoor sports facility that stretched across nearly 16 acres in Northwest Portland.

There were heavy footsteps and Kay twisted in her chair, catching her first glimpse of the visitor. Everything about the bulky man said informality, from his sheepish, apologetic smile to the faded jeans and half-zip pullover he wore. She also took note of his age, probably close to 50, and thus no cub reporter. More fuel for her trepidation.

A crisp breeze floated by and Kay pulled the blanket higher in her lap. Under a light coat she was dressed casually, with a navy cardigan sweater over an Oxford shirt and khaki slacks. Her elegance hadn't diminished even the slightest through the decades. She sat up straight as a ramrod and wore her thick, silvery hair neatly combed and pulled back into a single braid, accentuating the sort of graceful neck and high cheekbones that could have portended a past modeling career.

"Hope I didn't keep you waiting, ma'am. No one warned me about I-5."

"Mr. Maloney, I presume?" Kay asked, pulling off a pair of wire-rimmed reading glasses affixed to a gold chain around her neck. Her eyes shimmered with vitality and intelligence. "Please call me Kay. You'll forgive me for not standing."

"You're forgiven," the man smiled, taking note of the collapsible walker at her feet and the aluminum cane hooked over the chair's backrest. He clasped her outstretched hand. "And thank you for agreeing to meet with me. I know it was an unusual request."

She gestured toward an oblong canvas bag on the ground.

"I brought you Will's old chair. Do you know how to set it up?"

"Seems like all I do on the weekends," Maloney chuckled. "My sister drags me to every one of her kid's lacrosse games."

He removed the folding chair from the canvas case, pulling apart the accordion-like apparatus and placing it next to Kay's.

"Quite a view here," he remarked, lowering his girth into the chair.

"You should come back this evening. The defending city champions are playing."

"The kids play in March?" Maloney asked, surprised. He gestured to one of the fields further away, where a lone caretaker was taking advantage of a rare break in the rains to give the outfields a trim. The man sat atop his John Deere, steering the mower into a time-tested pattern that would not miss a single blade. "Is that why the landscape guy is cutting the grass?"

Kay laughed. "He's the groundskeeper, not a 'landscape guy'. Volunteers here a few days a week. Things have changed a bit since you were a child. They play from early spring to late fall now."

Maloney grunted. "Everything has changed since I was a child."

"So," Kay smiled, "you're writing a story about the old Washington Senators?"

"Just the 1945 team. As I said on the phone, we have a new team in Washington, the Nationals, and my editors want to do a story on the 60th anniversary of the '45 team. A feature story, above the fold. Thought it might stir up interest as we get closer to Opening Day."

And what are you stirring up here, Mr. Maloney?

The Internet had much to say about him. He was no sportswriter, having manned the Metro desk for the *Washington Post* since he was a junior stringer fresh out of journalism school at Columbia. His rise in the newsroom was meteoric, and within a few years he developed into an award-winning investigative journalist and crack researcher. He was reputed to own an endless trove of well-placed sources and a flair for old-fashioned intuition.

"So, what made you think to seek me out? My husband wasn't on that 1945 team."

"I spoke to one of Will's old teammates, Dick Holloway."

"Dick Holloway! How is Dick? As incorrigible as ever?"

"He's not well, I'm afraid. His heart is failing."

Kay's face fell. "Oh."

"I'm sorry," Maloney said, his regret seemingly genuine. "I thought you'd want to know."

Kay sighed heavily. "You get to be my age, Mr. Maloney, you hear such news too frequently."

She hadn't seen Dick in decades and could only recall a man so full of life and energy. He was one of the great athletes of an older generation, a borderline Hall of Famer who played professionally for more than two decades. When his baseball career ended, he took to selling life insurance for a small agency in upstate New York, living out the rest of his life with his wife in Ithaca. They had no children, and when Judith succumbed to cancer in 1993, he was all alone. Twelve years by himself, most at the misnamed Hopewell Gardens, where Kay's husband had visited him years ago. When he returned to Portland, Will had described the nursing home in the grimmest of terms, the facility resembling a set piece from *One Flew Over the Cuckoo's Nest.*

"It took some prying, but Holloway filled in a lot of the back story about your husband. What he was like before the war, how he'd changed after he came back. Said he had no idea where Will Jamison ended up, or whether he was even alive. But he left me with the best advice I'd ever heard on this job."

"What was it?"

"He told me to find the girl."

Kay gave him a wide smile.

"I know I said it already on the phone, but you have my sincere condolences. How long has it been?"

Kay looked away. "Too long, Mr. Maloney. It seems like Will was just here, sitting beside me, holding my hand." She closed her eyes for several moments, then straightened in her chair and turned toward Maloney.

"May I ask, why the interest in Will? There are plenty of veterans out there who have suffered as he did. You could have spoken to any of them. Books have come out–"

"He walked away."

Kay's face darkened. "I beg your pardon?"

"Your husband. He walked away. The Senators came within a game and a half of the pennant in 1945. Without him. They didn't lose any of their top players the next year, and got three starters back from the war, including their all-star, Will Jamison. A month into the '46 season, he works his way back into the starting lineup. Catches fire after that, and then one day just walks away from it all. Disappears."

The old woman said nothing, directing her eyes away again from Maloney.

"Ma'am?"

"You did your homework, Mr. Maloney."

"Not that well. He literally disappeared. I checked our archives.

The team said he was quitting baseball, suggested his heart wasn't in it anymore. There was speculation that maybe he hadn't recovered yet from his war wound. But that doesn't make sense, since he was playing so well."

Kay shook her head in confusion. "I thought you were writing an article about the '45 team. Will wasn't with the team in '45. He didn't return from Europe until the season was nearly over."

"You're right. My story is about the '45 Senators. But that's for the *Post*. Whatever you can tell me about your husband, well, that's just for me."

"But why? Why your interest in Will?"

Maloney leaned forward. "The man had it all before the war. An all-star, on top of his game, with money, fame, women. He enlists in the Army after Pearl Harbor. He doesn't wait until 1943 or 1944 like most other major league players. He signs up in January of 1942, a month after Congress declares war. He asks for front-line duty. Wins a Silver Star during the Battle of the Bulge. Comes home, and plays well enough to be an all-star again, then just walks away. Never to be heard from again. And only twenty-eight years old."

Kay studied the reporter closely. She felt the intensity behind his words.

"This is important to you. Personally. Why?"

Maloney sat back, silent. He had never spoken of this to anyone before. Not even his ex-wife.

"Mr. Maloney?"

"My dad was in Vietnam," Maloney began uneasily. "5th Marines. He was a company first sergeant. Saw some real hell at a place called Hue City during the Tet Offensive. I was twelve when he left, fourteen when he came back. He wasn't the same after he returned. Walked out on us for a while. He eventually came back, but he was drunk most days. Probably why he couldn't hold a job in civilian life. He wasn't the dad I knew as a kid. The one who took me to every 'Skins home game, taught me how to fish on the Chesapeake. By the time I was finishing high school, we hardly talked at all. And then…he died. The man was barely forty years old, younger than I am now. He never told me what happened in Vietnam. But something over there changed him."

Maloney paused, swallowing his emotion, staring ahead. Finally, he shook his head, unable to continue.

"I just want to know what makes a man like your husband walk away from everything. And everyone."

"Not everyone," Kay said. She took a deep breath before patting Maloney's hand gently, deciding it was time to trust her own intuition. "I assume you're aware it's not the cheeriest of stories."

She smoothed the blanket in her lap as she considered her next words. "Where do I begin?"

She slowly looked up, past Maloney, a smile spreading across her face. There was something in her eyes, a flicker of light perhaps, and she was suddenly warmed by a flood of memories from another time slowly coming into focus. She finally set her eyes back on his, and there was an entirely new demeanor, her exuberance unmistakable, as if she was suddenly decades younger.

"Have you ever been to Philadelphia?"

1942

Chapter 1

It was known by most as the City of Brotherly Love. Not, however, by the pair of brawny, white-clad sailors that had cornered a street tough on the train platform. The petty officers pummeled the thief with haymakers, making clear the policy of the United States Navy on pickpockets as police whistles shrilled across the station.

Will Jamison smiled to himself. This was the Philadelphia he remembered.

As was the backdrop. When Will joined the Washington Senators in 1938, he was surprised to learn there was little love among his veteran teammates for the monotonous road swings that marked their lives from April to September. Back then, as an awestruck 20-year-old from rural Wisconsin, Will took a different view. He looked forward to the travel as much as he did the games, luxuriating in First Class cars before filing through the stately depots in each city. He even treasured the train stations themselves, finding no two in America were alike, each a microcosm of the city they served. Vibrant, gritty, and humming with life.

Nowhere was this truer than the 30th Street Station in Philadelphia. A modern marvel, the facility featured an elaborate electronic intercom system, emergency medical space, and even a reinforced concrete roof over the main concourse where small biplanes could land. It was said Amelia Earhart touched down there once.

Just off the ticket lobby was the station's only bar. Will shouldered his way to the doorway, swimming upstream against the chaotic parade of commuters stampeding toward the trains. The entire station was mobbed with businessmen, families, soldiers, and sailors, all knifing their way past one another with matching urgency and sharp elbows.

Will sighed to himself. Beginning an amorous weekend with drinks at a raucous East Coast rail hub on an early Friday evening was not one of his more inspired ideas.

He pushed through the glass door, the space dimly lit and larger than he expected. There were few available seats at either the bar or the tables, his fellow travelers seeming to prefer a stiff drink to the stiff benches in the central waiting area. His view of the bar's interior was obscured by a curtain of tobacco smoke that dulled the glow of the glass-encased candles on each table. He didn't see her at first, but he knew she was there, her train having arrived from New York nearly an hour ago. Philadelphia was a logical meeting point, roughly halfway between her home in New York and his final destination in Washington. Close enough to make an overnight trip worthwhile. Large enough to provide the anonymity they each required.

At 24 now, Will was one of the most famous professional athletes in the region. By name, at least. Only those who came out to the stadiums would recognize him in person though, and here in Philadelphia, that served as a blessing. Avoiding the public spotlight was often a challenge for Will, particularly when he was in Washington.

For what he had planned this evening, it was imperative.

He stepped to the side to allow a departing family to whisk by with their baggage. The pair of teenage girls trailing their parents gaped at him before covering their mouths and sharing a giggle. At an imposing six-foot-three, Will was used to it. He was what women thought of as a rugged man, broad-shouldered with a lean frame, though far from handsome, with an angular face, thin nose and pointed chin. His almond-shaped eyes were easily his best feature, a shade of blue his mother often described as two pieces of sky. The sandy-brown locks that once peeked out from the bill of his ball cap were now shorn close on the sides and back, blending evenly with the garrison cap he wore tipped at an angle. Will knew that few would mistake him for a cinema idol, but he had learned to laugh off such thoughts years ago. He was an ascending Major League Baseball star, and in 1942, that made him akin to American royalty.

Will wanted to stretch his back, still sore from the 700-mile trip from Indiana. No longer an impressionable rookie, the shine on rail travel had lost its luster, especially now that he was traveling on the government's dime. Consigned to Third Class, where the passengers were packed in like cattle, he had little to do but gaze out at a country still bearing the scars of the Great Depression, a bleak tapestry of dilapidated housing, shuttered factories, and other economic wreckage.

Still, visiting grand cities such as Philadelphia, New York, and Boston remained intoxicating for Will. The entire population of his hometown in southwestern Wisconsin could fit comfortably within a single city block of any of the sprawling metropolises. Even Chattanooga, where Will spent nearly three seasons playing minor league ball in Washington's farm system, had been an enlightening experience to a young man hundreds of miles from home.

He was just a teenager, less than a year out of high school, when he arrived in Tennessee. It took some time for Will to acclimate to his new environs, particularly the searing summer heat of the South, where he nearly melted under the weight of his catcher's gear and the unforgiving glare of the sweltering Tennessee sun.

It took no time, however, for Will to acclimate to minor league pitching, lacing balls all over the field from his very first swing as a professional. And throughout those initial, invigorating months as a Chattanooga Lookout, Will discovered a new pursuit, one that had eluded him during most of his adolescence back home.

Young ladies from across eastern Tennessee flocked to the home games at Engel Stadium, batting their eyelashes at the budding athletes who might someday be promoted to the major leagues. More than a few were drawn to the tall, powerfully built player from Wisconsin with the muscled shoulders and earnest smile.

Will was quickly showered with warnings from his new teammates, who shared cautionary tales of local girls latching onto what they hoped might be a ticket out of Tennessee. He turned a deaf ear, too enthralled by the newfound attention he was receiving from these bold, shapely young women whose accents and charms shattered his meager defenses. He soon found himself with a debutante hooked on each arm, his social life and confidence soaring, right alongside his batting average.

It was the latter that captured the attention of Ted Haynes, chief of scouting for the Washington Senators. In May of 1938, a day after watching Will catch all 18 innings of a doubleheader on a blistering hot day, Haynes awakened Will at his boarding house in the pre-dawn hours, tossing the dazed player a one-way train ticket to Washington and giving him ten minutes to pack everything he owned.

It took less than two. Will was making $30 a week back then. His worldly belongings included his clothes, his playing gear, and nothing else.

Once Will arrived at Washington's Union Station with his sparse belongings, he was ferried by limousine to the team offices in the Senators' home stadium. Ushered into the private suite of Clark Griffith, the sprightly owner wasted little time in signing Will to his first major league contract. Only afterward was the need for urgency explained, a rash of injuries having felled both the starting catcher and his backup. Before the ink was dry on his contract, the team threw Will to the wolves, starting him in his very first game as a Senator. Against the New York Yankees.

He finished that rookie season with a .261 average. Hardly an earth-shattering number, but promising enough for team officials, convinced the rookie's swing would make the eventual adjustment to big league pitching. They also coveted his catching acumen and Howitzer-like arm, as well as his mastery of blocking Dick Holloway's notorious screwball.

The team's faith in Will's abilities paid better-than-expected dividends in the years that followed. By the end of the 1941 season, his batting average had climbed to a stellar .340, second-best in the American League. His electrifying season that year was overshadowed by other historic feats, namely Ted Williams conquering the mystical .400 barrier and Joe DiMaggio's unprecedented string of hits in 56 consecutive games. It was little wonder Will Jamison had still not become a household name outside Washington, a relatively small town among the pantheon of major league cities.

And it wouldn't start now. Just nine months after his last hit in Griffith Stadium that capped the '41 season, Will wasn't suiting up for the diamond. His home whites with the blue piping had been traded months ago for the olive drab service jacket and trousers he now wore as an enlisted man in the United States Army, leaving him nearly unrecognizable in a train station teeming with hundreds of men in similar uniforms.

Unrecognizable. Will smiled to himself. *Perfect.*

Chapter 2

Will's gaze settled on the bar. Even with her back to him, his prize was easy to sight. She was engrossed in a book, as always, but almost the second Will spotted her, she turned, glancing over her bare shoulder, her porcelain skin clearly visible in the muted light. Her eyes found his and he felt the usual jolt, the same jarring sensation as the day they first met nearly three years ago.

Even in the dreariest of surroundings, Kay Barlow was still a stunner. Just 22, she was slender and tall, an inch or two under six feet, with long, athletic legs sculpted by years of classical dance that began in her youth. The light from a nearby candle glinted off the sequined black cocktail dress she wore, two thin straps crisscrossing her shoulders. Her dark, luminous hair had just a tint of red to it, like a dull penny. It was perfectly coiffed and fell astride one eye, a seductive look made popular recently by another Brooklyn native, the young actress Veronica Lake. A touch of color emphasized her high cheekbones, and her full, sensuous lips were lightly coated in crimson.

Will crossed the room, unshouldering his green Army duffel and setting it next to her valise. He leaned in to kiss her cheek, pausing as his lips pressed against her face to savor everything about her. She smelled marvelously familiar, her lavender-scented hair mixing with the Elizabeth Arden perfume on her neck. Her skin was velvety and soft as cotton. He reluctantly pulled away, climbing onto the seat next to her.

"Well hello, Mr. Jamison."

"Hello, Mrs. Barlow."

He tapped the book sitting next to her on the bar. "*The Last Tycoon*? I hope that's not what you're looking for in a man. I'm on the Army's payroll now."

"Then I guess the first round is on me. Do you know Fitzgerald?"

"Yep. Donald L. St. Louis Browns. Lousy shortstop."

She laughed, an almost musical sound he missed these last eight months. "More like F. Scott, the writer. He died a couple of years ago. This was his last book."

"Does it have a happy ending?"

"I'll let you know. How was your train?"

He desperately wanted to tear off her clothes, and she was asking him about his trip from Indiana.

"What's so funny?"

"My trip was fine," he said, quickly erasing the smirk. "Yours?"

"About as comfy as a tin of sardines. The train was full of soldiers and sailors. I had to sit in the cafe car, where I was pawed by a drunken horde of Free Masons."

That she had attracted attention from male passengers was hardly a surprise. But he also knew that a man's brusque and unmannerly hands were the last thing Kay wanted touching her. She had enough of that at home.

"I'm guessing the drunken horde could see well enough. Perhaps that dress was a mistake."

She looked at him playfully, and he loved the way her eyes squinted every time she did so. "Do you think it was a mistake?"

"I would never, ever call that dress a mistake."

Kay gave him an approving smile. "Nicely done, Mr. Jamison. I see that the Army hasn't dulled you at all." She gestured toward the two stripes on his jacket sleeve. "They made you a sergeant."

"Corporal," he corrected.

"Are you done with training?"

"We finished basic in April, and we're still waiting to be assigned to a new division. Probably why they gave us these 10-day furloughs."

"You said on the telephone you had to go to Washington. Why?"

Will shrugged. "Promised the team I'd stop by. It was either Washington, or go see my folks in Wisconsin."

"Why didn't you? Wisconsin, that is."

"I saw them after I graduated from basic."

She looked at him expectantly, waiting to hear more.

"What?"

"Why don't you want to see your family again?"

"If I went to Wisconsin, I wouldn't be sitting here."

"Surprise," she said sourly. "A dodge."

The bartender appeared, offering Will a brief stay.

"Two glasses of champagne," he ordered.

"Well, well," Kay said, pushing away the glass of club soda she had been sipping. "What are we celebrating?"

"Victory in the Pacific," he said, watching the bartender pour. "Defeating the Nazis. How this night will end."

Other women might have blushed, but not Kay. She merely shook her head, feigning offense at his audacity as they clinked their glasses and sipped the champagne.

"Well, at least you have your priorities in order, Wilson James."

He grinned. *Wilson James.* In a fit of nervousness, that was how he introduced himself that August day three years ago when they first met. He had left his teammates at their hotel in the Bronx, choosing to breakfast at Siegel's, a local delicatessen he found just blocks from Yankee Stadium. The two were seated next to each other at the counter, and when she introduced herself as Kay Barlow, it didn't take Will long to make the connection. Eddie Barlow was a thickset, career journeyman mired in mediocrity. The New York Yankee, Will learned later, was also an alcoholic who often took out his on-field struggles on his wife, who he married when she was just 18.

That morning at Siegel's began the single most unforgettable day in Will's life. As that first conversation unfolded, they both sensed an extraordinary connection, like two lifelong friends reunited after years apart. She was young, not even 20 yet, but surprisingly streetwise and full of wit and insight, and she made him laugh, sharing stories of her working-class upbringing in Brooklyn as the only child of two tightly wound music instructors. Hour after hour passed, as Will became entranced by her poise, her genuine warmness, and those piercing, probing eyes.

Their breakfasts remained untouched. They stayed until Siegel's emptied for the lunch crowd and Will had to rejoin his team for a two o'clock game. As they walked out together, he realized he had never had a conversation like that with a woman, nor had he ever felt such a fierce, primal attraction. It was electric. They faced each other on the sidewalk, neither wanting to part, and Kay readily agreed to meet him afterward, on the other side of the Harlem River. That same evening, they brazenly strolled arm in arm through a light drizzle in Central Park, her husband just blocks away in their Upper West Side apartment. Three hours of effortless conversation later, the sprinkles of rain turned into a steady shower, and Will somehow found the daring to suggest they seek shelter at the nearby Park Central Hotel. Once there, they quickly stumbled into a night of fiery lovemaking that even Will's adventures in Tennessee had not prepared him for. It was also when he first saw the discoloration on her arms and back.

A shrieking train whistle from outside the bar brought Will back, and he pushed away the flute.

"What is it?"

"Is he still hitting you?"

Kay blinked, surprised by the abrupt change in conversation. She turned away, pursing her lips in embarrassment. After a few moments, she faced him again, attempting a wry smile.

"He stopped using his fists."

"You think that's funny?"

"No, Will," she said sharply. "I don't think that's funny. Not when he throws me up against a wall. Not when he slaps me on the side of the head." Kay stopped, and then her voice was quieter. "Not when he shoves me through a glass door."

Will felt his whole body tense. "He did that?"

She nodded, unable to meet his eyes. "The first year we were married. I was in Bellevue for three days."

Will's hand tightened around the stem of his glass. There was a tension-filled silence, until she finally placed a hand on his, caressing it gently.

"Can we start over? We have so little time, and I didn't take a train all the way to Philadelphia to talk about my husband."

Will didn't want to talk about him either. They both knew why they were here, and that it would never lead to anything lasting. And still Will felt so strangely protective of her. The only pinstripes Eddie Barlow deserved to wear were from a penitentiary.

"Why won't you leave him?"

She sighed. "We've talked about that. It's not that simple."

"Why not?"

"Where would I go? Back to Brooklyn? No, thank you."

"Come to Washington."

She smiled. "You're sweet, Will. But you don't live there anymore."

"I could set you up. Rent you a place. No one would know."

She shook her head. "He would find out. Please, Will. It's my life. And I can take care of myself."

Obviously, he thought dryly, but kept that to himself.

Kay reached into her purse and pulled out a pack of Chesterfields. She placed one between her lips as the sharp-eyed bartender struck a match and touched the flame to the tobacco. She was inhaling the rich smoke when Will suddenly leaned over and plucked the cigarette from her fingers, mashing it into a glass ashtray.

She glowered at him, incredulous, her hand still hanging in the air. But there was amusement in her eyes, his distaste for tobacco smoke well-known, and at once they both seemed to breathe easier, the mood lightened.

"You know, in the movies, the gentleman lights the cigarette for the lady."

He grinned. "I think we both know I'm no gentleman."

She lifted her glass and raised it in the air. "I think we need another toast. What shall we drink to? And don't say my dress."

Will loosened the knot in his tie and lifted his own glass. "How about to Siegel's Deli?"

"Bingo," she said, as they clinked their glasses again and sipped the sweet liquid.

"So, where will the evening take us, Will?"

"Well, I came up with a couple of options."

"Good. I like options."

"Let's start with Plan A."

She leaned in. "Tell me about it."

"It starts with the table I have reserved at Bookbinder's. Heard of it?"

"No. I've never been outside this train station. I'm a New York girl."

"Oldest restaurant in the city. Down by the docks. Biggest lobsters you'll ever see. They serve them in pools of butter."

"Mmm," she said, drumming her manicured nails on the bar. "An aphrodisiac. Sounds like a good start."

"After dinner, we go to a place called the Candlestick Room near Washington Square. They have a jazz trio on Friday nights."

Kay brightened. "Where we can dance?"

"I don't dance."

"Then why would you want to go there?"

"Good point. We'll skip that and go right to the nightcap. In our room at the Carleton, one of the city's best."

"I have to admit, I like Plan A. The wine and dine plan."

He put one foot on the floor. "Well, we can leave–"

Kay clasped his forearm. "Not on your life, mister. You said I have options. What's Plan B?"

Will returned to his seat with feigned exasperation. "Oh, all right. Plan B."

He waited a moment, his face serious now as he regarded her jade-colored eyes with a quiet intensity that made the back of her neck tingle with anticipation.

"Plan B is we go to the Carleton right now. And maybe stop and pick you up a change of clothes."

"I thought you liked this dress."

"I love that dress. But once the room door closes, no way does it come off in one piece."

This time, Kay blushed. But her eyes had not moved away from his and he felt the energy and passion that was already surging between them.

"Well, Will, that is not much of a plan. Not as...sophisticated... as the first one."

"No, but perhaps a bit more...spontaneous. It's been eight months, you know."

She tapped her chin with her index finger in mock deliberation. "Both of these plans have merit. How will I choose?"

"Let me help you," he said, leaning into her and dropping his voice almost to a whisper. "What color underwear are you wearing?"

Kay's cheeks colored again, and Will could never have imagined himself speaking to a woman in such a manner just a few years ago. But with his stardom in Washington came self-confidence. And he always felt more emboldened with Kay, well-versed in her proclivities.

"I'm going to guess that you're wearing black."

"That's a pretty good guess. You read palms too?"

"My experience tells me that women tend to wear black underwear when they have certain...expectations."

She scowled in indignation. "Exactly how much *experience* do you have, mister? Maybe it's because I'm wearing a black dress."

His eyes glanced down at her long legs. "Black stockings. Silk or something else?"

A question that was shaped by the war effort. Synthetic stockings for woman were becoming more prevalent now that the government had rationed the public sale of silk. It was needed for parachutes.

"The former."

Will scratched his chin. "Garter or no garter?"

"Your nerve apparently knows no bounds. Garter, of course."

"Well, I vote for Plan B then."

Kay laughed. "I didn't know that was in doubt." She clicked her fingernails again on the bar. "Plan B does have its merits."

Will stood, draining his glass and pulling his money clip from his coat pocket. He tossed a few bills on the bar and picked up both their bags. "I have a car waiting."

She rose to her feet, collecting her wrap, her book, and small purse. "A car? You do think of everything, sir."

"Well," he said, as he led her to the door, "I do have a minor confession."

Kay stopped. "What's that?"

He looked back at her, offering a mischievous wink. "I never bothered to make a reservation at Bookbinder's."

Two hours later, Will and Kay were on the thickly carpeted floor of their palatial suite at the Carleton Inn, a posh waterfront hotel in Penn's Landing. Will lay on his side, clad only in his Army-issue, olive drab boxer shorts and dog tags, his head propped up with one hand while the other held a bottle of Coca Cola from the icebox. The rest of his uniform, along with Kay's dress and undergarments, were strewn across the floor in a trail leading from the door to the bed.

Kay was next to him, sitting with her back to the wall. They were each in a state of weary bliss, and Kay's eyelids were heavy as a ceiling fan noiselessly pushed a soft breeze across their legs. A corner of a bed sheet covered her, but only from the waist down. Next to Kay was a near-empty flute glass, barely visible in the faint glow of a nearby table lamp, as the gravelly voice of Louis Jordan carried from a radio across the suite.

"Thank you for sparing my dress."

"Only because I hope to see you in it again someday. No promises, next time."

"So, when are you meeting with the owner?"

"Griffith? Lunch tomorrow. Then I see the boys the next day."

"Do you miss it?"

"Baseball?" he asked, taking a long swallow from his soda pop. "A bit. They have a team at the base. The Army is practically begging me to play."

"If you miss it, why not play?"

He shrugged. "The way I see it, I can be a soldier or a ball player. But not both."

"And you want to be a soldier. Why?"

Will sat up next to her and leaned against the wall. "What do you want to do with your life, Kay?"

She curled her lip, the frustration etched on her face. "Is this going to circle back to why you enlisted, or are you just trying to change the subject?"

He grinned. "I'm just trying to change the subject."

Kay resisted the urge to pour what was left of her drink over Will's head, hardly the first time he had evaded a question that touched on the personal. She forced herself to set her emotions aside. They had precious little time left together, and Kay had promised herself to make the most of every minute this evening. Besides, she had unexpected news to deliver.

"I'm going to leave him."

Will looked at her in surprise. "Well, hallelujah. When did you decide that?"

"A few minutes ago."

"So, you leave. Then what?"

She shrugged. "Then I'll finish nursing school. I'll work at a nice hospital, bring comfort to those who need it, fall in love with an idealistic doctor and live happily ever after."

Will gave her a look of sadness. "What about me?"

She laughed. "You, mister, are not the marrying type. As you've reminded me nearly every time we're together. And your lack of conversation skills, beyond discussing the color of my underwear, would drive me up the wall."

"Obviously we are completely incompatible. So when is your current husband expecting you home?"

"My husband is on a road trip in Detroit and Cleveland."

"So, we have time for round two?"

"Well, if two rounds are all you have left..."

Will sat up, reaching for her glass and placing it with his empty bottle on a nearby coffee table. He then slipped his hands under the sheet and pulled Kay on to her back next to him, their faces inches apart.

"At some point, I'm going to need some dinner," she whispered, as Will's cheek touched hers, and his warm breath filled her ear. She tugged his boxer shorts off.

"Restaurant or room service?" he asked, pulling the sheet away and pressing himself against her. He waited for her to answer, but this was Plan B, and she was through with conversation, instead wrapping her legs around him, pulling him closer with sudden urgency.

Chapter 3

WASHINGTON, D.C.

"Hey Mac, we're here," rasped the driver, twisting his body to face the passenger slouched in the back of the cab.

Will stirred, rubbing the sleep from his eyes. It had been a long, vigorous night in Philadelphia, the hours with Kay passing like minutes. He hoped to catch some shuteye on the Capital Limited, and had just settled into his seat with his garrison cap pulled down low over his eyes when he was recognized by a passing porter. The man was giddy, and heartily pumped Will's hand as word quickly swept through the train jammed with Washingtonians. Autograph seekers and well-wishers engulfed the star player, and even after arriving at Union Station two hours later, a gaggle of children continued to fill the aisle.

Admittedly, Will relished the attention. He hadn't always in the past, when fleeting moments of solitude were too often lost to fans who thought a chance encounter was an opportune time to discuss the quality of left-handed relief pitchers on the Senators roster, or whether Buddy Myer or Jimmy Bloodworth had a better glove at second base. Shielded from such public mobbings for months, Will was surprised by how much he missed it all. Particularly from the kids. Will could never turn away from a star-struck youngster, gladly shaking every small hand that reached out and signing whatever magazine or scrap of paper was thrust his way.

His indulgence on the train that morning, however, left Will without a minute's rest, and he practically collapsed in the taxi once he reached Washington, his eyelids falling the second the car was in gear. The interior was ripe with the odor of the unbathed driver, yet Will dozed happily, comforted by the traces of Kay's perfume that lingered on his service jacket, and the memory of that final, impassioned embrace as they said their farewells, their trains heading in opposite directions.

Stifling a yawn, he paid the cabbie and exited the taxi. A liveried attendant from the restaurant waited patiently nearby, relieving Will of his Army duffel while holding an open door that allowed the aroma of roasting meat to tantalize those passing by during the noon hour. The Old Ebbitt Grill, just a block from the White House, had catered to the uppermost echelon of Washington power brokers for nearly a century. It was a favorite of American presidents from Ulysses Grant to Teddy Roosevelt, and each time Will passed through the grand doors, he was warmly welcomed by the doting staff. Though he was far less refined than the other patrons, he was also far less imperious.

He brushed past the mass of business-attired martini drinkers who packed the lengthy, polished mahogany bar. The stench of cigar smoke hovered in the air, along with the blare of boastful and self-important voices that rose up from the liquored-up bureaucrats and their benefactors. There were other servicemen in uniform besides Will, most with stars, eagles, and gold braid adorning their epaulets. Frowns crossed their faces when they spied the paltry stripes on Will's sleeve, sniffing at the offense of a common enlisted man forgetting his station and trespassing in their privileged sanctum.

Will found the maître d', the fussy man offering a short, deferential bow. He snapped his fingers and another attendant appeared, leading Will to a quiet corner of the restaurant, away from the din and smoke of the bar. An older man and younger woman awaited his arrival, both rising from their table in greeting.

"Will," bellowed the man, extending his hand. "Welcome home. Damn fine of you to join us."

Clark Griffith was the owner of the Washington Senators and the most renowned non-political figure in the city. He appeared every bit his 72 years, yet there was a strength and energy in the man's vise-like grip as he squeezed Will's hand. Griffith was decades past his prime, but Will could see the fire that still burned in the old ballplayer's eyes. Unlike most other team executives who came from private industry and inherited wealth, Griffith was a former player, a standout pitcher who began his professional career before the turn of the century. At his zenith, Griffith strung together six consecutive 20-win seasons, a notable feat in any era.

Commonplace at the time, Griffith was conferred with a small ownership stake when he was hired to manage the Senators in 1912. In later years, he mortgaged several land holdings in the West, raising enough capital to increase his equity in the franchise. He then partnered with a business associate to acquire a majority interest in the team, and with his partner's proxy, the enterprising Griffith found himself with sole control of 60 percent of the stock. The board astutely elected the plainspoken former player as team president and even renamed their stadium in his honor.

Remarkably fit, the Old Fox, his nickname around town, looked just like that. He wore a tailored gray, double-breasted suit, black wingtips with a high-gloss shine, and a red necktie knotted in a perfect Windsor. He had large ears, a pointed nose, and a long-sloping forehead. His neatly combed hair, a mane of silver, was slicked down with a scented pomade, and he owned two of the bushiest eyebrows Will had ever seen on a man.

"You remember my goddaughter?"

Will smiled at the woman on Griffith's left and took her proffered hand. "Ms. Pritchard, isn't it?"

Her blue eyes sparkled. "You have a good memory, Mr. Jamison. It's Vivian, please."

They took their seats and Will cast the woman a long look. She was in her early 30s and dressed conservatively in a charcoal skirt with a white blouse buttoned to her neck. Her shoulder-length, butterscotch hair was fastened in a tight bun, with a stylish hat perched on top. She had a round face and pleasant smile, and the sort of well-proportioned figure most men fancied, Will included.

While her apparel and cultured manner suggested a prim and demure woman, Will knew Vivian Pritchard was anything but. Her story was well-known in Washington's loftier circles. A Vassar girl and daughter of a corner-cutting industrialist who managed to prosper during the Depression, Vivian came to Washington as an administrative aide to a California congressman her father patronized. In time, she was appointed to a staff slot on the committee, a rarity for her gender, and the Washington rumor mill quickly became rife with speculation as to how such a fetching young woman could have secured that sort of prized position. Exasperated with the insinuation and lewd gossip, Vivian sought counsel from her godfather, who recognized her financial wizardry and astute negotiating skills. He lured Vivian to the team, offering a role with substance where she oversaw much of the team's payroll. Her standing in the organization today was an extraordinary accomplishment, and Will doubted there was a single other woman working in the senior offices of any of the other major league teams.

As the trio exchanged small talk, a waiter arrived, delivering glass dishes brimming with fresh shrimp and wedges of lemon. They went to work on their appetizers as another waiter filled their glasses with iced tea. The shrimp cocktail was delicious, the sauce spiced with horseradish and Worcestershire. Yet Will tasted little of it, his thoughts drifting back to the Carleton, and Kay buttering a croissant for him as they dined in bed that morning.

Was that just four hours ago?

"I said, I understand we will be seeing you at the stadium tomorrow."

The words startled Will. From the tone, Will knew Griffith had repeated himself, and was rankled to not have the full attention of his guest.

"Yes, sir," Will said, quickly recovering. "The PR folks wanted to let the press snap a few pictures of me with the team."

Griffith looked at the ceiling and squinted, as if searching his memory. "I seem to recall a player who cringed at the notion of getting his photograph taken. Fought us tooth and nail every time we asked him to pose for pictures or participate in any promotional activities."

"Well, I cut myself a deal this time. If Charlie lets me suit up and throw around with the boys for a bit, the press can take as many damn pictures as they wish."

He turned quickly to Vivian. "You'll excuse my language?"

"She's heard worse than that, Will. Ty Cobb cursed her out once for refusing to have dinner with him."

Will laughed. "I've heard stories about Ty Cobb."

"They're all true," Vivian frowned, the experience clearly distasteful. "The man is a loathsome boar. And married. And old enough to be my father."

Griffith focused again on Will. "How long has it been since you tied on a pair of cleats?"

"Almost seven months," Will answered. "The exhibition games you had us play down in Havana, a month before Pearl Harbor."

It wasn't as if he hadn't had other opportunities. The military was providing recruits with access to organized athletics and there were baseball fields at virtually every training base in the country now. The post commander at Fort Benjamin Harris, outside Indianapolis, had invited Will to play, and the competition was tempting. It was a formal league, each roster sprinkled with one-time minor leaguers and college players. The colonel even offered to bus Will and a team of Army all-stars to the Great Lakes Training Center outside Chicago, where the Navy was believed to be assembling a team ringed with top shelf professional talent.

Will resisted every offer, the reaction from the Army brass ranging from understanding to indignation. Some accused him of a phony high-mindedness manufactured by public relations handlers back in Washington. Will stood firm. As much as he missed the game, he was determined to distance himself from baseball right now.

He set his fork down. "Mr. Griffith, it's great to see you and Ms.

Pritchard again, but I have to ask. Why am I here?"

Griffith bristled. "You make it sound as if I have an ulterior motive here. I can't have lunch with one of my players?"

"Sir, with respect, I've played for you for four years, and I've never heard of you having lunch, even once, with one of your players."

Griffith laughed. "Fair enough." He scraped the remaining sauce from his dish with a hunk of bread and chewed it down.

"I want you to re-join the team," he said, brushing the crumbs from his fingers.

Will nodded. "I will. When the war is over."

"No," said Griffith, no longer smiling as he tapped the table with his index finger. "Today."

Will glanced sideways at Vivian. She too had stopped eating and was studying him intently.

"You can't be serious."

The owner leaned forward, planting his elbows on the table as he wagged a finger at Will. "We're a game over .500, and we've managed that with our best player absent all season. We're mostly healthy, and we have a real shot at a pennant run this year. But not with a second-rate catcher. And not without a legitimate number three hitter."

"Mr. Griffith, we've talked about this. We agreed–"

Griffith slammed an open hand on the table, startling Will. "We never agreed. I acceded to your request. What the hell else could I do? The papers would have a field day with me if word got out that I tried to stop a player from enlisting. They would have painted me as some unpatriotic millionaire who cared more about gate receipts than I do my country."

"Do you?"

"Will!" exclaimed Vivian, appalled.

The table was silent, and Will looked down at his lap. It was an unfair slight and Will regretted it. The man had done too much for him. He looked at Griffith contritely, but the owner dismissed the tension with a wave of his hand. He had heard far worse in his business dealings. The old man then patted Vivian's forearm. She was still glaring at Will.

"It's all right, Vivian." Griffith looked again at Will. "You know about the Commissioner's letter to the President? After Pearl Harbor?"

Will nodded. Everyone knew about it. Baseball Commissioner Kenesaw Mountain Landis had penned a letter in January, asking the President if the league should suspend play with the country at war. The owners were skittish, worried the public would vilify them for insensitivity and promoting sporting matches while millions of men were preparing for war. They sought assurances from the White House that there wouldn't be any public condemnation if they chose to play the 1942 season. Roosevelt obliged the owners as they hoped, lauding baseball's vitality to morale at home and urging the game to continue.

"Rest assured, I'm not unpatriotic," said Griffith. "And the President wants us to put a quality product out there. I want you back, Will, in a Senators uniform, and behind home plate."

"I didn't mean to question your patriotism, Mr. Griffith. But I'm in the Army now. My contract with you ended last year."

"We'll see about that." He turned in his chair. "Vivian?"

On cue, Vivian reached into her large purse and withdrew two sets of papers. She placed them between herself and Will.

"What's that?" Will asked.

"That is your new two-year contract, Will. $28,000 to play the rest of this season. $32,000 to play next season."

His eyebrows shot up involuntarily, unsure he had heard her correctly. He pulled the papers toward him as he verified the numbers. The Senators had already finished a third of their schedule, after all. Why would they offer him a full season salary? And an overly generous one at that. But the figures were there in ink.

He was still dubious. "Come on. That's DiMaggio money."

"And now it's Jamison money," said Griffith. "You are as important to this franchise as Joe DiMaggio is to the Yankees."

"We're not the Yankees."

"No, we're not. They have all of their top tier players right now, while our crown jewel has left the team. You and DiMaggio are only a few years apart. Do you see him enlisting? What about Bobby Doerr, Lou Boudreau, hell, the entire National League?"

"Hank Greenberg signed up. So did Bob Feller."

"The single best players on their respective teams. And neither the Tigers or the Indians will have a prayer this season."

"Look, Mr. Griffith, I'm flattered, but–"

Griffith held up a hand. "We're not finished. That's as high as I can go, or Holloway, or Case, or God-knows who else will all want new contracts to match this one." He reached into the inside pocket of his coat and fished out a slip of paper, pushing it across the table toward Will.

Will leaned over and examined the paper without picking it up. He shook his head, mystified. "$10,000?"

"For you. That cashier's check cannot be traced back to me or this club. It is a one-time...well, let's call it a bonus. For your selection as an all-star last season."

"That's $38,000 just to play out this season," Vivian noted. "Three months."

Griffith leaned toward Will. "What do you say, Will? Do we have a deal?"

Will sat back in his chair, dazed. No Senator had ever been offered such a sum. Griffith's pockets simply were not as deep as his fellow owners, and even if he had the resources, such extravagance was not his style. Will knew he was a fine player, but he never imagined earning such riches playing a game he loved with a passion.

He couldn't even pretend to be tempted, though. There was no sum of money that was going to keep him out of the war. He was reluctant, however, to insult his patron again, and thus had to play the only card he had left.

"Mr. Griffith, even if I wanted to stay, I couldn't. The Army owns me now. I just can't quit."

Griffith slowly shook his head, as if hearing the arguments of a simple child. "Son, don't be naive. I'm no Rockefeller, but I'm still one of the most influential men in this city. Half the United States Senators have box seats at the stadium. I've known Roosevelt for more than 30 years. Had breakfast with the man just last week. You don't think I could get you out of the Army with one simple phone call?"

Will remained silent, his eyes shifting from the contract, to Vivian, to Griffith.

"You are serious."

"This is baseball, son. I'm always serious."

Vivian leaned closer to Will, so close he could smell the Chanel fragrance she wore on her neck. "Think of the team, Will. The team that gave you your first professional opportunity, and took a chance on a circuit player from the Wisconsin sticks. We've given you our loyalty these last few years. Do we have yours?"

Loyalty. The word had an effect on Will. Vivian was dead right, he owed the team everything, most notably for signing him from obscurity, and Will hoped to finish his playing career someday as a Washington Senator. But there were other loyalties too, and neither Griffith nor his goddaughter would likely ever understand his reasons for trading one uniform for another. No sum of money or emotional appeals were going to change that.

Will's eyes were drawn away, to the large window that fronted F Street, and the sidewalk crowded with workers and sightseers who were part of the mid-day rush. He thought of those outside the power circles of Washington. The millions of Americans who had already felt the harsh impact of the war in their families and communities. The team owners, fixated on pennants and profits while every day thousands of American boys were volunteering to defend their nation. That was nowhere close to true of Clark

THE BATTER'S BOX   25

Griffith, a good man who valued so much more than just the almighty dollar. And yet it seemed Griffith was willing to pay nearly any sum to keep his star player out of the war. Will was struck by the irony; his own father would have paid nearly any sum to get him into the war.

His response, however, was automatic.

"No," he said, his voice firm.

His former employers both seemed to deflate a bit as they gazed at him in stony silence. Griffith was unreadable, but Vivian was unable to mask her emotions. She finally turned away, and Will could tell it was more than frustration. She was seething.

"If you will have me back someday," Will continued, directing his words to the owner, "it would be a privilege to play for you again. I know how much I owe you. This team gave me my shot. You made me what I am today. And I promise you, I will pay you back someday."

Vivian scoffed out loud as Griffith raised an eyebrow. "Owe me?" he asked.

Will nodded.

Griffith sighed audibly and turned to his goddaughter. "Vivian, excuse us for a minute, will you?"

Vivian's eyes widened in surprise, but she dutifully complied, dabbing the corners of her mouth with her napkin as she rose from her seat. She gave Griffith a cursory peck on the cheek, not even glancing at Will, who had politely stood. Vivian stormed away from the table, and Will lowered himself into his chair again, fully prepared for an eruption. Griffith was accustomed to imposing his will on others.

Surprisingly, however, the old man's voice was gentle and very much conciliatory.

"Son, do you have any idea how much I want another World Series?"

"Sir, I–"

Griffith silenced him with an open palm. "I managed major

league teams for twenty years, Will. Those teams won nearly fifteen hundred games. But in all that time, I never won a single championship as a manager. Sure, this team won it all in '24, but I was in a suit by then, in the owner's box. Not the same thing, Will. Not the same thing."

The older man was awash in remembrances. Finally, he spoke.

"I know what you're thinking, Will. Owner. Millionaire. Lighting my cigars with burning hundred dollar bills, right? Let me tell you a story. When I was seventeen, I got paid ten dollars to pitch a game. They made me sign a paper, told me I was a professional ball player now. Gave me my first shot of rye whiskey afterward. It was in Hoopeston, Illinois. We played a team from Indiana, just across the border. The infield was mostly sand from the nearby quarry, and the grass, if you could call it that, was full of rocks and weeds. Not exactly Yankee Stadium, eh? Or the '24 World Series. But I sure felt like a major leaguer that day. I pitched four innings. Gave up a few hits, and a couple of runs. Pocketed the most money I had ever seen in my life. And you know what, son? It was the single greatest day of my life. I'd trade the '24 World Series in a heartbeat just to play on that sand and rock-filled field in Hoopeston again."

Griffith leaned in. "I admire you, Will. Admire your youth. Your vigor. Your conviction. If I was fifty years younger, I'd enlist right beside you. I am envied in this town, Will. Envied for my standing in the community, my team, my stadium. I have prospered since my playing days, though probably not as much as you think. But you know what I love most about this team? We play in Washington. The capital of the greatest nation on Earth. On any given day, any man in this town can bring his little boy to the ballpark, and sit in the stands with our servicemen, Members of Congress, hell, even the President of the United States. Those stands, Will, that is America. I love the team we have on the field, but everything I do as an owner, and you do as a player, is for those folks in the stands. When this war is over, I want you to come back. And when you do, your uniform will be waiting for you in your locker. You'll wear it tomorrow, and then I'll see it's not touched again until you return for good. Until that time, I will pray for your safe return. Owe me? Son, you only owe me one single thing."

Will was overwhelmed. Felt the drive and virility in this old man, and a newfound affection for him. More than affection. *Loyalty.* He would come back to this team one day, no question. And play his heart out for this man.

"What's that, Mr. Griffith?"

The owner bared his teeth. "When it is time for you to fight, you kick the living shit out of those bastards for breaking up my team."

Chapter 4

Will pushed through the glass doors, a bell tinkling above. The fact that the jingle wasn't lost in a boisterous sea of voices told Will it was a Sunday, the only day off for the laborers that filled every seat in Dixie's Café during the work week. Just a handful of tables in the restaurant were occupied, with the counter nearly deserted other than a single Negro nursing a cup of coffee. For a man of color, the counter was the only option in segregated Washington, even in one of the city's few racially mixed wards. There weren't many Civil War veterans left alive, but there were plenty of folks in the Nation's capital still determined to keep the two races apart.

The neighborhood was known to locals as Foggy Bottom. The name had been derived decades ago from the smoke-filled air that emanated from the four-story Heurich Brewery, the glass factory, and other assorted manufacturing plants perched along the narrow stretch of the Potomac River separating the capital from Virginia. The residents were a working-class mix of black and white, with a healthy dose of German and Irish immigrants. Plus one Major League Baseball star from the Wisconsin sticks, who first took up residence here during his rookie season with the Senators.

Will felt half-naked, having left his service jacket at the hotel. It was a concession to the oppressive June humidity. His dampened skin had already molded the olive drab trousers and khaki blouse to his body. Slipping off his garrison cap and looping it around his belt, he weaved past the tables and booths, nearing a counter chipped and worn after decades of service. He smiled when he saw the heavyset waitress sweep across the dining room, a large tray of food balanced precariously on one shoulder. Her thick chestnut hair was streaked prematurely with gray, plied on her head and held in place by an army of hairpins, and a heavy veneer of rouge and eye shadow colored her face. Underneath it all, Will had never known a more gentle soul.

Lucinda had been a fixture at Dixie's for nearly 30 years, hired as a teenaged cashier and eventually graduating to waitressing. She was clothed in what passed for a uniform at the diner, a white cotton blouse and skirt, with a smudged apron tied around her ample figure. Though she was only in her mid-40s, years of waiting tables had added a constellation of lines and creases to her complexion.

The woman was a bottomless reservoir of good cheer and kindness, all the more remarkable considering her life of hardship that began in squalor in a Baltimore tenement. Though Lucinda hadn't been dealt a favorable hand in life, she never uttered a word of complaint, caring only for the welfare of her customers, white and black alike. She worked six days a week and still had limitless energy, the woman a blur in constant motion.

Not today though. Will watched Lucinda finish delivering her order and return to the far end of the counter, where she hunched over a newspaper, chewing on a thumbnail. He cleared his throat audibly and Lucinda glanced up, caught in a double take as her mouth fell open and a small cry escaped. She rushed to the front of the counter, wiping her cheeks before wrapping her thick arms around Will.

"I hope that isn't how you greet all your customers," he said, pretending to gasp for breath.

She pulled back and gave him the once-over. "Look at you, General MacArthur! So dashing in that uniform. It's like Errol Flynn swooped in here."

Her tone was light and merry, but Will could not miss her reddened eyes. He eased himself onto his customary counter stool while Lucinda retreated behind the counter again, reaching for a coffee pot as she pushed a cup and saucer toward Will. He watched her as she poured. Her smile was still in place, but her distraction was obvious, her thoughts elsewhere. Something was off.

"Mr. Jamison, sir?"

Will turned, surprised by the voice of the messenger boy he hadn't seen arrive. The teenager had a face full of freckles, an unruly mop of curly hair, and a jaw that was working overtime on a piece of gum. "You remember me, Mr. Jamison?"

"Sure do. You work in the team offices, the mailroom, right? Is it Gary?"

"Gabe. Gabe Valentine."

"What brings you down here, Gabe?"

The boy pulled a small envelope from his back pocket and handed it to Will. "Mr. Swiderski sent me, thought you might be here. This came for you this morning, from an official courier."

Will raised an eyebrow as he opened the note. "How did Mr. Swiderski know where to find me?"

The boy stammered out some sort of response, but Will was no longer listening, lost in the muddled words on the paper, searching for their meaning. He lowered the missive, deep in thought, and absently pressed a folded dollar into the boy's hand. The kid gave an enthusiastic thank you and hurried away, his errand complete.

Lucinda leaned over the counter. "Bad news?"

"Good news. I think. I'm to report to the War Department on Thursday. A meeting with some colonel."

"Lucky you. That's just a stone's throw from here."

Will slipped the note into his breast pocket and buttoned the flap. "Maybe they've finally figured out what the hell they're going to do with my company. Hopefully send us to a combat division."

The waitress quickly looked away, reacting to something in Will's words. He noticed.

"Luce, what is it?"

She shook her head. "It's nothing, Will. And I haven't seen you in months, since the team left for Cuba. What are you doing back here?"

Will put his hand on her forearm. "Luce."

Lucinda sighed deeply and rested the coffee pot on the counter.

"You remember my oldest son, Danny?"

"Sure. The skinny towheaded kid who used to wash dishes here on the weekends."

She nodded. "That's Danny. He was drafted late last year. Could have taken a deferment, with his daddy gone and all, but he wouldn't do it. So he went into the Navy, and now he flies in those torpedo planes."

"Your kid is a Navy pilot?"

"No, he sits behind the pilot. Operates the radio and shoots one of the guns."

Will was having difficulty picturing a teenager like Danny, with hardly a muscle on his frame and his face covered in acne, firing a backseat .50 caliber machine gun at Jap Zeros.

"Well, good for him."

"He's on the *Yorktown*," she said, a catch in her voice.

The USS *Yorktown*. Will understood her unease now. The entire country had been riveted to the radio the last few days, as breathless reports filled the airwaves of a massive naval battle raging around a tiny, obscure atoll named Midway, nearly 4,000 miles from the West Coast. Early accounts were optimistic, suggesting a decisive, unheard of victory for the American Navy. One that was desperately needed.

Throughout the opening months of the war, the ill-prepared Americans had been overwhelmed by Japanese ground and naval forces muscling their way through U.S, British and Dutch-controlled islands and territories. Strongholds like Wake Island, Guam, and the Philippines were quickly lost in spite of gutsy efforts to fend off the attacks, the American forces lacking in both numbers and modern weaponry and equipment. Simply overmatched everywhere, the Allies had been reeling across the Pacific.

What the United States desperately needed was time. Time to fully mobilize, train millions of servicemen, and convert factories and assembly lines to the production of war goods. In the midst of ramping up the war effort came this possible miracle at Midway. The news came streaming to the mainland 48 hours ago, with reports that American carrier-based dive bombers had sunk two and possibly three Japanese aircraft carriers. Then more sobering reports surfaced of an unnamed American aircraft carrier that had also been lost.

Lucinda was wringing the towel with her hands as the tears formed again in her eyes. "What if it was Danny's carrier that was sunk?"

Will squeezed her hand. "You don't know that. Don't even think that. Do you realize how many ships the Navy has over there?"

"I read the newspapers, Will. We only have four carriers in the Pacific."

"Okay, so only a one in four chance the ship that went down was his. And even if it was, he would have gotten off the carrier before it sank."

Lucinda wiped away her tears. "I'm sure you're right. Look at me, I'm a mess."

He looked her in the eye. "Still the prettiest waitress in this dive."

"The only waitress in this dive," she countered, but she was smiling again. She looked at him closely and put a hand to his cheek. "It is so good to see you, Will. What do you want Cecil to fix you? Oatmeal and half a grapefruit?"

"Hell no, Luce. You wouldn't believe the muck our mess cooks serve. Give me three eggs, real eggs, over easy. Some bacon that has some meat on it, and a stack of toast that hasn't been blackened into hockey pucks."

Twenty minutes later, Will was mopping up the last bit of yolk from his plate with a piece of expertly buttered toast. He had finished the sports page from Lucinda's paper for the second time, pouring over box scores to see how the boys were faring. It was during his third cup of coffee that Will knew he was stalling the inevitable.

He sighed, and signaled Lucinda for his check. He had known for weeks this moment was coming, his emotions zigzagging between boyish enthusiasm and outright fear. He grimaced to himself, irked now by a misplaced vacillation that was unnecessarily chewing him up inside. He straightened in his seat, finding his resolve, determined once and for all not to put this off another minute.

It was time to play ball again.

Chapter 5

Beads of sweat dribbled from Will's nose and chin as he laced up his cleats. Embedded in the bowels of 30-year-old Griffith Stadium, the clubhouse was more than a dressing and showering area for the players. It was a hideaway. A place where they could sequester themselves from admiring fans and haranguing sportswriters, and maybe have a quiet drink or smoke, all with a semblance of privacy and comfort.

Well, privacy at least. The clubhouse was stifling, with the region's notorious early-summer humidity settling over the city and seeping into every crevice of the stadium. Lacking windows and modern ventilation, the air had thickened to a point where deep breaths could nearly choke a man. Electric fans clattered away in the far corners, futilely attempting to simulate the slightest of breeze, and leaving the space as airy and tranquil as a sealed bank vault.

Will stood, straightening his belt and smoothing the flannel jersey across his chest, a strange turbulence churning underneath the thick fabric. Throughout his playing career, nerves had never been an issue, his play impervious to whatever pressure he faced. The jeers and insults hurled by an opposing crowd rarely affected him, nor did facing the likes of Bob Feller or Lefty Gomez. Today was different though, and Will could feel his heart pounding through his rib cage. He had been away from the game for seven months, and though his Army training had kept him in decent physical shape, he wasn't close to baseball shape. He hadn't swung a bat in forever, and while he could recite from memory the technical specifications of the M1903 .30 caliber Springfield rifle, he didn't stand a chance these days of catching up to a Dutch Leonard fastball.

He sighed, reminding himself yet again how meaningless

this all was. He had nothing to prove here, and not a single scout or coach to impress. He could concern himself with sharpening his skills after he returned from the war. Today was simply an opportunity to throw the ball around a bit and catch up with old teammates, away from prying eyes. Will knew he was a fraction of the player he was the previous season, and the boys were going to give him some good-natured hell for it. He would just have to take his lumps.

Not for the first time, Will regretted his past promise. When he informed the club of his enlistment back in January, the front office had pleaded for one last public appearance. At the time, he hadn't thought returning would be much of a burden. Perhaps a few publicity shots in his crisp Army uniform, clasping hands with Clark Griffith as a symbol of the team's support of servicemen and the war effort. In return for his appearance, Will had made one request. An opportunity to practice with the team, away from the cameras. He wouldn't admit it to anyone, even Kay, but the separation had been far more difficult than he anticipated.

Pulling his cap on, Will fled the airless clubhouse for the auxiliary tunnel that ramped up to the playing field. He passed through the dugout and stepped onto the field, every worry instantly swept away by a pulsating glee. Lowering himself to one knee, he brushed the soft grass blades with an open palm, the sensation catapulting him back four years, and the very first time he inched onto this same field as a rookie.

His memories were interrupted by a series of sudden shouts from across the field. Will followed the voices to the outfield, where a dozen Senators in their home whites were lined up, chasing down shag balls. Others were positioned around second and third base, fielding sharp grounders, while a few were milling near the visitors' dugout, chatting with some of the visiting Philadelphia Athletics in their gray uniforms with the distinct blue trim and scripted "A" on the front.

"What'sa matter, Jamison, players don't report to their managers on those candy-ass Army teams?"

He turned toward the voice behind him, the thick New England accent paining his ears. Will had been so focused on the field, he walked right past Charlie Longman, the crotchety 62-year-old manager of the Senators. Longman was perched in his choice position, on the dugout's top step, leaning over a railing as a chaw of tobacco bulged from his cheek. His waistline had expanded noticeably in recent years, part of the physical decline of a man who had once been one of the game's most dominating pitchers. Back in his day, Longman's ability to doctor a baseball was considered the work of a true craftsman. He was even teammates with Tris Speaker once, the legend giving Longman the moniker "Bloody Chuck" because of his penchant for brushing back hitters with high fastballs.

Will retreated to the dugout. "Morning, Skipper. Good to see you too."

Longman spat a stream of tobacco juice over the railing. "I don't got lots of time for ex-Senators that ran from their team like a Frenchie from a rifle."

"My country needs me, Skip."

The manager lifted his cap and ran a hand through what was left of his thinning hair. "Your country doesn't have an eight game home stand against Philly and Chicago. Anything left in that throwing arm?"

Will windmilled his right arm. "I think I can loosen it up a bit, make that throw down to second base on three or four hops."

"Just like your rookie year," Longman grunted, holding out a palm. "The boys are hoping you'll cover every piece of action."

Will grinned, handing over a thick wad of bills. "Well, I'd sure hate to disappoint the boys. Where's my gear?"

The noon hour passed and the sun was high in the sky now, beating down on the field as the mercury climbed into the upper

90s. Opening pitch against Philadelphia was just two hours away, but the players had serious business to attend to. Standing behind home plate, Will straightened the protective mask strapped to his face. The musty, padded leather was sodden with grime and perspiration, but to Will, it was as comforting as a blanket to a baby.

As was his return to Griffith Stadium. The structure dated back to 1911 when it was built for a paltry sum square in the middle of LeDroit Park, a mostly Negro residential neighborhood less than two miles from the White House. After fire destroyed the original wooden stadium, new grandstands were fashioned from steel and concrete. The stadium underwent a number of expansions and upgrades over the years, and by the 1930s, the double-deck stands could hold more than 32,000 spectators.

The outfield was as sizable as any in the major leagues, dwarfing other venues like Fenway Park and Yankee Stadium. It was just one of the ballpark's many unique features, including a 30-foot high cement wall in right field fronted by a massive hand-operated scoreboard, and the 50-foot high bottle-shaped sign advertising National Bohemian Beer, affixed to the center field fence. Light panels had also been mounted the previous season on large poles atop the grandstands and outfield bleachers, allowing the Senators to join other ballclubs offering evening games, increasingly popular among working-class fans.

Will lowered himself into position behind home plate. Despite his break from the game, it was all second nature, the movements fluid and unchanging, and honed over thousands of innings caught. Every muscle and joint tensed with anticipation as he gently rocked on the balls of his feet and eased himself into a perfect balance. He swiped his throwing hand across the dirt, drying any residual moisture and adding the texture his fingertips would need for achieving an optimal grip on the ball. His throwing arm was folded behind his back, his hand grazing the numbers stitched into the back of his sweat-soaked jersey. His body became still, coiled like a new spring, ready to be released.

His eyes darted from the pitcher to the runner at first. The boys had chosen to start with Stan Spence. Hardly their swiftest runner, Spence was still a savvy, rangy veteran with long strides who knew how to get a jump on a pitcher. He had already taken his lead—six, maybe seven steps off the bag—and was now bent forward, his eyes focused on the back foot of the pitcher. He sidestepped twice more towards second base, a move both bold and not bold. It was an ambitious lead, but Spence knew Dick Holloway inside out, including the wily pitcher's peculiar mechanics.

Holloway worked from the stretch and Spence waited for the pitcher's signature leg kick, a wasted motion that many thought all but guaranteed a stolen base for a crafty runner. Spence knew better, of course. The lost time would be quickly compensated for by a scorching fastball, one that had vanquished American League hitters for years.

Will ignored the game within the game between Holloway and Spence. He punched his fist into the worn catcher's mitt, a small cloud of dirt escaping the leather, and gave Holloway his target. He was tall for a catcher, so he reflexively lowered the glove, leveling it with the hitter's knees.

Imaginary knees, of course, as there was no hitter at the plate. This wasn't a hitting competition.

Holloway gave Spence a cursory glance over his shoulder as he brought the gloved ball to rest at his waist. His left leg kicked up, and though Will's eyes were locked on his pitcher, he saw the flash of movement as Spence took off from first, his burst perfectly timed. Holloway pushed off from the rubber, grunting as he flicked his wrist and the ball flew from his hand.

From behind home plate, Will cursed at the ball's unexpected downward flight path. He had seen this pitch a thousand times while catching Holloway, but hadn't expected it now. Dropping his mitt down, he managed to get under the pitch and pick it cleanly just before it touched the plate. He felt the ball's impact with his glove in the same instant he heard the well-known thud of leather on leather. Will sprang to his feet, one explosive movement, his bare hand reaching toward the glove that was already opening. It released the ball into his hold, the weight familiar as his dirt-smudged fingertips found the seams with ease. He reared back, his arm firing forward in a blur, a whipsaw release that first caught the attention of scouts years ago.

Though Will hadn't thrown in what seemed like ages, his natural strength did not fail him as the ball rocketed across the infield, sailing past Holloway and impaling the shortstop's glove. Will pulled the mask from his face, slamming it to the ground after watching the ball land a few inches higher than intended. The placement mattered little though, as the sliding Spence had beaten his throw to second base, the tag applied just after his right foot touched the side of the base.

The umpire scissored his arms and shouted the runner safe, triggering a chorus of cheers from the large cluster of Senators and A's gathered to watch the contest. Will spat and kicked up a cloud of dirt in frustration as the runner leapt to his feet and raised his arms in triumph. Spence then strutted over to Tommy Heileman, the portly team equipment manager designated as both umpire and banker for the competition. Heileman held up a fistful of 20s, Will's 20s, and waved one in the air before handing it to Spence. The veteran player kissed the bill and tipped his cap to the catcher in a teasing salute.

"O for 1," Heileman called down.

"Dick threw a damned screwball," Will protested angrily.

"Quit your griping, Field Marshal," answered a grinning Holloway. "Can't all be fastballs."

"They can when it's my money on the line, you jerk," Will growled, pulling his mask back on and resuming his stance behind the plate, as the players howled in laughter.

Next in line was Roberto Estalella, their plucky, Cuban-born third baseman, who rubbed his hands greedily as he took his own lead off first base.

Will stood and slid the mask to the top of his head. "Forget it, Bobby," he called down, gesturing with his thumb for Estalella to take a hike. "I want George!"

There were hoots and jeers as Heileman shouted back to him. "Hey, we're trying to give you a chance here, Jamison."

"I want George."

Heileman shrugged, then waved Estalella off the infield dirt. A spry young man took his place, bouncing on his toes as he flashed a self-assured grin toward home plate. George Case was widely considered the fastest man in the American League. The fleet six-footer from New Jersey had led the league in stolen bases the last three seasons, and flagged down fly balls and line drives in left field that most major leaguers couldn't dream of reaching. The man ran like a gazelle.

Will bent down again, watching Case match Spence's earlier lead. The runner then took three more steps before digging his spikes into the dirt. Will gave an admiring grunt. Case certainly didn't lack confidence.

Dick Holloway was less impressed, and took Case's lead as a personal affront. Will held down three fingers, causing Holloway to give a curt shake of the head. The catcher narrowed his eyes behind his mask and flashed the same three fingers again, this time followed by a punch to his mitt, as if adding an exclamation point. Holloway surrendered, smiling to himself, and fired another pitch. As the ball neared the plate and began its customary dip again, Will's glove dropped with it, envisaging the flight of the pitch. This time, just as the ball touched his glove, Will was already coming out of his crouch, the spring uncoiling.

Case never had a chance.

An hour later, Will was back in the broiling clubhouse, freshly showered and lacing up the brown leather shoes that had been issued to him months ago at Fort Harrison. He wore a satisfied smile, having thrown out half the roster while losing just the single 20 to his former teammates.

Batting practice had been less of a show. He was behind on too many pitches, even those he knew Dutch Leonard was easing up on. The rust was expected though, and Will considered it a good day, the brief reunion with his teammates just the tonic he needed. The itch had been scratched.

He finished with the shoes and began buttoning his blouse, already stained with perspiration.

"Not the worst hitting I've ever seen."

He turned, seeing Charlie Longman leaning against the door frame, his arms crossed.

Will smiled. "Not the worst compliment I've ever heard."

"Hell, Will, a few days in the cage, you'd be back to your old self. You're still the future here, son."

"I've heard about that kid you got down in Chattanooga. Maybe he's your future."

Longman nodded. "Cole Legler. He's a good one, no doubt. But he don't have your arm. Word is he's thinking of enlisting too. You guys are killing me."

The manager continued. "Spoke to the old man. Said he tried to talk you out of it."

"Yep."

"Said he failed, and you're hard over to fight."

Will wiped his forehead with a handkerchief. He was roasting. "I'm not looking for a fight, Charlie. Just serving my country. It's not like I'm the first ballplayer to sign up."

"Mmm," said the manager, looking at his feet.

Will could sense the man's discomfort. "What's on your mind, Charlie?"

"Just don't want to lose a good man here," Longman murmured.

Will nodded, and the two men stood silent for a few awkward moments. Will was about to offer a farewell when Longman spoke again. He looked up, but not at Will, his eyes on the wall behind him.

"I knew another ballplayer once who signed up to fight. Long time ago. Kid was a second baseman, trying to break in with Pittsburgh the first year I was coaching there. He was all bat, no glove. Probably weighed 120 pounds, soaking wet. But boy could he stroke that bat. He was seventeen when he got his first spring look with the team. We sent him down to double-A to develop. He came back the next spring, and we sent him down again. Kid was scrappy, wouldn't give up."

Longman paused, lost in his thoughts.

"He come back the next spring?" prompted Will.

Longman shook his head slowly. "Nope. President Wilson got us into that worthless war, and the boy was determined to join the Army. So he signed himself up and shipped overseas."

"What happened to him? He play for you again?"

"He wrote me and his ma, about once a month. He was an only child, mind you. Told us not to worry, that he would be coming home soon enough."

Will blinked. "Jesus, Charlie. I didn't know."

"I don't talk about it. But I think about Robby every day. He was a good kid. Smart with the books, could've played college ball somewhere. They said a sniper got him, half a mile behind his own lines. They were taking turns, getting a break from the trenches, getting a hot meal."

Longman looked down at his feet, and Will knew to turn away while the man discreetly wiped his cheeks.

The manager cleared his throat. "I gotta get back on the field. You keep your ass out of trouble, Jamison."

Before Will could say anything, Longman turned abruptly and padded back toward the dugout.

Chapter 6

The Hotel Saint Jacques was one of the city's most exclusive luxury properties, tucked away behind a string of grandiose foreign embassies lining Massachusetts Avenue in Northwest Washington. Will was fond of the leafy neighborhood, having visited it frequently some two years ago while dating a buxom, doe-eyed secretary from the British Embassy. She was taken with his celebrity and courtly manners, a rare pairing in a city filled with the ruthlessly ambitious. He was turned on by her accent. Will's international relations, as Dick Holloway phrased it, lasted a month.

The accommodations at the Saint Jacques were opulent, the lavish furnishings and white-glove service a bit extravagant for Will's tastes. The room rate was also outlandish, but Will considered the sum a bargain in exchange for the anonymity the hotel provided. He could walk freely about, unrecognizable among the foreign diplomats and businessmen milling in the lobby and gilded corridors. Will doubted a single one of them had ever sat in the Griffith Stadium bleachers. Or knew what a bleacher was.

He sat on the edge of the wrought-iron bed with a telephone in his lap, having hung up twice already on the nasally voiced operator asking if he needed assistance. Taking a final deep breath, he lifted the handle from its cradle for the third time, vowing there would not be a fourth. He gave the operator the number of the telephone exchange in Lancaster, then checked his watch while awaiting the connection. It was a quarter past four in the afternoon in Wisconsin.

He willed his mother to answer the call. As selfless a person as Will knew, she was his one confidant, their closeness reflected by the effortless banter of their conversations that flowed with such ease. It was a stark contrast from his father. Their exchanges were strained, every word tinged with friction. The back and forth was like a tennis match, lurching wildly between heated quarreling and awkward silence, with little desire among either man to bridge the gulf that continued to widen each passing year.

After a few moments, the switchboard operator in Lancaster picked up, and Will recited the home telephone number from memory. Seconds later, the connection was made.

"Hello?"

Will sighed. "Hey Dad, it's Will."

"William, where are you? Still in Indiana?"

"No, Washington. I got a couple of days furlough to come back and see the team, take care of some paperwork. Thought I'd call."

"Ah. Well, it's good to hear your voice, son."

"How's Mom?"

"She's fine. She's doing some volunteer work at the Red Cross in Platteville. Drove down with Helen and Margaret."

"How're the stations?"

"Lousy," his father grumbled. "Damned ration books are killing us."

That was no surprise. With America ramping up its industrial production and the mass conversion of factories and assembly lines, the government had imposed rationing on the general population, issuing coupon books for civilian purchases of basic commodities needed for the war effort, including fresh meat, gasoline and rubber. Shortages of fuel and tires were hardly a winning formula for the filling station business. Will wasn't overly concerned though, knowing his old man had learned after the Depression years to stash away quite a bit of cash. Plus his folks owned their house in the clear, thanks to Will and the contract he signed in '40.

"You hear from Jack?"

His father perked up. "Wrote us a few weeks ago. He's a gunnery officer now on a destroyer in the North Atlantic. Got them a U-Boat last month. But he asked for a transfer, wants to fight the Japs.

Maybe they'll make him a captain, send him to one of them big aircraft carriers out there. Wouldn't that be something?"

The pride in his father's voice was unmistakable, as it always was when he spoke about Jack. Oddly, the partiality had never sparked a hint of jealously or animosity in Will toward his older brother. After all, their father wanted Jack on an aircraft carrier, the foremost target of the Japanese Imperial Navy. Maybe he hadn't heard about what happened to one of the carriers at Midway, or the sinking of the USS *Lexington* the previous month in the Coral Sea.

"Look Dad, I don't have much time. I've got a meeting down at the War Department and–"

"The War Department?"

Three magic words that Will immediately regretted. There was suddenly new life in his old man, his father's interest in the conversation a little less feigned.

"Know what it's about?"

"Not really," Will answered.

That was true. The summons had offered no explanation. Will certainly had a good idea, but he was prepared to electrocute himself rather than prolong this discussion any further.

"Well, where they sending you?"

"No one knows. Our company is still at Fort Harrison."

His father was incredulous. "What the hell are they waiting for? The Huns to land in England?"

Will shook his head as he looked upward, marveling at his father's ability to chastise the Army for taking so long to send his son to war. He thought about the contrast with Lucinda at the diner, a mother filled with dread about her son's fate.

"Any chance you can get in the 1st?"

And there it was. The question Will had heard from his father at least 20 times since the day he was inducted. The 1st Infantry Division, known as the Big Red One for its distinctive shoulder patch, was one of the Army's most revered units. Formed during the previous war, the 1st Infantry was part of General Pershing's original American Expeditionary Force, amassing a record of accomplishment in the trenches. It was also his father's old division.

"I don't know, Dad. The chances–"

"That there's a fighting unit. You can be sure that's where the action will be."

Like it was for you? Will wanted to say the words, but bit them back.

"I'll see what I can do. When do you expect mom home?"

"Late tonight. They won't leave Platteville until after supper."

"Tell her I'll try and call again tonight or tomorrow."

"Sure, sure. Look son, about the 1st, you want me to call someone? I can–"

"It's fine, Dad. I'm sure it will be the 1st."

A lie. He had no idea where they would send him. But he needed to end this discussion, as his father's voice was driving him over the edge now. They both may have sensed the tension as a sudden quiet settled over the line. With an abruptness that both relieved and disheartened Will, they said their goodbyes.

He gently replaced the receiver, bracing for the expected wave of emotion. His father's fixation on Will's military service, to the exclusion of virtually all else, had embittered Will since the day he enlisted. Longer than that, he knew. The fissure in their relationship began years ago, when Will finally acknowledged some difficult truths about his father.

In the spring of 1918, the Germans embarked on one last desperate offensive to end the four years of stalemate that marked the Great War. The operation was initially a trouncing success, marking Germany's deepest penetration of the war into French and British-held ground, but it also left the Germans exhausted, undersupplied, and highly vulnerable. That was when General Pershing's fresh American divisions were thrown into the line. The Americans were inexperienced, having sat out most of the war to that point, but eager to fight and unsullied by years of trench warfare that others had suffered through. A series of defeats for the Germans ensued, their lines crumbling all along the Western Front, including a rout at the hands of the American 1st Infantry Division in the Argonne Forest.

Many years later, Will learned his father had seen none of it. He had been a junior lieutenant, serving as a supply officer miles behind the front lines. Will never begrudged his father that. Henry had neither sought nor evaded combat service, simply filling a role the Army had logically assigned a young man who in civilian life had successfully started and managed a small business, and who knew something about the purchasing and transport of goods. Pershing's force was the largest single fighting force in American history, and it needed the organizational skills of men like Henry Jamison to equip and sustain it. Henry, perhaps seeing so many others in the 1st Infantry come home with decorations and Croix de Guerre medals pinned to their uniforms, saw things differently.

Will was barely a toddler when Henry returned from Europe. His earliest memories of his father were a couple years later, at the family supper table, when Henry shared tales of the Great War with his two little boys. They were too young to understand their meaning, but Will and Jack were still mesmerized by Henry's colorful storytelling, their dinners cooling as they hung on every word. Their father was a hero, so they repeated the stories to their friends and classmates, and spent their Saturday mornings pinning maps of northern France to their bedroom walls and drawing pictures of tanks and biplanes.

Their fascination eventually began to wane. As they grew older, and the stories repeated so often it was as if they were played from a phonograph, the boys began to sense something was amiss. It was certainly noticeable with their mother, whose distress grew more obvious to the boys each time their father spoke of the war. There were other oddities as well. Most notably, their father's accounts were never precisely the same, expanding bit by bit, in both detail and length. As did his role.

The stories rapidly spread beyond their own home to those of others, or anywhere Henry could corner a friend or neighbor. The tales of his war service made Henry a legend among some and a respected man in the community. And throughout those years, as Will suffered lie after lie, an unkind reality gnawed at him. His father was a fraud.

Will's mother, Grace, rarely reacted to Henry's stories anymore, other than a dutiful smile or nod of acknowledgment. She abhorred the falsehoods, but fretted over the consequences of challenging Henry, whom she truly loved. Of greater concern to Grace was Henry's inability to see how distanced he had become from his two sons. She knew that Henry loved the boys, but in pushing them toward military service, she feared he had lost sight of how much he was also pushing them away.

Grace was fervently devoted to her sons. She loved each fiercely, but she worried little about Jack. Even as a young boy, Jack had been filled with purpose and confidence, and blessed with an inner strength that enabled him to meet and master every life obstacle he faced.

Will had a more tenuous childhood, starting in grammar school when his diminutive size attracted frequent taunts and occasional beatings from the older boys. Grace was aware of the torment Will was subjected to, but there was little a mother could do other than bandage his cuts, and soothe his hurt feelings with assurances that things would get better.

If Will's mother was a comforting presence, his father was an invisible one. Henry avoided the boy after he got into such scrapes. Will was convinced his father was embarrassed and ashamed of his son's weakness, and though Grace tried to convince her son otherwise, she suspected it was not far from the truth. The only encouraging words Will ever recalled hearing from his father came when he told the boy the whippings and bullying would make him stronger.

They didn't, of course. It was only Jack's protective fists that made the older boys eventually leave him alone. That changed when Will entered high school, and finally hit the growth spurt that stretched out Jack years earlier. Midway through his sophomore year, he had sprouted to an inch taller than his upperclassman brother, with even wider shoulders and thicker muscles to boot.

But it was far more than the physical changes that would shape Will's future. More than anyone else, his mother began to notice a quality in her son that was becoming more evident each passing day. It was an unfaltering determination and perseverance that came to define Will Jamison. Though he was still more reserved than his gregarious brother, Will tackled every aspect of his high school years with a signature doggedness. By the time he neared adulthood, Will had developed into a right-minded, driven young man, who never allowed himself to fail or fall short of his own expectations. He certainly had his faults, but Grace's worries about Will began to recede, to the point where she eagerly awaited how this young man would make his mark on the world.

Chapter 7

Will shifted his weight again, hearing the squeal of broken springs and feeling the wrenching swirl of the coffee and donuts he had washed down earlier at Dixie's. The stomach pains were only adding to the worries that were slowly consuming him.

The tattered sofa seemed symbolic of the Department of War itself, a musty relic pleading for refurbishment. It was also clearly designed to make visitors as uncomfortable as possible. The coarse upholstery had the texture of sandpaper, with a foul odor reminiscent of Dick Holloway's locker.

The cramped, bustling office was lodged deep within the War Department and buzzed with the din of typewriter keys and ringing telephones. Housed in the old Munitions Building along Constitution Avenue, the Department was just a 20-minute walk from Dixie's and Foggy Bottom. Within its walls, a legion of administrators supervised an unprecedented buildup of the armed forces, from recruitment drives to the mass production of war matèrial. The year before, across the Potomac River in Arlington, officials had plunged a ceremonial shovel into a mound of dirt, breaking ground for a mammoth new consolidated military headquarters. But that project, with its curious eight-sided design, was not expected to be completed until the following year.

Will strolled into the ancient structure an hour ago with a bounce in his step, eager to finally learn where he would be sent and what his role in the war would be. His shoulders sagged the moment he reached this windowless suite of offices, greeted by the stenciled letters on the frosted glass insets.

Public Affairs Division.

The words had a visceral effect on Will. He was all too acquainted with the functions of a public relations operation, having been repeatedly drawn into his share of contrived dog and pony shows during his playing days in Washington. He now understood why he had been ordered here. He was to become his own dog and pony show.

Will had heard the arguments for months. Most notably, the impact on morale at home if any harm came to men like him, and hence, the War Department's preoccupation with their duty assignments. He heard talk of options the Army was considering. Exhibition games were at the top of the list, as were other publicity stunts designed to raise money for the war effort. To some extent, Will felt an obligation to follow the Army's wishes, and accept whatever non-combat role the Army prescribed, unable to deny his value to the Army in front of crowds and cameras. Nor could he ever forget the incalculable debt he owed to the game. A game that had changed the entire trajectory of his life.

He hadn't even picked up a mitt until his 13th birthday. Lacking the size and power to wrestle for the school team like Jack, Will took up baseball instead, surprising himself and those around him with a hidden cache of natural talent. As he began high school, Will's athleticism coincided with his physical growth, and his dominance on the freshman team soon became the talk of the barber shop and other places townsfolk liked to gab. At the start of his sophomore year, Will was approached by the manager of the varsity squad, who informed him there was just one position on varsity open for competition in the spring among the underclassmen. The manager assured Will that if he was willing to wear the cumbersome equipment and catch their hard-throwing senior pitcher, a varsity letter would await him. That sold it. A letter was unprecedented for an underclassman, and he would be alone among his tenth grade friends, a feat not even his brother had accomplished. The letter would also surely draw the attention of the girls who had long made shunning Will a sport of its own.

He was hardly content with just wearing the equipment, though, setting his mind instead to play the position in the spring better than anyone expected. Enlisting Jack's help, the two brothers took to the backyard every morning that winter before school. Even when the snow fell and the temperatures plummeted, they swept and scraped what they could off the grass so Will could practice.

And practice he did. They had just one drill, separating themselves by less than ten feet, with Jack throwing ball after ball at his brother's feet. Some were catchable, others skipped off the ground and scampered by. Jack tossed dozens of such throws every morning, and Will ranted and raved at himself as he struggled at first to catch or block the balls within reach.

They kept at it, though, as Will took a beating, mostly from the hard ricochets off the frozen ground that slammed into his torso and limbs. The inside of his forearms soon took on a permanent purple tint from the deep bruising. But as the outside temperatures began to warm, the number of balls getting past Will rapidly dwindled. By April, he was a human wall, stopping virtually everything Jack threw in and around his path.

Spring tryouts arrived, and the returning upperclassmen watched Will work behind the plate in awed silence. He made the varsity team that spring as the starting catcher, and was later named to the all-county team. Two years later, he carried the Lancaster Purgold, and the rest of the town, to its very first State baseball championship.

A week after hoisting that championship trophy, Will received his high school diploma. It was May 31, 1935, the same day he was paid a visit by a regional scout for a Midwest minor league association. He offered Will a signing bonus of $50, not unwelcome in those post-Depression years, and a fistful of bus vouchers to get him to Monterrey, Mexico. He was to spend three months there playing league ball with a hundred other similarly skilled young men, all auditioning for a gallery of low-level pro scouts.

Will was jubilant about his first professional signing, but there was little rejoicing at home. Jack had been gone for months, having left his low-wage position at the local shoe store and enlisted in the

Navy. His father had shown little interest in Will's success on the field, and playing for some dirtwater Mexican team for 40 bucks a month didn't seem to Henry like much cause for celebration. But with the economy still stalled and the filling stations scarcely keeping the family housed and fed, Henry grudgingly accepted Will's vocation. Not without sharing his doubts with his wife, including a late evening drunken tirade about how worthless of a son Henry had been saddled with. Will heard every word of it from his bedroom.

Just three years later, Will was settling into his first major league season in Washington. Not long after, in the midst of his stellar 1941 campaign, Will was named to the American League all-star squad, and Washington became abuzz with rumors that Clark Griffith was going to reward his rising star with the most lucrative contract in the history of the franchise.

That off-season, Will was visiting his folks in Lancaster in early December, having just returned from a series of exhibition games in Cuba. It was a bright Sunday afternoon, with snow flurries on the way, and Will was grudgingly helping his father fix the carburetor on the Buick. His mother came running outside to usher them indoors where they listened to a stricken radio newsman detail the attack on the U.S. Pacific Fleet at Pearl Harbor. Jack, thankfully, was still with the Atlantic Fleet. The family camped in their living room the rest of the day and evening, immersed in the breathless radio reports that teetered on the edge of hysteria.

As the family gathered with neighbors the next day to hear Roosevelt's "day of infamy" speech to Congress, Will knew his life was about to change. For months, he had sensed that war was on the horizon for America, and as he listened to his President ask Congress for a formal declaration, he was moved by Roosevelt's words, and somehow knew intuitively that he was going to be a part of it. The very next morning, Will shared with his parents his intention to enlist. Though just six months ago, it felt closer to six years.

"Can I get you some coffee, Corporal?"

Will looked up at the orderly. Like so many other faces he had passed in the halls of the War Department, it was full of youth and vigor. He shook his head, wishing he could loosen the knot of his tie. The reception area was suffocating, as plumes of cigarette smoke from the clerks and secretaries drifted to the ceiling where they settled into a static haze. Another orderly answered his phone, mumbled a few words, and stood, gesturing for Will to follow. The boy quickly ushered Will into a large office, where a ruddy-faced man with the eagles of a full colonel on his collar tabs sat behind a metal desk covered with mounds of paper. An olive-skinned private first class with thick glasses placed a steaming mug of coffee on the colonel's desk while another officer in a naval uniform, standing stiffly in his creased Navy blues, appraised the newcomer. Will came to attention and saluted, grateful he had thought to have the hotel press his own uniform that morning.

"Corporal Jamison, reporting as ordered, sir."

The colonel stood and returned the salute. He then broke into a wide smile and extended his hand across the desk.

"Max Augustine."

Will was taken aback by the sudden informality, and shook the offered hand. "Sir."

"Stand at ease, Corporal." Augustine gestured to the other men. "That's Lieutenant Commander Hollingsworth, my deputy, and Pfc Figueroa, who pretty much runs this place. Welcome back to Washington, Will. May I call you Will?"

"Yes, sir. It's good to be back, sir."

"Liar," chuckled Augustine. "My apologies for keeping you waiting so long. We had a small brush fire to put out with Congress. I understand you just made squad leader in your company. Congratulations on the extra stripe."

The colonel's jocularity surprised Will, his casual manner uncommon among the few high-ranking officers Will had encountered. Augustine looked to be in his early 40s. His Class A service jacket hung on the chair behind him, and his sleeves were rolled past his elbows. Wire-rimmed reading glasses rested on a hawkish nose, giving him the outward appearance of a librarian. He had broad shoulders and a thick neck though, and the firmness of his handshake suggested to Will that though Augustine was past his prime, this man very much belonged in a uniform.

Will shrugged. "Not sure I've earned it, Colonel. Haven't seen a German or Jap yet."

Augustine picked up a manila folder and held it in the air. "I appreciate your modesty son, but I've read your jacket. Your company commander, Lieutenant Bishop, is a West Point man, well-regarded in your regiment. Says your squad is the most squared away in your battalion."

Will remained quiet, his face impassive, but he felt surprising pride and self-worth. Bishop doled out few compliments.

Augustine pulled a sheet of paper from the folder and waved it. "I presume you know this request of yours was forwarded to my office, after endorsement by every senior officer in your chain of command."

Will held his breath, recognizing the letter he and Bishop had carefully crafted weeks ago. He remained at parade rest, his hands locked behind his back, but Will could feel every muscle in his body tighten. Another deep rumble came from his stomach. It was clear now why he had been ordered here. Will clenched his jaw, feeling the heat spread rapidly across his body, his temper on the rise.

It was hardly inconspicuous.

"Why don't you have a seat, son," said Augustine, his voice gentle now as he exchanged a look of concern with his deputy.

"I'll stand, sir." The edge in Will's voice was unmistakable.

"It wasn't a request, Corporal," injected a frowning Hollingsworth.

Will nodded toward the paper Augustine held in his hand. "I want to stay with my company, sir," he said.

"I understand that, Will. I admire the sentiment. And I have no doubt you have earned that stripe the hard way. But whether you like it or not, Will, you are special. There are a million men in this Army now, and we'll need millions more before we take on Hitler and Tojo. We had a huge influx after Pearl Harbor, yourself included. But those numbers aren't nearly enough, we'll need–"

"I get it, sir, but–"

"We're going to be significantly expanding the draft soon. Did you know that? The White House wants nine million men in the combined services by the end of next year. Nine million! The Army numbered less than 300,000 a year ago. Recruitment campaigns are underway all over the country. All those ships, airplanes, tanks and bullets we plan to roll off the assembly lines? We need to pay for those, and somehow manufacture ten times those numbers in the next two years. To raise the kind of capital we need, we're selling war bonds to the public."

"Yes, sir. I've heard this before, and I know other players–"

"We need *you*, Will. No one is questioning your patriotism, or your courage. You demonstrated that the day you volunteered. But you can do much more for the Army, and your country, stateside, than you can in a foxhole somewhere overseas. And you're hardly alone. Like you said, others are doing it." Augustine paused. "I'll cut to the chase, Will. The Army wants to send you to Fort Huachuca, Arizona. Help start a baseball league for the 84th Infantry Division."

"A baseball league," repeated Will, rolling his eyes to the ceiling and not even trying to mask the disgust in his voice.

"That's right. There is another option. Commander Hollingsworth is of the mind you should join a whistle stop tour we're organizing to sell war bonds across the country. So you have options."

Options, Will thought.

An image of Kay, naked in their bed at the Carleton Hotel, suddenly came to mind. Plan B. Now that was an option.

"Take the tour," suggested Pfc Figueroa, with a toothy smile. "We already got Lana Turner and Hedy Lamarr!"

"Thank you, Javier, for your input," said Augustine, unable to hold back a smile as Hollingsworth shifted his contemptuous scowl from Will to the Pfc.

Will shook his head. "Respectfully, sir, I want to stay with my company."

Hollingsworth's exasperation was boiling over. He started to speak but Augustine quickly held up a hand to silence him. "Tom, give us a minute. And take Javier with you."

His subordinate leveled a final glare at Will but excused himself as ordered. Figueroa followed, closing the door as he left.

Augustine tapped out a Pall Mall and offered one to Will, who shook his head. The colonel struck a match and pressed it to the tip of the cigarette. He gestured toward the door.

"That sign on the outer door. *Public Affairs Division*. Ten bucks says you made up your mind about me the second you read those words."

"You owe me ten bucks, sir. I never size a man up before I see him step to the plate."

The colonel nodded, waving his cigarette in the air. "You want to see how he holds the bat. Where he stands in the box. How aggressive his stance is. Whether it's open or closed."

Will blinked. "How'd you know that?"

Augustine gave him a rueful smile, flicking ash into a tin can. "Care to guess what I did before the war?"

"Newspapers?"

"Nope."

"Lawyer."

Augustine flinched. "No need for insults, son. No, Will, I was the public relations manager for the St. Louis Cardinals."

Will grinned, unable to help himself. "No kidding?"

"No kidding." Augustine spun his chair to the veranda and lifted a framed photograph, handing it to Will.

Will examined the picture. It was Augustine, several years younger, in a business suit and fedora, standing next to Dizzy Dean, the legendary Cardinal from the 1930s. Both men were beaming.

"The man was a hell of a pitcher," Will remarked, handing the picture back to Augustine.

"The man was a hell of a braggart. He was one of the best, and he knew it. He'd still be pitching today if injuries hadn't derailed his career." Augustine narrowed his eyes. "Dizzy had swagger and bluster, but he backed up everything he said, and did everything that was asked of him. Always for the good of the team."

"Not very subtle, Colonel."

Augustine smiled, stubbed out his cigarette and held up his palms in surrender.

"You know Will, I never played myself, but I do know a thing or two about the game. I saw you play at Sportsman's Park last year and in '40."

"Small world."

"Smaller than you think. Years ago, when I was even younger than you, I too was an infantryman. In France. Served under Black Jack Pershing. The old man commissioned me himself, pinned my lieutenant bars on after Soissons."

Will smiled, finally relaxing a bit. "A battlefield commission? And from the ranks? You must have been a hell raiser."

Augustine was more serious now. "Hell raiser? Interesting choice of words. No, Will, the Huns raised plenty of hell for us. Look son, I don't often feel the need to establish my *bona fides* in this position, but I wanted you to know that you're not sitting across from some rear echelon desk jockey."

There was a pause, and Augustine seemed to be trapped in the past. An unpleasant one. His focus returned, and he tapped an index finger on Will's letter. "My job is to talk you out of this. You know that now, right?"

Will nodded, stiffening.

Augustine leaned back in his chair. "Well, I'm not going to do that. You and I are going to pretend I did, so when I'm asked by my superiors, I can say that I begged and pleaded with you, but to no avail. Got it?"

Will cocked his head, confused. "Sir?"

Augustine sighed. "Let me put it this way, Will. Even if I had gone through all of that, presented arguments so compelling and poignant the angels sang and I brought tears to your eyes, it wouldn't have mattered, would it?"

"No, sir."

"And if I ordered you into a non-combat role, say, to play in some exhibition games, or go on a public relations tour where you could put your hand on Rita Hayworth's ass, that order would probably find its way into the press, wouldn't it?"

"Probably. But not the part about my hand on Rita Hayworth's ass. I like that idea."

Both men laughed.

"As I thought. Giving the Army a nasty black eye. Which is why we're skipping all of that. I'm going to tell you what the rest of your outfit will soon learn. Your entire battalion is transferring to Fort Benning, Georgia, in less than a month. You're going to form a new division, the 10th Armored. Battalions of tanks, armored cars, and where you'll serve, in the mechanized infantry."

Will felt a wave of relief washing over him, though he wasn't entirely sure what mechanized infantry meant.

"Colonel, are you saying–"

Augustine held up a finger. "All I ask for is one favor." He leaned back in his chair and laced his hands behind his head. "Tell me why. Tell me why you're so bent on going to war."

"I just want to serve my country."

Augustine nodded. "We all do. Hell, not long ago, me, Hollingsworth, Figueroa, we were all in civilian clothes. We're here now, as are you, and we all have our reasons."

Will remained quiet, but he liked Augustine, and felt he owed something to this man.

"I'm a good player, Colonel. Maybe one of the best. But the Japs *attacked* us, and I can't help it that I don't want to think about baseball right now. Like you said, sir, there are going to be millions of men enlisting or drafted for the war. All going into combat. How am I supposed to live with myself knowing I wasn't one of them because I could hit a baseball 400 feet?"

It had all come out so quickly, and Augustine was silent for a full minute as he processed the rapid-fire words. The young man's conviction was undeniable. Augustine sensed Will was still holding something back, but the colonel knew he had pressed enough.

"Fair enough," Augustine said, standing. He offered his hand again. "And truly admirable, Will. I hope you find whatever you are looking for."

Will shook it. "Thank you, sir. I can't tell you how much I appreciate this."

"Just a word of warning. Where you want to go, I've been there. And I don't ever want to go back. Whatever you think it's going to be like, it will be ten times worse. When you've seen your buddies torn apart by machine guns, their corpses impaled on barbed wire, and rats feasting on their guts in the trenches, you'll have a different view of things. Let's see if you're still thanking me when this damned war is over."

Will stood, brought his heels together and saluted. He started to leave the office, but his hand froze on the doorknob.

"Colonel," he said, turning back to Augustine. "I have a favor to ask. It's a bit...out there."

"Will, you wouldn't believe the crap we deal with here." He smiled. "What do you need, son?"

"There's a lady who waits tables at a coffee shop down in Foggy Bottom. Her name is Lucinda Walker, and she's got a boy, Danny, who's in the Navy. On the USS *Yorktown*. The papers are saying we lost an aircraft carrier at Midway, but they haven't said which one. That poor lady is beside herself. She doesn't know if her boy is dead or alive."

Augustine took off his glasses and tossed them on the desk. He suddenly looked noticeably uncomfortable, and he spoke in a quieter tone now.

"Everything the press reports they get from this building. It'll be out tomorrow, Will. We lost the *Yorktown*. The Japs crippled her a few days ago. She remained afloat long enough to get her crew off. They hoped to salvage her, but a Jap sub got through a screen of destroyers and put two torpedoes into the ship yesterday, sinking her."

Will exhaled, feeling hope again. "But the crew got off."

"Yes, most of them."

"So, he's likely alive."

"If he's a crew member, yes."

"He was on a torpedo plane."

Augustine darkened. "Our torpedo squadrons took a beating in that fight. We lost a hell of a lot of them, from every carrier. No casualty lists yet."

Will nodded, his stomach lurching again. He pulled on the doorknob and hurried to the nearest exit to find some fresh air.

Chapter 8

There were enough servicemen packed into Washington's Union Station to retake the Philippines. Some were still in civilian clothes, waiting to be inducted, but most wore assorted uniforms, sharing smokes and barracks humor as they waited to be whisked away to the scores of military bases still sprouting up across the United States. A mix of enlistees and draftees, they would all soon be molded into infantrymen, pilots, tankers, engineers, artillerymen, sailors, radiomen, medics, and myriad other specialties that comprised a modern fighting force.

For Will, there would no return to Indiana. As Colonel Augustine had promised, he was to report directly to Fort Benning and await the arrival of the rest of his battalion. A week ago, Will would have been ecstatic about the prospect of joining a new outfit forming in Georgia, one tantalizing step closer to shipping out for a combat theater. Instead, he was sullen, beset by conflicting emotions as he leaned against a marble column, thumbs hooked in his trouser pockets and his duffel at his feet.

Part of it, Will knew, was Augustine and his talk of corpses hanging on barbed wire. That ghoulish image had stayed with Will. He was hardly naive about modern warfare, and more aware than most of the magnitude of death and destruction transpiring in Europe and Asia. Still, Augustine's evocative words, and the discomfiting look in the man's eyes, had chilled him, giving Will a taste of something he hadn't yet experienced. Foreboding.

Equally vexing were the recent travails of his personal life. Thoughts of Kay were pulling at him like never before. When they parted in the past, he had little difficulty shelving any lingering attachment, and shifting his focus back to the field and whatever young lady in Washington might be in his orbit. Will presumed Kay did the same, and attended to her life in New York and sham of a marriage.

Now, she would not leave his thoughts. From the moment his train pulled out of Philadelphia, Will replayed over and over in his mind their intimate hours at the Carleton, and found himself dwelling on everything about her, physical and otherwise. No woman had ever weighed on him like this before. It was a stark reality that was both deeply unsettling, and as exhilarating as anything he had ever experienced.

A good problem to have.

It was one of his mother's favorite expressions, the pithy words reflective of her unrelenting optimism and ability to embrace even the most elusive of silver linings. It was certainly fitting now.

He heard a clock somewhere above chime loudly, the hour edging closer to a spate of noontime departures. Will had purposely arrived early, itching to escape this blasted town and the infernal humidity. He patted the inside breast pocket of his service jacket, feeling the comforting outline of his orders, and found the massive overheard wall clock. It was 11:15 in the morning. Twenty minutes until his Atlanta-bound train arrived from Ohio.

Will thought about the last time he waited here, on the very same platform. It was the previous October, shortly after the end of the '41 season. That train carried him to Newark, where he met Kay for the second time that year. They were able to spend three days together, with Kay granted rare leave from her husband. He was with some of his Yankee teammates in Atlantic City for a celebratory drinking and gambling binge after their club easily bested the Dodgers in the World Series. When Kay told Will of this, the other pursuits readily available in Atlantic City immediately crossed his mind.

"I actually feel sorry for the hookers," she said, reading Will's thoughts with a sardonic smile. "Eddie's a lousy lover even when he's not loaded up on gin."

Will smiled with her, but they both knew Kay's biting remark was pretense, a feeble attempt to mask her revulsion and hurt over what she knew to be true. A candlelight dinner and carafe of wine later, she opened up about her home life, sharing a blunt narrative of her marriage that Will sensed had never been spoken aloud before. He already knew of the abuse, as Kay could hardly hide the marks from Will in the bedroom. But more revealing was the penitence she confessed for allowing herself to be swept off her feet by such a man, capped off with a bitter observation that her union with Eddie had fallen to a point where she cared more about the welfare of a faceless prostitute in Atlantic City than the man she had fallen for while still a teenager.

They sat for hours that night, the restaurant staff allowing the couple to remain long after the kitchen closed. It marked a turning point in their relationship, one no longer simply defined by sexual desire and chemistry. For the next two days, Will did everything in his power to make Kay forget about the brute she was shackled to at home. They strolled through parks, her arm hooked inside his. They took in a museum, then a matinee of the latest Barbara Stanwyck movie. Kay was astonished to learn that Will had never been to downtown New York, so they rolled the dice the following afternoon, venturing from Newark into Lower Manhattan in full view of throngs of New Yorkers. Neither fretted much about being discovered. Will would have been easily recognized in Washington, but on an island of millions, where Gehrig and DiMaggio were the hometown heroes, all anyone saw was another blissful couple delighting in the great city.

It was a whirlwind tour. She took him to see the Statue of Liberty, Battery Park, and the majestic bridge that spanned the East River, linking Manhattan to her native Brooklyn. They could even see the distant contours of Ebbets Field, where the Dodgers played in Brooklyn's Flatbush section. They walked along Wall Street, home to the barons culpable for a decade's worth of financial ruin. She could have worked for the visitors' bureau, proudly sharing the history of the city, the distinct architectural styles that Will never would have sighted on his own, and the diversity of cultures and ethnicities that comprised the populace of each borough. They finished the day at Kay's temple, the capacious, 30-year-old New York Public Library in Midtown, with close to two million books on its shelves.

He didn't see it nine months ago, but as Will reflected back, it was plainly obvious to him now. Those days with Kay were the best of his young life.

The crackling of the Union Station loudspeaker brought him back to the present. It was a public address announcement, the muffled voice echoing through the cavernous station like the voice of God. Will tuned it out, forcing his thoughts to return to last October. In their final moments together that weekend, he and Kay talked about seeing each other again sometime after Christmas.

It wouldn't happen, as the minute the first bombs and torpedoes rained down on Pearl Harbor on December 7th, everything changed.

Will had been transfixed by news of the war for the previous two years, engrossing himself in the newspaper accounts of what was happening overseas. Though the papers were light on details, Will nonetheless found himself riveted by the scale of hostilities across the globe. There was the epic struggle between nearly three million men of Hitler's *Wehrmacht* and a mostly peasant Russian army fighting to repel the invaders threatening Leningrad and Moscow. Before that, it was the remarkable pluck and resiliency of Londoners throughout the heart-stopping Battle of Britain, where the residents remained even after much of the historic city was reduced to rubble and ash by ceaseless waves of German bombers.

Will took note of the fighting in East Asia as well, though he considered the Japanese a far less threatening adversary. They were, after all, an island nation with limited resources, half a world from Los Angeles and San Francisco. It was the pugnacious Germans, and their fascist Italian cohorts, that Will saw as the real menace. Hitler continued to build a potent force of men and machinery that was growing and modernizing every passing month. He had a disciplined, battle-hardened army that numbered in the millions, thousands of Stuka dive bombers and Messerschmitt fighters that dominated the skies, and divisions filled with tanks and other armor that had already steamrolled across most of Europe. The speed and surprise of their *Blitzkrieg* attacks enabled the Germans to obliterate early opponents, including the Poles, the Belgians, and the Dutch. They triumphed again and again, with relative ease and few losses. All in a matter of weeks.

As Hitler continued to rack up conquest after conquest, Will's animus toward the Nazis intensified. He had long despised bullies, and the Nazis were sparing no one, jailing and persecuting the most vulnerable within their borders while invading the meekest around them. Will had never cared much for browbeating or swagger, and Hitler's chest-thumping and hateful tone toward the Jews, the Poles, and anyone else the *Der Führer* considered racially impure, was too much for him. It struck a raw nerve.

Will was baffled by the indifference among his countrymen toward the German aggression, most likely resulting from faith in the alliance among the French and British that would surely halt the German stampede. France, however, capitulated to Hitler in the summer of 1940, stunning the world. Even Will was astounded that an industrialized nation of 42 million people, with a formidable army augmented by naval and air forces, and a country that had fought the Germans to a standstill for four years in the last war, could collapse in less than a month in this one.

By late 1941, two years after the first German divisions and tanks punched through the horse cavalry and other antiquated forces of Poland, signaling the start of the new war, the expanse of the Third Reich covered all of Europe, save Britain and a few neutrals. It stretched across the Baltics and Mediterranean, down to the African continent, and deep into the breadbasket of Russia. They had secured oil fields, vast deposits of ores and minerals, and a swath of other natural resources that could fuel the German war machine for years to come.

Will recalled the *Encyclopedia of the Great War* his father had given him as a child. He treasured that book, the pages worn and dog-eared from reading each of the entries about the war over and over again. He remembered how desperate the French and English were for America to join the fight, their own casualties numbering in the millions after four years of horrific conflict, fighting for yards at a time.

Two decades later, it seemed history was repeating itself. The dimension of the fighting, however, had sharply escalated from earlier in the century, and was now truly a world war. By the time Will enlisted, Hitler had more than seven million soldiers under arms, and Will recalled asking himself what kind of an army the United States could possibly assemble to counter the Herculean force sweeping across Eurasia.

The answer was now all around him. Across the train platform, there stood a cross-section of the gathering force of Americans that had answered the call to duty. The middle-aged, career naval officer, in his starched dress whites, giving his distraught wife a final kiss as three solemn children stood nearby. The scores of ardent young men scattered throughout the immense station, travel vouchers and small suitcases in hand, waiting to be shuttled to induction centers and training camps. Even the small boy, pulling a squeaking wagon full of empty tin cans he had collected from the station's restaurants, to be donated to the war effort, perhaps forming a future artillery shell casing.

They would all be a part of it. And as Will considered the men around him, he pushed aside the apprehension that nagged at him since he spoke to Augustine. He felt himself filling with pride again for his country, and, truth be told, himself. He was reminded why the decision to enlist had come so easy, and why, to this day, he had never harbored a second thought about it. They were all here for the same reason.

It happened so quickly after Pearl Harbor. He returned to Chicago, where he kept his off-season apartment, and after the new year and a call to the team offices in Washington, he signed up at a recruiting office on Wacker Avenue. He stood outside in a small blizzard waiting his turn, relieved when the bull-necked sergeant failed to recognize either his face or name. Within a few weeks, Will had cleared out the apartment and was on a train to Indianapolis. From there, a short bus ride brought him to Fort Benjamin Harrison, his new home.

Over the next 12 weeks, Will was transformed from professional athlete to common infantryman. He learned how to march in formation, square away his cot and uniform, and knee-jerk to commands hollered in his ear. His platoon hiked 20 miles through sloping foothills and dense forests carrying 60 pounds of equipment. They were given instruction on how to fire and disassemble every light weapon in the Army's arsenal, operate a field radio, and dress bullet and shrapnel wounds. He became an expert marksman. They taught him judo, how to spear a man with a bayoneted rifle, and how to cut an enemy's jugular with a combat knife.

He got to know the men in his squad. Their backgrounds, personalities, and abilities were as varied as the men Will suited up with at Griffith Stadium. As with his baseball life, Will made few close friends and kept mostly to himself. They knew who he was, as word had spread quickly across the base. There was an occasional baseball enthusiast who wanted to talk Will's ear off about their hometown team, or get an autograph for their girl or kid brother, but most left him alone, too spent by the infinite drilling and forced marches to treat him differently than the other GIs. That suited Will just fine.

As the weeks passed, Will was making an impression, both with the men in the ranks and the officers in command. All were struck by Will's severe focus and his determination to shine as a soldier. They pointed to his work ethic on the parade ground and his proficiency on the firing range and obstacle course. He used his precious down time not to unwind with his platoon mates, but to field strip his rifle or review the Army's field manual.

Will was jerked back into the present as a wave of newly arrived passengers paraded by, shouldering past Will and the others around him. The sun was cascading through a glass segment of the ceiling, and he caught a glint of light bouncing off the auburn hair of a taller woman stepping down from one of the passenger cars. It reminded Will of Kay, and just the thought of her again sent a surge of excitement through him. He made a mental note to call her the minute he arrived in Atlanta, not knowing how long it might be before they were able to speak again.

The passengers continued to file past Will, hurrying to make their connecting trains or reach the street exits to awaiting buses and taxis. He saw the auburn-haired woman again, her pace slower than the others. Though still a ways off, she was walking directly toward Will, and he was struck by the resemblance. Same willowy figure. Same slender legs.

It was the smile that did it. A familiar, playful smirk, framed by the soft, full lips that had been etched into Will's conscience since that first breakfast at Siegel's.

"You look like a man who's seen a ghost," Kay said, beaming now as she finally stopped just inches away.

Will was too dumbstruck to move. "What are you doing here?"

She grazed his cheek with her hand. "I wanted to see you off."

Will's heart was racing. "You came all the way down from New York to see me off?"

"It's not exactly like you're leaving on a road trip to Detroit. You're going off to war, mister."

"How did you know I would be here? I never told you when I was leaving."

"Dick Holloway told me."

"Dick?"

"He and Eddie came up together, played minor league ball in Altoona. Judith, Dick's wife, is one of my closest friends."

"I can't believe you're here," he said, shaking his head.

Her smile faded a bit, her confidence waning. "Is it okay that I am here?"

Will almost laughed at the absurdity of the question. He wanted to bury his face in her lavender-scented hair.

He met her eyes instead, and she had her answer.

"When do you go back to New York?"

Kay glanced at her watch. "My train leaves in about 18 minutes."

He looked at her sideways. "*My* train leaves in about 18 minutes."

Another radiant smile. "I'll ride as far as Charlotte. Then I'll turn around, and catch a train north."

"Why Charlotte?"

"Why not? I have to turn around at some point. Gives the two of us four whole hours to talk. Imagine all the personal questions I can ask."

"Oh, I can imagine."

She looked past Will and gestured toward a cafe at the end of the platform. "I think now would be a good time for me to get us some coffee."

"They have coffee on the train."

"I know. But it gives me an excuse to scram. I have it on good authority that an old friend or two of yours will be coming by to say their goodbyes."

"Who?"

"You'll see," she teased. "I'll return shortly."

As she started to glide past, Will was overtaken by a sudden urge to kiss her. He gently latched onto her wrist, stopping her in mid-stride and pulling her close as he caught a passing whiff of her perfume. Kay's eyes widened in surprise and he instantly released her, startled by his own impulsiveness. He swiveled his head, nervously scanning the crowd to see if anyone had noticed. They were in Washington, after all, and even in uniform Will was still identifiable, particularly among the press photographers canvassing the platform. All it would take is one newspaper bit and their secret would be out, a tongue-wagging scandal ripe to be fanned and sensationalized by the Washington and New York papers, marring both their reputations for years to come.

Kay read his face immediately, finding something endearing about both his boldness and his sudden panic. She looked at him longingly, wanting to throw herself into his arms and expose them both. Surely he knew how much she had fallen for him. How she would leave her husband, today, at this very moment, if he asked her to.

They stared at each other as Will fell silent. There were so many things to say he didn't know where to begin.

"What is it, Will?" she quietly demanded, willing him to speak his mind.

"I...I want..."

"You want what?"

"On the train, I want you to ask me those personal questions. I can't promise I'll answer them, any of them, but I want to try."

His face relaxed, as if even saying the words had unburdened him from some great pressure.

Kay, for her part, stood motionless, smiling a thousand smiles. A reaction that made Will realize he may need to manage her expectations a bit.

"Or maybe," he said, "I just want to hear your voice."

"Then maybe," she replied, "I'll stay on a bit longer."

She clasped his forearm, squeezed it tightly, and headed for the cafe.

"Get a load of Sergeant York here!"

The voice rose above the commotion from the train platform, and before Will could turn around, another joined in.

"Is that what we're sending against the Japs? Might as well surrender now and start eating fish heads."

Will grinned, recognizing the speakers even before he laid eyes on them. He started to throw a couple of fake punches at his old buddies, Dick Holloway and Stan Spence, then saw the other men crowding behind the pair. It was the entire team, coaches included, each man decked out in regular clothes.

He shook his head as if aggravated, trying to disguise the sentiment that suddenly overwhelmed him.

"What the hell are you clowns doing here? You have a game at two."

"Correction," said Holloway in his trademark Texas drawl, holding up a finger. "We clowns have a game at four. The Old Fox pushed it back."

"Why?" Will asked, noticing Charlie Longman for the first time, standing quietly with the other coaches at the back of the pack.

"Why, the man asks," laughed Holloway, clapping Will on the shoulder. "Because our best player is flying the coop, abandoning his teammates in their hour of need against the Red Sox. Griffith wanted us to get down here and throw you out of town. Make sure your sorry ass boarded the train."

The men all laughed, and Will grinned appreciatively. He had a few close friends on the team, Holloway chief among them, but hadn't expected any sort of gesture like this. He had always respected them, but now he felt a particular closeness to each man. He was indeed abandoning them, in a sense, and yet they were here. Every single one of them.

Will shifted his feet, his discomfort evident. He rarely displayed any sort of emotion in front of others, but their presence here affected him, more than he would have expected.

"Yeah, well, try and not get your butts whipped by the entire league. If this team is in the cellar when I get back, I'll beat the tar out of each and every one of you."

There were a few chuckles, but the gathering was mostly somber now, and Holloway was looking at him blankly.

"Thanks for coming down, boys," Will said, his voice quieter now and nearly inaudible on the crowded platform. He wanted to say more, but could not find the words.

A sharp whistle shrieked in the distance, signaling the approaching train from Cincinnati that would continue south to Richmond, Atlanta, and beyond.

Dick Holloway stepped forward, looking foreign to Will in his navy Brooks Brothers suit, scarlet pocket square, and fedora.

"Sounds like your ride, Will. You keep your head down over there. And remember, you cement-shoe catchers can't run, so find yourself a big old tree to hide behind, and stay there. You hear?"

The two men shook hands. "I'll come back soon, Dick. I have to. No one else can catch that crazy screwball of yours."

Holloway clutched Will's hand tightly, his smile fading. "I'm proud of you," he said, pulling Will closer and speaking low in his ear. "If I had half the guts you do, I'd be right behind you."

With that, Holloway turned and started for the long corridor leading to the Massachusetts Avenue exit. The other players and coaches, nearly two dozen men in all, took turns offering Will a few encouraging words and a slap on the back. As the men departed the platform, edging past the herd of servicemen and other passengers pressing closer to the incoming train, one Washington Senator remained, his hands stuffed in the back pockets of his ill-fitting, rumpled suit. Will stepped toward Longman as the train rolled into the station.

"I love this team," Will said, raising his voice over the roar of the train and gesturing to the backs of the few players still visible. "Never wanted to play anywhere else. I'll be back, Charlie. Those boys are like brothers. Not sure I realized that until just now. They... this team...means everything to me."

Longman said nothing. He just stepped toward Will and wrapped one arm around his shoulder and pulled him in for a short embrace. The man's concern and emotion, more than Will had ever seen from his own father, was a surprise, and Will found himself at a loss for words. The crusty manager finally released him and began walking away.

Will threw his duffel over his shoulder as he wiped away the wetness in his eyes and joined the long line queuing up to board the train. The mass of fellow servicemen was comforting to Will. He loved his teammates, but these were his new brothers, a thought that gave Will sudden purpose, just as it had on the day he was inducted. He saw Kay across the platform, giving him the cheeriest of smiles as she meandered her way through the crowd, two steaming paper cups in her hands. His eyes never left hers, and there was so much unsaid as she handed over one of the cups and slipped an arm inside his. Will breathed in deeply, the scent of lavender filling his lungs as he took in the uniforms around him. He found himself once again struggling with the pull of competing obligations, realizing now he was as anxious to return from the war as he was to join it.

A good problem to have.

1944

Chapter 9

DECEMBER 18, 1944
SOUTHERN BELGIUM

Will was hunched in the back of a jeep, futilely blowing warm air into his bare hands. He turned the collar up on his field jacket and tucked in his chin, hoping his steel helmet would take the brunt of the hurricane-like gale that walloped them all without mercy. While the windshield afforded some protection for the two men seated in front, it did nothing for Will, perched atop a crate of bazooka rockets, his feet resting on his field pack. He gritted his teeth, envious of the men buttoned up in their tanks, able to bask in the ambient warmth that radiated from their machinery.

The wintry air whipped across the low-lying plains and sloping hills, gathering into a stout crosswind that hammered the line of vehicles. It was 27 degrees Fahrenheit, with a late evening wind chill dipping into the misery-inducing teens. After hours of exposure, the men riding in the jeeps and armored vehicles were chilled to the bone, each silently cursing the Army, the war, and the Belgian winter.

It was a powerful force of men and armor, and one that was very much alone in the countryside. For weeks, the 10th Armored Division had been fighting as part of a multi-pronged army, but on this black night, they were on their own. Even the senior officers were disquieted, knowing how vulnerable they were out here to an emboldened, formidable enemy that, according to scuttlebutt, had bulldozed through most of the existing American defenses in this sector and now lurked somewhere out in the darkness.

Will's armored infantry battalion had been issued winter gear just a week ago, a stroke of good timing and fortune considering the Army's notorious supply foul-ups. Whether his lined field jacket and woolen shirt and sweater would be enough to fend off the elements here in southern Belgium was anyone's guess. His saintly mother had thankfully knitted Will a scarf, wrapped tightly now around his neck and tucked under the collar of his jacket. He had no gloves, but the wool cap he wore under his steel helmet at least provided his ears some protection from the biting cold.

His hands were the immediate problem, and he gave up blowing on them, jamming each into the pockets of his field jacket. It was only a slight improvement, as his bare skin was now pressing against the cold steel of several hand grenades. A cartridge belt was strapped around his waist, holding clips of rifle ammunition, his canteen and a sheathed bayonet. The stripes on his sleeve denoted his rank as a Staff Sergeant, permitting him to carry the holstered Colt .45 caliber pistol on his right hip.

The jeep pushed through the night, part of a lengthy column of armor that belonged to Combat Command B (CCB) of the 10th Armored and stretched for nearly two miles. CCB, one of the division's three brigade-sized components, was comprised of some 70 tanks, 3,500 men, and an array of other armored vehicles, artillery, and other weaponry. Will was fortunate to be in one of the lead vehicles, knowing the company of combat engineers who brought up the rear of the column in their half-tracks had it far worse. Those men were left to choke on the pungent exhaust that belched from the dozens of tanks they trailed.

The column had been on the move for nearly 16 hours. Most of the division had been quietly bivouacked that morning, far behind the lines, outside Rémeling, France. They had recently completed their first significant combat action of the war, supporting an assault on the city of Metz, a German stronghold in northern France. Though the 10th Armored had acquitted itself well, the German defense had been ferocious, leaving the division bloodied and weakened. They were eventually pulled from the line and shuttled to Rémeling to rest and take on replacement troops, as high command wanted the 10th Armored at full strength for the eventual push to Berlin. General Patton was readying his Third Army to deliver the knockout punch of the war.

The lieutenant riding shotgun swiveled around in his seat. "Where're you from, Sergeant?"

"Wisconsin, originally," Will answered, raising his voice to be heard above the roar of engines and the howling wind. "Small town you've never heard of. What about you, sir?"

"Bridgeton, New Jersey. Probably makes your small town look like New York City."

With the ice between the two relative strangers finally broken, Will was curious if the new platoon leader would continue. Since they pulled out of Rémeling, Lieutenant Lucas seemed pensive and uncertain, and Will sensed the man wanted to talk. As if on cue, the officer turned in his seat again.

"Can I ask you a question, Sergeant?"

"Sure thing, sir."

"I know you took some casualties at Metz. Sorry to hear about Lieutenant Davison. I heard you two were close. He going to pull through?"

Will's voice was flat. "Lost his left leg, sir. But he'll make it."

"There were eight other replacements with me. That's nearly a quarter of the platoon."

"The whole battalion got shot up, sir. Captain Bishop bought it on the first day. He was the Dog Company CO since the day they formed the 10th Armored, back in '42. Stray shell from a Kraut .88 killed the captain, first sergeant, and company clerk. Lieutenant Patterson was Bishop's exec. Battalion gave him the company, and he got shot by a sniper two days later."

"Jesus," whispered Lucas, facing front again.

"Wasn't too bad, sir, considering. The infantry divisions in Metz got hurt a lot worse than we did."

"Krauts ain't giving up yet," ventured the driver, a youthful, pale-faced private first class named Hayward who was also the lieutenant's runner. "And sure as shit won't be too keen on GIs in their backyard."

Will grunted in agreement. Most sergeants would have chewed out a Pfc for sticking his nose into such a conversation, but Hayward was a sharp kid who didn't miss much. Will leaned to the side, trying to study Lucas. The lieutenant's eyes were focused on the windshield, his arms folded together as he chewed his lower lip. The new platoon leader wasn't a difficult man to read.

He gave Lucas a tap on the shoulder and spoke in his ear. "We'll spread out the replacements, sir. Plenty of us still here who've been around the block. We'll get the new men squared away."

Around the block. Will was a whopping 26 now. He had his very first taste of combat just last month, nearly three years from the day he enlisted.

"Is that a nice way of saying you'll get *me* squared away, Sergeant?"

Will grinned. Judging from the lieutenant's tone, Lucas wasn't one to take himself too seriously, something Will appreciated. But the man became quiet again, likely giving thought to the weight of his responsibilities. Or the fact that he was replacing a fallen officer, wondering how long he himself would last. It was one lesson of war Will had learned quickly. Every promotion was another step toward an early grave.

His thoughts turned to Cameron Davison, Lucas' predecessor. He and Will had been friends, even with the difference in rank, and Will hadn't truly appreciated the man's ability until he was gone. Davison was experienced, confident, and decisive. Everything Lucas appeared not to be.

He pulled a pack of Beaman's from his pocket and popped a stick into his mouth, nearly fracturing a tooth on the rock-hard gum. He knew it was pointless to dwell on Davison. The man was gone, and Will's role was to support their new platoon leader. He was the platoon sergeant, the lieutenant's right-hand man, and as they plunged ahead into the unknown, now was when Lucas needed him the most. And Will needed Lucas to focus on the task at hand, not fixate on thoughts of failure and death.

Something big was surely stirring out here. Big enough to compel the brass to rouse the entire division from camp, detach it from the Third Army, and send it dashing north to shore up the First Army.

"You go to West Point, sir?"

Lucas turned in his seat again, looking at Will with a raised eyebrow. "Do I look like I went to West Point?"

Will laughed, despite himself, hoping the officer would not be insulted. Ira Lucas most definitely did not look like the Academy-trained officers that strutted around the division, each aspiring to be the next George Patton. Lucas was barely five feet, seven inches tall. He had the lithe build of a teenager, but his thinning hair and slightly stooped shoulders were those of an older man. Will guessed him to be around 30, relatively old for someone with only a single bar on his epaulet. He also wore eyeglasses so thick Will wondered how the man could see down a rifle sight.

His reaction managed to get a chuckle out of Lucas. "National Guard. Joined a few years ago, before the war started."

"No kidding?" asked Will, genuinely surprised. "Why aren't you with one of the Guard divisions?"

"I was. My Jersey regiment was part of the 35th Infantry, but then a few of us got orders to report to the repple depple."

Repple depple. Army lingo for a replacement depot, where freshly arrived soldiers, or those recently discharged from the hospital, waited for their new assignments, usually as replacements for units that had lost men in battle.

"So, you're Third Army." There was no masking the relief in Will's voice. The veteran 35th Division had a first-rate reputation within Patton's force, and had been in the thick of the post-invasion fighting from the hedgerows of Normandy to the current contests along the Moselle River.

Lucas hesitated. "Yes. In a manner of speaking. I was the

battalion S-2."

He looked away when he spoke those last few words, and even Will's shoulders sagged a bit. The lieutenant had been an intelligence officer, probably posted some distance from the front lines. Lucas' embarrassment was evident, the man's combat experience as lacking as his self-confidence. Will thought of his father, another man consumed with misplaced shame over a role he did not choose. Will straightened, determined not to judge Lucas, or hold him to his father's ridiculous standard.

"Sir, most of us hadn't seen a lick of fighting until five weeks ago. The platoon isn't exactly filled with combat vets."

"Is that supposed to make me feel better, Sergeant?"

Lucas delivered those words with a tight smile, appreciative of what Will was trying to do.

"It's the truth. This is your platoon, Lieutenant, and you need to know what you got. And what you got is a lot of good men. They're well-trained, and they know how to fight. But we just got to France in September."

"I heard you lost a lot of officers in Metz," Lucas noted. "Probably why I got shanghaied at the repple depple."

They did. The junior officers in the 10th Armored had been trained to lead from the front, and too many had been lost during their first foray into combat. Afterward, General Morris, the two-star who commanded the 10th Armored, sent half a dozen trucks to the replacement depot to grab every available man with bars on his shoulders. It was a modern day press gang.

Most of the men killed or wounded at Metz had been with the division since the day it was formed, back in 1942. They had trained for more than two years in the States, a continuous regimen of drills and exercises across the flatlands of rural Georgia, and later the tree-topped bluffs and grassy valleys of eastern Tennessee. They learned the complexities of integrated forces of armor and infantry, and studied the tactics and vulnerabilities of their German counterparts. Each day that passed, the division melded into a more fluid fighting force, and yet the men, the vast majority of whom were volunteers and not draftees, became increasingly impatient.

They wanted to fight, but as the war entered its third year for the United States, the division was still anchored on American soil. The 10th Armored was like a snarling dog, tethered to a stake, straining to join the contest on the other side of the Atlantic.

It was a particularly frustrating time for Will. He knew he had evolved into a good soldier and he was proud of the stripes on his sleeve. But he was at a tipping point, so much so that he began to privately wonder whether the Army might have sidetracked an entire division just to keep one public figure out of harm's way. It was absurd and irrational, and yet the idea gnawed at him for months.

There were glimpses of hope. The division's vehicles and equipment were upgraded in the summer of 1943, suggesting deployment was on the horizon. That included the arrival of their new armored half-tracks. The half-track was the workhorse of the armored infantry, an open-air personnel carrier with space for up to a dozen men in the back, plus another two or three in the cab. It carried a mounted heavy machine gun, and on level ground it could reach speeds of up to 40 miles per hour. Instead of rear wheels, the vehicles had a track propellant system, much like a tank, allowing it to forge across rougher terrain.

When autumn arrived, so did their first tanks, a mix of M4 Sherman medium tanks and M5 Stuart light tanks. There was talk that the division would soon join Patton's army, then clawing its way up the boot of Italy. But no such orders came. By the time winter settled in and the campaign in Italy had stalled, it was clear the 10th Armored was being held back for what everyone knew was eventually coming, an invasion of the rest of German-occupied Europe from across the English Channel. But when the crossing would occur, where it would occur, or even who would be a part of it, remained one of the most closely guarded secrets of the war.

Then D-Day came. June 6, 1944. American, British, and Canadian troops stormed the beaches of Normandy, France, followed by weeks of fierce fighting as Allied forces struggled to break out from their small beachhead. While a number of divisions poured into Normandy throughout the month of June, the 10th Armored wasn't among them, leaving Will and 12,000 other restless men stewing in discouragement and the Georgia humidity. The division finally landed in France in September, after most of the country, including Paris, had been liberated. They trained for an additional month in Normandy, and then in October, the division was finally ordered forward. They were to join the Third Army, now holding the westernmost flank of the Allied army. An army that was closing in on Germany itself.

Until it wasn't.

Though Patton had driven his forces to within spitting distance of the German border, his supply situation had become critical. His tanks, the heart of his army, were running out of fuel. Fuel that still had to be trucked overland from the beaches of Normandy, nearly 500 miles away. And those treasured barrels and other stores had to be shared with other American and British armies fighting the Germans elsewhere in France, Holland, and Belgium.

And so, the 10th Armored, along with the rest of the Third Army, waited. Again.

Most of Patton's men were grateful for the halt, the army physically spent after four months of continuous fighting across France. Not Will Jamison though. It had been 32 months since he enlisted, scrapping a promising and lucrative playing career. Thirty-two long, tortuous months of tangling with the Army bureaucracy to ensure he would get into this fight.

Among professional athletes, he was hardly alone now, as droves of other major leaguers had joined the Armed Services in the last two years. Bob Feller was on a Naval ship somewhere in the Pacific. Ted Williams was flying planes for the Marines. Even Joe DiMaggio had finally signed up.

It wasn't until November that the 10th Armored finally saw its first combat action. Patton wanted to strike into the Saar basin, a region rich in the natural resource deposits on which the German war machine was dependent. Even this late in the war and close to defeat, the Germans were manufacturing armor, weaponry, and munitions at an astounding rate, and stemming the arterial flow of iron and coal into German factories was imperative for the Allied advance.

In the Third Army's path stood Metz, an ancient fortress city just 30 miles from the German border. Hitler understood the city's strategic importance and ringed it with a bastion of heavily fortified outposts, bolstered by an ample garrison of thousands of troops.

When word came that the 10th Armored had been ordered into the fight around Metz, Will was exultant. Their time had finally come.

His fervor to join the fight evaporated their very first day under fire. Engaged against an implacable German defense that belied any notion they were facing a defeated enemy comprised of second-rate conscripts, the 10th Armored found itself in a dogfight, and Will had never been more frightened in his life.

Throughout their long, arduous training, the infantrymen and tankers had learned to support each other over open ground. In Metz, they were fighting in an urban environment, and the deeper the division penetrated into the city, the more ineffectual the tanks became. For the armored infantry, including Will's company, it became a fight in the streets. Block to block they fought, as the Americans cleared out buildings and houses, while the Germans targeted them from windows and rooftops. Snipers were everywhere, and hand grenades rained down from above. They lost Lieutenant Davison on the second day after the officer stepped on a mine. Will had to take over the platoon after pinning the screaming officer down while a medic twisted the tourniquet on what was left of his shredded leg. In time, the American forces managed to splinter the German defenders and the remaining garrison surrendered. But not without significant bloodshed that rattled the once-confident 10th Armored men, Will Jamison included.

With the enemy in flight, Patton pressed on. The 10th Armored clashed with the Germans again, this time in the contested triangle of territory between the Moselle and Saar rivers. On November 19th, the division crossed into Germany, fighting their way past the Siegfried Line with surprising ease.

All told, the 10th Armored had shone in their first action, fighting as courageously and effectively as any of Patton's veteran commands. But the division had also sustained significant losses and exhausted itself, earning some well-deserved recuperative time before the final Allied drive into the heart of Germany.

Bivouacked at Rémeling, the men received fresh uniforms, warm showers, and hot food. They passed time playing cards and writing letters to home, as word circulated that they would not see any further action until at least after Christmas.

That all changed in a heartbeat after the initial distress calls from the First Army, far to the north in Belgium, flooded the switchboards at Allied headquarters. Parts of the First Army were holding what had been considered a largely dormant sector along the Belgium-Luxembourg border, an area so devoid of German activity that the American commander in the area had paid little attention to it. Word came that the surprise German attack had smashed though the patchwork American lines in shockingly short order.

By dawn, the first elements of the 10th Armored were on the road to Belgium. Combat Command B hastily mobilized, loading their trucks and half-tracks with as much ammunition and other stores as they could carry. They had little idea where they were heading and what they would face. They hoped that whatever Germans were left out there weren't nearly as tough and resilient as those they faced in Metz.

Almost every man in Will's platoon had the same thought as they shouldered their packs and rifles and climbed aboard their vehicles. The war was almost over, and the Germans were reeling on both the Western and Eastern fronts.

What could they possibly have left?

Chapter 10

It was nine in the evening when the column reached the outskirts of a sizable town. Curtains were pulled back from the candlelit windows of the houses lining the streets, the residents stirred by the earthshaking American armor and the high-pitched squeal of tank treads churning across roads that nearly buckled from the weight.

The lead vehicles slowed as they neared the town square, bringing the entire column to an eventual halt. Under the light of a street lamp, Will spotted Major William Desobry, their commanding officer, hop out of his jeep and follow a retinue of other senior officers into a nearby hotel guarded by a squad of military policemen. Orders were passed on to refuel the vehicles as quickly as possible, and the men were allowed to briefly climb down and stretch their legs or relieve themselves. The air soon filled with voices trading laughter and crude jokes, their warm breath and tobacco smoke creating small clouds of vapor. A short time later, Desobry emerged from the hotel, grim-faced and alone, and assembled his officers in the street for a hasty conference, Lieutenant Lucas included. The large huddle quickly broke and Lucas returned to the jeep.

"They got crates of rations around the corner, Sergeant. Send two men to grab what we need, and load the platoon back into the half-tracks."

"No hot chow?"

"No. C rations on the truck. Major Desobry got orders, we're moving out."

Will yawned. "The entire column? We just got here."

"No, just Team Desobry. The other teams are moving on elsewhere."

That got Will's attention. Their team was less than a third of the column.

"Where the hell are we?"

"Bastogne."

Will grunted, another name he would soon forget. The division had passed through so many towns and villages since they left Normandy two months ago. He detailed men to retrieve the rations and ordered the squad leaders to herd the rest of the platoon back into their vehicles. Will blew more warm air into his hands, certain the temperature was still dropping. Another hour in the back of the jeep and his face would be a frozen slab of meat.

"They say where they're sending us, sir?"

"Not far. There's a village a few miles north of here," Lucas replied, wiping his eyeglasses on his shirt sleeve. "I think it's called Noville. Colonels O'Hara and Cherry are heading to other villages. Each team has orders to hold the villages and roads, and delay the enemy from advancing here to Bastogne. Team Desobry is getting this Noville place."

Within each combat command of an armored division, the tanks and infantry were divided into teams. Will's platoon was part of a mechanized infantry company attached to Team Desobry. Named for its commanding officer, each team was a high-powered, rapid reaction force comprised of tanks and other armored vehicles, and supplemented with infantry, combat engineers, and other supporting units. Team Desobry's principal firepower came from its 15 medium Sherman tanks, five light Stuart tanks, and five tank destroyers.

"Hold against what?"

"Major Desobry didn't say. Said he would brief us when we got there. But apparently the Germans have launched a pretty big offensive in this sector."

Will was dubious. "With what? And why the hell would they attack all the way up here?"

Even as the words left his mouth, he felt a hollowness to them.

They were in the Ardennes, a picturesque expanse of thick forests, rolling pastures, and quaint farming communities. It was a deceptively peaceful setting, as Belgium, and specifically the Ardennes, was hardly a stranger to military conflict. From his childhood obsession with the Great War, Will recalled that the Germans had marched through the Ardennes in their attack on Belgium in 1914. In 1940, they came through here again, this time to circumvent the French defenses along the Maginot Line, defying widely held assumptions that the thickly wooded Belgian landscape would serve as a natural barrier against invading tanks. That mistake enabled Hitler's forces to easily knife through Belgium and strike into the belly of France nearly unopposed.

Could they be doing it again?

Will dismissed that thought. This was not 1914 or 1940. The Germans had been badly whipped and steadily pushed back since D-Day, losing most of France, Belgium, Holland, and Italy. Not to mention the complete collapse along the Eastern Front. Patton was in Germany, and speculation was rampant that the war would be over within a few weeks.

The soldiers collecting rations soon returned, and Will and Lucas climbed into the jeep as Hayward thumbed the ignition. Major Desobry, standing in the passenger seat of his lead jeep, twirled his finger in the air, signaling the column to move out. His reconnaissance platoon accelerated ahead in their jeeps and armored cars. Once those units were away, Desobry waved the rest of the column forward.

The half-tracks and tanks lurched forward, grinding their gears as they made their way out of Bastogne. They headed northeast, forced to maintain a slow pace, the darkness mixing now with a thick fog that greeted the column as they pulled out of town. The headlamps of Lucas' jeep illuminated the half-track in front of them, but beyond that short distance, they could hardly make out the highway ahead.

Will pulled his rifle from the floor of the cab and inserted a clip of ammo from his cartridge belt. He loved the M1 Garand, the standard-issue rifle of the U.S. Army. It fired a .30 caliber cartridge from a clip that held eight. When the last bullet was expended, the rifle automatically ejected the clip, and the owner inserted a new one. The M1 was deadly accurate up to 500 yards and reliable no matter the weather elements.

They had also been assured in training that its length and weight made the M1 ideal for hand-to-hand combat and bayoneting an enemy. To his private relief, Will hadn't experienced that yet. He didn't harbor any qualms about firing his weapon at another human being, and he had already killed more than a few Germans in Metz. Whether he was capable of jabbing or slashing another man open with the sharp edge of his bayonet, well, that was another question. One he kept to himself.

Will chambered a round and hoisted the rifle, tucking the stock snugly under his armpit. Both Hayward and Lucas noticed.

"You see something you don't like, Sarge?" asked Hayward, the Pfc's hands gripping the steering wheel tighter as his head rotated from side to side.

"Keep your eyes on the road. I can't see a damn thing. That's what I don't like."

Lucas cleared his throat. "Major Desobry said the Germans haven't made it this far. The road should be secure."

"Secure," Will muttered. It was the same word they used to describe Metz when Dog Company was sent in to mop up the remaining resistance that someone had deemed nominal. Cam Davison stepped on a mine, and the company was trapped in a deadly crossfire on a street sandwiched by buildings full of fanatical *Waffen* SS troops. The SS men were reinforced by two Panther tanks that made quick work of the four Shermans that had accompanied Dog Company. It was a miracle the entire outfit wasn't slaughtered.

"Secure is some of our tanks on the shoulder," Will said sharply, and harsher than he intended. "We haven't seen a checkpoint or even a single MP posted up here. That sound secure to you, sir?"

"I guess not," Lucas said quietly, as he pulled his own M1 from between his legs and rested it across his lap.

Will knew he sounded like an insolent ass. It wasn't insubordination so much as it was ridiculing the man's inexperience. As if Will was some sort of seasoned veteran. He wasn't, and reminded himself again of his responsibility to his new platoon leader.

They passed through Foy, a small hamlet of houses just a couple of miles outside Bastogne, and advanced toward a second village a few miles beyond that. Noville, the lieutenant had called it. Though there was hardly any moon, the fog had thinned somewhat, allowing them to see the silhouettes of houses on the rim of the village and a few other structures in the distance. Lights flickered in a few windows, but there seemed to be little activity in the village itself. Will checked his watch in the glow of the headlamps behind him. It was nearly ten in the evening.

The vehicles halted a few hundred yards from the village where the reconnaissance platoon awaited. Lieutenant Showalter of the 90th Cavalry Squadron approached Desobry's jeep at the head of the column. After conferring with the major, Showalter returned to his armored car and the advance guard drove cautiously into Noville. The remainder of Team Desobry idled their engines, waiting for an all-clear.

It came less than ten minutes later, as the red-faced Showalter came running down the road, having left his platoon in Noville. There would be no radio communication until they knew where the Germans were. The lieutenant saluted Desobry, pausing to catch his breath. The wind had died down considerably, and with 2nd Platoon near the head of the column, Will could hear every word of their conversation. Even panting, Showalter's thick Mississippi accent was unmistakable.

"Town is secure, suh."

"Civilians?"

"They've skedaddled, suh. Most of 'em, anyways. Anyone left is hiding now in their cellars."

"They've probably seen this movie before. Cover?"

"Houses and barns, mostly, suh. Reminds me of some of those tiny farm towns we saw in Georgia. They got a church, a school, and I think a beer hall."

"A beer hall?" asked Desobry, brightening. "That's the best news I've heard all day. Climb aboard, Lieutenant. Time to lay out a welcome mat for the Krauts."

Desobry stood in his jeep, circled his finger in the air again, and the column came to life, moving steadily into the sleepy village.

Chapter 11

Like so many other rural communities that dotted the French and Belgian countrysides, Noville had a rustic, Old World elegance that bore little resemblance to anything Will had ever seen back in the States. The village was mostly a collection of modest stone houses, barns, and other small structures, all centered around a centuries-old church with an adjoining presbytery. There were no commercial buildings, other than a four-table cafe and a grain store that stocked dry goods and a few groceries for the villagers. Most living in Noville were employed in farming and other local trades, while some worked in Bastogne or elsewhere nearby.

With the first sounds of Desobry's advance guard, the villagers roused themselves and dressed quickly by candlelight, hastened by chilling memories of other foreign soldiers arriving unexpectedly. Headlamp beams danced against their dwellings as the tranquil little village was transformed into a chaotic hub of activity. By the time the main column arrived, most of the inhabitants had abandoned their homes, clutching small valises and family valuables. They fled the village by foot, some pulling milk cows and horse-drawn carts behind them. No one bothered exchanging a word with the soldiers. It was obvious the well-armed Americans were staying, and expecting a fight.

Several villagers stood near the church, fascinated by the choreography involved with dispersing so much machinery among Noville's narrow confines. One of Desobry's staff members directed traffic with a flashlight, scattering the half-tracks and armored cars throughout the village while leaving the tanks on the main road. The vehicles were topped off with fuel again, as riflemen fanned out across Noville and began digging into the earth, establishing their perimeter lines and positioning machine guns and anti-tank batteries. Every other man was ordered to rest, the sleep coming easier for some more than others.

Unlike Bastogne, Noville lacked street lamps, leaving the men to work mostly in the dull moonlight that came and went with the shifting clouds. Fortunately, the village layout could not have been simpler. The main highway from Bastogne extended in a straight line, through the village of Foy, and then on to Noville. Entering Noville from the south, it split the village down the middle for roughly 400 yards before reaching the northern approach. There, the road led to the next village, Houffalize, almost due north and six miles away.

Within Noville, houses lined the main road on either side. Additional roads connected Noville with other neighboring communities, and a few packed-dirt passages led to homes and barns on the village periphery. The tallest structure was the church tower, reaching nearly 200 feet from the ground. The steeple would provide a commanding view come daybreak, but stood out as a glaring bullseye, surely to attract the attention of every German artillery spotter left in western Europe. Across from the church stood a large schoolhouse where the team's medics began setting up an aid station, and just a few doors down was the squat, two-story brick house where Desobry established his headquarters.

Will and Lucas stepped through the door, the living room awash with officers and senior enlisted men, and a cloud of noxious tobacco smoke hanging in the air. The only light came from a handful of candles someone had scrounged. The radio operator had raised Bastogne, and he and Desobry were huddled in a corner, the major pressing a headset to one ear while clamping a hand over the other. The officers and non-coms conversed in whispers, knowing Desobry was straining to hear whatever distant, tinny voice was broadcasting over the radio waves.

The duo took their place among Desobry's other subordinates who led the various components of the team, the men standing shoulder to shoulder in a semi-circle as they waited for Desobry to finish. Three officers stood out to Will. Captain Schultz, the bearded, no-nonsense West Pointer who commanded the team's armor. Captain Newhouse, the relatively new CO of Dog Company, who served as Desobry's lead infantry officer. And Captain Geiger, the always-jovial Headquarters Company commander, sharing a quiet laugh with the young lieutenant who headed the detachment of combat engineers.

Will turned his attention back to Desobry just as the major ended his transmission. He had served under Desobry before and held the officer in high regard. Roughly the same age as Will, Desobry was unique among senior leaders in the division, having no formal military education. He was born in the Philippines to a career Army officer, but passed on attending West Point in favor of Georgetown University, a Jesuit school in Washington, D.C. He was tall, fit, and pencil thin, with a charismatic smile and cheerful demeanor. He was also a reliable, pragmatic officer with an innate command presence, and his rapid ascent to battalion-level command came as no surprise to those who served under him. Will had seen his share of Desobrys on the baseball diamond. The man was a born leader.

They first met nearly two years ago at Fort Benning, when Desobry arrived as a newly commissioned lieutenant. Will had always shied away from newspapermen and photographers, so he wasn't easily recognizable in person to the men he served with. He was to Desobry, who had been a frequent visitor to Griffith Stadium during his years at Georgetown, and even attended the 11-inning game when Will belted a franchise-record six hits.

The room fell silent as Desobry returned the handset to his radio operator. He kept his face neutral, knowing every eye was on him, but Will had served under the man long enough to know that something was amiss.

"Well, folks," Desobry began, "welcome to scenic Belgium. Here's what I've been told. Two days ago, the Krauts launched an all-out offensive here in the Ardennes. They cut a lot of the telephone lines, so communications have been all fouled up. There appears to be a hell of a lot of divisions involved, and G-2 is still trying to figure out their number and composition. The First Army was spread pretty thin in this sector, and the Krauts mowed right through the infantry divisions holding the line. The 9th Armored was in reserve, and was sent forward to support what was left of the infantry. They couldn't hold, and have been falling back since. At this point, it seems the 9th is fighting nothing more than a delaying action."

Desobry had carefully chosen those last few words. His officers exchanged surprised looks, fully understanding their meaning. What was left of the American army up here was in full retreat.

"We don't know what the German objective is," continued Desobry, "but the brass believes they need Bastogne, which is the town we passed through earlier. There's a network of roads and highways that connect in Bastogne, and therefore whoever has Bastogne, controls every major road in this sector. If the Krauts are trying to move all their armor somewhere, they'll need those roads."

One of the infantry platoon leaders spoke up. "So why are we out here, sir? Why didn't we stay in Bastogne?"

Captain Newhouse shot the junior officer a withering glare, but Desobry was unfazed by the interruption.

"We have to keep the Krauts out of Bastogne long enough for reinforcements to arrive and fortify the town. Our job is to hold an arc on this side of Bastogne, and throw up roadblocks everywhere we can to slow down the German armor. This village, Noville, is north of Bastogne. Colonel O'Hara is southeast of the town, and Colonel Cherry is due east. That's our arc. Each team is blocking a major access point to Bastogne."

A hand went up. "Major, you said the German tanks got past both our infantry and the 9th Armored?"

"Yep."

"So, whatever the Germans are attacking with, and rolled over a bunch of our divisions with, we're supposed to stop all that by ourselves?"

"If they come our way, yes. If we can't stop them, then we slow them down. The 101st Airborne is on its way to Bastogne. We need to buy them time."

An uneasy silence filled the room.

"They're sending paratroopers to fight Panzers?"

It was Captain Newhouse who asked the question, using the German vernacular for tank. The man grasped the disconnect better than anyone else in the room. He was a former paratrooper with the 82nd Airborne Division who transferred into the armored infantry after badly dislocating his shoulder during the jump behind German lines on D-Day.

"They're the closest division available. I'm sure other units are also on the way."

"I wouldn't sell those 101st boys short," offered Captain Geiger. "They have a hell of a reputation."

"They're tough as nails, Gordy," responded a terse Newhouse. "But light infantry isn't designed or equipped to take on Panzer divisions."

Desobry gave a rare, wolfish smile. "But we are. And our orders are clear. We have to hold out as long as possible. Every minute counts."

Another of the infantry platoon leaders spoke up. "Sir, some of my squads are down to four or five men."

Desobry nodded. "I'm aware. We're not getting reinforced or any more replacements, so you'll have to make do with what you have."

"Any chance of hot chow?"

"No chance. We'll have C rations for breakfast, and C rations for lunch."

"What's the fall back plan?"

"We're not falling back," Desobry snapped loudly. The question had come from Major Hustead, Desobry's executive officer, and an uncomfortable silence fell over the room. Desobry rarely lost his temper, and to bark at his exec in front of others was entirely out of character. Whatever Desobry had been told on the radio had him on edge, a state rarely seen by the men in this room.

He clearly regretted the outburst. The major removed his helmet, running his fingers through his short blond hair as he let out a long breath.

"Sorry, Charles. But Colonel Roberts made it clear, there's no give on this one. We are to hold this town, indefinitely. But we're sure as hell not going to sit on our asses and wait for the Germans to knock on the door."

Desobry nodded to an aide who stood on his toes and tacked a crude sketch of the surrounding area on the wall behind Desobry. Will wanted to laugh; it was like they were back in the Stone Age. The posted drawing was not only one-dimensional, it lacked any information about elevation, scale, or distance. The 10th Armored's dash into the Ardennes was so swift and unexpected that they hadn't had time to acquire an adequate supply of topographical maps. That was no small thing and would hamper their ability to organize a coordinated defense. No one had a deeper frown than Captain Schultz. Unfamiliarity with the terrain would be a particular disadvantage to his tanks.

"As you can see," Desobry said, "this piece of dog shit for a map tells us almost nothing. But it does tell us where Noville is in relation to Bastogne and some of the other roads and towns in the area. As for our defense here, HQ Company will hold the village, with Dog Company's heavy weapons platoon in support. Colonel Roberts controls the artillery in Bastogne. I'm not sure how much of it we can count on, since we have to share it with Cherry and O'Hara. As for air support, this crappy weather isn't supposed to lift anytime soon, so we're on our own for the time being."

"Any other good news, Des?" It was Hustead again, but this time he had a twinkle in his eye.

"Yeah," Desobry grinned, "Christmas is next week. And we've

got plenty of ammo and fuel." He pointed again at the hand-drawn map. "I'm sending Dog's rifle platoons down these three roads to set up outposts. 1st Platoon will head east on this road, to Bourcy. 2nd Platoon, you'll take the highway, the road we just came in on, which leads north to Houffalize. 3rd Platoon will head northwest and hold the road to Vaux. Each platoon will have tank support, though we can't spare much. Don't venture too far, say, no more than 400 or 500 yards down the road. If you run into Krauts, use whatever you have—mines, bazookas, spit wads—to slow them down. Hurt them. Then get the hell back here to the Alamo. Unfortunately, you won't have field telephones and we've been ordered to stay off the radios. So use your runners and keep me informed. I need to know what's happening out there. Lieutenant Lucas, where are you?"

Lucas stepped forward in the dim light. "Here, sir." There was a trace of unease in his voice, the officer surprised to hear his name called out.

"What are your effectives?"

"34 men." Even as he said it, Lucas cast a sideways glance at Will, who gave a subtle nod of confirmation.

Desobry crossed his arms. "Colonel Roberts thinks the main road from Houffalize is the most likely path the Germans will take here. Is 2nd Platoon ready to fight?"

"Yes, sir."

The hesitation and self-doubt in Lucas' voice was unmistakable, and before Desobry could press the lieutenant, Will spoke up. "Sir, if those are Panzers out there, and they've got Mark IVs and Vs, can we get a M10 or two instead of the Shermans?"

Desobry shook his head. "Negative. We only have five, and I can't risk the tank destroyers out there in the open. They'd have no cover. We need to keep them here in Noville. Each platoon will get a team of engineers, they can mine the fields for you. That should help keep the Krauts on the roads and off your flanks. Put your best men on the bazookas, you'll need them."

Desobry scanned the sea of faces around him. "Any questions?"

The room was still.

"Then let's get into position. We have some visitors to welcome."

The room broke and the men filed out of the smoke-filled command post and into the street. Pockets of men were everywhere, fervidly digging gun pits for the heavier machine guns and mortars. Dog Company's half-tracks idled nearby, and the platoon leaders began shepherding their men into the vehicles. The engines came to life as the infantrymen tossed away their cigarettes and half-eaten C rations and climbed back aboard.

"What do you make of things, Sergeant?" asked Lucas, as the two men stood watching 2nd Platoon load into their half-tracks.

Will shrugged. "Depends how long they expect us to hold this place. But I'm with the major. It's time to remind these Krauts who's winning this little war."

"One thing I don't understand, Sergeant. Why didn't you want the Shermans?"

Will smiled, remembering Lucas was regular infantry.

"They're not my first choice, sir. The Sherman is a good tank, and when they take on a German Mark IV, it's a pretty even fight. But the Panzer divisions carry a lot of Mark Vs too. Panthers. They're bigger than the Mark IVs, and have much thicker armor up front. The Sherman has to hit them on the side or the rear, which isn't easy in a tank battle. The M10 is a different ballgame. A tank destroyer, TDs we call them. They got a 76-millimeter cannon that will rip open a Panzer like a tin can. The TDs have pretty thin armor, so they can't take a hit, which is why Desobry doesn't want to risk them on open ground. A Kraut tank shell will go through a TD like cardboard. But they're fast as hell and can zip all over the place. Like a boxer, who sticks and moves. It'd be nice to get some M18s. Bigger gun, even faster than the M10, but the M10s will do. Just wish we had more of them."

The lieutenant mulled it over. "You know your armor, Sergeant."

Will shrugged. "When you're in the armored infantry, you have to know what the big fellas can do. Which one packs the bigger punch, and which one can take the bigger punch."

"I guess I have a lot to learn here."

"Lucas!"

The two men turned, surprised to see Desobry approaching.

"Sir?" asked Lucas, saluting in unison with Will.

Desobry spoke in a low voice. "Lieutenant, I know you just joined us and this will be your first action. You understand what I'm expecting from you?"

"Yes, sir. We hold the Germans out on the road, and send a runner to keep you apprised of our situation."

Desobry nodded. "One of the recon squads took a peek down the highway. There's a rise, about a thousand yards out. It's a bit farther out than I'd like, but set up there. Tactically, I'll leave things up to you. You've got an experienced platoon and you'll have a couple of Shermans backing you up. But I don't need any heroes out there. Sucker punch them. They hit you in strength, you get your ass back here. We can defend the village, but we can't defend the open country. Got it?"

Lucas nodded. "Got it."

Desobry clapped Will on the shoulder and gave both men a wink. "You listen to Sergeant Jamison here. Man can not only drive the ball to the opposite field, he also knows how to fight German tanks from the ground. Lieutenant, you listening to me?"

Lucas had been, but now his head was turned, distracted by a number of GIs walking slowly down the main road, south toward Bastogne. The headlamps of the parked vehicles cast long shadows of the men against the houses lining the road.

"Who the hell are these guys?" Desobry said softly, hands on his hips.

There were roughly two dozen of them. They were filthy and bedraggled, and as they shuffled by, Will could see their hooded eyes and hunched shoulders, each man appearing ready to drop from exhaustion. They moved deliberately, many with their arms, legs and heads swathed in bloody bandages. The goliath leading the group was even taller and huskier than Will. Hand grenades hung from the lapels of his field jacket, and his Thompson submachine gun looked like a toothpick in the man's meaty hands. He saw the oak leaf on Desobry's helmet, slung his weapon, and offered Desobry a half-salute.

"Sergeant Edelman. CCR, 9th Armored."

"You look like you've been in a hell of a fight, Sergeant."

"Yes, sir. We're about done in."

"Charles!" Desobry called out. Seconds later, Major Hustead trotted up to the group.

"Sir?"

"Get these men into the schoolhouse. Dig up some rations, and hot coffee if we have it."

"Yes, sir," Hustead said, motioning for Edelman's men. They fell in behind the executive officer and followed him away.

Desobry turned back to Edelman. "I have no idea what's coming this way, Sergeant. What can you tell me?"

"We came from east of here, sir. We were sent up to support the 106th Infantry, but the Kraut armor clobbered them and broke right through their lines. Our team had the right flank, and the Krauts hit us in force. Picked off our Shermans and Stuarts like it was a turkey shoot. We were ordered to retreat, and then had to fight our way through a regiment of mechanized infantry. Got separated from the rest of our company, and followed the road here."

"Mechanized infantry? You're sure?"

"Yes, sir. Got close enough to see their insignia. 2nd Panzer Division." Edelman paused. "If I was a betting man, I'd say that entire division is headed this way."

The words hit the 10th Armored men like a mule kick. Even if they had Teams Cherry and O'Hara with them, a German armored division would outnumber their force by four to one. And it was a veteran division. Team Desobry was isolated, vastly outgunned, lacking air and artillery support, and now likely facing an onslaught of tanks and crack troops.

Finally, Desobry spoke. "Sergeant, I need you and your men here, with us. Find Captain Geiger, he'll place you somewhere on the perimeter."

Edelman's eyebrows went up. "You're staying?"

"You got somewhere else to go, Sergeant?"

Edelman gave Desobry a long, blank look before tapping his Thompson and breaking into a crooked smile. "Got any ammo, sir? We all ran out hours ago."

Chapter 12

It was well past midnight and Will was in the backseat again, turtling himself in the collar of his field jacket. Pfc Hayward wrestled with the steering wheel, fighting the windstorm that buffeted the jeep as the small column steadily advanced on the road assigned to 2nd Platoon. In Noville, the men were at least shielded by the various structures, but out here in the open countryside, the blustering gusts hit them with the brute force of a Joe Louis roundhouse.

As with the earlier drive to Noville, the platoon moved through the darkness unsure of what awaited in the distance. Though the Ardennes was swarming with Germans, First Army headquarters still had little inkling of their precise whereabouts or objectives, and so the vehicles moved at a crawl up the highway, slowed further by a thick fog that lingered over the road.

Even with their collective lack of sleep, every soldier in the small force was alert. The vehicle-mounted machine guns were fully manned, the gunners squeezing the spade grips as they traversed their barrels back and forth. The men riding in the back of the half-tracks peered over the armored sides, rifles and submachine guns loaded and at the ready.

Will held his M1 tightly. To others, his grim bearing suggested composure, but inside, Will felt the same wrenching in his gut as the other men, knowing their vehicles could be in the crosshairs of an unseen German tank sitting squarely in the road ahead. Or that a battery of 88-millimeter guns, the lethal German artillery pieces, might suddenly let loose a barrage capable of annihilating the platoon in a matter of seconds.

Fortunately, they weren't going far. Even at this slack pace, the vehicles were already climbing the small rise Desobry spoke of, not even half a mile from the edge of Noville.

There were four half-tracks ferrying the armored infantry platoon and their team of engineers, plus two Sherman tanks trailing in support. Besides the .50 caliber machine guns mounted on their half-tracks, the infantrymen were armed with a mix of lighter weapons, including two .30 caliber machine guns and two 60-millimeter mortars. The platoon was also equipped with four lightweight, shoulder-fired rocket launchers, commonly known as bazookas, the deadly anti-tank weapon prized by the infantrymen. At least, those who didn't have to carry them.

Before they reached the crest of the slope, Lucas touched Hayward on the arm and the driver slowed the jeep. The lieutenant raised himself up, grasping the frame of the windshield as he threw a single palm in the air to halt the column. The night quickly became quiet again, other than the soft churning of the tank engines.

Will followed Lucas out of the jeep and the two men climbed to the crest, scanning the ground ahead. With the higher elevation, the haze had lessened somewhat, and a shard of pale moonlight emerged from the cloud cover, winking at the Americans and offering a momentary encompassing view of what lay ahead.

Both men halted in mid-step. In the distance, they could see silhouettes of soldiers, scattered across the road and fields ahead and moving in their direction. The two Americans instinctively raised their rifles, but as the approaching figures came into focus, Will relaxed his trigger finger, gently pushing the lieutenant's gun barrel down with his other hand.

Their gait and posture resembled that of old men. They were filthy and disheveled, and their vacant expressions matched those of Sergeant Edelman and the 9th Armored survivors they had encountered earlier in Noville. From their insignia, Will could tell these were more First Army men, drubbed and routed by German forces that until two days ago, no one in the Allied high command thought existed. Many were missing weapons, and most were in the same wretched physical condition and mental state as Edelman's men.

"You ever seen anything like this, Sergeant?" asked Lucas softly.

"No, sir," Will replied, as two more passed by, not even slowing to acknowledge the presence of an officer.

Lucas wasn't the only one thrown by the retreating Americans. The 2nd Platoon men were all standing in their half-tracks, studying the whipped stragglers as they passed by, clearly unsettled by the sight.

"Hayward," Lucas called to his driver. "Pass the word for the men to unload. Packs can stay in the vehicles. Have the squad leaders, and whoever is in charge of the tanks, assemble here."

As Hayward scurried away, Will stepped off the pavement, unsheathing his bayonet. He lowered himself to one knee and used the sharp blade to scratch at the ground, relieved when he felt the bayonet easily pierce the surface. Even with the onset of winter temperatures, the soil was still saturated from the heavy autumn rains. Outnumbered and outgunned by the advancing Germans, the softened ground might be their only advantage, allowing the defenders to dig in and provide themselves some cover. The spongy earth would also slow any German tanks veering off the road to flank or bypass the American position.

He returned to the jeep, joining the squad leaders who had gathered around Lucas. There was another man Will didn't recognize, a burly figure chewing a wad of tobacco. He wore the headgear of a tanker, and the stripes on his sleeve matched those of Will. The man's stubbled face seemed to be permanently creased into a scowl, and he leaned his hip against the hood of the jeep, his arms folded in nonchalance as they all listened to Lucas direct where he wanted the men and weapons placed.

It was a textbook strategy. Each side of the road would be flanked by extended lines of riflemen, bazooka teams, mortar squads, and machine gunners. The half-tracks would be positioned some distance behind, ready to spirit the men to safety, but their mounted heavy machine guns would provide additional support to the men on the line. It would all be fairly predictable to the oncoming Germans, but given how little Lucas had at his disposal, Will couldn't disagree with the tactics.

When Lucas finished, he turned to Will. "What is your assessment, Sergeant? Can we hold?"

Will resisted the urge to remind the lieutenant that their orders weren't to hold, just to wound the enemy and slow him down, buying the garrisons in Noville and Bastogne every possible minute and hour. He didn't want to embarrass Lucas in front of the others, especially the tanker Will caught rolling his eyes more than once.

"Yes, sir," Will answered. "If we can keep their tanks off the road. Those fields will have some give, and if the Krauts are in a hurry, they'll want to stick to the highway. We bottle them up right here, we might be able to hold out a bit."

The lieutenant nodded, reassured by Will's optimism.

"Start digging," Lucas ordered the others. "Minimal noise. First and Second Squads to the left of the highway. Third and Fourth Squads on the right. Lengthen your lines best you can, but don't leave them too thin." He turned to the tank commander. "Sergeant—what's your name?"

"Harding," the man said, spitting a stream of tobacco juice.

"Sergeant Harding, where do you want your tanks?"

"Back in Noville, Lieutenant," snorted the sergeant.

Harding was clearly pleased with his little joke, one that fell flat with the others. They generally tolerated the occasional wisecracking from the tankers, a unique breed to say the least, but none cared for Harding's flippant manner while an entire Panzer division was bearing down on them.

Lucas tipped the front of his helmet up, and for the first time, Will saw a hint of anger in the man. "Sergeant, can the smart-ass remarks. A straight answer, please."

"Sure, sure, Lieutenant," Harding said, as if consoling a child. "I'll set up on the road, right behind your lines. We'll take out anything the Germans send this way. Blast the fuckers to hell. I'll put Plumtree's tank on the left, where that depression starts. He'll back me up and support your men."

Will pursed his lips and looked at the tanker in contempt. It was the most asinine plan he had ever heard. If the Germans had as much armor as they had been told, any tank sitting on the road, this close to the main line, would be obliterated in a matter of seconds.

He could see Lucas was dubious, as any sane infantryman would be. But with no experience commanding armor, the lieutenant likely felt obligated to accept the tanker's judgment.

"Very well. But I don't want a shot fired until I give the signal. I'll be close by, and you'll either see or hear me. You may fire independently once you get my signal to open up."

Harding started to protest, wanting to fire on the Germans at his own discretion, but he chose not to argue with the platoon leader. For now.

"Just don't forget to tell us when to pull out," he sniffed instead. "We'll need to beat those Krauts back to Noville, and I wouldn't want them Panzers to chew up you infantry boys. Sir."

The mockery in Harding's voice was unambiguous, but Lucas either didn't notice or didn't care. He gave the men their final instructions and the group dispersed, with Lucas joining his squad leaders to oversee the placement of their heavier weapons. The tanker was already halfway to his Sherman when Will caught up to him.

"Harding!" he called, slinging his M1 over his shoulder.

The tanker turned. Though both were old 10th Armored hands from the States, the two men were strangers and had never spoken. Harding relaxed, relieved to be talking to another non-com.

"You believe that 90-day wonder?" he asked, shaking his head in disgust. "Fucking dimwit doesn't have a clue what he's doing up here."

The 90-day wonder phrase had been coined a year ago, a derogatory reference to how quickly the Army was producing new second lieutenants and rushing them to the front with scant training or experience.

Will moved closer, surprising Harding, until their faces were inches apart. Harding wasn't as tall as Will, but his neck and shoulders bulged with muscles.

"Seems to be a lot of that going around," Will countered, glaring down at the shorter man.

Harding was caught off guard by Will's menacing tone. "And who the fuck are you?"

"Jamison, Platoon Sergeant."

"Well, Jamison," Harding scowled, "you ain't my platoon sergeant. You just keep that greenhorn out of my way. The little pissant is aiming to get us all killed."

"Greenhorn?" countered Will. "Exactly how much action have you seen, Harding?"

"Plenty," the man said, puffing out his chest. "Our tank company supported the 90th Infantry at Metz. My boys and I took out two Kraut tanks from a thousand yards."

"This won't be a thousand yards, asshole. If you leave your tank up here, the Krauts will light you up like it's the Fourth of July. And have you seen how soft this ground is? Your other tank won't be able to maneuver. He'll be useless out there."

Harding put his hands on his hips, and spat out tobacco juice, just missing Will's boots.

"You a tanker, Jamison? 'Cause you sure as hell don't look like one."

Will narrowed his eyes. "You want to turn your tank into a fucking coffin, that's your choice. Maybe you'll get lucky, and the Krauts will be as stupid and incompetent as you are. Maybe not."

Harding opened his mouth to respond but Will jabbed a finger in his chest. "And if you ever talk to my lieutenant like that again, I'm going to ram one of your armor-piercing shells down your fucking throat. You got me?"

Harding's jaw fell an inch as he glowered at Will before a threatening grin slowly stretched across his leathered face.

"I got it, now. That little lieutenant, he your girlfriend? That it?

Well, maybe when this scrap is finished and we're back in Noville, you and I can have a little chat. Maybe see if you can back up that lip of yours."

Both men had their fists clenched as they stared each other down. Will had every urge to deck the smug jackass but knew there was no time for such nonsense. He would make time in Noville. He slowly backed away.

"You put your tank up here with us, Harding, you and your crew are dead men. Dead men."

The tanker shouted something in return, but Will had already turned and walked off, no longer listening. He was livid and burning with frustration, slapping the hood of a half-track as he passed by. He cared nothing for the fate of that arrogant prick, but they needed the man's tanks.

He reached the half-track that belonged to the engineers, the men busily unloading their equipment from the back. The squad was under the supervision of a gangly corporal who was passing heavy crates down to one of his men on the ground. Will shook his head in disbelief. The engineers were surrounded with explosives and every one of them had a cigarette planted in his mouth.

"Meyer!"

The corporal stuck his head over the side of the half-track and saw Will looking up at him. Meyer grinned as he flicked his cigarette away and climbed down.

"Yo, Sarge," he said, red-faced from the exertion. Even the simple greeting was corrupted by the man's nasally New York accent. Before the war, Meyer drove a cab in the city, and Will always wondered how out-of-towners could have possibly understood him.

"When are my engineers going to start mining those fields?" Will demanded.

Meyer scowled in return. "When are your Senators going to start playing with their heads out of their asses?"

Will brightened immediately.

Lev Meyer was a Jew from Long Island, and an unapologetic Brooklyn Dodgers fan. Some considered Meyer little more than a good-natured smart-ass, but Will knew better. He was skilled, resourceful, and a rock under enemy fire. Though he had been attached to Dog Company since the 10th Armored arrived in France, Meyer had actually landed on Omaha Beach three months before that, on D-Day. He came ashore with the 29th Infantry Division, part of the very first wave, into the teeth of the most ferociously defended landing zone in Normandy. The combat engineers were responsible for clearing beach obstacles that day and forging a path through the German defenses. Meyer's landing craft had floundered as it neared the shore, but the wiry engineer, carrying 60 pounds of equipment, had waded through the surf, somehow evading the storm of machine gun fire pouring from the heights above. He was the only engineer assigned to his regiment to survive the assault that fateful morning. Remarkably, Meyer had never lost his jaunty energy, or his penchant for creative insults.

"Corporal," Will said, the use of the man's rank a subtle reminder of Meyer's place in the food chain. "Did your bums even win a single game against the Yankees in the '41 Series?"

"That's a cheap shot," Meyer retorted, defying the food chain as he wagged a long, bony finger in Will's face. "My bums actually did win a single game against the Yankees in the '41 Series."

Both men grinned, then Meyer turned serious, motioning for Will to follow him around the half-track. Will could hear the platoon attacking the ground with their entrenching tools like an army of ants.

"We've got a problem," the engineer said, gesturing toward the silhouette of a lone straggler weaving past the 2nd Squad's foxholes. "They keep coming in. On the road, and through the fields."

Will chewed his lower lip, understanding Meyer's predicament. The engineers couldn't lay their mines while there were still American soldiers out there.

"Okay, but you can dig the holes for the mines, right? When

these guys stop coming in, we'll know the Krauts aren't far behind. That give you enough time to put in the hardware?"

Meyer scratched his jaw. "Cutting it close, but we'll make it work. Another snafu, though. All we got are these six pound mines. I don't know who the hell grabbed those worthless pieces of shit before we left France. They won't blow the mud off a Panzer's treads."

Will cursed out loud. Together, the explosives and Harding's tanks would give them a chance. But without more potent mines, they had no chance. The Germans would slog their way across the fields and flank the roadblock within minutes.

"So, they're useless?"

Meyer was quiet for several moments, then raised a finger as an idea formed.

"By themselves, yeah. But we got enough that we can stack them, two or three high. That'll do some damage. At least make the bastards consider getting their asses back on the road. We also have some TNT we can jerry-rig. Just give us a little warning. Maybe ten, 15 minutes to set everything."

"You'll have it. Start digging those holes."

Meyer barked out orders to his men as Will moved toward the main line of defense. He made a quick inspection of the entrenchments, appreciating the urgency the men worked with. It was one of the rare instances Will would acknowledge the value of their two long years of training. He came to where the 3rd Squad was deployed, on the immediate right side of the road, and found the squad's bazooka team. Corporal Minske was laying on his blanket, puffing a cigar, while Pfc Delgado was a few feet away, digging a foxhole with his small spade.

Will put his hands on his hips. "Joe, you want to explain this?"

Minske, a stocky, pug-faced assembly line worker from Detroit, sat up in surprise and quickly stubbed out his cigar.

"The kid is paying off a debt, Sarge. We were playing cards yesterday, and loser had to dig our holes for the next month. He lost."

Will looked down at Delgado, waist-deep in the hole he was digging, his cherubic face barely discernible in the dark. "Is that true?"

"Yes, Sergeant."

"Who taught you how to play cards?"

"He did," Delgado said, pointing at Minske.

Will had to quickly turn away before Delgado could see his smile.

"Carry on," he said, winking at the grinning Minske as he walked away.

Will liked Hector Delgado, but the kid had been with the platoon for three weeks now, and it was time he learned some things on his own. He had been an electrician's apprentice before being drafted, and like Meyer, found himself trained as an engineer. He was rushed to France, where there was an acute demand for men who could build temporary bridges and facilitate river crossings, but with the unexpected volume of casualties in the fighting around Metz, some genius in division personnel decided to redirect Delgado from the engineers and assign him to a rifle squad instead.

He met Delgado for the first time last month in Rémeling. The Pfc had just reported in and was standing at parade rest while Will sat on a camp chair in his tent, reviewing the transfer papers. The platoon had a number of teenagers, but Delgado in particular looked as if he was just entering high school.

"One of my bazooka teams needs a loader," Will had told him. "You're it."

The kid's eyes lit up. "I get to shoot the bazooka, Sarge?"

"No. Corporal Minske gets to shoot the bazooka. And he's good at it. You get to follow him around like a lap dog, carrying a haversack of ammo. When he fires a rocket, you load a new one."

Delgado wrinkled his nose. "But I ain't never done that, Sarge."

"It ain't brain surgery, kid. You slide the rocket into the back of the tube, pull the safety pin, and connect the wire. Minske will show you how. Then you tap your shooter on his helmet and get the hell out of the way. The back blast will blow you to bits if you're caught in it."

"Can we take turns shooting?"

Will rolled his eyes with impatience, though he desperately wanted to laugh.

"Yeah, you can take turns shooting. Minske will take his turns shooting the bazooka. You'll take your turns shooting your rifle. You know how to fire a rifle?"

"Yep."

"*Yes, Sergeant.*

"Yes, Sergeant."

"Good. But remember, we're an armored division. Our job is generally to fight other armored divisions. Those bazookas are the most lethal weapons we have in this platoon. That means you, as a loader, have one of the most important jobs in this platoon. Do you understand?"

"Yes, Sergeant."

"Do you have any questions?"

"When do I get to–"

"Do you have any *other* questions?"

Delgado opened his mouth to answer, but Will cut him off. "You say one word about shooting the bazooka and you'll be digging latrines for a month. Any. Other. Questions?"

"Yeah, Sarge, any chance I could get an autograph for my kid?"

Will blinked, not sure what part of the question surprised him the most. "You have a kid?"

"Yep, a baby boy. Me and my girl ain't married yet, but we will be when I get home."

"How'd you know I played?"

"Shoot, Sarge, everyone knows you played. I seen you myself, in Philly."

Will's memories were interrupted as he nearly tumbled into another foxhole, the man digging inside of it whispering a harsh admonishment to the unknown figure above. Will stepped more carefully, thinking again of the bazooka team. Their hole was closest to the road, so they were going to be in the thick of it. Delgado was young and inexperienced, but eager to please. Minske was solid, and beyond the hazing, Will was sure the veteran had shown Delgado the ropes.

Hearing Delgado speak of Philadelphia made Will think of his last visit to that city, his insides warming as he thought of his companion that night. A vision of Kay in her black cocktail dress came to him, and it stopped Will in his tracks. What he would give to have one more night with her at the Carleton. To caress those long legs, to look into those magnetic, green eyes, and breathe in her perfumed scent. During those prolonged months of training in the States, he received a number of letters from her, letters that were now bundled with a boot lace, wrapped in plastic and safely stored in the bottom of his field pack. He could not write her back, of course, with her husband at home, but he managed to speak to her by telephone a few times before the division sailed for Europe. Kay gave Will her aunt's address in Brooklyn where he could write her, and he promised he would. A promise he failed to keep, and since arriving in Europe, there hadn't been a single letter from her.

He certainly thought of her often, though, reading and re-reading the saved letters so many times he had most of the prose memorized. Will had never felt this close to a woman before. He recalled the farmhouse the platoon passed on the short drive from Noville. How wonderful it would be to be inside a house like that, on a night like this, curled up on a featherbed next to her, the pair oblivious to the wind that rattled the walls around them.

"Sarge?"

The voice belonged to a machine gunner. He and his loader were looking up at Will from their pit, wondering why the rough-hewn platoon sergeant had an airy smile on his face. A smile that abruptly disappeared, replaced by a string of curses and a gruff order for the men to finish preparing their weapon. Will directed his attention to the front again. The visibility was still abysmal, but it seemed the stragglers were finally dwindling, only a few in sight now.

Will returned to the jeep and retrieved his own entrenching tool from his pack. 2nd Platoon was running out of time.

Twenty minutes later, every set of American eyes was searching the ground ahead as they awaited the enemy's arrival. True to his word, Harding's tank was parked just 30 yards behind the main line, perched atop the road like a heeled Doberman. It was mostly concealed by the darkness, but if a single flare was sent aloft, the tank's outline would stand out for a mile.

Will gripped his rifle anxiously, as did the two men he shared the large foxhole with. He had known both Ed Janikowski and Ray Sloan since the early days in Georgia. Will always considered Sloan a bit of an odd duck. The lanky, 22-year-old cowboy from New Mexico was a bit slow with both his words and thoughts, but he was steadfast under fire, which was all Will really cared about.

With Cam Davison gone, Janikowski was Will's closest remaining friend in the outfit. The corporal just turned 29 and had served in the Army for more than a decade. The son of Polish immigrants and eldest of five children, Janikowski had enlisted at the crux of the Depression because the little money that came in from the family dry cleaning business wasn't enough to feed so many mouths. He was a slim man, but few who knew Janikowski were deceived by his size. The corporal had fought in the division boxing contests back in Georgia, and owned a right cross that had broken more than a few jaws on the streets of his working-class Chicago neighborhood. He took quite a few blows in the process, however, leaving him with a permanently crooked nose.

Janikowski had been in combat since the very first Allied offensive in North Africa. He was a veteran of Kasserine Pass, the patch of barren desert in Tunisia where the U.S. Army had their initial taste of combat in early 1943. They were inexperienced then and poorly led, and had the misfortune of facing off against Erwin Rommel, Hitler's most capable ground commander, and his notorious, battle-hardened *Afrika Korps*. The Americans were thrashed that day in humiliating fashion, as waves of GIs literally ran from the battleground. To this day, Janikowski still bemoaned the officers who panicked, resulting in the near-slaughter of his entire company. Days after the fiasco, then-First Sergeant Janikowski cornered his company commander, a West Point man, berating and then shoving the young captain for losing his nerve and abandoning the company in the middle of the fight. Janikowski lost his stripes for that, busted all the way down to private and transferred stateside to a new armored division that was forming. Nearly two years later, despite the man's lingering bitterness, Will came to realize how fortunate they were to have Janikowski fall into their lap. At Metz, he had proven to be invaluable and a calming presence among a platoon filled with jittery, untested men.

Now, the three men, whose paths would have never otherwise crossed in America, were crouched side by side in a Belgian foxhole. The fog had thickened, worsening their visibility, if that was possible. Over the howling wind, the men strained to see or hear any sign of the approaching enemy. They hadn't seen a single straggler since a knot of men from the 28th Infantry Division trickled through after spending much of the night in a running firefight with the Germans. With the enemy on their heels, the sergeant in charge offered his haggard men to Lucas to augment the small force at the outpost. Lucas declined, sending them back to Noville where they could rest. They would be needed later.

Once those men were clear, Lev Meyer and his team took to the fields, laying their mines and other explosive deathtraps before racing back to their own holes minutes ago.

They finished just in time.

Chapter 13

The entire platoon was in position now, their conversations hushed as a stillness settled over the surrounding farmland, the only audible noise the turbulent wind that continued to sweep across the open ground. The tension was trying the nerves of every man on the line, but they all held fast, each soldier searching for the first sign of the untold numbers of German tanks and assault troops expected to emerge from the darkness.

The silence was short-lived, interrupted by a series of distant explosions, followed by a lengthy eruption of far-off small arms fire. The men at the Houfallize Road outpost listened stoically, nervously trading theories about what was happening and where. Within minutes, the final echoes of gunfire tapered off, and the unnerving quiet returned.

Will was certain the exchange was to the east, where 1st Platoon had dug in on the Bourcy Road, less than a mile from their own outpost. Less clear was why the fighting had ended so abruptly. Did 1st Platoon turn back the Germans? Or had they already retreated to Noville?

Another gust pushed across their position, and behind the wind came a new, more ominous sound, known to every man serving in the armored infantry. It was the low growl of machinery and the churning of tank treads. The men readied their weapons, heeding the order from Lucas to hold their fire in case the vehicles were American. The possibility was enough to make Will's stomach tighten. The fields on both sides of the road were laden with explosives, skillfully concealed by Meyer and his engineers, and with such poor visibility, the bazookamen and tankers might be compelled to fire at any shape coming down the highway. Will spat, frustrated by the platoon's blindness.

"Give me that BAR, Sloan," Will ordered, holding his M1 out to the man beside him.

The wiry New Mexican looked at Will with curiosity as he exchanged weapons and handed over an extra magazine. Will stuffed it inside his field jacket and climbed out of their hole.

"Where the hell you going?" asked Janikowski, incredulous.

"Stay here," Will hissed, "and make sure no one takes a shot at me."

He scaled up the embankment and trotted forward on the pavement, cradling the bulky gun as loose gravel crunched under the weight of his boots. The Browning Automatic Rifle had been a mainstay of the U.S. infantry since the previous war. Weighing less than 20 pounds, it was capable of firing several hundred rounds per minute, providing rifle squads with the equivalent of a light machine gun that could be carried by a single man. Sloan had been lugging the weapon for his squad since their training days in Georgia.

After some 50 yards, Will dropped to one knee, thumbing the safety off the weapon. The engine noise was much louder now and the outlines of two tanks, one behind the other, suddenly loomed ahead. They were less than 100 yards away, their form and markings still unidentifiable.

He lifted the BAR and braced it against his shoulder, taking steady aim as he felt his heart pounding. He took a deep breath and squeezed the trigger, firing a short burst over the first tank. The shots reverberated loudly across the open fields and the lead tank ground to a halt. Will could make out a figure in the turret, obscured by a mounted machine gun pointed in his direction.

Will lowered the BAR and cupped one hand to his mouth. "Who goes there?"

There was a shouted response, harsh words that were mostly lost in the stiff wind.

Was that English?

A sharp crack from behind Will tore through the night as

Harding's Sherman roared, the first shot from his main gun landing just in front of the lead tank. The blast created a flash of light that briefly illuminated the field, long enough for Will to see the outline of the behemoth in front of him. It was no Sherman, and Harding had guessed correctly. Unharmed, the Panzer fired its main cannon before rolling forward. Will dove to the ground as its opening salvo slammed into the side of Harding's turret, the sharp explosion lighting up the sky. Will scrambled down the embankment and sprinted back to his lines, knowing he was racing across their own minefield now. The heavier guns of 2nd Platoon opened fire, but the weapons did little good, the high-caliber machine gun bullets bouncing harmlessly off the Panzer's armor plating. The German tank fired again, this time striking the front of Harding's tank, and the wounded Sherman burst into flames. The Panzer's machine gun opened up, raking the American position with withering fire and driving most of the GIs deep into their holes.

A stream of bullets zipped over Will's head as he ran, close enough that he could hear the lead slicing through the air. He heard Janikowski and Sloan calling to him and dove head-first into the trench, the two GIs breaking his fall. They pushed Will off with a string of curses, as the scowling Janikowski ripped the BAR out of his hands, returning it to Sloan.

"You crazy asshole!" Janikowski fumed, shoving the MI back into Will's hands. "What the hell were you doing?"

"Sightseeing," Will panted, as he joined the other two on the parapet. Improbably, he thought of Dick Holloway and managed a smile. "Who said catchers can't run?"

"Everyone," growled Janikowski, searching for a target.

By now, the second German tank had moved up the road and joined the fight, the two Panzers launching a hailstorm of shells and tracer rounds that streaked across the blackened night. Harding's tank was afire, but it wasn't clear if the other Sherman had engaged yet. Just at that moment Will heard its main cannon fire, the shot falling wide of the lead German tank. Will swallowed hard. The Sherman had gambled by revealing itself in the field behind 1ˢᵗ Squad. As the crew frantically reloaded, the two Panzers rotated their turrets to the right and fired nearly simultaneously. One shell landed short, but the other struck the Sherman in the right tread. With the American tank immobilized, the two German tanks lurched forward, thirsting for a kill shot.

There was sudden movement to Will's right. It was Minske, running forward from his hole, his bazooka up on his right shoulder. He slid to one knee, pausing to line up the lead Panzer in the sighting mechanism as the crew of the Sherman emerged from their hatches, knowing they had mere seconds before the Germans blew their tank apart.

Minske pressed his trigger, and the electrical current sent a rocket whooshing from the tube. At point-blank range, the rocket smashed into the Panzer, punching a hole in the frontal armor. The explosion tore apart the German crew inside, but the smoking, crippled tank plowed ahead, the driver likely slumped over the controls and his corpse pushing on the "sticks" that maneuvered the tank. It careened off the embankment and nosed into the gully at an awkward angle, completely out of action.

A bazooka rocket from another crew just missed the second Panzer, the projectile grazing the turret and exploding harmlessly in the adjacent field. Realizing it was now vulnerable to multiple anti-tank guns, the Panzer reversed its engines, retreating into the darkness.

Will could hear Lieutenant Lucas calling for the men to cease fire. Harding's tank was smoldering, a thick plume of smoke snaking into the sky. Two riflemen ran to check if any of the crew had survived, but one look inside the blood-streaked turret ended any such hope. The other Sherman was equally useless, unable to maneuver with only one functioning tread. The crew had volunteered to man their guns, but Lucas saw the futility of that and ordered the tankers to join the other men on the line.

Remarkably, other than Harding and his four crewmen, the

Americans had not suffered a single casualty in the brief clash.

Lucas appeared, easing into the hole next to Will. His face was flushed and his eyeglasses were splotched with mud, but the man was otherwise a surprising picture of calm.

"How we doing, Sergeant Jamison?"

The two men ducked as a stream of machine gun fire kicked up dirt around them and more shells rained down from above. The Germans weren't finished. Whatever supporting forces they had were now firing machine guns and mortars at the Americans.

Will had to shout over the din. "They're probing us, sir. It ain't gonna be just two tanks next time!"

Sloan rammed a fresh magazine into his BAR. "We pulling out, Lieutenant? Looks like we're all out of tanks."

Janikowski glared at Sloan in contempt. "Are you out of your fucking mind? We still got crates of bazooka rockets, shithead!"

"Yeah, but no tanks."

Lucas looked again at Will. "The corporal is right. We still got the bazookas and some firepower. How do we use it?"

Will gave it some thought. "They've probably figured out we don't have any tank support left. If I were them, I'd risk the soft ground, and push my tanks and men into the fields so I could take the road from the flanks. That won't be easy. Their treads will kick up a lot of mud and the mines will stop at least a few of them."

Lucas followed Will's train of thought. "But if they want to flank us, maybe they just send a feint on the road?"

Will nodded, surprised Lucas had caught on.

"Okay, Sergeant, leave your best bazooka man here in the center. The road will be his. Spread the other bazookas out. When the Kraut tanks start pushing across the fields, we shoot off every rocket we've got, then get the hell out of here. What do you think?"

Will raised an eyebrow. "I think you got a hell of a lot more training than ninety days."

Lucas gave him an embarrassed grin. "Pass the word to each squad. I'll send a runner back to Major Desobry."

For reasons unknown, the German fire came to a stop, and no more tanks came. Will thought they might be waiting for daylight, but Janikowski rightly pointed out that favored the Americans as much as it did the enemy.

There certainly wasn't any protesting among the men about the lull. Will managed to wolf down a couple of D ration chocolate bars, hardly Switzerland's finest but calories he needed. He was tempted to close his eyes, knowing he hadn't slept now in nearly 24 hours. None of them had. If he got out of this alive, Will vowed to sleep for a week.

His eyelids were half-closed when Janikowski cuffed him on the shoulder. Will heard it immediately, the snarl of German tanks rolling again in their direction. The men reached for their weapons, each soldier filling with angst as they realized the noise was much louder than before.

The Germans were attacking in force.

The platoon rose as one to the top of their foxholes. Rounds were chambered and those on the half-tracks fed fresh belts of ammunition into the heavy machine guns. Will rested his rifle on the parapet, his eyes falling on the freshly dug soil that lined the rim. He watched the tiny pebbles and grains of dirt dance around each other, the ground shaking from the vibration of so many tons of German steel lumbering their way. Squeezing his left eye closed, Will stared down the gun sight with his right, waiting patiently for a target to appear in the open hatch of the lead tank. That man would be the eyes of the German vanguard and the first to sight the American position. Nearly a full minute passed before the outline of the lead tank emerged, and Will cursed under his breath.

Panther.

In recent years, the Germans had manufactured a variety of medium-sized tanks. The backbone of their fleet was the 27-ton Mark IV, comparable in size and firepower to the 33-ton Sherman.

The 47-ton Mark V Panthers were different, more fearsome beasts. Most notably, they were outfitted with thicker armor up front that the Sherman's main gun could not penetrate.

The Panther was hardly the only worry. There were other tanks lined up behind it, their silhouettes taking shape as the column rumbled closer. Some spilled down the embankments and into the adjoining fields. Though invisible at the moment, Will knew supporting infantry was out there as well. At least two companies, he guessed, likely more. Either interspersed with the armor, or following closely behind, using the tanks as protective shields.

The Panther was just over a football field away, and Will could see the shape of the tank's commander in the turret, the man speaking into a radio transmitter. Will slowed his breathing, pinpointing his aim to where he imagined the man was wearing an Iron Cross on his tunic. Center mass, his firing range instructor from ages ago had called it.

His index finger tensed on the trigger. He accounted for the wind, but was confident the shot would not miss at this range. Will squeezed the trigger and felt the rifle buck against his shoulder. Half a second later, blood geysered from the man's neck as he straightened for a second before slumping over the open hatch. The turret officer in the tank behind the Panther, what looked like a Mark IV, quickly dropped inside his own hull. Will fired but the German had already disappeared, the hatch closing behind him.

The Panther's gunner angrily searched for a target, the turret rotating towards the half-tracks behind the 3rd Squad just as another rocket left Minske's bazooka. Will lost sight of the projectile but heard a sharp sound of metal striking metal, the rocket bouncing off the front of the massive tank in a burst of sparks.

"Goddamn it, Minske!" Will shouted, pounding his fist into the ground. The bazooka man surely knew it was a Panther, but wrongly assumed that a close-range frontal shot would bust through the thick armor.

"Take out the fucking treads!" cried Will.

Pfc Delgado rammed another rocket in the tube and hastily connected the necessary wires. The young man's hands were shaking as he heard the distinct mechanical whir of the Panther's turret rotating in their direction. He rapped Minske's helmet twice just as the Panther peppered their lines with machine gun fire, forcing both men to dive for cover.

Get up, Will thought.

As if reading Will's mind, Minske calmly rose to one knee, chewing on an unlit cigar butt as he shouldered the bazooka again. He pulled the trigger on the launcher and watched the rocket fly towards the Panther, striking the front left tread. The massive tank came to a sudden stop, lost in a cloud of smoke. It took a few seconds for the wind to clear the air, revealing a tread that was now a mangled mess of steel. Minske could hear gears grinding as the driver tried to move the tank off the road so others could press ahead, but to no avail. The Panther would not budge.

Meanwhile, the Mark IV, smaller but still formidable, began maneuvering to the right of her sister tank, where the narrow shoulder was more level with the road. In a stroke of luck for the Americans, the Mark IV's right tread inched off the shoulder, and began digging into the edge of the embankment, softened by weeks of saturation. The Mark IV lost traction, and the tread became immersed in mud as the driver labored to maneuver the tank back onto the road.

His tube loaded again, Minske aimed the bazooka at the stationary Mark IV, as easy a target he would ever have. Just as his finger touched the trigger, there was a burst of fire from the Panther's machine gun and Minske was thrown backwards, the bullets catching him in the chest and throat. Delgado cried out and crawled to Minske, but the corporal was already dead, his torso a mess of blood and bone. The Panther's machine gun opened up again, and Delgado flattened himself on the ground as bullets streaked over his head.

Peeking out from the rim of his foxhole, Will watched Delgado turn toward his own hole. It was just yards away, but it may as well have been miles. The young man was pinned down in the open, overcome with fright and unable to make his way back to safety.

Will called out, trying to raise his voice above the chatter of weapons from both sides.

"Delgado!"

The shaking Pfc could not see him, but he turned his head, recognizing the voice.

"Get up, Hector! Use the bazooka!"

Delgado gave a short nod of acknowledgment. His eyes shifted to the bazooka, still laying where Minske had dropped it, just as a second German machine gun began firing, punching into the American lines. But he remained still, paralyzed with fear.

Will's eyes moved from the Mark IV, still struggling to move forward, to the wounded Panther, the two tanks now abreast of each other and trading fire with the Americans. They had unwittingly formed their own roadblock, preventing the other German armor from advancing on the road.

That gave Will an idea. He fed a fresh clip into his rifle and scrambled out of the trench, ignoring Janikowski's tirade as he darted up the embankment, across the road, and toward the far right of their position. The German fire lessened the further he moved down the line. He slid into the last foxhole, finding a lone 4th Squad soldier firing short bursts from his BAR. The man agreed to cover Will, who sucked in a deep breath and bounded out of the hole, this time in a dead run directly toward the German lines. He nearly fell in the dark as the ground dipped into a depression, his boots sloshing through several inches of icy water.

Miraculously, he had not drawn any enemy fire. Either the Germans hadn't spotted him, or they were unconcerned about one lone rifleman madly charging their position. Will was roughly halfway to where he figured the German lines were when he made a sharp left, now on a perpendicular path toward the two German tanks, hoping he was invisible to the crews inside their hulls.

They had peepholes, but would surely be watching the American lines ahead, not their own flanks. He wasn't quite invisible to the German infantry scattered in the fields. Bullets began tearing into the ground around Will, whistling past his ears as he ran on. He was nearly to the highway when he heard a forceful shout in English, followed by a volley of fire from the American line.

Lucas was ordering covering fire.

The platoon's machine guns peppered the German lines, quieting much of the return fire. Will finally reached the highway, climbing up the embankment again and collapsing against the Panther's left tread as he gasped for breath. He set his M1 down and pulled the Colt .45 handgun from its leather holster. Grabbing a handhold, Will climbed onto the tank, just as the turret rotated to the left, a gunner sending steady bursts of machine gun fire into the American lines. Thankfully, with so many tracer rounds firing, Will's men could see what he was up to and ceased firing at the German tanks.

Without warning, the Panther's cannon roared and Will nearly lost his balance as the giant machine shuddered. He steadied himself, his ears ringing from the blast, and saw the dead German commander he had shot minutes ago. The officer's upper body was protruding from the open turret hatch, face down, his overcoat bathed in blood. Holstering his sidearm, Will grabbed the man's arms and hefted him upright, dropping the corpse into the turret. As his body crumpled to the base of the hull, Will heard shouts of panic in German. He pulled a grenade from his pocket, yanked the pin and threw it inside, slamming the hatch shut. Seconds later, there was a muffled explosion and the machine gun fell silent. Will leapt from the tank, barrel-rolling to his feet. He plucked his M1 off the ground and zig-zagged back to his own lines while the platoon threw up a curtain of protective fire. He dove into his trench, crashing into Janikowski's legs once again, the man letting loose a flurry of words Will wasn't sure he had even heard before. Will's chest was heaving, and despite the temperature, he was lathered in sweat.

"Holy shit, Sarge!" exclaimed Sloan excitedly, still firing his BAR. "Who said catchers can't run?"

Janikowski untangled his legs from Will's. "That was the stupidest fucking thing I've ever seen! Why can't you stay in your hole?"

Will gave a faint, pained smile, his breathing still heavy. "Remind me never to do it again."

They were interrupted by a piercing explosion as one of the American half-tracks took a direct hit from the Mark IV's cannon. A reminder that the fight was far from over. As the Panzer's crew reloaded, the driver was finally inching the wayward tread back on to the road. If he could maneuver the tank again, it would uncork the bottle, freeing the other German tanks behind it. The Mark IV fired again, its shell landing just behind another half-track. The German gunner began lowering his elevation as the tank's machine gun stopped firing. Perhaps reloading as well.

Will peered out of the foxhole and saw Delgado was gone, having used Will's escapade to safely retreat to his hole. Will called to him and the young Pfc's helmet popped up. Delgado followed Will's eyes to the Mark IV, and then to the mud-splattered bazooka, on the ground next to where Minske had fallen.

Delgado gave Will a toothy grin, and the boy was suddenly on his feet. He ran past Minske's corpse, scooping up the loaded bazooka and hefting it on his shoulder. Will shouted encouragement, and ordered those nearby to lay down suppressing fire. Delgado balanced himself on one knee as the Mark IV's machine gun began firing again. He pressed the trigger, his first time firing the big gun.

Fortunately, at that range, the young man could not miss. The rocket hit the Mark IV square in the front of the hull. Unlike the Panther, though, the rocket sliced through the armored plating and detonated inside, blowing the turret clean off. Delgado raised a fist in triumph, and even Will joined the rest of the platoon in a raucous cheer. The disabled Panzers sat side-by-side, the two smoking hulks completely blocking the road.

Other German tanks, meanwhile, were steadily making progress crossing the fields, supported by half-tracks filled with *Panzergrenadiers,* the German version of mechanized infantry. A lead tank ran over one of Meyer's TNT bundles and the blast brought the Panzer to a halt, black smoke pouring from its engine block. A bazooka rocket flew through the night, striking the tank in the seam between the turret and the hull. Several other German tanks fired almost in unison, as if in angry response. The fusillade tore into the American position, one shell hitting a foxhole and blowing the three occupants into the air like broken rag dolls. Will heard the screams, followed by the anguished cries for their lone medic.

The casualties were mounting. Will knew he should consult with Lucas, but they were out of time.

"Meyer!" Will called out. The engineer was two foxholes over. "Yo!"

"I need you and your men to get the wounded to the half-tracks."

Most men would have balked at such an idea in the face of intensive enemy fire, but Meyer had lived through far worse. Without another word, his engineers scrambled out of their foxholes and began retrieving the wounded men, carrying or dragging them to safety.

The Germans fought on, determined to break the back of what they now knew was an inferior force. An empty clip flew out of Will's M1 and he quickly reloaded, knowing they were all running low on ammunition. A Panzer in the field to his left fired a round, the shell landing in the midst of the 1st Squad. The medic could not keep up.

Fuck this, Will thought to himself. It was time to pull back to Noville.

As if to confirm that thought, a new sound brought a shudder to nearly every man on the line. In that brief instant, Will knew the fight was lost. It was the distinctive, shrill whistle of a German artillery shell. Not from a tank, but from a towed artillery piece far behind the German lines. It passed over their position, detonating well behind the half-tracks. Several more followed, and Will quickly crawled toward Lucas' foxhole where he found the lieutenant and his runner firing their rifles. He shouted to be heard over the cacophony of gunfire and explosions.

"Sir, they've called in artillery! Time to haul ass!"

Lucas gave him a short nod. "Tell the .50 cals on the half-tracks to cover our withdrawal, and put up as much fire as they can!"

Will retreated to where the remaining half-tracks were positioned, shouting instructions to the machine gunners. He turned back to the line, seeing Lucas pulling the men back, emphatic and standing tall as he directed each squad to carry out both their wounded and the heavier weapons they would need in Noville. Will couldn't hold back a smile, realizing how much he had misjudged the former National Guardsman.

With the 10th Armored men fleeing their foxholes, the Germans pressed the attack. Helping to pull the last men aboard the half-tracks, Will thought he heard the distinct sound of an American .30 caliber machine gun coming from the main line. From atop the half-track, he scanned the fields ahead, following the tracer lines back toward one of their machine gun pits. He could make out the gunner's upper body above the rim of the hole. As Lucas shouted for the trucks to move out, Will hopped down from his and ran forward, wondering what asshole didn't hear the order to bug out. He dove into the pit next to the gunner, astonished to see Delgado. A blood-soaked bandage was wrapped around his left thigh.

Will grabbed his sleeve. "Let's go, Hector! We're pulling out!"

Delgado finished firing a long burst. "Can't run, Sarge. My leg. You go!"

The belt of ammunition ran out, and Delgado reached for another. "They're trying to get around us!" he shouted, pulling back the bolt and pressing the trigger again.

Will looked to where Delgado was training his aim. Two German armored vehicles were bolting across the field, oblivious to the mines, trying to cut off the retreating Americans. And here was Delgado, a scrawny, terrified kid, trying to save them all.

He grabbed Delgado's arm, more forcefully this time. "We're leaving now. I'll help–"

There was a sudden explosion and Will was thrown backward by a wave of hot air. He landed sharply on his back, the wind punched from his lungs as Delgado fell on him. A warm wetness splashed across Will's left cheek as clumps of earth rained down on the two men.

Will spat out a mouthful of dirt, coughing the cordite out of his lungs.

"Hector," he gasped. "You hit?"

There was no response, and Delgado's limp form did not move. Will gently pushed Delgado to the side, and in the early morning twilight, he could see part of the boy's head was missing. Will shrieked and stumbled back in the hole, unable to keep from gawking at the grotesque, shattered skull, and a face unrecognizable now, torn apart by a large piece of shrapnel.

He felt a yank on the back of his collar, and hands pulling on his biceps. He was lifted from the gun pit, falling to the ground beside Lucas and Janikowski.

"Oh, Jesus," whispered Lucas, staring at Will's face in horror.

"Will, you okay?" Janikowski snapped his fingers in front of Will's eyes. His hand grabbed Will's jaw and roughly swiveled his head from side to side. He turned to Lucas. "I don't think that's his blood, sir. It's probably Delgado's."

"Okay, let's get him out of here."

They heaved Will to his feet, and the three men fled to the last remaining half-track as shells continued to fall around them. Arms reached down and pulled Will up, laying him on the floor of the vehicle. The other men hunched down behind the armored sides, shielding themselves from the storm of German fire. The driver put the vehicle in gear and they hurried away from what was left of the outpost, leaving a number of their dead behind. Will looked upward, the glow of daybreak edging across the horizon as the crimson splotches of blood slowly congealed on his face.

Chapter 14

Dawn was breaking, but with a thick fog continuing to shroud Noville, the rising sun was reduced to barely a faint glow in the distance. The riddled vehicles carrying the remnants of 2nd Platoon passed through the perimeter defenses following a tense exchange of passwords and countersigns. With waves of German tanks and infantry converging on Noville from multiple directions, the Americans were all on edge.

Will had pulled himself up to the riding bench, squeezing himself between Janikowski and Sloan. The men in the half-track were quiet, cigarettes clenched between quivering lips as they tried to collect themselves in the aftermath of the frenzied chaos at the roadblock. The ferocity of the German attack was like nothing they had experienced before. Even in Metz.

Their vehicles were quickly waved onto a side road, and the drivers shut down the engines as the men sluggishly climbed down and awaited orders. Major Desobry appeared, followed by Captain Schultz, the latter frowning at the absence of his two tanks. They intercepted Lucas before the lieutenant had one foot out of his jeep.

Janikowski stood in the half-track looking down on his friend, glassy-eyed and slouched low on the bench. He pulled Will to his feet, leading him off the half-track and to the nearby command post. As they stepped inside, Will tried to push Janikowski away, but a wave of dizziness washed across him and his knees began to falter. Janikowski grabbed the bigger man under his arm and eased him gently to the floor, propping his back against the wall. Desobry came through the door, visibly surprised when he spied Janikowski kneeling beside the prone sergeant.

The major hurried over. "Oh, Christ. How bad is it, Corporal? Why the hell isn't he with the medics?"

"He ain't wounded, sir," answered Janikowski, rising to his feet. "That's Pfc Delgado's blood. It was pretty bad. Thought I best bring him in here, so the platoon don't see him like this."

Desobry dropped to one knee, wincing as he examined Will's face. "Sergeant?"

There was no response. Will was in a trance, unable to see anything but an image of Delgado in that gun pit. An 18-year-old who placed his own life ahead of so many others, only to have fate lash out against his daring with a ghastly death. Will's mind replayed those sickening final seconds, over and over again. The explosion, the warm spray of blood, the fragments from the boy's head. He squeezed his eyes closed but the grisly vision remained.

Desobry put a hand on Will's shoulder. "Will," he said louder, shaking him roughly.

Will blinked his eyes several times before he was able to focus on Desobry, the major still gripping his shoulder tightly.

"Sir," Will said, the response automatic.

"You okay, Sergeant?"

Will nodded distractedly.

"Talk to me, Will."

Will hesitated, struggling to put his thoughts into words.

"Delgado," Will started, his voice shaking. "He was right in front of me. His head..."

Will's voice faded and Desobry turned to Janikowski behind him. "Rejoin your platoon, Corporal. I'll keep an eye on him."

Janikowski nodded, too tired to salute. He slung his rifle over his shoulder and exited the command post. Desobry took the canteen from his belt and doused a handkerchief with cold water. He used the wet cloth to wipe the dried blood from Will's face, his own stomach convulsing as he picked off the pieces of brain matter that had crusted on the sergeant's cheek and forehead.

"Stay put, Will," Desobry said softly when he had finished. "We'll find you some coffee."

The last few words had fallen on deaf ears, Will's eyelids

drooping as his chin fell to his chest. He was fast asleep.

Time passed, though Will had no idea how much. His eyes fluttered open as he felt someone tugging on his ankle. Instinctively, Will yanked the sidearm from his holster, leveling it at the stranger in front of him.

It was a civilian. He was older, with white hair, a thick mustache, and the pallid skin of someone who spent considerable time indoors. A green Army blanket covered Will's legs and the man was unlacing one of Will's boots. There was a young boy, also on the floor, pulling on Will's other boot. They were each wearing threadbare coats and thick wool mufflers, and stared wide-eyed at Will and the barrel of his pistol.

"Hell you doing?" Will whispered hoarsely, his mouth dry.

The older man let forth a burst of French. When it was clear Will didn't understand, the man turned to the child and repeated himself. He spoke rapidly but calmly, and when finished, he gestured toward Will. The boy cleared his throat and spoke in English that was only slightly accented.

"*Capitaine*, this is *Monsieur* Amand."

"I'm a sergeant, not a captain. Is he a doctor?"

The boy laughed, until the older man shot him a reproachful look.

"*Non, sergent*," the boy said, serious again. "He is the schoolmaster."

Amand spoke several sentences to the boy, who turned again to Will.

"He says your feet are wet, and we must dry them fast before they, how do you say, get bigger?"

"Swollen."

"*Oui.*"

Will nodded, remembering the frigid water he had splashed through while charging the German tanks. He holstered the .45 as the pair resumed pulling the boots from Will's feet. They then peeled off his damp socks, the boy recoiling from the stench.

Will's attention shifted across the room, where Desobry and two other officers were hunched over the kitchen table, studying a map. The radioman was seated cross-legged on the floor, eating breakfast out of a can as he listened intently on a headset. Another aide was carrying in crates of supplies from outside. Will drank from his canteen, then eyed the schoolmaster again, the man now pulling off his own shoes and socks.

"What's he doing?" Will asked the boy.

More words were exchanged between the two villagers. "*Monsieur* Amand is wearing two pairs of socks," explained the boy. "He says you must take one pair."

Will stared at the older man. "You're giving me your socks?"

The boy quickly translated.

"*Oui*," Amand responded, lacing his shoes up again.

"Why?"

"*Pourquoi?*" asked the boy.

"*Ami*," said the man, starting to work one of his socks over Will's toes. Will put his hand on Amand's to stop him, then began pulling the sock on himself.

"*Merci, mon ami*," said Will, and the old man smiled warmly at him in return.

Will turned to the boy. "What's your name?"

"Philippe. Philippe Dupard."

Amand said a few words and mussed the boy's hair, laughing and winking at Will.

"What'd he say?"

Philippe looked embarrassed. "He says I am his best pupil."

A shell exploded down the street, followed by several more. The walls shook and chunks of plaster fell from the ceiling. Everyone instinctively glanced upward, wondering if the next round would fall in their laps. But nothing more followed, and Will finished pulling on the socks. They were made of thick, homespun wool, and felt marvelous.

Amand spoke again, and the boy quickly translated.

"He says the shoes must dry before putting them on again."

Will ignored the advice and reached for his boots. "Where'd you learn to speak English?"

The boy looked at him, confused. "From *Monsieur* Amand, of course."

Will stopped lacing his boot, looking back and forth between the two villagers.

The schoolmaster smiled at Will. "I taught him."

Will blinked. "You speak English?"

"*Naturellement*. Very much so."

"Then why the fu–." Will saw Philippe studying him and checked himself. "Why're you using the boy as a translator?"

"It is the best way for him to learn," explained Amand. "And with all of these Americans in Belgium, his English will be most useful in the future."

Amand nodded at the boy as he softened his voice. "Philippe has no real home anymore. His parents were murdered when the Germans came through here in 1940. His sisters were taken away by the SS. He has been living with the Lemaitre family, near Bourcy, where the Germans are now. As for me, well, the school here in Noville is my home." He waited, and Will saw something flicker in the man's eyes. "This village had suffered through four years of occupation. What the SS did when they first came through here...it is unspeakable."

The older man looked away, toward the door. Outside, where the enemy was. "We were liberated, more than a month ago, by Americans. I will not stand by while the Germans attempt to take this village again."

Will finished with his boots and threw the blanket off his legs. His head felt clear now, and he rose to his feet, unsteadily at first. Amand and Philippe stood with him and the boy wrapped a small arm around Will's waist, aiding his balance. Will gave the boy's shoulder a squeeze in gratitude.

"Kid, you ever find yourself in Griffith Stadium, you look me up."

Philippe wrinkled his nose. He looked to the schoolmaster for help, but Amand was equally confused and could only shrug. Desobry, meanwhile, took notice that Will was standing again, and approached the threesome.

"*Monsieur,*" he said, addressing Amand. "The Germans will be here any minute. I would advise you and the boy to either leave Noville, or find a cellar somewhere."

"You are using the schoolhouse for wounded men, no?"

"Yes, and we've marked it with red crosses. But no guarantee the German tanks and artillery will see it's an aid station."

"That is where I will go. I can assist your medical people."

"And the boy?" Will asked.

Amand and Philippe shared a knowing smile. "We have a hiding place for him," said Amand. "Under the floorboards in the school-house. It has worked well in the past."

Will grasped the man's hand. "Thank you for the socks."

"No, Sergeant," said Amand, covering Will's hand with both of his. "Thank you for being here. For fighting these wicked men on our behalf."

Will mussed the boy's hair, just as Amand had done, and Philippe's face broke into a wide grin.

The two civilians said their farewells and left the house. Desobry watched Will bundle himself up.

"Going somewhere, Sergeant? You look a bit wobbly."

"Back to the line, sir. I'm fine."

"You want a medic to check you out?"

"I'm not wounded."

"Maybe you need some sack time. I can–"

"I said I'm fine, Major," Will barked. "Just back off, for Christ's sake!"

The other officers turned in surprise, and Will clamped his mouth shut, a second too late. He looked at his feet, unable to meet Desobry's eyes.

"Sergeant Jamison," Desobry began, his voice cold. He stopped there.

Will nodded, accepting the silent rebuke. "Sorry, sir. Not myself right now. Just looking to get back to my platoon."

With a nod from Desobry, his subordinates resumed their duties and the major stepped closer, keeping his voice even. "I think we're all a little squirrelly right now, Sergeant. Your men were placed with 3rd Platoon, holding the north end of the village. You drove past the position on your way back into Noville. It's where the Krauts will likely hit us first. We've spread the bazookas and anti-tank guns along the perimeter, but tell Lucas I'm keeping a section of Shermans as a ready reserve. If he needs them, send a runner."

"Yes, sir," Will said, snapping as sharp a salute he could muster.

Desobry ignored it and placed a hand on Will's shoulder instead.

"I need you out there, Will. You're the best I got. Hold that ground, keep your men together. I don't want to see a single Kraut in this village."

Will nodded an acknowledgment. He found his helmet and started for the door, swinging it open as a blast of cold air swept into the house.

"One last thing," Desobry called.

Will turned, one foot out the door. "Sir?"

Desobry gestured to the corner of the room, where several rifles were stacked against the wall. Most likely collected from the men wounded at the outposts. "You may need one of those."

Will gave an embarrassed smile, having forgotten he was unarmed. He quickly picked out an M1, slinging it over his shoulder as he pulled a bandoleer of ammunition from an open crate and stuffed his pockets with hand grenades. The weight of the weapons and ammo gave Will comfort, as did the strength he could feel returning to his body. He left the house and broke into a light jog, anxious to find his men. The main road had been cleared of vehicles, dispersed long ago among the side roads and structures to conceal them from the enemy's heavy guns.

Not that any German forward observer could see his hand in front of his face right now. Though the sun was climbing higher in the eastern sky, the fog remained obstinate, leaving the surrounding terrain completely veiled from the Americans. After passing a Sherman tank peeking out from behind the beer hall, Will found the 2nd and 3rd Platoons. They were well dug in, straddling both sides of the road. Still unable to see more than a few feet ahead, Will nearly toppled into a mortar pit. The crew directed him to Lucas, who had placed himself in a forward position, just yards away from the road and a cemetery. Will could see the shapes of several grave markers ahead of Lucas, but almost nothing beyond that. As he drew nearer, he heard Lucas quietly conferring with Pfc Hayward.

"Not so loud, Lieutenant," warned Will, crouching down at the edge of the shallow trench. "You'll wake the dead."

Lucas turned, looking up at Will in the surprise.

"Sergeant," he said, the relief evident in his voice. "You're back. You sure you're okay? You don't look good."

"You're no Cary Grant yourself, sir. How're things looking?"

"For us or the Germans?"

Will gave an appreciative smile. He was liking this man more and more. "Let's start with us."

"We've got about 50 men between the two platoons, and some idiot left me in charge. We can't see a damn thing past our holes. Hitler could be standing right over there for all I know. We heard a hell of a racket half an hour ago, sounded like the Krauts moved every tank left in the Third Reich in front of us. Not a peep since."

Will shook his head at the futility of holding out against such overwhelming odds. "I saw one Sherman back there. Anything else?"

"No other tanks, but Desobry gave us an anti-tank gun. The crew is set up behind the last house, and they're sighted on the road."

That was good news. The British-designed M-1 Anti-Tank Gun

fired an armor-piercing round that was lethal to most German tanks. It was a towed gun, and therefore had limited mobility, but if the gun was positioned to fire on anything coming down that road, it would cause all sorts of headaches for the German advance.

Will looked across the cemetery, the fog fusing now with the morning light. He could barely see a few feet ahead.

"Any idea how far out they are?"

Lucas took a swallow from his canteen. "If I had to guess, less than a thousand yards. But that's just a guess."

"How are we fixed for ammo?"

"Everyone is loaded up, and we've got plenty for the bazookas and .30 cals."

"Desobry is keeping a section of Shermans in reserve. He says if we need them, send a runner."

Lucas nodded. "If we can–"

His words were cut off by a series of thumping noises in the distance, followed by the high-pitched whistles of German artillery shells streaking across the sky.

"INCOMING!" someone yelled unnecessarily. Most of the men were already in their holes, and Will jumped into the trench with Lucas and Hayward. The three men got as low as they could, covering their heads with their arms as two shells landed nearby, showering them with dirt and stones.

Another salvo arrived seconds later, one blast ripping apart a 3rd Platoon machine gun crew. More incoming rounds shrieked overhead, a full cannonade now, as dozens of shells pounded the thin American defenses. Even through the booming, deafening explosions, Will could hear the agonizing screams of the wounded men. The ground shook violently, and it seemed just a matter of seconds before their hole would be hit, blowing each of them to bits if they were lucky. Burying them all alive if they weren't.

The explosions continued for several minutes, each man overcome with sheer terror. Will sensed movement next to him, and saw Lucas clawing at the dirt, trying to climb to the surface.

Will grabbed him by the back of the collar as another shell exploded in front of them.

He had to shout into the man's ear to be heard. "Where the hell you going, sir?"

Lucas tried to pull free, but Will would not release his grasp. Another shell landed nearby, dumping mud and rocks on the men again.

"I'm getting out of here! Let me go!"

Will threw the lieutenant against the side of the trench. "Are you nuts? You'll get torn apart out there!"

The panic-stricken Lucas was shaking. "We can't stay here! We'll die in here! Let me go!" He was nearly out of the hole when Will grabbed him by the collar again. Lucas threw his right elbow back, catching Will square in the chin. He grimaced from the sharp pain, then grabbed the lieutenant's shoulder and spun him around, delivering a right cross that connected with Lucas' left cheekbone, sending the man's eyeglasses flying through the air. His eyes rolled to the back of his head and he slumped to the ground.

Will snatched the glasses from the mud, slipping them into his pocket as he and Hayward cowered in the trench next to the prone Lucas. The Germans were shelling the village from all sides now, terrorizing the Americans under the bombardment. Some of the men turned to prayer, while others suffered the indignity of their bowels emptying. For most, there was little to do but burrow deeper into the ground. Will felt the vibrations from every blast, certain the earthen walls were going to cave in from the pressure. He clamped his hands over his ears, unable to drown out the earsplitting explosions. A shell hit just a few feet away, the concussion throwing all three men into the air. They landed in a heap at the bottom of the trench, Lucas still unconscious. Hayward was bawling now as he curled himself into a ball. Another shell landed just a few feet away, followed by a series of whistling inbound shells, and Will threw his body on top of Lucas. Dozens of shells landed on the two platoons, the explosions ripping through the air without pause and sending shrapnel and debris flying in all directions.

Will pressed his face into Lucas' back. He tried to breathe, realizing he was on the verge of a horrifying death. Though no one could see or hear him, Will was sobbing, something he had not done since he was a little boy, as the tears poured from his face and pooled on the back of Lucas' field jacket.

The shelling lasted another 15 minutes, the seconds ticking by so slow it seemed as if time had stopped. And then, finally and abruptly, there was silence, the barrage lifted.

As the last pieces of earth fell to the ground and the smoke began to clear, no one moved, the American position eerily still. Those unscathed were frozen with fear and shock, some unable to accept they had survived. Will's ears were ringing, but he could hear the moaning of the wounded, and the babbling, incoherent voices of those driven half-mad by the barrage.

Will pulled himself off Lucas, quickly wiping his cheeks with the back of his sleeve. Hayward was cowering in the bottom of the trench, still weeping, his head in his hands. Lucas finally stirred and slowly rolled on to his back. Blood trickled from his nose and down his chin. The side of his face was also turning a deep purple, adding to the evidence he would surely use for Will's court martial.

Every man in Noville had been subjected to the prolonged barrage, but as their hearing and senses gradually returned, there was no time to recover. German armor could be both heard and felt throughout the village perimeter. Whether it was reflexive, or simply because the men had no other choice, they climbed to the tops of their holes and shouldered their weapons. The steady growl of tank engines was gathering, clearly heading their way.

"Hayward," Will said, grabbing the runner by the arm and pulling him to his feet. "You okay?"

"Yes, Sergeant," the dazed youngster responded, his voice shaky and quiet as he wiped his eyes.

"I need you to take the lieutenant to a hole further back. Where he can coordinate things. Can you do that?"

Hayward nodded and helped Lucas to his feet. The officer was holding his jaw and would not look at either man, but he followed Hayward without protest, wordlessly accepting his glasses from Will.

Will peered over the side of his hole and saw the fog had still not lifted. It may have worsened, as he could only make out the helmets of the men in the foxholes around him. Will cupped his hands around his mouth and called out.

"Who's got a bazooka?"

Two men nearby answered, and Will immediately recognized one of the voices. "Is that you, Quinn?"

"Yep."

"You ready?"

"They got Rosie and Deluca," Quinn snarled, referring to his squad mates. "Any of those Kraut assholes come down the road, they're mine."

It was Janikowski's suggestion months ago to put the men with attitudes on the bazookas. With Minske dead, Will was grateful Tommy Quinn was in the next hole. He was a brawler.

The sound of the oncoming Germans grew louder and Will shouted instructions to the men. Quinn was closest to the road and would take the first shot, signaling the other bazookas and the anti-tank gun to let loose. The problem was the fog. They still couldn't see an inch past the graveyard. Anything beyond that, they may as well have had their eyes closed. At least the Germans would be equally blind.

The ground trembled again, and from the din it was clear that more than one tank was bearing down on them. Out of the fog they emerged, two Panthers, leading a small number of *Panzergrenadiers*.

Will heard Quinn's bazooka fire, followed by the metallic clang of the rocket bouncing off the heavy armor of the lead Panther. He was readying a tirade of curses for Quinn when the anti-tank gun fired, its armor-piercing round blasting through the frontal plating of the same tank. The Panther burst into flames and Will heard celebratory shouting from the anti-tank gun crew. The second Panther maneuvered around the first and fired, its shot crashing into the beer hall. The blast took out an entire section of the building, brick walls and wood flooring crumbling to the ground in a pile of smoking rubble.

The Panther had clearly spotted the Sherman. Will gave a cold smile, knowing the American tank should have been the least of the Panther's worries. Two bazookas fired in succession at the Panther, one missing long but the other striking the tank's left track, bringing the German tank to a halt. The anti-tank gun crew smelled blood and struck the wounded Panther in the turret with a fatal round. Both tanks were now completely out of action.

The German infantry attempted to charge across the open field, cloaked by the fog, but without their armor leading the way, they had little support. The volley of lead from the American machine gunners and riflemen mowed a number of the Germans down and kept most others pinned to the ground. The *Panzergrenadiers* quickly retreated back into the thick haze, carrying their wounded and leaving their dead behind. The surviving crewmen from the second Panther tried to abandon their vehicle but were caught in a vicious crossfire, their bodies thrashing about as they were torn apart by large caliber bullets.

Lucas finally called a cease fire, and the battlefield fell silent again. Across the cemetery, the two Panthers lay in the road, smoldering, the corpses of their crew members draped around them.

By some miracle, the American suffered few casualties. It was a relatively tepid assault, a minor probe to gauge the strength of the Americans on this end of the village. While they had repulsed the modest German force rather easily, there was no celebrating among the defenders. Nor did they bother to taunt the German infantrymen who were still withdrawing back to their lines.

They knew this was just the beginning.

Chapter 15

The twin wisps of black smoke swirled around the demolished German tanks before snaking into the overcast sky. The twisted steel remains sat atop the highway like two charging beasts, felled by a big game hunter as they made a final lunge for their prey.

The German artillery had fallen silent after a series of morning barrages. Those manning the perimeter lines took advantage of the reprieve, mostly to care for and evacuate the wounded while cold rations and ammunition were brought forward. Though the 10th Armored men fared well in fending off the initial probe, the Germans were surely priming for a mass assault. There was talk in the ranks about withdrawing, the men carping among themselves about the lack of any fallback plan should the Germans break through. How long could the small force be expected to withstand an entire Panzer division?

Major Desobry, at least, appreciated their plight. He knew the approaches to the north and northeast were the most likely focal points of the impending German attack, yet there was little he could send to reinforce those positions, sparing only an additional Sherman tank and two bazooka teams. A few more stones for David's slingshot.

It was nearly ten in the morning, and the fog was still clinging to Noville, denying the Americans much of a view beyond their own lines. From the experience at the outpost, Will at least knew the highway to Houffalize led to higher ground, maybe half a mile away. Anything else was pure guesswork, as they could see virtually nothing past the cemetery and the destroyed German tanks.

Their spirits were briefly lifted when pots of coffee miraculously appeared after the last round of shelling. Sent from Desobry's command post, there was barely enough for half a cup per man, and it was lukewarm at best. But for the beleaguered men in the entrenchments it was a Godsend, and they grasped their tin mess cups with both hands, savoring each sip as if they were enjoying the finest champagne in all of Europe.

As the minutes passed with still no sign of the Germans, wishful conjecture took hold among the men that Noville may have been bypassed. Will dismissed that idea. It was clear now the Germans needed the juncture of three major roads, and the village controlled the juncture. False hope, though, was better for the men than no hope, so he kept his dour view to himself.

The exhausted men prepared themselves as best they could. They picked at their rations, scrounged for bazooka rockets and grenades, and tried to catch whatever few minutes of sleep were possible. Janikowski, who could doze through most anything, was curled in a ball next to Will in their foxhole, snoring peacefully under a thin blanket.

Will returned his attention to the box of K rations in his lap. He had little appetite but forced down several bites anyway, knowing he would need every ounce of strength before the day was through. Will's intestines fought back, refusing to digest any more of the chopped ham and eggs likely canned during Roosevelt's first term. He threw away the dry crackers and focused on the Hershey bar, evoking warm memories of Endicott's Candy Store in Lancaster. He tore off the wrapper and bit into the hard chocolate, savoring every morsel. Pocketing the Wrigley's Spearmint and packet of instant coffee, he was left with one last item, what most men considered the treasure in these cartons, the miniature pack of four cigarettes.

Though the stench of cigarette smoke had always been anathema to Will, he had become accustomed to it in the Army. He had no choice. Nearly everyone in his outfit was taken with tobacco. Lev Meyer chain-smoked Chesterfields. Janikowski was a Lucky Strikes man. Even Sloan, the Santa Fe cowboy, had a permanent wad of Yankee Girl chaw in his cheek.

Will twirled the small pack of Camels. He gave a quick glance to Janikowski, mumbling in his sleep something about a girl named

Pauline, and tore open the cellophane. Like an impish boy reaching into the cookie jar, he placed one of the Camels between his lips, striking a match and pressing the small flame to the end of the cigarette.

Will sucked in deeply, his mouth filling immediately with the rich smoke. He reflexively blew it out, his face souring from the foul and unpleasant taste. He figured he could tolerate it a bit longer, so he took another drag, holding this one for a few seconds before exhaling again. He looked at the cigarette derisively, feeling nothing.

He inhaled once more, even longer this time, and held it for a beat or two. Parting his lips, he tried sucking the smoke into his lungs, but his throat constricted, causing a fit of coughing as he fumbled the cigarette into the mud.

Will took a swig of water from his canteen and spat it out, missing the retched aftertaste of the ham and eggs rotting in his gut. He was determined to smoke his first cigarette, though, and finish it. So he fished out another and searched for the matches.

"Here." It was Janikowski, still curled under his blanket, but fully awake now and watching Will with bemusement. He handed over a gold Zippo lighter.

"Keep it. I got another I took off a dead Kraut in Metz. Take shorter pulls at first. Normal breaths, not long, deep ones. You'll get the hang of it."

"Who says I want to get the–"

Will cut off his own words, hearing heavy footsteps nearby. He tossed away the cigarette and both he and Janikowski reached for their rifles.

"That you, Sergeant?" came a soft voice from above. Even whispered, the lieutenant's voice seemed resounding across the open ground.

Will stood, stretching his back and arms. "Yes, sir."

Lucas lowered himself to his haunches and rubbed his gloved hands together, his rifle slung over one shoulder. There was little concern about snipers in this haze.

"How are you men faring?"

Will shrugged, throwing two sticks of gum in his mouth to kill whatever was still festering. "We're okay, sir. Wish we had more bazookas."

Lucas rubbed his jaw absently, and Will could see the left side of his face was still swollen. "I'll see if Major Desobry can send us anything more. That all?"

Will nodded, hoping to diffuse the simmering tension between them. "The men are a little down. Maybe the USO could stop by?"

Lucas grinned. "I played golf with Bob Hope last week. Let me ask him."

Janikowski was looking out toward the German lines. "You played golf with Bob Hope?"

Lucas winked at Will. "It was a jest, Corporal, I–"

"Lieutenant," warned Janikowski with quiet alarm. "You better get in here!"

Will and Lucas both turned in the direction Janikowski was looking, surprised at the man's urgent tone as there was still nothing but silence coming from the German lines. It took less than a heartbeat for them to realize the danger, and that it wasn't what they could hear. It was what they could see.

The cemetery had generally marked the extent of their visibility, the main road melting into a dark mist beyond that point. No longer. Will's eyes first took in the symmetrical row of trees lining the far edge of the cemetery. They hadn't been able to see those before, and were, Will realized, the first trees he had seen since they arrived. There was more, as they could now see well beyond the cemetery, and as the seconds ticked by, the road came increasingly into focus, foot by foot.

The fog was lifting.

Lucas waved a warning to others nearby before sliding into the foxhole next to Will and Janikowski. The three men raised their weapons to the parapet, hearing ammunition clips being rammed into rifles and bolts clicking as every man on the perimeter readied himself. The wind had picked up, and with it, the remaining fog rose slowly from the ground, as if pushed upward by a magical hand.

"Son of a bitch," murmured Janikowski.

His voice was not alone, as Will heard a stream of other curses from the men positioned nearby.

For the first time since the armored column arrived the previous evening, they had a clear view of their surroundings. Facing Noville were two long ridges boxing in the village. The highest was to the east, toward Bourcy. Another was due north, and perpendicular to the highway that led to Houffalize. The elevation provided the Germans atop the ridges with a commanding view of Noville and beyond. Worse, every inch of ground adjoining Noville sloped upwards, as if the village was in the base of a shallow bowl, with the ridges forming the rim. Stretching across that rim was an imposing, menacing sight that the American defenders could only gape at with hopelessness.

It was a breathtaking mass of German machinery. Row after row of tanks, the snouts of their cannons looming over Noville like the Sword of Damocles. Will could see dozens of them on the two ridge lines alone, hordes of Mark IVs flanking the larger Mark V Panthers.

Will tapped Lucas on the arm. "Sir, your runner."

Lucas nodded. "Hayward!" he called out, no longer concerned about noise.

The young soldier quickly appeared, scooting into their hole, his face a mask of fear.

"Find Major Desobry, tell him what we're seeing. We're going to need whatever tanks he's got in reserve."

Hayward scurried from the hole and ran back toward Desobry's command post, returning just a few minutes later, breathless but his eyes full of sudden vigor. To everyone's incomprehension, the German tanks had still not moved or fired.

"Are we getting more tanks?" asked Lucas.

"No, sir. The major said he can do better. We just got a platoon of Hellcats from Bastogne."

"Hallelujah," Will said emphatically, clapping Hayward on the back.

Lucas looked at Will, quizzically. "Hellcats?"

A light had finally returned to Will's eyes. "Tank destroyers," he said, baring his teeth. "The best."

Chapter 16

"Listen, Will," mumbled Janikowski, between mouthfuls of the fruitcake he received at last week's mail call. "I know you don't wanna hear this–"

"Then keep your trap closed," Will said sharply. He knew what was coming.

"The lieutenant, he ain't up for this."

Will peered over the edge of their foxhole, making sure no one else was within earshot.

"You're right," he said, turning back to Janikowski. "I don't want to hear it."

"Davison would've hoofed it back to the CP two or three times by now. Made the major see how things are–"

"Keep that crap to yourself," Will growled, irritation in his voice.

"Fine. I'll keep it to myself. But I got my ass kicked once in this war, and it ain't happenin' again. This is your platoon, and if Lucas ain't ready to make a decision, you're gonna have to make it for him."

A decision. Janikowski was speaking in code, but his insinuation was clear. If no order came from Desobry to pull back, someone on the line might have to exercise some discretion. Will was quiet, refusing to respond. He could not encourage this, though a voice inside was telling him that Janikowski was right. The men were nearing a breaking point.

There was a quiet along the front, but only because the Germans had inexplicably paused once again. In addition to the mounting casualties that were deluging the makeshift aid station, Noville itself had sustained substantial damage, with several houses absorbing direct hits. Many were burning, the intense blazes fueled by wooden roofs and furniture. The main road was strewn with so much rubble and debris it was nearly impassable. Amid the destruction, someone had quipped that Noville would soon become "no ville." Gallows humor.

Lacking air or artillery support, and with the number of serviceable tanks dwindling, there was little Desobry could do but wait for the Germans to make their next move.

It had taken the Germans long enough after the fog lifted, nearly 20 minutes, to make their first move. Puffs of smoke finally appeared along the ridges, followed by the delayed gun reports as the Germans launched a seismic barrage, sending thousands of pounds of explosive ordnance into the village. The men were well dug in, so casualties were initially light, but several of the team's armored cars and half-tracks were less fortunate, destroyed or rendered useless by the shelling.

After the last German gun fell silent, Desobry counterpunched, sending forward four of the newly arrived tank destroyers to meet the expected charge. The M18 Hellcats were the most lethal and agile of the American tank destroyers. Their inventive crews had mastered the "shoot and scoot" for the nimble Hellcats, using their speed to evade return fire from their less dynamic foils. It wasn't just cat and mouse; the Hellcats could deliver a powerful blow. The 76-millimeter turret gun was like a sledgehammer, capable of punching holes in even the thickest German armor.

On Desobry's order, they emerged from their protective cover behind the few structures still intact, expecting an onslaught of Panzers. Instead, the Hellcat gunners licked their chops, astounded by what they saw from their viewing scopes. High atop the ridges, the German tanks still hadn't moved. The outline of each Panzer was framed perfectly against the oatmeal gray sky, presenting clean and stationary targets. It was a shooting gallery.

The Hellcats fired as one, every single shot in their opening broadside finding its mark and immediately taking out four of the Panzers. The German commander quickly grasped how exposed his armor was and at last gave the order to advance. Dozens of tanks plunged down the ridges, converging on the village from both the north and east. As the ground flattened out and the German armor neared the main American lines, bazookas and anti-tank guns joined with the Shermans and Hellcats in knocking several more of the oncoming Panzers out of action.

Just three of the German tanks in that initial surge managed to reach the village. One intrepid Mark IV actually breached the perimeter, zipping down the main road at nearly 40 miles per hour. It was a courageous but doomed undertaking. The tank was eventually slowed by the many mounds of rubble, then quickly blown apart by hits from three different bazooka crews.

The Germans were undeterred by their initial losses and would not let up, attacking the length of the perimeter throughout the rest of the morning. The Americans fought with tenacity and grit, refusing to buckle and repulsing the attackers each time. The Germans finally broke off the attack at midday, leaving behind scores of destroyed tanks and armored cars.

Even the Americans were in awe of how resoundingly they had repelled the initial assault. The clash had been almost entirely one-sided, and reports of the deadly accuracy of the Hellcats and bazooka teams flowed into the team's command post. They had scored hits on nine of the 14 Panzers that attacked from the north ridge, many of those ablaze now and billowing smoke. Eight more were lost that came from the ridge to the east, plus the two Panthers from the initial probe. The American losses were nominal in comparison. They lost one of the Hellcats and four of their other armored vehicles. None of the infantrymen had been killed, and only 13 wounded.

It had been a pasting, but there was little respite or celebrating inside the American lines. They knew the Germans weren't retreating. They were regrouping.

The shelling resumed minutes later, the enemy determined to flatten every last remaining structure in Noville and expose what was left of the American armor. With their spotters no longer impaired by fog, the German artillery and heavy mortars fired with devastating effect. Hundreds of shells crashed into Noville, systematically reducing houses, barns, and whatever else was left into piles of fiery wood and smoking wreckage.

And now, with the barrage lifted, and Janikowski offering his last cigarette to Will, Pfc Hayward appeared, scrambling into the trench between the two men. A bloodied bandage was wrapped around his left arm.

"Major Desobry wants all platoon leaders on him, Sarge." There were occasional shells still falling, and Hayward had to shout over the noise. "Lucas wants you to go!"

Will raised an eyebrow. "Why isn't he going?"

"He broke an ankle, Sarge. The medic is splinting his foot up."

"Shit. Where's the CP?"

"Same house as before. Halfway down the road, on the right."

Same house? How was any house back there still standing?

Will scampered down the main road. He passed the beer hall just as a mortar shell tore through what remained of the building's roof, the explosion showering him with bricks and other debris. He picked himself off the street, coughing dust out of his lungs, and staggered into the command post.

About a dozen others were gathered around Desobry, a mix of officers and senior non-coms like Will. There was also a new man, a sturdy fellow wearing a clean uniform, brown leather jump boots, and the notorious Screaming Eagle patch of the 101st Airborne Division on his sleeve. He was a stark contrast to Desobry. The major appeared to have aged 20 years since Will last saw him just hours ago, his eyes bloodshot from weariness and worry.

"Listen up, everyone," Desobry started, his voice more upbeat than Will would have expected. "I'll be brief, because one well-aimed shell and we'll have a mess cook in charge of this outfit. As I'm sure you all know, our position is no longer tenable. Before anyone asks, I have already requested permission to withdraw. If not to Bastogne, at least to the high ground between here and

Bastogne. That request was denied. Our orders are to continue to hold this village and these roads."

There were murmurs of protest, and Desobry screwed his face into a scowl, his patience waning. One of the other platoon leaders spoke up.

"Major, they must have forty tanks on those ridges."

"If it makes you feel any better, our observers say they started with sixty. Unfortunately for us, they won't be stupid enough to cluster their tanks on that high ground again."

"They don't need to," grunted another officer. "They can just sit back and lob those mortars and eighty-eights at us all day."

"Agreed. We can't fall back and if we stay put, the Kraut heavy guns will wipe us out. Our only hope is to push their tanks and artillery off those ridges."

The men quietly absorbed Desobry's words. He was right, of course, and lacking permission to retreat to Bastogne, they had no alternatives. But that didn't make the news any more welcome.

"What are we attacking with, sir?"

The question came from First Lieutenant Brandywithe. He was one of Desobry's more experienced officers, having fought the previous year in Italy, and his platoon was holding the southern end of the village. Will was surprised Desobry hadn't given him command of the more vulnerable northern approach.

Desobry turned to his right. "Bob, what can you pull together?"

Captain Schultz, commanding the team's armor, rubbed his stubbled chin as he considered his response. "As of now, we've got eight Shermans, a few Stuarts, and maybe three or four destroyers we can spare for an attack. We have to keep at least a few of the destroyers in the village, can't risk them all out in the open."

Will frowned, feeling defeated already. The Stuart light tanks were useless against the German tanks, outfitted with thin armor and little more than pop guns compared to what the Panzers carried. And Will had little faith in the Shermans anymore.

Desobry likely shared the same outlook but remained poker-faced. He gestured to the paratrooper at his side. "The good news is, we're being reinforced. This is Lieutenant Colonel LaPrade, with the 101st Airborne. His battalion is arriving soon, and he'll be leading the attack. Sir?"

The 101st man stepped forward, chewing on the stub of a cigar. A West Point graduate, he was roughly the same age as Will and Desobry, but his hardened features and steely eyes reflected a wealth of combat experience. The 101st had parachuted behind enemy lines twice in the last six months. First in Normandy, ahead of the invasion force during the early morning hours of D-Day. Then in October, into Holland, as part of the calamitous Operation Market Garden, a plan that led to the near-annihilation of an entire British airborne division.

When the Germans launched their attack in the Ardennes, the 101st, like the 10th Armored, was in northern France, recuperating from their losses in Holland. They too were rushed in to block the German onslaught. Unlike the 10th Armored, they hadn't had time to supply themselves, and marched into Bastogne last night lacking winter clothing and equipped only with the food and ammunition they carried. That element aside, the 800 paratroopers of LaPrade's battalion were combat-hardened men. They would more than double their own number and give the 10th Armored men a badly needed lift.

LaPrade's eyes gleamed with the fervor of a self-possessed man impatient to get into battle. He tossed his cigar butt away and moved to a large blackboard that had been pilfered from the schoolhouse and was now leaning against a wall. Someone had already diagrammed Noville and the proximate ridges.

"My men will be walking in from Foy shortly," LaPrade began in an authoritative voice, pointing to the village halfway between Bastogne and Noville. "When the attack begins, Able Company will press straight north, up these ridges, here and here. Baker Company will attack to the northeast. We'll hold Charlie Company back as a reserve. Major Desobry has agreed to send tanks up each of these roads in support. My bazooka teams are good, but they're only carrying a few rounds each. Anything your teams can spare would be appreciated."

Desobry cleared his throat. "I have a man under orders to steal anything in Bastogne that isn't nailed down. Bazooka ammo is at the top of his shopping list. He should be back soon."

LaPrade gave him an approving nod.

"We have to push the Krauts off those ridges," Desobry concluded. "Jumpoff is at 1400. We'll have artillery support from Bastogne beforehand, and some smoke to cover our movement." His eyes swept the room. "Any questions?"

"Sir," Will said, stepping forward. "What about us? Dog Company?"

Desobry avoided Will's eyes. "1st Platoon will stay put, in case the Germans decide to swing around to the south. But we need every man we can spare in this attack. 2nd and 3rd Platoons will support Colonel LaPrade's force."

LaPrade grinned at Will. "The Krauts won't be expecting us to attack, Sergeant. You don't want to miss the look on their faces, do you?"

Will felt no humor. He could only think about how weakened his platoon was. How close to the end each of his men were. How even if they pushed the Germans off those ridges, they could not possibly hold the ground once the enemy counterattacked. He bit back the words he wanted to say, and clenched his jaw instead.

"No, sir."

Desobry and LaPrade took a few more logistical questions and then Desobry dismissed the men. Will lingered, pulling the major aside.

"I know what you're going to say," preempted Desobry. "But I can't have those paratroopers out there by themselves. They're not built to take on armor."

"It's not that, sir."

Desobry studied his sergeant, unused to seeing him so tentative.

"What is it, Will?"

Will lowered his voice. "You sure you don't want Lieutenant Brandywithe with us? Lucas is in bad shape. No way can he make it up those ridges."

Desobry laughed in relief, punching Will on the arm. "Is that all? Don't you worry about it, Sergeant, I'll have my best man out there."

At just after two in the afternoon, as the brief barrage from the American artillery in Bastogne winded down, Colonel LaPrade signaled for the attack to begin. His battalion had marched into the village following the same path as Team Desobry the previous evening. LaPrade didn't bother to assemble the men into formation, simply double-timing his fresh paratroopers as they arrived into skirmishing lines alongside the 10th Armored men. The Americans marched toward the ridges, hopeful that the remaining Hellcats and Shermans on their flanks, coupled with the veteran bazooka teams among the 101st Airborne and 10th Armored men, could fend off the enemy armor while the riflemen pushed the *Panzergrendiers* back. They had just begun to climb the sloping ground when they realized their timing could not have been worse.

At almost precisely the same minute, the Germans launched their own attack, barreling down the hillsides again in their tanks and armored vehicles. The two forces collided across the open ground as tanks and infantry quickly became entangled, grappling with each other in a savage brawl. Neither side was able to gain an advantage, and after nearly two hours of frenzied fighting, down to bayonets and fists in some pockets, both sides limped back to their respective lines.

It had been a stalemate. While the Germans had moved no closer to Noville, the Americans were unable to dislodge the German tanks and artillery from the high ground, leaving the defenders in Noville in the same precarious position as before. The paratroopers and infantrymen had to fight their way back to Noville, carrying a number of their wounded. Will took note of how diminished the 10th Armored men were as they shivered underneath field jackets and overcoats blotted with mud and blood. He counted helmets, and not including the severely wounded, there were 18 men from 2nd Platoon left, including Janikowski, who seemed to have nine lives. His pal Ray Sloan was less fortunate, shot twice in the leg, according to Janikowski, and taken prisoner. The platoon had entered Noville with 34 men, and in less than a day, had lost nearly half its strength. 3rd Platoon appeared to have even fewer men left, not a single man left above the rank of corporal.

They were all on the verge of collapse. Some had been fighting continuously for more than 12 hours, and nearly everyone had been nicked to some degree during the fighting. Their medic was out of morphine and running low on sulfa powder and field dressings. The men patched themselves up with whatever bandages were available, and called for stretcher bearers to carry the wounded to the center of the village where they could be evacuated to Bastogne.

The Germans appeared to be equally sapped and halted any further attacks, giving both sides a short timeout. The Americans dug into whatever rations they had left and passed around their remaining smokes. Those that could, climbed under their thin blankets and tried to sleep.

For Will, the lull brought on a quiet despair, as he mentally counted those helmets again. He thought of those they had already lost here. Minske, Delgado, the others. Men he was drinking beer with a few days ago. Looking at pictures they shared of their wives and kids. Minske had a six-month old daughter he never knew, a little girl who would now take her place among Delgado's son and an entire generation of fatherless children.

The break in action stretched for hours, with only light shelling and an occasional minor probe of their lines. By nightfall, it was clear the Germans were through for the day, and the men's spirits were buoyed when the garrison was reinforced by five more

M18 tank destroyers from Bastogne. The Germans offered one prolonged barrage during the night, if for no other reason than to disrupt whatever rest the Americans were getting.

Morning arrived, and with it another intensive bombardment. The Germans were targeting the remaining structures in Noville, though their gunners were blinded once again by another wreath of fog blanketing Noville, fusing now with thick smoke from the houses and barns still afire. There were smaller clashes along the edges of the village, but the armored infantrymen and paratroopers refused to yield, fending off one German attack after another.

It was early afternoon when Hayward appeared at Will's foxhole with a summons from Lucas. They scurried to the rear, the Pfc taking time to confide that the lieutenant was in a great deal of pain, more than he was letting on.

They found Lucas sitting in his trench, his legs stretched in front of him, writing on a small pad of paper. A makeshift splint was affixed to his right foot.

Will gave a half-salute. "Sir, how's that ankle?"

Lucas gave him a wry smile. "My ballroom dancing career has been put on hold, and I could use a nice cup of hot cocoa. How do I look?"

"You look like shit."

Lucas chuckled, but Will saw right through the man's guise. He was pale and sickly, and the wear from the burden of command was evident in his eyes. Hayward was right, Lucas was in considerable pain.

Will slung his rifle over a shoulder and squatted into his old catching position. "Letter to your girl, sir?"

Lucas closed the pad and stuffed it into a pocket. "Nah, just writing my dad."

"What's he do?"

"He's the chief of police in Bridgeton."

Will raised an eyebrow. "They have a police department there?"

"Yep," Lucas grinned. "My dad."

Will noticed a ring for the first time. "You're married."

"Ten years," said Lucas, pulling a small billfold from inside his field jacket. He removed a worn black and white photo of a young woman on a playground swing.

"That's your wife?" Will couldn't hide his surprise. The lieutenant's wife was a looker, with shoulder-length hair, features so dark they were almost Mediterranean, and a warm smile. She was wearing a pair of shorts that showed off quite a bit of leg. Judging from the smile on Lucas' face, Will's reaction was a common one.

"Yes, that's Susan. It was taken years ago, before the kids."

"You have kids? How many?"

"Three, now. Ashley is six, Julia is four, and I have an eight-month old I haven't met. Annie."

"You have three girls?"

Lucas laughed. Will's tone made it sound like Lucas had contracted some sort of incurable disease.

"It's not that bad, Sergeant. You'll have a family someday."

They were interrupted by several bursts of small arms fire to the south. Another test of their defenses, as the Germans continued to probe for a vulnerability in the American perimeter.

"So, what's the plan, sir? Another attack? Maybe throw some pitchforks at those Kraut tanks?"

Lucas exhaled. "Did you hear about Desobry?"

There was a stab in Will's gut. "What about him?"

"He was wounded. Late last night. Bad."

Will suddenly felt numb, his mouth dry. "How?"

Lucas massaged his ankle, his face contorting as he hit a tender spot. "A shell hit right outside his CP. He's got a bad head wound. That colonel from the paratroopers was killed."

"LaPrade? Jesus. How bad is Desobry?"

"Medics think he'll live. They got an ambulance for him and evacuated him to Bastogne. If he got through. The Krauts have likely taken the road we came in on."

"So, we're surrounded," said Will, unsurprised.

"More or less. We'll know for sure soon. We've been ordered back to Bastogne."

Will felt the back of his neck suddenly burning, his frustration boiling over.

"Well, that's fucking great. We've been here for two days now. Lost half the company trying to take those goddamn ridges. The major is in a hospital, if he's lucky, and now that the brass has finally given us permission to get the hell out of here, the Krauts have cut us off."

Lucas was quiet. He was as irked as his sergeant, but as an officer, he had to maintain some level of respect for their superiors. Still, Lucas too felt an unnatural urge to curse someone out.

Will took a deep breath, trying to regain his self-control. Lucas still needed him. What was left of the platoon still needed him.

"Who's in charge?" he asked while rubbing his forehead, his tone more even now.

"Major Harwick. He was LaPrade's exec. Says we'll have to fight our way out of here. He's sending a company of paratroopers and some of our armor out first, to punch a hole through the German lines. We got a lot of wounded. They'll be loaded on to the half-tracks and jeeps, protected by a ring of tanks. Everyone else rides in whatever vehicles are left. The Hellcats will form the rear guard."

It was a reasonable plan, and though the odds were stacked against them, Will felt a spark of optimism now that they were leaving. It was five miles to Bastogne, and it would be a harrowing journey for what was left of Team Desobry. But Will knew they would make it. They had to. Bastogne meant hot food, sleep, and defensible ground. An entire division of paratroopers was rumored there, and hopefully the balance of the 10th Armored. Bastogne meant survival.

He gestured toward Lucas' ankle. "Can you make it?"

Lucas winked. "I'll be faster than you, Jamison. I hear catchers can't run."

Will couldn't help but smile. "Twenty-two stolen bases my last season. When do we jump off?"

"Soon. 1400." Lucas patted his M1. "This is my crutch, so I'm going to get a head start. I'll meet you in whatever staging area they're using. I'm relying on you to get the men back."

Ten minutes later, Will left a screen of men to hold their position and led what was left of the two platoons to the center of the village. Others had already assembled and the men began climbing into the battered half-tracks and armored cars. The lead tanks and paratroopers had moved out minutes ago, and Will could hear the Shermans in a shootout with their counterparts, trying to break the German encirclement.

Major Harwick, a lean, mustached young officer who carried himself with the same self-assurance as LaPrade, addressed Will. "You ready to move out, Sergeant?"

Will saluted. "Yes, sir. We're just finishing up with the wounded."

There was an excited shout, and both men turned to see a lone rifleman rushing down the street. He was one of the men Will had left on the perimeter to screen their withdrawal.

"Sir," he said to Harwick, breathless and red-faced. "We can hear Kraut tanks. A mess of 'em. Coming down the road."

They had run out of time. Harwick and the other officers began shouting out orders, hastening the loading of the wounded men. The scene quickly became chaotic, and Will knew they were minutes away from catastrophe. The Germans would soon discover there was virtually nothing left at the perimeter to defend the village. The Hellcats would offer some cover, but they could not hold back that many Panzers on their own.

Will spun around, searching for the man he needed. He cupped his hands together. "Meyer!"

There was no response, and he shouted the name again.

One of the other engineers hurried by Will, pointing a thumb over his shoulder. "He's back by the church, Sarge, with the medics."

Will ran to the church. The presbytery had been flattened by the first round of German shelling, but the tower and main structure were still standing. A German commander perhaps, with a sense of decency? He found Meyer holding one end of a litter, a cigarette dangling from his lips as he helped load the wounded man on to the hood of a jeep.

"Lev!"

The engineer looked up, offering a weary smile. "Will! Glad to see you're still in one piece."

"You got any of that TNT left?"

"Plenty."

Will gestured toward the church. "Krauts are coming down the ridges and will bust right through this place. We need to slow them down, keep those tanks off our backs. Can you bring the tower down on top of the road? And quickly?"

"You helping? My guys are with the wounded."

"I'm helping."

Lev surveyed the steeple. He welcomed any sort of engineering challenge, but he also understood how little time they had. His decision took mere seconds, a confident smile stretching across his face.

"Blowing up a church. This will set the Jews back a thousand years."

The two men returned to where Will had left Harwick, the major signaling for the main body to get underway. As Will explained his intentions, Meyer retrieved haversacks of TNT and spools of Primacord from one of the half-tracks. Harwick gave Will an appreciative clap on the shoulder and climbed into an awaiting jeep. The last vehicles moved out, followed by the remaining tank destroyers.

Will and Meyer hurried toward the church and pushed through the doors, packs of explosives draped over their shoulders. Inside, the engineer showed Will where to place the TNT and how to connect the detonating wire. The two men worked diligently, even as they heard the telltale squeal of tank tracks coming down the road.

Will set his last charge and called up to Meyer, who was in the tower.

"Let's go Lev, we got about one minute."

"Don't rush an artist, Will," Meyer called down. "Gotta do this right or the place will just cave in on its footprint."

Will moved to the doors and peeked down the street. No tanks were in sight yet, but a steady churning was growing louder. He heard Meyer clomping down the wooden steps, turning to see the man holding his last pack of TNT up with a smile.

"One more," Meyer said, "and we'll–"

It was the last words Will heard from the engineer. There was a roar from the street, and then the world around Will erupted. He was lifted off his feet, his body slamming into something solid, and then there was nothing, as if someone had turned off every light in Belgium, plunging Will into a bottomless well of black silence.

Chapter 17

In the two days since the team's half-tracks first rolled into Noville, Will had endured a battering. The endless shelling and waves of Panzers had drained the last ounces of strength from his body, and his spirit was equally bankrupt after witnessing the suffering and death of so many. No two years of training—no ten years of training—could have prepared the men for all they had braved in Noville. With each step forward and every passing second, the aching in his muscles and joints had worsened. His insides were no better, with a sharpness in his gut that alternated between ravenous hunger and wrenching nausea.

Yet the moment the blast leveled the church and tossed Will through the air, all of it, every feeling from head to toe, inside and out, vanished in the blink of an eye.

Engulfed in a murky blackness, he could see even less than he could feel. As blinding as the worst of the fog had been, there were always discernable shapes and forms. At the least, a comforting outline of another man at his shoulder. Now, there was nothing.

It was quiet at least, blessedly quiet. The blaring from the mayhem and many instruments of death and madness so prevalent before were absent now, as were the heart-piercing cries of the wounded and the dying.

The silence, regrettably, did not last. There was a high-pitched tone at first, distant and faint. And then something else behind it. A muffled, halting noise. He finally felt something, his body in spasm, and realized he was hearing the sound of his own uncontrollable choking.

He was conscious now, enough so that he knew his body was face down and sprawled across something hard. The hacking continued, his lungs seemingly clogged with sawdust, before his airway finally cleared and his breathing slowed into something more rhythmic again.

He remembered now. The church exploding. A direct hit, either from artillery or a tank. How long ago was that? Had he been out for minutes? Hours?

He was alive, that much he knew.

The stench of cordite and burning cinders was in his nostrils. There was a heavy object resting on the left side of his face, cold with a coarse surface. He slowly opened his eyes, then squeezed them shut to ward off the bright daylight and dust particles that fell from his eyelashes. His head and hips were rotated to one side, and whatever rubble his body was stretched across was digging into his chest and stomach. The church had likely collapsed, the blast throwing him clear. Or not clear enough.

Shit. Where was Lev?

The engineer had been on his way down from the steeple. Did he escape the blast? Or was he buried by it?

A draft of air shot up his right thigh, so cold Will knew his pants were torn and his bare skin exposed. He needed to move his head, both to assess what was around him and ensure his neck was uninjured. He waited a full minute to gather his strength, relieved that the ringing in his ears was already fading. After a single deep breath, Will raised his head, slowly, allowing chunks of brick and shards of wood to slide from his face and neck. He lowered it quickly the second he heard the nearby voices.

German voices.

He kept his eyes closed, swallowing hard to relieve the tickle in his throat. Though his body was still rife with discomfort, Will knew he had to remain prone. The voices were close, but conversational, their tone lacking tension or agitation. The sounds of those safely behind their own lines.

Will fought the impulse to run, an impulse he knew would lead to certain capture, if he wasn't shot first. Could he even get up? There was pressure along his back, some sort of long, heavy object, like a beam or other support. He chanced a subtle movement and shifted his upper body. There was some give, enough to suggest to Will that he wasn't pinned down and could manage his way out.

Near as he could tell, he had escaped any serious injury. His helmet and wool cap were gone, and he felt a trickle of blood rolling down his ear and on to his cheek. A ruptured eardrum? Perhaps not, as his hearing seemed fine now, and he heard a soft moan, even nearer than where the Germans were standing. It had to be Meyer.

A vehicle passed within a few yards, loud and heavy. A tank, or a personnel carrier, close enough he could feel the vibration.

There were footsteps, and more voices. The moans were louder now, and in between, Will could hear Meyer's voice, mumbling something incoherent. The Germans moved closer, and Will pressed his lips together, aware of the vapor his warm breath was creating in the below-freezing temperatures. Meyer's voice suddenly changed, stronger now, and pleading. Will silently begged his friend to quiet himself. Or should he? If Meyer was seriously wounded, he would need medical attention. Maybe the sooner the Germans attended to him, the better.

Another odd sound, almost a crunching noise. One of the Germans had stepped onto the rubble, and seemed to be moving closer to Meyer. Will forced his muscles to relax as his body went limp, hoping he would be mistaken for a corpse.

Those hopes were quashed by the sharp report of a gunshot, so close it caused Will's body to twitch in surprise. He froze, panic gripping his heart as he held his breath for his life. Meyer was quiet now, and the German sounded as if he was climbing down from the rubble. The back and forth with his buddy on the ground hadn't missed a beat, as if he had taken a leak or tied his shoes, and not just finished off a man in cold blood.

There were new footsteps, another soldier arriving, barking something at the others. Laughter followed, a joke possibly.

He heard the same sound again, another man climbing the

pile, this one closer to Will. The soldier was clumsy, and he could hear the man stumbling and cursing as he kicked away bricks and other debris with each step. The voice seemed youthful. Will could no longer hold his breath, his chest felt as if it was caving in. He tried to exhale cooler air that wouldn't vaporize, then quickly sucked in another breath. The German was jabbering amiably with the others while he climbed, one boot finally landing inches from Will's face. He braced himself for a bayonet jab or a hard kick. His chest tightened, and though his lungs weren't working, his heart was in overdrive. He felt sudden warmth around his groin, his own piss spreading across his pants.

Only a blind man wouldn't have seen Will's body shuddering, and he suddenly felt the press of cold steel on his cheek. He couldn't help but squirm, clenching his eyes closed and refusing to look at the man behind the trigger.

And then, a miracle. The gun barrel was suddenly withdrawn, the soldier stepping away. After a few more cautious steps through the rubble, Will heard the thud of the man's boots hitting the road. The men moved off, their voices waning, and he exhaled again, nearly hyperventilating as the tears came, stinging his eyes. His heart was hammering away so hard Will thought it was going to burst from his chest.

He still did not dare move. Someone else could be watching, a sentry perhaps. He would have to remain still until nightfall. He was weighing his chances when he heard a series of shouts from across the street. More soldiers, this time barking commands in both German and French.

French?

Will gambled, knowing he could not feign death forever, and slit his eyes, opening them a fraction of an inch. Adjusting to the daylight, panic shot through him. Just across the road, the Germans had marshaled the remaining civilians in the village. There were more than a dozen, lined up along the shoulder, kneeling with their heads bowed.

A cold chill passed through him, sharper than even the outside temperatures, as he recognized the distinctive uniform of the officer in charge and the three men standing guard. A uniform he had seen on the streets of Metz. The men were part of the *Schutz-staffel*—the SS—the vicious military wing of the Nazi Party. Their green overcoats were a stark contrast to the more slate-gray coats and tunics of the *Wehrmacht*, the regular German Army men that filled the ranks of the 2nd Panzer Division.

The villagers were a mix of men, women, and children. Families, Will surmised, that had sought shelter in their cellars when the Americans first arrived. Or taken prisoner and brought in from neighboring communities and farms. Some were expressionless and resigned to their fate, while others were filled with dread, sobbing as their heads hung down. A few seemed on the brink of hysteria.

Then, he saw him, standing at the end of the row, and Will's heart sank further, shaken by the recognition. It was Amand, the schoolmaster.

The sight of the kindly, elderly man on his knees hardened something inside Will. His fear became rage. Rage over innocent civilians being held at gunpoint. Rage at the callous murder of Lev Meyer. Rage how helpless and powerless he was to intercede. There was one consolation, at least, the absence of the boy, Philippe.

He could see just the four SS men guarding the civilians, though Will's vantage point was somewhat limited. Rescuing the civilians was futile, as their captors would gun him down in seconds. They were also hardly the only Germans in the area, as columns of vehicles and marching *Panzergrenadiers* were passing through at regular intervals.

As Will contemplated his options, a trio of other soldiers materialized, these men wearing the familiar uniforms of the *Wehrmacht*. One of them drew himself to attention, saluting the SS officer as he took note of the civilians. The officer returned the salute, and gestured for the men to move on. Will appraised the *Wehrmacht* man. He was a sergeant, like Will, and his age and hardened features suggested a man who had likely fought in both wars this century. The grizzled soldier queried the officer, his voice deferential, but even from across the road, Will could sense the thinly veiled contempt the sergeant held for the younger Nazi. Will had heard there was often tension between the *Wehrmacht* and the zealots in Hitler's SS. The sergeant's body language suggested that was playing out in front of him. The two other *Wehrmacht* men quietly fell in behind their sergeant.

The officer gave a brusque response, and the sergeant's eyes narrowed. He said a few words in return, gesturing at the civilians, but the sneering officer interrupted, his words harsher now. The sergeant shook his head, and Will heard the single word he uttered, spoken in a forceful, resolute voice.

Nein.

The SS man, his mouth agape at the insubordination, shouted a command and the men behind him leveled their submachine guns, pulling the bolts back and aiming their barrels at the sergeant. The *Wehrmacht* men began to raise their bolt-action Mauser rifles, but their sergeant calmly motioned with his hand for the pair to stand down. He took a step toward the officer and said something quietly, then turned and walked away, motioning for his men to follow. One of the SS thugs started to follow, but the officer held him back, chuckling dismissively at the departing men.

Then, without another word, the Nazi calmly drew his Luger pistol and shot the villager closest to him. The bullet struck the gray-haired woman between the eyes, her head disappearing behind a red mist as her body dropped heavily to the gravel. Two other villagers, both young men, leapt to their feet and ran but the officer waved off his men and coolly shot the two Belgians in the back, bringing them each down with a triumphant smirk.

Three shots, three executions.

Will wanted to cry out, unable to comprehend the butchery. He had to keep himself from retching, and felt his hands forming into fists.

More shots rang out. The officer wasted no time, methodically shooting one civilian before moving to the next. As if he was dispensing with burdensome paperwork. His men watched with only casual interest, their faces lacking emotion, suggesting how routine such atrocities had become.

Amand was last. Will could not turn away, or even avert his eyes. At first, he thought the schoolmaster was simply staring at some faraway point, desperately trying to free his mind from such unimaginable inhumanity. But he wasn't staring into the distance. He was staring at Will. And as their eyes met, he saw a flicker of recognition in the older man, offering Will a barely imperceptible smile as he waited for the fatal shot.

It did not come. The officer had stopped in front of Amand, blocking Will's view, and was frowning at his jammed Luger. He began to clear the weapon, then seemed to change his mind. He turned to one of his subordinates and said a few words, his tone light-hearted. His man laughed back, then pointed his gun at the remaining villager and pulled the trigger. The automatic weapon shook in the Nazi's hands, and Will squeezed his eyes closed, unable to watch. The gun finally fell silent, the barrel still smoking as the last brass cartridge tumbled to the ground.

Will had to force his eyes open. Amand was prone on the gravel. The schoolmaster's body and limbs were bent grotesquely, and blood dribbled from bullet holes across his back and neck. Will could taste the bile in his mouth, and fought to keep from vomiting or crying out in revulsion. The SS men were not taking prisoners, soldier or civilian.

His eyes returned to Amand, the man face down in a pool of his own blood, and a cold fury took hold of Will. He was unsure he could even stand now, his body mostly numb. Numb from the unrelenting cold. Numb from the sickening carnage on the sidewalk and the scale of death and brutality he had witnessed these last two days. He needed sleep. He needed it all to end. Will forced his eyes closed again, desperate to escape this hell, trying to imagine himself in a different place.

The place that had always brought him such comfort and solace.

He could not remember her name. It had been two and a half years since he saw her last, and though her name had always been seared into his heart, it escaped him now. Was it simple forgetfulness, or had he lost his mind with the lunacy around him? The face he could recall, and so he focused on that, and then the rest slowly came to him. The contours of her neck, her shoulders, her breasts. The freckles standing out against the creamy skin of her naked back. The purity in her eyes.

His breathing began to ease as he focused on her facial features, soft and inviting. Just inches from his own as they laid together in that hotel bed in Philadelphia, their eyes locked on one another. He would always remember that very moment, when it seemed as if their souls had finally latched on to one another for good. He brushed her thick, sensual lips with his fingertips, savoring the feel of the cool skin of her thigh hooked across his legs. Her eyelids gradually closed as her breathing became rhythmic, no longer able to ward off the sleep the twosome had pledged to avoid on their final night together.

Will blinked his eyes open, surprised to see the village shrouded now in the early evening dusk. He had fallen asleep, even with his body still laying awkwardly across the wreckage. The Germans had moved off, away from their crime scene, leaving those they had murdered to the elements. The street seemed deserted now with only an occasional passing vehicle. There were sounds of fighting in the distance, artillery mostly. He waited another hour, allowing the darkness to fully envelop Noville.

It was time. Will was cramping now, and as the temperature continued to fall, there was the risk of hypothermia. He slowly began to wriggle his body. His joints had stiffened, but he otherwise seemed uninjured as he carefully freed himself, laboring to make as little noise as possible.

There wasn't a German in sight, but his eyes quickly fell on the unmoving shape on the far side of the debris pile. He slithered his way across the mound, and even in the dim moonlight, Will could see Lev's field jacket around his stomach and pelvis stained with frozen blood. There was also a small black hole in the back of the engineer's head. Will reached for Meyer's dog tags, his eyes shifting away from the far more gruesome exit wound. He climbed to his feet, his leg muscles crying out in protest, and futilely searched for a rifle in the darkness. Pulling the .45 from his holster, he checked the magazine and slowly climbed down from the pile, taking inventory of what he had at his disposal. There was one additional magazine for the .45 and no more grenades. His canteen was half-full, but he had no food other than a pack of Wrigley's. He still had his bayonet, and a six-inch combat knife sheathed in his boot.

Will took several swallows of water, then jammed two pieces of gum in his mouth, realizing how famished he was. With his .45 in one hand and his knife in the other, he moved swiftly toward the schoolhouse. The periphery was heavily damaged, but it had avoided any direct hits and may have been the only structure in Noville still intact. He darted through the open door, his .45 pointed ahead. The wood floor was splotched with dried blood and littered with soiled bandages and other medical waste. The medics had been busy. Will listened for the sounds of others, but the school-house appeared deserted.

"Philippe!"

He kept his voice to a loud whisper. He remembered Amand saying something about the floor boards, but he had no idea where to look.

"Philippe!"

There was a soft scraping noise from a corner of the room. Will decided to take a chance, pulling out Janikowski's Zippo and holding the flame close to his own face.

"Philippe! It's me, the American!"

More scraping.

"*Par ici.*"

The boy's voice carried across the room, and Will moved in that direction, holding the lighter in front of him. Philippe had pushed a few of the floorboards up and was climbing out of the crawl space he had wedged himself into. Will blew out the flame and helped the boy to his feet.

"You okay?"

"*Oui.* Yes." The boy seemed shaken, and his face was filthy, but his voice was steady.

"Listen to me. We have to get to Bastogne, where the American lines are. You need to stay behind me the whole time, unless I tell you different. Don't make a sound, okay? You understand?"

"Yes. Monsieur Amand?"

Will hesitated. "He left with the other Americans. I promised him I would come for you. Okay? Follow me."

Hearing nothing from the road, they quietly exited the schoolhouse, the village still mostly dormant. A pair of tanks rumbled down the main road, and Will and Philippe hid behind the smoldering remains of a house. When the Panzers had passed, they moved in a crouch away from the road, following the most direct path out of Noville. They circled behind where the presbytery had previously stood, then dashed between two more houses, nearing the edge of the village. Kneeling behind a brick water well in the middle of a yard, Will searched the open fields ahead. There was just enough moonlight to see a network of entrenchments, and the glint of helmets bobbing up and down.

The Germans seemed lax, a sign the front lines were some distance away. Many stood lethargically in their waist-deep holes, leaning against the edges as they smoked cigarettes and ate from tin cans. Others simply milled about, standing in the open with their rifles slung, conversing in voices that were low but hardly whispered.

Even in the dark, Will could make out the large barn to his left. It was just outside the village and therefore closest to the German perimeter. An idea formed, but one that depended on the Germans' attention focused ahead on the fields, not back toward Noville.

He kneeled in front of Philippe.

"When we go, I need you to run as fast as possible to that barn. Stay behind me. If I turn, you turn. If I slow down, you slow down. Got it?"

The boy nodded.

Will relaxed his body, waiting for an opportunity. It came a minute later when a battery of long-distance artillery opened fire somewhere on the other side of Noville. As shells rained down on Bastogne, Will and Philippe sprang to their feet and ran to the barn. They made it undetected, flattening themselves against the side wall. Will scanned the German line, but there was no change, only the men in the entrenchments standing between the two of them and open countryside. If they could make it into the fields, they might have a chance. The Germans would have difficulty finding targets, even with the moonlight.

But there was an obstacle, and it was sitting squarely in the center of the German line, maybe 40 yards away. A machine gun nest, manned by two soldiers. He could see the outline of the nasty-looking barrel, pointing out toward the field. At short range, the gunner could spew enough bullets in their direction that a curtain of darkness wouldn't matter much.

Will pulled the slide back on his .45 and grasped the butt with both hands. He exchanged a purposeful nod with Philippe, then silently counted to three. They fled the cover of the barn, scampering across the yard as fast as their legs could carry them. Rather than running away from the machine gun, Will headed directly towards it, approaching from behind. His footsteps were heavy, and as they neared the enemy soldiers, a voice from another nearby hole called out in their strange, guttural language, more confused than concerned.

Will slowed as he reached the machine gun pit. The two men appeared to have been sleeping, but now their eyes widened in surprise as the large American suddenly appeared in front of them. The man on the left jumped to his feet and Will shot him in the face, blood splattering from the back of his head. The second German reached for his rifle and Will fired twice more, hitting the man in the chest and stomach. The German flailed at the holes in his body before crumpling to the ground. Will kicked the machine gun off its tripod and led the boy across the empty field. There was a flurry of shouts behind the two as several rifles fired wildly into the night. Will and Philippe did not stop, even after the gunfire tapered off, putting as much distance as possible between themselves and the Germans. They ran for nearly half a mile before stopping, both falling to their knees and gasping for breath. Will reached for his canteen and gulped down half the remaining water, then passed it over to Philippe who drank the rest. He looked for the North Star to get his bearings, but struggled to find it behind the patchwork of clouds that dotted the nighttime sky.

And then Will laughed at himself as Philippe looked on in puzzlement.

Stars? I really need the stars?

Across the field, there was a faraway glow on the horizon. Even from this distance, the thunder of artillery could be heard, followed by the deep thuds of shells slamming into buildings, tearing them into splinters and rubble and setting them afire. The Germans were at it again, trying to eviscerate another Belgian community in their path.

Fuck the stars.

Will knew exactly where Bastogne was.

Chapter 18

There was an artistry to the Ardennes. Within its borders were infinite pockets of dense woodlands, each framed by expansive stretches of rich terrain, grassy meadows, and meandering streams. Much of it was breathtaking, resembling the boundless fields Will had tread as a small boy. In wintertime, Will and Jack would spend their weekend afternoons trampling across the empty, harvested acreage with carefree abandon. They were oblivious to the freezing temperatures, refusing to don hats and gloves or heed their flushed cheeks and ears. They armed themselves with toy Colts and Winchesters, and their imagined battles were serious affairs. When the boys finally tired, they slogged back through the snow to the house on Adams Street, their mother waiting in the doorway with warm blankets and mugs of steaming hot chocolate.

Just like now, Will grumbled to himself as he stomped through a mound of cow manure, too weakened to detour around it.

With the moon wrapped in a thick cloud cover, the night had turned completely black, making little difference whether a man's eyes were open or closed. Will didn't dare shut his, though, aware of the depth of his exhaustion and the risk he might drift into a slumber, even standing up. He could at least still feel the gentle tug at his waist, Philippe's hand tightly clutching the back of his cartridge belt.

It had been less than an hour since they left Noville, and the trek to Bastogne had begun easily enough. Lightly armed, he kept the pair off the roads, hoping to avoid a clash with any more Germans. They made good time those first few miles, moving deliberately but steadily across the rolling farmland.

As the adrenaline rush from blasting through the German lines outside Noville subsided, an overpowering fatigue set it. With each step forward, Will felt his energy waning. He yearned for sleep, and the minor obstacles that began appearing in their path, from a small herd of milk cows to a four-foot rail fence, took every remaining ounce of strength to navigate with the boy. He considered stopping at one of the farm houses they passed, the draw of warmth, food, and dry clothes nearly irresistible. As was a bed. His body ravaged from the prolonged exposure and relentless fighting, Will nearly passed out at the thought of a warm bed. He hadn't slept off the ground in more than three months.

He tried to banish those thoughts from his mind. They had to keep moving. He had no idea how much longer Bastogne would remain in American hands, and if the town was evacuated he and Philippe would be trapped behind German lines. So they trudged on, his fatigue so draining he had to concentrate just to put one foot in front of the other. He figured they had a mile or two to go, depending how far outside Bastogne the American perimeter extended. As they drew nearer to the town, the sounds of fighting sharpened, and he willed himself to become more alert, each step bringing them closer to peril. The exchanges of gunfire were no longer in the distance or echoing across the open ground. They were just ahead.

Will abruptly halted as his ears picked up the sound of nearby men and equipment. He and the boy dropped to their stomachs. The voices were indistinct, but it was clear they had reached the German lines around Bastogne. He squeezed the butt of his .45 tightly while slowly snaking his way ahead on his elbows, Philippe closely behind.

The voices ahead became clearer. There were two of them, the men sharing a quiet conversation. He listened for another minute or so, contemplating his options, and realizing he had only one. Raising his head a few inches from the ground, Will scanned the field ahead. The Germans were likely in a foxhole, maybe ten yards ahead of him. Closer than that, he realized, as a light breeze carried a whiff of cigarette smoke past his nostrils.

Just at that moment, his left elbow came to rest on a large stick, snapping it in two.

"*Hans?*"

The voice sounded confused and almost childlike, but not distressed.

Will quietly pulled the slide back on the Colt, hoping the wind would cover the metallic sound. He motioned back to Philippe to stay put, the boy returning a nod of understanding. Then Will was on his feet, charging ahead.

"*Hans, bist du es?*"

It wasn't a foxhole, but a shell crater, and the two Germans were lounging in it, their backs propped against one side. They were smoking and drinking from tin cups, the much heavier man holding a flask, their rifles on the ground next to their packs. There was little reaction when Will first appeared, the men perhaps expecting their buddy to return. It wasn't until Will leapt into the crater that the two Germans saw his GI uniform, their eyes widening in alarm.

The younger of the two, a teenager, scrambled to his feet as he reached for his rifle. Will aimed his .45 and then quickly cursed himself, realizing a gunshot would bring others to the crater. That he had not thought of this earlier was a sign of his diminished state. Will took his finger off the trigger and palmed the .45, charging the young soldier as he raised his Mauser. Rearing back, Will smashed him with the pistol butt, hitting the boy square in the nose. There was a splash of blood and the German crumpled to the ground, unconscious, but at least spared the awful pain of several fractured facial bones.

The older German, pasty-skinned and wearing a thick overcoat as large as a tent, had remained on the ground and was fumbling now with the bolt of his rifle. Will turned on him, pulling his combat knife from his boot. The man began to cry out, but his voice froze as the blade sliced through the air. The German batted Will's arm with his rifle and the weapon discharged, the shot ringing through the night as the redirected blade sliced into the German's thigh. He howled in pain and Will quickly clamped a hand over the man's mouth. Dropping his Mauser, the German's hands frantically reached for his attacker's throat, but Will's knife struck again, slashing the man's jugular. Will held his adversary down as blood poured from the man's severed vein and carotid artery, and within seconds the German slumped to his side, a peaceful, almost serene glaze settling over his dead eyes.

Still kneeling on the man's chest, Will panted for breath. He was sure the gun shot would bring other Germans to the crater, and though his barehanded killing had Will's mind racing in a frenzy, he pushed those thoughts aside, summoning his last reserves for one final sprint to the American lines. With only a few hundred yards remaining, Will knew the worst was behind them. He and Philippe were going to make it. They were going to survive this, and when it was all over, Will would find his way back into the arms of his girl back home.

Kay.

He actually smiled in relief when her name came to him. Maybe she wasn't his girl, but she would be someday, the moment he escaped this insanity and set foot again on American soil.

It wasn't September anymore. He had enough of the war.

The Battle of the Bulge spanned nearly six weeks and involved more than one million German and American soldiers. It was the single largest clash of World War II, and stands today as the greatest battle in the history of the United States Army.

No one on the Allied side saw it coming.

Following the invasion of Normandy in June 1944, the Allies began steadily pushing the Germans back across the Western Front, even as Hitler was secretly amassing a colossal force well behind his lines. On December 16, 1944, the Germans unleashed 30 armored and infantry divisions, numbering more than 400,000 men and 1,200 tanks and other armored vehicles, against just three American infantry divisions and a single armored division posted along the Belgium-Luxembourg border. Three of the American divisions were almost completely inexperienced while the fourth had been decimated in recent fighting elsewhere. The Germans steamrolled past the American positions and began pressing west. Hitler's improbable objective was to drive all the way to the Belgian port of Antwerp, some 125 miles away, and split the Allied army in two. To do so, his armored divisions needed to capture critical networks of roads and bridges, and rapidly, before mass reinforcements from the Americans and British could reach the beleaguered forces attempting to slow down the German march.

It is unclear how the Allies may have fared if it had not been for the extraordinary efforts of several individual units throughout the Ardennes region, including the American 10th Armored and 101st Airborne Divisions, each thrown into the fight shortly after the German offensive began. The delaying actions of Combat Command B (CCB) of the 10th Armored, including Teams Cherry, O'Hara, and of course, Desobry, impeded a major thrust of the German advance for nearly two days. This delay gave the 101st Airborne a crucial window to move into Bastogne, barricade the town, and fuse together a motley band of lightly armed paratroopers and remnants of other units to defend its vital junction of hardtop roads. What was left of CCB's tanks and armored infantry eventually withdrew from their assigned outposts to join the paratroopers in Bastogne for what would become an epic stand.

Together, the 101st Airborne and 10th Armored men weathered a siege by overwhelming forces for nearly five days. Lacking reinforcements, air support, food, medicine, and ammunition, and subjected to constant sub-freezing temperatures and falling snow, some 18,000 Americans withstood day and nighttime shelling and repulsed repeated assaults by nearly 45,000 Germans. At one point, the German commander sent a message through the lines, demanding the surrender of the beleaguered garrison. Brigadier General Anthony McAuliffe, commanding the combined American forces in Bastogne, famously answered with a one-word response.

"Nuts."

And so the defenders of Bastogne held on, exhausted, sickly, and frostbitten. Without the town, the Germans were denied access to the roads needed to traverse unforgiving terrain replete with vast forests, saturated fields, and winding river valleys. The German offensive soon stalled, and the Allies poured fresh reinforcements into the Ardennes. The first relief elements of General Patton's Third Army arrived from France after Christmas, punching through the German lines and effectively ending the siege of Bastogne. The tide in Belgium was irreversibly changed, though it would take weeks to push the Germans back to their original lines.

The Battle of the Bulge, so named because of the shape the initial German incursion created in the Allied lines, continued until late January, 1945. The losses on both sides were staggering. More than 80,000 Americans were eventually killed or wounded, while German casualties exceeded 100,000 men.

Strategically, the costs were catastrophic for the Germans. Unlike the Americans, they had nothing to replenish the men and tanks that were lost. The remaining German forces, battered and demoralized, were swept back into Germany, ceding all of the territory they had initially gained. Most consequential, because of the volume of men and armor the Allies assembled to push the Germans back, a vast, vengeful invasion force was now perched just across the German doorstep.

On April 30, 1945, three months after the Battle of the Bulge ended, Adolf Hitler shot himself in a Berlin bunker, and the war in Europe soon came to a close.

More than 60 million people perished during World War II. Two-thirds of that number were civilians. The war left millions more displaced and homeless, and a continent in ruins. Those Americans who participated in the bloodshed and destruction, and witnessed the cruelties and deprivations firsthand, returned to a country that was spared from such tragedy on its own soil. A country that was itching to celebrate its resounding victory, sweep aside the past, and usher in a new, post-war era of growth, prosperity, and global peace.

The veterans who came home to America, nearly 16 million of them, were also eager to leave their war experience in the past. Most simply wished to reintegrate into society, reclaim their past lives, and assimilate back into their communities and families. For many of those who served in combat, this proved to be more difficult than they anticipated, the men scarred by their experiences, and, because of the times, blind to the healing that needed to occur.

Some of those scars were physical. Some far less visible than others.

1946

Chapter 19

"How's it look, Will?"

He knew the question was rhetorical. Griffith Stadium always looked magnificent, a vibrant kaleidoscope of vivid, dazzling colors. The maintenance crew that cared for the playing field saw it as an artist sees a canvas, cultivating every square inch like it was the Gardens of Versailles.

Whoever asked the question had already brushed past Will in the dugout, joining the cluster of players gathered along the third base line and leaving him gazing out at the sight with wondrous awe. While the veterans stretched their limbs and exchanged playful barbs, the rookies huddled together like baby ducklings, swept up in a mix of exuberance and terror as their first Opening Day drew nearer. Will should have followed his teammates onto the field, but his feet remained cemented to the top step of the dugout, his eyes drawn to the lush sea of grass in the outfield and the steel and concrete-encased structure that encircled it.

It was strange to be so awestruck by this field. He had played on it hundreds of times before the war, not to mention the string of recent practices following his return to Washington last week from spring training. Today felt different, though, as Mother Nature had finally dispensed with the incessant wintry temperatures and overcast skies. It was a crisp 61 degrees, without a trace of a breeze in the air, and the sunshine pouring down from above seemed to give each man a special energy, and the playing surface a bright, vibrant hue.

Will absorbed it all. He breathed in the atmospherics, the minty scent of freshly cut grass filling his nostrils, while from somewhere nearby, the stadium organist ran through his notes, practicing a repertoire that would rouse tens of thousands of spectators filling the stands in the coming days. He was comforted by the soft touch of the flannel practice jersey against his skin, looser than he was accustomed to, a consequence of the weight shed during the war.

The last Senator bounded out of the dugout and trotted onto the field, leaving Will alone with his thoughts. His eyes swept across the manicured infield, framed by the charcoal-painted grand-stands and blue umbrella sky, transporting Will back some 15 years, when his father brought Will and Jack to their very first game at Comiskey Park. Envisioning himself playing in such a venue before thousands of onlookers, the sight had captivated Will and bound him to baseball forever. Now, as he watched his teammates line up for a series of calisthenics, a wistful smile formed on his lips and Will breathed a single word to himself.

"Playable."

That single word whisked him to the past again, this time to Chattanooga, and a teammate named Amos Pratt. Pratt was a hard-nosed, hard-drinking, and hard-swinging third baseman from West Texas. When young Will arrived in Tennessee to join the AA affiliate, Pratt was leading the Southern League in runs batted in for the third consecutive season. He was also 32, nearly a pensioner by minor league standards. He had multiple stints and call-ups with the Senators under his belt, but Pratt's prowess in the minors never followed him to the big leagues, and it became apparent that the erstwhile bridesmaid was destined for the minor league life of broken-down buses and musty motel rooms.

To Will's surprise, Pratt never showed even a hint of sourness over his fate. He embraced it. More than any other player Will had played alongside, Pratt was intoxicated by the game of baseball. He would have suited up anywhere, at any level, from fabled Fenway Park to an empty lot in Washington's most poverty-stricken neigh-borhood. In every inning of every game, Pratt raced on to the field with the spirit of a young boy. Even after a lengthy downpour liberated the team from the taxing grind of game after game across the Sun Belt, Pratt would look across the rain-soaked field, puddles dotting the soft earth around the base paths, and proclaim to all that the conditions were, in his word, playable. When a late-season storm blanketed eastern Tennessee with five inches of snow, closing schools, businesses, and roads, Pratt again declared the field playable.

And now, as Will looked out across sun-splashed Griffith Stadium, he was reminded how hallowed this real estate was, and how little he appreciated it before the war. The men who doted on it around the clock like parents of a newborn baby had achieved what the players on the field could only dream of: perfection. Every blade of emerald grass was clipped with the precision of a fine watchmaker. The surface of the outfield was as smooth as a millpond. The chocolate-colored infield had been raked fastidiously to ensure a texture that would stand up to the searing heat of a Washington summer. And the fresh chalk lines, from home plate to the outfield foul poles, marked the sacred boundaries.

"Definitely playable," he said, his voice still just a whisper.

"What was that?"

Will turned in surprise. He was no longer alone and hadn't realized he had given voice to the old refrain.

"Nothing," Will answered, a bit too quickly, wondering how long Charlie Longman had been standing behind him.

The manager grunted. "You're late."

"I'm here."

"You got a contract yet? That cocktail napkin you signed last month won't get you past next week."

"I met with Griffith yesterday," Will replied. "He said they'll have something for me to sign today."

"Good. Then steaks are on you tonight. I heard Buck and Doc worked you out again yesterday. They still don't think that leg will hold up for an entire season."

The same doubts Will had been privately harboring for months. Since taking the first steps to rejoin the team, he had been adamant with club officials that the wound had fully healed, a dubious claim met with immediate suspicion by the team physician. Privately, Will had his own misgivings. Fifteen months had passed since the shell fragment had lodged itself in the flesh of his left thigh just as he and Philippe reached the American lines outside Bastogne. The Army docs had given him a clean bill of health prior to his discharge, but Will knew the leg was still a problem. He could feel it each time he lowered himself into position behind home plate. In his workouts, what began as a fairly benign sense of pressure gradually sharpened into more than discomfort. It was worrisome, considering a 154-game season loomed ahead.

Long-term, Will had been advised that the leg would get no better or no worse. If it was simply a matter of pain tolerance, as suggested by the team physician, Will figured he could gut out the season. Pain he could endure. Fatigue, however, was altogether different, and gave Will pause. Catching was the most physically demanding of all positions and would place considerable strain on his weakened leg muscles. He had tried lessening the pressure by favoring his right leg, but found that even the slightest alteration in his mechanics fouled up his technique. He could not change overnight the tradecraft that had been honed over thousands of practice hours.

It frustrated Will to no end. He never imagined that a piece of iron the size of a penny, a scratch compared to the grievous wounds of so many others, could jeopardize his playing career.

"It's fine," Will answered. "Good as new."

Longman guffawed. "Bullshit. Or I guess they don't make artillery shells like they used to."

The manager rubbed the back of his neck, eying Will carefully. "You okay with Legler?"

"Yep," Will answered, turning his attention back to the field.

"You sure?"

Will shrugged, feigning indifference. He was far from indifferent, though, and fully aware of the implications of what Longman was hinting at.

"Yeah, I'm sure. The kid finished the season as the starter. It's his job to lose."

The manager took a seat on the bench and folded his arms over his girth. "I'm disappointed to hear that. I thought for sure you was going to tell me the kid was on borrowed time."

Longman knew him well. Riding the bench would place a boulder-sized chip on Will's shoulder. But it was the sort of chip he had used in the past to fan a flame within, and harden his determination on the field.

"Come on, Charlie. I haven't played in nearly five years. Did you think I was going to dive back in and start crushing balls so hard you had to bench one of the organization's best prospects?"

"I guess–"

Will held up a palm, the carefree look on his face replaced by one full of confidence and determination. A look Longman had not seen in years. And though his eyes glimmered with good humor, Will's voice was filled with resolve.

"Give me a week."

It had been just three weeks since the two players first met at the team's spring-training facility in Orlando. The equipment locker tucked into the back of what passed for a clubhouse at old Tinker Field reeked of mildewed cowhide and mouse droppings. Will was on his knees, rummaging through crates of aged catching gear as he cursed his inability to find a set of matching shin protectors. Though Will had been vigorously working out nearly every day for two months, his focus had been solely on his physical conditioning. Once he belatedly joined the team in Florida, he deferred to the coaches' wishes that he allocate every minute to sharpening his offensive game. It was time now to return to his old position, and with Dick Holloway awaiting on the mound, Will was hurriedly searching the team's stores while the rest of the club limbered up for batting practice. Batting practice Will also sorely needed. First pitch against Boston was in 24 days.

There were footsteps behind him, the sound of metal spikes on cement, and Will turned to see a towering figure, the man's size 14 feet crossing the clubhouse in long strides. He was younger than Will, in his early 20s, with the bronzed skin of a California surfer.

"Nothing but junk in there," the young man said, his voice amiable. "Most of it belongs in a museum."

Will stood and faced the newcomer, whose broad smile revealed rows of even teeth. He was a giant. There were few major leaguers as tall as Will, and this guy had at least two or three inches on him. He was not only taller than Will, but thicker all around, almost entirely muscle.

"Hoping to find my old stuff. No luck."

"They've got my road gear somewhere around here. You're welcome to it, until they find you a new set."

Will smiled, holding out a hand. "Appreciate it. Will Jamison."

The other man extended a sizeable paw. "Cole Legler. You don't know me, Mr. Jamison–"

"It's Will. And of course I know you. You were in double-A when I left here in '42. Then went into the Army Air Corps, right?"

"Right," said Legler, surprised Will knew his background. "Joined in '43. Four of us from Chattanooga, all into the Air Corps. The Army taught me to fly, ended up as a co-pilot in a B-25."

How the hell did this moose get in a cockpit?

"Against the Japs?"

The younger man shifted his feet. "Well, guess I was in the same theater as the Japs. Army brass managed to keep our bird out of the heavy stuff."

Not a blowhard, Will thought approvingly.

"Ancient history, Cole, and you were hardly the only one. Took me better than two years to get to Europe." He paused. "I watched you last fall from the stands. You've got a hell of a swing."

Legler brightened. "Thanks. Just wish I had your arm behind the plate."

"From what I saw, you're not far off. Your footwork just needs some fine tuning, but you know that."

Legler grinned. "Were you scouting me?"

Will scoffed, pretending Legler hadn't pegged him right. Which he had.

"More like an observation. One teammate to another."

Even Will could hear the insincerity in his own voice.

Legler nodded his agreement, keeping up the pretense that this was nothing more than friendly banter between mutually supportive teammates. "If you don't mind me saying so, Mr. Jamison–"

"Will."

"You've got a hell of a chance here, Will. With Roscoe down, all they got is that college boy they just signed to Chattanooga, and he ain't ready. We need another big bat, even if it's off the bench."

Will didn't know if he wanted to take a swing at Legler, or buy him a beer. Legler was sending a message, and Will couldn't help but appreciate the younger man's brashness. Success at this level was all about confidence. Confidence that not only had to be felt, but radiated and projected on to others. And Legler was oozing with it.

Plus, the kid had stirred something inside Will, something he hadn't felt in a long, long time.

Will was keenly aware of the younger player's advantage. Legler had produced impressive numbers last season, first in Chatta-nooga and later in Washington. Moreover, Legler wasn't competing against Will Jamison, the 1941 all-star. Will was a shell of that player right now, and hadn't caught a game in four and a half years. A long climb awaited, but with Will's wartime experience came perspective. Whatever tests he faced on the field, it all seemed so trivial now compared to what he survived in Belgium.

Bastogne, like Noville, would be etched in his memory for eternity. Following Will's return to the American lines, two paratroopers had carried him to a battalion aid station, where a local civilian nurse changed the blood-soaked dressing wrapped around his leg. Hours later, a combat surgeon gave Will a few belts of French brandy before removing the jagged piece of shrapnel from the back of his left thigh. Though Will belonged in a field hospital, he was sent back to the line that same day. With Bastogne surrounded, every able-bodied man who could pull a trigger was sent forward to join the tenuous perimeter defenses. Will considered himself able-bodied enough and reunited with what was left of his old unit that made it back from Noville. He found Ira Lucas, still hobbled with a fractured ankle, commanding a street barricade, one of many hastily assembled across the town to block the enemy's advance.

Three days later, the cloud cover over Bastogne finally broke, and crates of precious supplies parachuted down to the earth. Wave after wave of C-47 transports dropped food, ammunition, and medical supplies into town, re-supplying the besieged Americans. Within a month, American reinforcements were flooding into the Ardennes, and with the Germans back on the run, the 10th Armored was finally pulled from the front. The Battle of the Bulge was over.

It was then that the division's mail caught up to them, and Will was dealt a heartbreaking blow. The news came in a letter from Jack, half a globe away. Their mother had passed away a month before Will and the rest of the 10th Armored saw their first combat at Metz. She had fallen severely ill at home one evening, a brain aneurysm they later determined, and died within hours. Will hadn't heard anything from his father, who relied on Jack to deliver the news while floating in the South Pacific some 12,000 miles away.

Will was devastated. He hadn't even been aware that his mother had health problems, yet such was the fragility of life that she collapsed and passed away in the same day. It pained Will beyond measure that neither he nor Jack attended the funeral.

Following Hitler's death and the German surrender, there was talk of the division participating in the invasion of the Japanese home islands, but two atomic bombs ended that discussion, and the war finally, and mercifully, came to an end.

For Will, the war ended in a hospital in France, where he was sent to rehabilitate his leg after surgery. Remarkably, he had been a soldier for more than 1,000 days, but only spent a mere 48 of those engaged in combat. They were enough.

As millions of servicemen returned to the United States, the process of transitioning them back into civilian life lasted weeks for some, and even longer for others. It wasn't until October of 1945, nearly five months after the war in Europe ended, that Will walked off his troop transport and into the Brooklyn Navy Yard. Once free of the Army, he returned to Lancaster, anxious to see his brother and surprised by the obligation he felt to make peace with his father. It was a far more tearful reunion than Will expected. He was practically tackled by Jack, who drove up from Chicago to welcome Will home, and even the greeting from his father seemed heartfelt. There was something off about Jack, their conversations back at the house more awkward than Will was accustomed to. But Will guessed they were all a little off after what they had been through.

The détente with his father evaporated quickly, with Henry promptly reverting to old form. The questioning of his two sons about their wartime experience had all of the empathy of a prosecutor hammering a reluctant witness. Henry pressed them each, enthralled by their decorations and eager to hear the stories behind them. There was something in his father's voice that unnerved Will, something between envy and resentment. So Will truncated his recollections, perhaps wary of recalling such disturbing memories in detail, perhaps simply to defy his father. Henry's frustration mounted, the man clearly chomping at the bit to trumpet the heroics of the Jamison boys to others in their small community. It all led to yet another of the heated exchanges that marked their every conversation before the war. This one escalated quickly, and by the next morning, Will was gone, without a single farewell.

He returned to Chicago, taking a small apartment in his old building, just blocks from where he had enlisted at the outset of the war. A surprise phone call from Clark Griffith came, the owner offering warm words and every assurance that the team wanted its catcher back. Will didn't doubt Griffith's sincerity, but knew there was more than just benevolence at play. The Senators had come within a hair of the American League pennant the previous year, and with the World Series in rare sight, Griffith needed his former all-star back on the field.

Charlie Longman brought Will back to the present, stomping into the dugout, past the handful of players taking refuge from the sudden squall passing over the stadium.

"Jamison," Longman barked, a plug of tobacco bulging in his cheek. "Just got word the boys in legal are whipping up your paperwork. No more of that provisional bullshit. They're offering you a two-year contract."

Will thought he had seen it all in this business, yet he still could not keep his mouth from falling open. From the corner of his eye, he saw Cole Legler's head whip around, his surprise evident as well. The 30-day contract Will had signed the previous week was a stopgap, and standard for returning players whose medical status was considered undetermined. Will hadn't balked for a second when Vivian Pritchard had suggested it.

"I'll get you an at-bat on Opening Day," Longman continued. "The home folks will love it. And we'll see if we can't get you some time behind the plate in the series. Friday we go to New York, open with a doubleheader on Saturday. The rookie will catch the first game, second game is yours."

Will blinked in astonishment. "I haven't played–"

"Skip," interrupted Legler. "I thought–"

"We ain't paying you to think, rookie."

"I'm not a rookie, this is my–"

"When you talk stupid, you're a rookie." Longman turned back to Will. "Any questions?"

His tone made it clear there were to be no questions, and for a second, Will was back in Noville, listening to the commands of Major Desobry.

"Uh, no. I guess not. Thanks for giving me the chance, Charlie."

The manager shook his head in exasperation, as if Will had not heard what he said. Longman grabbed him roughly by the elbow, leading him out to the auxiliary tunnel and out of Legler's earshot.

"The chance? Fuck chances, Will. I appreciate your service and all, and I know you got a cigar box full of medals somewhere, but your job is here now. This team did okay during the war, and Griffith is pleased as shit. Thinks this year we'll be even better. But let me make it clear to you. The Yankees, and everyone else who got their boys back, don't want to just win, they want to crush us into dog meat. They don't think we're fit to shit in the same crapper as them. Griffith wants to prove that last year was no fluke. As for you playing, you earned it, before the war, and Griffith has a long memory. Just don't make an ass out of him. Or yourself. Understand?"

Will nodded.

"Go get some swings in, then I want you to work with Legler behind the plate. He's our catcher right now, and the kid's got the footwork of a one-eyed elephant. Teach him what you can, he's your teammate after all. Try to remember that as you two are pissing on each other's legs. Got it?"

"Got it."

Longman grunted a goodbye and started up the tunnel to the clubhouse.

"Hey, Skipper."

"Yeah?"

"The kid is going to make a hell of a backup."

For the first time that day, Longman smiled.

Chapter 20

(AP) April 19, 1946 — The Washington Senators fell to the Boston Red Sox, 8-2, on a blustery Wednesday afternoon before a near-capacity crowd at Griffith Stadium. The visitors swept the season-opening series, sending Washington to the American League cellar with an 0-3 record to begin the year.

Mickey Harris went eight innings for Boston, striking out 11 men and notching his first victory of the season. Bobby Doerr belted a three-run blast off Washington starter Ray Scarborough, who was chased from the game after surrendering three consecutive doubles in the top half of the 7th inning. The home fans were finally able to cheer their team in the bottom of the 7th when Washington slugger and decorated war hero Will Jamison stepped to the plate, pinch hitting for starting catcher Cole Legler. In just his third at-bat of the season, Jamison drove in Washington's only two runs with a drive that came within inches of clearing the right field wall. Jamison also saw his first action of the season behind the plate, catching the final two innings as the home fans await his return to all-star form. The Senators will look to awaken their bats in the Bronx, where they will face the American League favorites in a four-game series at Yankee Stadium beginning Saturday afternoon.

It was Friday morning, a rare day off for the Senators with the season still in its infancy. A late afternoon train would shuttle the team to New York, followed by a trip to Boston later in the week for an early rematch against the Red Sox. It was a tough draw, opening the schedule with 12 consecutive games against the two powerhouses. The Senators fared well during the war years while the league's best talent was away, but the games ahead loomed as their first real test.

There was an early spring chill in the capital, with the morning temperatures hovering in the 40s. Will was bundled up in his heaviest coat, standing on the sidewalk as he peeked through the large plate-glass window at the bustle of Dixie's Cafe. It was a visit he had been anticipating for months. On those desolate, rain-filled days in France and Belgium, standing under a mess tent waiting for chipped beef on toast or some other culinary slop, he longed to be back in the warm confines of Dixie's. While his platoon mates jostled with each other in the chow line and debated the merits of Ava Gardner versus Ingrid Bergman, Will could only think of the day he could indulge again in rich, savory foods that weren't derived from powder and preservatives.

He missed far more than Cecil's cooking, though. The eatery was a second home to Will, and those inside a second family. For a man who had long eschewed the glare of the public spotlight, Dixie's was a safe haven, a place where the fans and autograph hounds largely left him in peace, and treated him like any other laborer in the city, for better or worse.

Will pushed through the glass door, the chime from above lost in the clatter coursing through the restaurant. Dixie's was packed, each table filled with a cross-section of Foggy Bottom life, as blue collar factory workers and Ivy League-educated diplomats sat shoulder to shoulder, waging friendly arguments about anything and everything, from the Senators' dismal start to whether the Democrats would survive the November elections. Others kept to themselves, as Will usually did, their noses buried in books and newspapers.

He hung his coat on a rack against the wall, nearly collapsing from the ambrosial aroma of frying bacon that wafted through the restaurant, and mentally added a double serving to the truckload of food he was about to order. The days of limiting himself to leaner options were long past, the hourly admonishments from Longman about his diminished weight still ringing in his ears. His manager was right, of course; Will's slugging power and durability behind the plate were dependent on filling out his once-strapping frame again.

He scanned the length of the counter, frowning at the lack of a single open seat. He was about to settle for a table when an older Negro, wearing the dungaree coveralls of a brewery hand, pushed away his half-eaten breakfast and threw down a couple of bills. Will darted across the restaurant to claim the open counter stool, lowering himself onto the worn leather as a sigh of contentment escaped his lips.

Opening a grease-stained menu, Will skimmed it quickly, smiling in satisfaction. The menu was unchanged, not a single item different from what he remembered before the war. Other than the prices, he noted, which had sharply increased. Even the selection of salads remained, though Will knew for a fact that not a single customer had ever ordered any of them. There was no chance any vegetable had ever left the kitchen at Dixie's, where fried bologna was a daily special.

His smile widened the second he lowered the menu and spotted Lucinda. She was at the far end of the counter, scribbling out an order from a large family. Tearing the order from her pad, she pinned it to the wheel in the window where hot food was passed through from the back kitchen. It was when she reached for a pot of coffee that she finally caught sight of Will. Her mouth fell open, one hand flattening against her chest as she gave a joyful shriek and ran to his side of the counter. Will stood, swallowing her bulk in his arms as she gave him a mammoth embrace.

She finally pulled back, but not before pecking him on the cheek, smearing it with lipstick. "Will Jamison, oh my Lord. I don't know what to say."

"How about, welcome back?"

Lucinda nodded enthusiastically. "Welcome back! When did you get here?"

"Not long ago. Wish I could have stopped in sooner. The team put me up at a rooming house on Capitol Hill until I could get my old place back on 25th Street."

She put a gentle hand on his arm. "I read that you got yourself wounded. Was it bad?"

"Nah, just a scratch." Will was quiet for a moment, but he needed to ask. "Your boy?"

Lucinda waived the question away. "That's right. You left when Danny was at Midway. He's fine, Will. His plane was away when the *Yorktown* was attacked, and he landed on another ship. He spent two more years on carrier planes, then broke a leg in a crash landing. He ended up in San Diego, and the Navy kept him there for the rest of the war as a gunnery instructor. He's working for the telephone company now here in town."

"Hey," called a surly voice from the pass-through. "Stop yapping with that bum and take some orders."

"Oh, you shush Cecil," Lucinda called back. "Nobody wants to eat your sorry cooking, you just go back to burning water."

There was laughter from others nearby, as Will gave Cecil a wave and the two exchanged grins. The burly cook gave him a mock salute through the window with his spatula, which Will returned before turning back to Lucinda.

"I've been waiting four very long years to say this. I'll have the usual."

"Well, is this the, I'm a star baseball player and I need to eat healthy, order? Or the, I've been eating Army food for four years and I need some of Cecil's flapjacks?"

"The latter," he laughed, patting his belly. Or where he should have had a belly. "I'm on a special diet. Need to pack on some pounds."

"Honey, I've been on that diet for 30 years. It's working just fine.

Give Cecil ten minutes to get some hot cakes and eggs out."

"And a double order of bacon. Crisp."

"And a double order of bacon. Crisp. I'll get your milk and coffee."

Half an hour later, Will's speared his last forkful of pancake, using it to scrape the remaining droplets of syrup from his dish. He stuffed it into his mouth and pushed the platter away, gratified but a bit downhearted. His favorite meal had come to a close.

It was mid-morning now and the crowd had thinned. Will reached for his billfold, signaling Lucinda to bring his check. Her attention however, was drawn to the street entrance. Turning on his stool, Will saw a slight young man removing his coat. He appeared to be around 20 years old. His blond hair was close-cropped and he wore charcoal slacks, a white dress shirt, and a poorly knotted striped tie.

What he was wearing on his right arm is what stood out the most. A chrome hook, in place of a hand and wrist.

Will turned away, hoping Lucinda would do the same, but she could not stop staring, her face full of sympathy and pity. The young man came to the counter, and Lucinda at least managed to look him in the eye, greeting him with a welcoming smile. Will counted money from his wallet, unable to tune out their conversation.

"Can I help you, sweetheart?" Lucinda asked.

"I'm here about the job."

"The job?"

"Yes, ma'am. The one you posted in this morning's newspaper. A busboy, one who can work weekday mornings."

"Well, Cecil does all the hiring here, and he's on the grill right now."

"I can come back–"

Lucinda laughed. "Nonsense. He should be caught up on orders, and I sure could use the help. You wait right here. I'll get him."

A minute later she returned, Cecil following close behind. He had been the only cook at Dixie's for better than a decade and doubled as a general manager. The diner had once been inherited by an elderly widow in Virginia who knew nothing of restaurants, let alone health codes and commercial leases, so she turned everything over to Cecil, who added the business side of Dixie's to his existing kitchen duties. A former merchant mariner, Cecil was close to 40 years old and shaped like a fireplug, with a hefty build and colorfully tattooed, muscled arms. He wore his usual white t-shirt and trousers, and was wiping his hands on a food-stained apron as he followed his waitress to the counter. Lucinda had obviously not told Cecil what to expect, as the cook visibly blanched when he saw the metal protruding from the young man's arm. Cecil quickly recovered, offering as authentic a smile as he could muster.

"What can I do for you, kid?"

"It's Warren. Warren Dawson. I'm here for the busboy job."

Cecil looked both apologetic and apprehensive. "Sorry, kid, but we're not hiring right now."

The words took both Warren and Lucinda by surprise. "But there was an ad in the paper," the young man protested. "I promise I'll work hard and–"

"Yes, yes," soothed Cecil, "I'm sure you'd do a bang-up job. But we filled the position."

"With who?" Lucinda questioned, looking at Cecil as if he had lost his mind.

Cecil's eyes narrowed in warning to her as he turned back toward Warren. "We filled the position. I'm sorry, kiddo."

The young man's shoulders sagged at first in resignation. He suddenly straightened, his face hardening as he flashed a quiet, contemptuous scowl at Cecil before stalking off.

"Hey fella," Cecil called after him uneasily, aware now that much of the discussion had been overheard by others. "Want to thank you for your service. Can we get you something to eat? On the house, of course. A piece of pie, maybe?"

Warren turned and faced the cook. His face was blank, and his voice even. "A piece of pie?"

"Sure," grinned Cecil. "Least we can do. How about it?"

Warren thought about it. "Cecil, right?"

"Right."

"You got eggs, Cecil?"

"Sure do, kid."

"Well, Cecil, why don't you take those eggs, shells and all, and shove them up your ass?"

The smile dissolved from Cecil's face, his eyes bulging as he balled his fists. No one spoke to him like that, especially in his own place. The entire restaurant was hushed now, waiting for Cecil's response, but the young man was already halfway to the door, leaving the sputtering cook with no choice but to turn on his heel and stomp off to the kitchen.

Like the other customers who were snickering among themselves and returning to their breakfasts, Will had witnessed every word of the exchange. Unlike the others, he found nothing amusing about it. He slapped his money on the counter and quickly caught up to Warren just as he pulled open the glass door.

"Hey, kid."

Warren turned, his body rigid with anger.

"I'm not a kid," he snapped.

"Take it easy, it's just a figure of speech." Will gestured at the hook. "Where'd you lose the hand?"

"Okinawa."

Will gave a grim nod. It was one of those obscure names that a year or two ago, no one had ever heard of. Now it was synonymous with the worst conceivable savagery. A small, rocky Pacific island, Okinawa became a blood-drenched nightmare for U.S. forces late in the war. Some 14,000 Americans were killed trying to wrestle the stronghold from a garrison of fanatical troops who considered the island, just over 300 miles from Tokyo, sacred soil. They fought to the death on every square inch, giving the Americans a taste of what an expected invasion of the home islands would cost. More than 100,000 Japanese perished on Okinawa, many by their own hand, refusing to surrender.

"How'd you lose it?"

Warren blinked, startled by the directness of the question. No one asked him that question. Not even his own mother.

She was hardly alone in her discomfort. Americans had enthusiastically supported the war effort, but were as jubilant as those in uniform when it ended, and eager for the nation to return to normalcy. The public didn't forget the veterans' service, though, and flocked to the parades in droves, feting the men with long ovations and infinite praise for their heroics and sacrifices.

For those like Warren who suffered disfiguring wounds—the amputees, the burn victims, and others—their return reception was often markedly different. Many were pushed into facilities that were under resourced, understaffed and tiled in bureaucratic quicksand. Some found themselves subjected to gawking stares and finger pointing from children and others who didn't know better.

All of which explained the suspicion that filled Warren's eyes when he heard Will's question. The tone, however, struck Warren as sincere, so he took a few moments to gather his thoughts before responding.

"My squad was clearing out a cave where a bunch of Japs were holed up. Jap officer came out of nowhere, charged us from behind with his Samurai sword and a grenade. Someone got him with a grease gun, but he'd already armed the grenade. The blast took out half the squad. Nearly tore my arm off. Corpsman tried to patch me up, but the docs at the aid station couldn't save much past the elbow."

Warren studied Will's face carefully, drawing a conclusion. "You served, right?"

Will nodded. "France, then Belgium."

"Wounded?"

"Not bad. Took a piece of metal in the leg."

"So, no hook?"

Will laughed, and even Warren broke a smile.

"You're pretty sharp, kid. Why do you want to work in a dump like this?"

Warren shrugged. "I'm starting college in the fall. Small school in Pennsylvania. GI Bill is helping, but I still need every nickel I can scrape together."

"Cleaning tables?"

"Not my first choice, mac. This is the 20th job I've applied for this month. Construction sites. Department stores. Even ice cream counters. Everyone seems to have a good reason not to hire someone with a hook sticking out of his arm. Me? I just want to work."

"You got something to write with?"

Warren nodded, curious now, and took a fountain pen from his pocket. "Still learning to write with my left hand."

Will removed two business cards from his wallet. He had Warren write down his address and phone number on one, which Will pocketed. He then jotted something on the other card, and handed the card and pen back to Warren.

"I'm going to have a chat with Cecil, see what I can do here. We go back a few years. I'm not sure what kind of mood he's in after your egg advice, but he's not as much of an asshole as he seems and probably knows he screwed up. Whatever he decides, I want you to call the number on that card and ask for Mason. Tell him you're calling about a job in groundskeeping. He'll be expecting to hear from you."

Warren examined the card, impressed. It belonged to the team's press liaison, and Will had learned long ago to always carry a few of the man's cards with him.

"You work for the Senators?"

"You could say that."

"But what if Cecil changes his mind? Actually offers me a job. Do I still call this Mr. Mason?"

"Cecil's ad said he only needed someone in the mornings, right? Mason can use you in the afternoons or evenings. You got a problem working two jobs?"

Warren could only shake his head, and Will could see the young man's eyes watering, the emotions of the last few minutes having a profound impact. He clapped Warren on the shoulder and the two said their farewells. Will watched the boy go, satisfied and unsatisfied. With his jaw clenched, Will turned and began weaving his way through the tables, feeling a quiet rage stirring within. He brushed past Lucinda at the counter, her face twisted in confusion as Will stalked through the swinging door and into the kitchen. He had worked himself into a barely controlled fury.

Cecil was feverishly working the grill and looked up in surprise.

"Will. What d'ya need pal?"

"I need you to hire that kid who was just in here."

Cecil sighed, returning his attention to the hotcakes he was flipping. "You heard what I told him. I ain't hiring right now."

"He's a vet, Cecil. Lost part of his arm in the Pacific, fighting the Japs."

"I feel bad about that. But I can't hire him."

"Can't? Or won't?"

"Can't," Cecil reiterated, his patience spent. There was an edge now in his voice. He pointed his metal spatula at Will. "And look, just because you're some rich ball player don't give you no right to tell me how to run my joint."

Will's voice was taut. "Why won't you hire him, Cecil?"

"I told you–"

"TELL ME THE FUCKING TRUTH!" Will shouted, slamming a fist on a stainless steel table holding stacks of dishes.

Cecil jumped, startled by the sharp outburst. Will's voice had carried from the kitchen, and the entire restaurant was quiet again.

It was too much for Cecil. First the crippled kid cursing at him and now Jamison acting like a beat cop putting the screws to a purse snatcher. He quickly scooped up the hotcakes with the spatula and threw them down on a chipped plate before turning to Will again, his cheeks apple red with anger.

"The truth? The truth is, people come here to eat. It's the last peace they get before they clock into jobs they don't like so much. Not everyone has your money, pal. These are simple, working people. They don't want to come here, get a plate of food, and then look at that."

"*That?* That hook you mean?"

"Yeah, that hook. It makes people...feel bad."

Feel bad.

Cecil softened his voice, but not by much.

"Look, Will, we go back a long way. I let you sit at the counter with the darkies, no questions asked. You know me. I respect the hell out of what that guy did over there, what all of you did, but I got a business to run."

Will nodded slowly and exhaled, letting the tension run out from his body. Cecil saw it, and relief swept across the cook's face. His lips had just begun forming a smile when Will charged him, his hands grabbing fistfuls of the cook's cotton t-shirt. In a sudden, violent motion, he shoved Cecil against the wall next to the large grill. The cook slammed against the plaster with such force that a stack of pans on the shelf above fell noisily to the floor. The blow knocked the air from Cecil's lungs as he crumpled to the hard surface.

Lucinda came rushing into the kitchen. She saw Will looming over Cecil with a venomous glare, his fists raised in the direction of the cook, whose face was screwed up in pain.

"Will! What in–"

He wheeled towards her. "Stay out of this, Lucinda."

Will turned back toward Cecil, who had managed to prop himself up against the wall. His face had turned pale and his breaths came in gasps as he tried to get his words out. "Please.... Don't..."

Will squatted down until he was level with Cecil, their faces inches apart.

"You know what?" he asked, jabbing a finger in the cook's chest.

"I don't want that kid working in this rat-infested shithole. And I'm going to make damn sure no veteran ever sets foot in here."

"Will," pleaded Lucinda, "you can't–"

Her voice coincided with a sharp twinge of pain behind his eye, and he felt the heat and wrath flowing through his blood. He whirled toward her as he picked up an empty pot and threw it as hard as he could against the wall.

"SHUT UP, LUCINDA!" he shouted. "JUST SHUT YOUR FUCKING MOUTH!"

He bolted past the waitress, now pale and speechless. And as he stomped out of the restaurant and headed home, forgetting his heavy coat, he knew. Even if Cecil was persuaded not to call the police and press charges. Or even if his public explosion managed to avoid an above-the-fold headline in the *Washington Star*. He knew.

It was the last time he would ever see any of them again.

Chapter 21

(AP) May 15, 1946 — The Washington Senators suffered their worst loss of the season, falling 14-1 to the Detroit Tigers on a balmy spring day at Griffith Stadium. Tiger Ace Hal Newhouser continued his sizzling start to the season, striking out eight Washington batters on the way to his third complete game. Washington's lone run came on a sacrifice fly in the fourth inning, when Will Jamison drove a deep fly ball to right field, scoring George Case on the sacrifice. Hank Greenberg had two home runs for the Tigers, while George Kell and Eddie Lake belted three hits each for the visitors.

It was an unusual day for Jamison, making his fifth consecutive start behind the plate. In addition to his run-scoring sacrifice, he socked a sharp line drive to left field in the sixth inning with his team trailing by 11 runs. Jamison tried to stretch the hit into a double but was called out after left fielder Roy Cullenbine fired a dart to second base, his throw beating the sliding Jamison by a whisker. Jamison blew his top at the call, shouting at umpire Stan Matthews in a profanity-laced tirade. Matthews wasted no time in ejecting Jamison, who lunged for the umpire and had to be restrained by first base coach Lou Cummings and two Detroit infielders. Several Washington players emerged from the dugout to escort Jamison off the field as he continued to berate the shaken Matthews. No word yet whether the league office will take disciplinary action against the former all-star. With the split series, the Senators fell to 12-12 on the young season and play host next week to...

"Fuck," grumbled Will, loosening the silk bow tie for the umpteenth time before yanking it from his collar.

He could field strip a M1 Garand while blindfolded but couldn't fasten a simple bow tie to save his life. He tossed it aside, choosing to wait until he got downstairs to enlist help. Jorge, the evening doorman, wore one every day.

He shrugged on the black coat, pulling at the French cuffs of his overstarched shirt while studying his reflection in the dresser mirror. The tuxedo was a size too small and felt like a strait jacket, a just comparison considering the evening ahead. Will fought the impulse to feed the formal wear to the building's incinerator and instead sighed in defeat, pouring himself another finger of Scotch and downing it in a single swallow. The tuxedo was hardly to blame for his foul mood.

It was a night Will had dreaded for weeks. The team's annual charitable gala at the Wardman Park Hotel was sure to be a star-studded affair, at least by local standards, drawing coverage in every major Society page from Washington to New York. The posh ballroom would fill with the city's elites, including Members of Congress, White House officials, Cabinet members, and the countless ranks of lackeys and yes men that circled the room like packs of hyenas. They would all eventually leave with lighter wallets after caving to the guileless pleading of Clark Griffith, the gala serving as less of a social event than a ham-fisted shakedown.

The team owner was passionate about his charitable work and dedicated himself as much to raising research dollars for childhood health diseases as he did to building a pennant contender. The self-made Griffith happily served as chair of the yearly fundraising drive, and though he himself wasn't considered much of a philanthropist, he had no qualms about goading others into donating.

The ballclub had a standing requirement for each player to attend. Will went enthusiastically after first joining the team, happy to support such an exemplary cause, but like the others, he came to despise the numbing small talk and unending salesmanship that was such a blemish on the event. Even now, he would sooner charge a regiment of *Panzergrenadiers* than waste an evening ingratiating himself to such men, or the equally repugnant lobbyists and journalists that floated over their prey like ravenous vultures. It was appalling to witness, the quid pro quo circling the room like a merry-go-round of political opportunism. Worst of all were those who latched onto the players, boasting about their own youthful glory days on the diamond, as if they had virtuously sacrificed a contract with the Yankees to answer the call to public service.

There would also be no shortage of eye-pleasing women in attendance, plying themselves into gowns that showcased their curves, and sure to draw leers from every corner of the room. Will would have his chances this evening, that much was a certainty. None with the only woman he cared about.

Months had passed since his return from the war, and Will still had not reached out for Kay. He considered a phone call when the team was in New York in April but opted against it. He had a small window to prove to Clark Griffith and Charlie Longman that he could return to his former caliber of play and would not risk any complicating distractions. It had been four long, agonizing years without her, but he figured he could manage another month or two.

There was a soft knock at the door, likely yet another of the grating salesmen who relentlessly canvassed his apartment building at all hours. Will sighed, knowing the Wardman ballroom could wait no longer, and pocketed the bow tie and embossed invitation. He gave the mirror one final glance, wishing he could bolt the door and sequester himself from the outside world for the evening. Even an hour with a blathering salesman at his door was far preferable to what awaited downtown. He quickly dismissed that notion, unable to imagine facing Griffith if he failed to show.

Another rash of knocks followed, more urgent now, and Will turned the last light off. He pulled open the front door, calculating how much injury he might cause to the salesman and his vacuum cleaner or set of encyclopedias after throwing them from the third-story window. He was about to let loose a string of colorful words but instead froze, stunned by the figure facing him in the doorway.

"So, mister," the visitor began, her eyes alight. "I have two options for you. Plan A, and Plan B."

She waited for a response, but Will remained mute and still as a statue, overcome by the cascade of emotions coursing through him.

Her auburn hair was shorter now, falling just above her shoulders, and framed an oval face that had only grown more striking since he last saw it. Her eyes were as soft and penetrating as he remembered, and even now were methodically dissecting him. But it was that arresting, seductive smile he could not get past. Stark white teeth surrounded by ravishing, raspberry-colored lips he had waited an eternity to kiss again. A smile that flustered Will to his core from the minute they first met.

She was, as always, fashionably attired, wearing a hip-hugging, turquoise cotton skirt that reached just past her knees. Her waist was wrapped in an oversized leather belt, while a snug, ivory-colored silk blouse stretched across her figure, as trim as when he saw her last. A double strand of pearls encircled her long neck, dipping to the tip of her cleavage, clearly visible beneath where the top of her blouse was unbuttoned.

His throat was dry and he felt unsteady, overcome by a stir he had not felt in years. He knew this moment was coming, but hadn't expected it so soon.

So soon. He had been back for seven months.

"It's been years since I heard you speak in person," Kay said, smiling in amusement as she checked her watch, as if late for an appointment. "How much longer do I have to wait?"

The words broke the spell and Will sagged a bit, realizing just how much he had missed even the soft lilt of her voice, tinged with the faintest trace of her native borough. With one hand glued to the door, Will finally managed to find his words.

"How...what are you doing here?" he stammered.

Even as he spoke, Will heard the absurdity of the question, and the bungled words of a smitten teenager with a knotted tongue.

"What am I doing here," she mimicked. "Well, I'm not here to borrow a cup of sugar."

He dropped his arm from the door, if only to prove that he could move. "How did you know where I lived?"

"I bribed the bat boy. Ten dollars. Your doorman let me up here, didn't ask for a penny. Probably got his money's worth looking down my blouse."

That made him laugh. "You should have talked the bat boy down. He would have told you for five."

"Aren't you worth an extra five?"

He waited for the clever retort, but the words eluded him. He was still fixated on her eyes and lips, and, he now realized, overcome with desire. Oddly though, it wasn't sexual, but something else. Something more. He wanted to hold her. To caress her soft skin. To inhale her sweet perfume and fragrant hair, and nuzzle against the nape of her neck. Seventeen months ago, sitting in a miserable foxhole, on the precipice of death, she was all he had thought of. What he had longed for. He wanted to be a part of her now. Part of her body, her thoughts, her heart. He wanted her. All of her.

Kay's smile faded. She was also sensing the charged current between the two. It was palpable.

"Will, I–"

He did not let her finish, stepping into the hallway and wrapping his arms around her waist. She threw herself into his embrace, and they clutched each other for a full, fierce minute. He finally released her, and as he pulled back, she seemed to notice for the first time what he was wearing.

"Look at me, coming here unannounced. You obviously have plans."

"Yes," he said, realizing he would be late now to the gala. He laughed.

"What's so funny?"

What was so funny was how little he cared about Clark Griffith at the moment.

"Nothing. Plans change. And I could use a drink."

"Me too. Can we stay here?"

"Sure. I don't have much booze left, but I have plenty of beer. And it's cold."

She agreed, happily, and followed Will into his flat. He switched on the lights, immediately embarrassed. He hadn't had time to personalize his temporary home with any furnishings beyond what came with the leased apartment. Even the paint was a dull mauve. The walls and hardwood floors were bare, and though the living spaces were large, the furniture was sparse and dated. There wasn't even a kitchen table, though Will rarely took a meal here.

He directed Kay to the worn, frayed sofa in the living room while he headed to his bedroom to change clothes. He returned wearing denim jeans, a worn Chattanooga Lookouts sweatshirt, and a pair of crew socks. He grabbed two Pabst Blue Ribbons from the icebox and joined Kay in the living room. She was curled up against what passed for a cushion, her shoes on the floor and her legs folded underneath her.

"So," he began, easing onto the sofa next to her and passing over a beer. "We have some catching up to do. I feel like Rip Van Winkle."

Kay blinked. "Will Jamison! Is that a literary reference?"

Will grinned. "Well, they had a library at Fort Benning. Had to find out how *The Last Tycoon* ended. I may have read a few other books back then."

"You read Fitzgerald?!?"

"Yep. Two movie studio guys, going head to head. Could've been Lou Gehrig and Lefty Grove back in the day. Or Ted Williams and Bob Feller. No offense, but the man's writing sort of put me to sleep. I'm more of a Zane Grey guy."

She smiled. "Westerns."

"Yep. And Grey was a baseball player. Played a few years in the minors. Imagine that."

Kay shook her head in wonder. "Imagine that. You never cease to surprise me, Will." She considered her next words. "I guess one good surprise deserves another."

"You took up baseball?"

"Better, I think. I left Eddie."

Will almost choked on his beer. He wiped his mouth as she held up her hand and proudly wiggled her ringless fingers.

"When?"

"Last summer. The divorce came through in February."

Will took another sip, averting her eyes, wondering if she thought-

"Don't worry, Will," she said, as if once again reading his mind. "I'm hardly expecting a marriage proposal. I told you long ago that I knew you weren't the marrying type."

"Whew," he grinned.

She offered a smile in return, but it was half-hearted at best.

"Besides, I didn't do it for you."

Will should have felt relief when he heard that, but instead looked at her sharply.

"Someone else?"

"Nope," she countered, taking a sip from her beer. "For me."

He exhaled, hoping she hadn't noticed his reaction. "What made you finally pull the trigger?" His eyebrows shot up. "He didn't do anything-"

"No," she quickly responded. "That stopped some time ago. Someone called the police and a couple of detectives came by. About the time you shipped out. They threatened Eddie, said they would go to the papers unless he laid off. I tried to imagine who would have called the police. Who could have possibly known?"

"Not many," Will said.

"No," she said, meeting his eyes. "Not many."

Will held her gaze, his poker face revealing nothing. And everything.

"It worked," she continued, "though it hardly turned him into an angel. Why did I finally leave him? I guess I finally saw the light, and grew up a little." She paused for several moments, combing through her memory. "I always wanted to believe that things could get better. That Eddie would go back to what he was like when we first met. I told you about that. He was all manners and charm back then, and I fell for it. I was in love, I guess, or thought I was. Maybe I was just looking for a way out of Brooklyn. But the day I took his name is the day the manners and charm disappeared. He was really struggling on the field that year, and the drinking got worse every day. And when he drank..." Her voice trailed off for a moment. "I think he was frustrated. Frustrated he couldn't hit the ball, frustrated I wasn't getting pregnant. I never told you that part. Eddie wanted children, boys to be precise. He was possessed by the notion of a son following in his footsteps. But nothing was happening. I even went to a special clinic in Connecticut. They told me I couldn't have a child. Ever."

She said it matter-of-factly, her voice almost toneless, but Will felt the emotional charge behind the words. He reached for her hand, knowing how heartbreaking the discovery must have been. They had never really spoken of children, but Will knew intuitively Kay would have made a wonderful mother.

"I'm sorry, Kay."

Will suddenly looked at her sharply, realizing the other implication of what she had said.

"Wait, *that's* what made you want a divorce? Because you couldn't have kids with the fucking asshole that slapped you around?"

Her eyebrows shot up in surprise at the sudden outburst, his tone shifting from sympathy to belligerence in the blink of an eye. The vulgarity also caught her off-guard. Will rarely cursed in front of her in the past, and on the rare occasion he forgot himself, he had been visibly embarrassed. It was the small-town Midwesterner in him. No longer, it seemed.

She set all that aside. "No, I wanted a divorce when I realized how relieved I felt that no child of mine would have to have Eddie as a father. I was feeling compassion for a child that would never exist. There was no hope for him, or for us. It was time."

"Did he try and talk you out of it?"

"Hah, he welcomed it. If I couldn't give him kids, what was the point of being with me? Not to mention he was hardly inconspicuous about his affairs anymore. We met with the lawyers, and agreed to end things."

Will smiled in approval and clinked the neck of his bottle with hers. "Well, good for you, Kay Barlow."

"Kay Maddux. My maiden name."

New name, new woman, Will thought. He recalled his past dismay with her inability to walk away from her husband, unable to comprehend why any woman would stay with such a man. It was a decision, Will assumed then, rooted in fear. Eddie Barlow was a violent man with a short fuse. Especially, Will presumed, when it came to open defiance from a woman he likely considered duty-bound to honor and obey.

Looking back, Will saw how shortsighted he had been, and how profoundly he had underestimated Kay. It wasn't fear that kept her in that prison, it was hope. Not borne from some childlike naiveté, but because Kay was simply one of those rare, unapologetic, and optimistic souls. A woman who had once taken to heart the notion of for better or for worse. Will could sense the change in her now, her voice and manner full of self-assurance. She had mettle too, having stood up to a goon like Barlow and told him she was walking out, knowing he could have very well punched her lights out.

Perhaps, Will thought to himself, the last four years were as impactful for her as they were for him. Or perhaps she hadn't changed at all, and he simply didn't know her nearly as well as he should.

"Penny for your thoughts," Kay said.

He finished his beer and set it on the coffee table.

"Just thinking how special you are." He kissed her hand. "We should celebrate."

"A little late," she replied, the smile returning. "I've been divorced for three months."

"Not the divorce. Us. Together again."

He took her bottle and set it on the table, then slid an arm underneath her legs, lifting her into his lap. Her body went slack, allowing his arms to pull her in close, their mouths now just millimeters apart, as her arms wrapped around his shoulders.

"I didn't come here for this," she whispered, as he felt her breath grazing his lips. "I want to, believe me. But you need to know, it's not why I came here."

"Then why did you come?"

Kay inhaled deeply. "To see if it was still there. Between us."

"Is it?"

She gave the question some thought, and Will felt a bolt of panic seize his heart as he waited for her response.

"That depends," she said slowly, her eyes glancing downward. "What color underwear are you wearing?"

He burst into laughter. More laughter than he had felt in years, and she quickly followed. Soon they were doubled over, and Kay had tears in her eyes. By the time they regained their composure, the question had already formed in Will's mind. Years ago, in this same situation, it was a question that never would have occurred to him, and the two would have already made it to the bedroom, their clothes strewn behind them. He had his priorities then.

He had changed. Or had she changed him?

Ask her, you fool.

"Why don't we get some dinner?"

Chapter 22

O'Malley's Pub was one of those Washington establishments with a history so farcical it could only be true.

It opened in the early 1920s as the Diamond Club, a Prohibition-era speakeasy that flourished in its early years. Adjacent to the glass works, the brassy nightspot drew heavily from Foggy Bottom's working-class Negro population, specializing in bootlegger bourbon, high-dollar craps games, and low-rent working girls. Federal agents closed it down in the early 1930s, and when Prohibition ended, the shuttered club was purchased by a wealthy New York restaurateur. He thought a more upscale, Irish pub atmosphere would be a perfect fit for the Washington business crowd, so he changed the name to O'Malley's, banished the gaming tables and prostitutes, and stocked the bar with Bushmill's and Guinness. It was an idea with promise, but O'Malley's faltered from the day it opened its doors, unable to lure more white professionals from their tony Georgetown enclaves a mile away. The owner quickly cut his losses, selling the place on the cheap after only a year to a local man named Ray Bellamy.

The new owner lived a few blocks down 24th Street and had driven a cab most of his adult life. The churchgoing Bellamy rebuilt the club's atmosphere, bringing in a piano player and swapping out the high-end booze for Jim Beam and Heurich's Senate Lager, suiting the drinking tastes of the blue-collar locals. He hired his son to run the grill in the back kitchen, and because permits and licenses were expensive in the city, Bellamy saved a bundle by keeping the O'Malley's name. And so it stuck, an Irish-named, Negro-owned dive, with a stable of regulars that, like the neighborhood itself, cut across racial and cultural divides.

It was still supper hour on a weeknight, so Will and Kay had the place mostly to themselves. O'Malley's wouldn't fill up with its regulars until past nine or ten. They sat at one end of the long bar, hungrily devouring greasy hamburgers topped with fried onions while the notes of the Duke Ellington Orchestra played on a nearby radio. The bartender, who was also the owner, watched them carefully as he cleaned glasses at a sink.

"Well, miss," Bellamy called over, "what's the verdict?"

Kay wiped her mouth with a napkin. "Oh my God. Will wasn't lying. This is the most scrumptious thing I've ever had."

A broad smile stretched across Bellamy's ebony face. He was born and raised in Foggy Bottom, his grandfather employed as a livery driver for President Ulysees S. Grant. Tossing a dishrag over one shoulder, Bellamy folded his spindly arms, beaming with pride.

"I'll let my boy know you said that. You can bring her in here anytime, Mr. Jamison."

Kay swallowed another bite, rolling her eyes in delight. "What's your secret?"

The owner mimicked locking his mouth and throwing away an imaginary key, chuckling as he moved off to attend to another customer at the far end of the bar. Will took a pack of Luckies from his coat and lit one with the Zippo he had been carrying since Belgium.

Kay's eyes went from the cigarette to the two empty beer bottles in front of Will. "Who are you and what have you done with my altar boy of a lover?"

Will grinned, flipping the Zippo closed and exhaling the smoke. He held out the pack.

"I don't smoke anymore."

It was Will's turn to be surprised. "Since when?"

"Since a year ago. May 8th, to be precise."

It took a few seconds to register. "V-E Day?"

"The day I knew you were coming home. That was my last cigarette. I knew how much you hated them. Or did."

Will took one last drag, then stubbed the cigarette out in a tin ashtray. "So, are you working?"

"I'm a nurse."

"That's right," he recalled. "You wanted to get back into that. Good for you, Kay. Manhattan? Brooklyn?"

"Down the street."

Will blinked. "Huh?"

Kay laughed. "Well, not quite. I'm at Sibley Memorial Hospital, just off North Capitol."

"You moved here?"

She nodded. "After the divorce I stayed with my aunt in Brooklyn for a while, then found work here when I heard you rejoined the team. I've been in a hotel near the hospital for two weeks now. Not exactly the Carleton in Philadelphia. A shoebox would be a closer comparison. There's barely enough room for me and the mice. But I found a flat in Dupont Circle, right on the bus line. I move in next week."

Will signaled for another beer, his sudden discomfort painfully obvious.

Kay noticed and pushed her plate away. "Try to contain your joy, Will."

"It's fine," he managed.

"Fine?" She crossed her arms. "Did I misread something here?"

"Come on, Kay, don't–"

"I thought we rather enjoyed each other's company, and that you would want to spend more time together." She paused. "Are you seeing someone?"

"No, there's no one else."

"The truth please. It's been four years, and I can under–"

"There's no one else," he insisted.

"Then what's the problem? You don't want to be with me?"

He was quiet again. The truth was, he wasn't sure what the problem was. His reaction made as little sense to him as it did to her. After obsessing over her for years, he should have been euphoric.

"You've been back for months, Will. No letter. No phone call. If your name wasn't in the newspaper every day, I wouldn't know if you were dead or alive."

Will still did not say anything, his eyes locked on the bottle in front of him.

"And here we are back at square one. I talk, and you say nothing. Just like my letters. I wrote and wrote, and heard nothing in return."

"Come on, Kay. I couldn't write back. What if Eddie–"

"I know that, Will, but that's not the point."

"What is the point?"

"The point," she said coldly, "is that talking to you is a one-way street, whether or not Eddie is in the picture. Am I wrong?"

Will remained still.

"Just say something, Will. Anything! For God's sakes, are you ever going to talk to me?" Kay threw her hands up in frustration. "Why do I feel like I'm always asking you the same damn questions?"

"Because you're always asking me the same damn questions," he shot back.

She glared at him but Will refused to meet her eyes. Kay shook her head in surrender, rising from the stool.

Will stopped her, a firm hand on her forearm.

"Please, Kay. Don't go. I'm sorry."

She pulled away from him. "What's the point, Will? You're not going–"

"I've never had a girlfriend before."

Kay stopped, surprised by the words.

"What?"

"I've never had a girlfriend before," he repeated, lowering his voice, conscious there were others at the bar now.

"Come on. Never?"

"Never."

She sat again. "How is that possible?"

"It's possible," he sighed. "I've been with women, obviously, and dated plenty. But never a steady girl."

"Why not?"

He shrugged. "I'd meet someone, and it would last a few weeks, at best. Then I'd end it. Or find a way to make them end it. Don't ask me to explain it. It's not anything I'm proud of. I want to change, Kay. I want things to be different with you. With us. I just don't know what you're expecting from me."

"What should I expect from you?"

A good question. A relationship had been unthinkable once. Not when he could bed other women. There were half a dozen women in this neighborhood alone he could sleep with in a heartbeat. And yet in all the time he had been back in town, he had not made a single call to any of them.

He turned to Kay, those green eyes still appraising him. In a single glance he saw everything that had drawn him to her since the day they met. The decency and kindheartedness. The sharp mind and infectious laugh. And still the most alluring woman he had ever known, by a landslide.

I love her.

He scoffed at the notion the second it crossed his mind. It was preposterous. How could he love her? He had not seen her in four years. And how would he, Will Jamison, know what love felt like? He had never loved any woman before.

Still, he knew. He knew, because back in Noville, with his sanity hanging by a frayed thread, it was thoughts of her that he clung to more than anything else. Thoughts that saved him from falling to pieces and fueled his determination to survive and withstand whatever the Germans dished out. He knew because every time he found himself in a shadowy corner since returning from the war, mired in despairing emotions and haunting memories that plagued him since he left Belgium, he thought of her.

Yes, he loved her. It wasn't preposterous, it was a certainty. But his love was also full of contradictions. Namely, as Kay pointed out, his unwillingness to reach out for her since his return. He needed time to readjust, he had told himself, and rejuvenate his career.

Eight months later, that excuse had run its course. His return to the game was complete, and he still hadn't lifted a finger to connect with her.

Why?

Why was he so conflicted about this? Kay had liberated herself from a failed marriage and an abusive husband, and she had come to him. What more did he want? He could say categorically that he would never find a better woman in this lifetime. As soon as his playing career ended, so too would the playboy lifestyle that marked his early years in Washington. Without his fame and bankroll, how many knockouts would want to be with a guy like him? Four years ago, he would have happily accepted that, and traded every girl he ever dated for just the one knockout who never cared what he did or how much money he made. To be with her, that was all he wanted then. What changed? Why did the notion of the impeccable Kay Barlow, or Kay Maddux now, as his girl, trouble Will as much as it electrified him?

"Will," she prompted.

He remained still, unable to face her. Unable to explain himself. What was there to say?

"It's odd," she noted, her voice tinged with sadness. "You've changed, and you haven't changed. I don't know if I'm talking to a stranger, or the same old Will."

He nodded, unable to disagree.

"Did something happen over there?"

"What do you think?"

"I don't need the condescending tone, Will."

"I'm sorry," he said, not meaning it.

She covered his hand with hers. "Tell me what happened."

"We won, Kay," he pronounced, full of sarcasm. She deflated again, withdrawing her hand. He knew he was losing her, the wilting conversation a victim of his own sabotage.

He finally turned to her, cringing at the hurt on her face, and foolishly thought he could still salvage things.

"Look hon, I'm thrilled you're here now. I really am. Things will be different, and I just need to get used to that."

She watched him closely, even as he looked away, taking a swig from his beer. Finally, she stood, recognizing his attempts to placate her for what they were, words without meaning. She reached into her purse and pulled out a few bills, placing them on the bar.

"What are you doing?"

"I've waited a long time, Will. Years. I can wait a little longer."

"Wait for what?"

"You. Us. When you're ready, and you certainly aren't right now, come find me. It's a small town."

She started for the door.

"Kay," he said, swinging off his stool and stopping her again with a hand on her forearm. "I'm playing better. I'll be back to my old self soon. Things are starting to fall back into place. I can feel it. Just give me some time."

"Is that what I am, Will? Something that falls back into place?"

"I didn't mean it like that."

"I saw the empty bottles, Will, in your apartment. We've been here an hour, and you've already downed three more. A ball player who likes to drink. I've been down that road before."

"That's not–"

"I've been waiting for something better for a long, long time. I deserve it. And I thought I had it."

She backed away, tears forming in her eyes.

"You know where to find me," she said, stopping and turning to him one last time. "For what it's worth, I hated hearing the word girlfriend as much as you did speaking it. I thought we had something more than that. Much more."

And then she was gone.

(AP) June 22, 1946 — On the first full day of summer, the Washington Senators continued their mid-season surge, topping the first-place Boston Red Sox 7-4 in the finale of a four-game series in the Nation's capital. It was the home team's eighth win in ten tries. The win moves the Senators to three games over the .500 mark, good for third place in the tight American League pennant chase.

Washington managed to keep the great Ted Williams at bay, limiting the 27-year-old to a single hit in five trips to the plate. The "Splendid Splinter" has been tearing up American League pitching since his discharge from the Marine Corps earlier this year and is on his way to a MVP season. But before nearly 40,000 fans today at Griffith Stadium, Washington starter Dick Holloway and two other Senator pitchers got the best of the three-time all-star. Holloway scattered six hits while only allowing two earned runs in seven innings of work. Will Jamison continued his resurgence at the plate, adding three more hits and four RBIs. The catcher has raised his season average to .294, impressive in his first full season back after four years of fighting the Nazis.

Jamison's hot hitting was marred by yet another incident involving the slugger. This came just days after his second ejection of the season when Jamison nearly came to blows with Tiger pitcher Stubby Overmire, following Overmire's plunking of Jamison in the back with a fastball. In today's action, Red Sox shortstop Johnny Pesky was attempting to score from second base on a line drive to left field. Pesky slid into the legs of Jamison, who applied the tag even as his legs buckled from the impact. After a nerve-wracking few minutes for the home crowd faithful,

Jamison managed to climb to his feet. Backup catcher Cole Legler had already taken the field to replace the injured Jamison, who then refused to come off the field. Washington manager Charlie Longman came out of the dugout to retrieve his star player and a shouting match ensued, with a stream of words from both men unsuitable for printing on these pages. One can only imagine what was on the mind of Clark Griffith as he observed the spectacle from his owner's box. His best player has returned to all-star form and lifted his team into contention again. But this is not the same Will Jamison fans fell in love with years ago….

Chapter 23

MUNICIPAL STADIUM
CLEVELAND, OHIO

"You've got to be fucking kidding me."

The words were muttered under his breath as Will glowered at the third base coach. But the man wasn't kidding. He had unquestionably touched his chin for the second time.

Pivoting on his right foot, Will stepped out of the batter's box, straddling the chalked line and holding the pitcher in place. He rested the bat on one shoulder and pinched the bill of his cap, a prompt for Buck Whiting to repeat the sequence. The third base coach, standing in foul territory just to the side of the bag, complied, cycling again through a series of hand and arm motions that would have flummoxed the U.S. Army Signal Corps.

Will was certain the first set of signs had been a mistake. It had to be a mistake. But there it was again. The second tap of the chin.

Bristling with dismay, Will glared down the third base line, willing the man to correct himself. Whiting was finished with the signals though, and looked away from Will's enraged eyes, doing his damnedest to look at anything and anyone other than his batter.

There had been no mistake.

Gritting his teeth, Will stepped back into the box. He was seething, but knew Whiting wasn't to blame. The call wasn't coming from him.

It was a warm, overcast day in Cleveland, with few empty seats in the stands. There had been patches of light rain throughout the afternoon, and though another mass of storm clouds was moving in from the east, not a single spectator had left. Not when one of the greatest players in the history of the Cleveland Indians franchise was on the mound.

Will motioned through a couple of check swings, chopping his bat through the air as the opposing pitcher and catcher exchanged their own signals. He burrowed his right cleat into the loose dirt as the gray-clad Washington base runners at first and second widened their leads as much as they dared. Tuning the unruly crowd out, Will waved the cocked bat over his back shoulder, the barrel drawing circles in the air. The pitcher worked from the stretch. As his front leg came up, Will surprised just about everyone in the stadium, twisting his body until it was square with the pitcher. Dropping the head of his bat over the front of the plate, he watched the fastball come blazing in, hard and inside. Very inside. Will had to jerk his upper body back at the very last moment to avoid the blistering pitch, missing his front shoulder by inches as it whistled past his ear.

Ball one.

A roar of approval arose from the rollicking crowd, nearly delirious from the brush back pitch that ratcheted up the tension even further between the two gladiators. The pitcher gloved the return throw and Will met his eyes for half a second, long enough to see the man's mouth curl into the most taunting of smiles.

Burning with humiliation, Will squeezed the handle of the bat, imagining it was the pitcher's throat. Or his manager's. The Senators had two runners on with nobody out in the fifth inning, trailing the Indians by four runs. Delivering in such pressure-packed moments had once been Will's hallmark, smashing hits and driving in key runs time and time again when the stakes were at their highest. The notion of a slugger like him bunting with runners on base would have been laughable once, a skill he brandished so little, he barely remembered how to knuckle the barrel of the bat.

It was a message from Longman, that much was obvious. Though Will's batting average had been steadily climbing for weeks now, it clearly hadn't allayed whatever doubts his manager was still harboring. Doubts that left Will batting just fifth in the lineup, long after he dislodged Cole Legler as the starting catcher. Will had held his tongue, figuring Longman would eventually return him to the number three spot he had held since his days in Chattanooga. A spot from which he had knocked in 310 runs during his four-year career in the majors.

Granted, the man standing just over 60 feet away, glove tucked under one arm as he rubbed the moisture from his hands into the ball, was no pushover. At an even six feet tall and 180 pounds, Bob Feller wasn't the most imposing presence on the mound. Yet the showy Cleveland right-hander was widely considered the most dominant pitcher in the major leagues.

He hailed from a tiny Iowa farm town that was probably a mirror image of Lancaster. As a third grader, the boy's throws measured nearly 300 feet, a distance most grown men couldn't come close to matching. During his teenage years, his father built a baseball field in the middle of their acreage of corn so young Bob could compete against local kids and even semi-pro players passing through. By the time he was 16, Feller was considered a phenom, and signed his first professional contract with Cleveland, famously receiving a single dollar and autographed baseball in return. He started his first game for the Indians in 1936, four months shy of his 18th birthday.

His major league career got off to a torrid start. In his first five years, Feller amassed more than 100 wins and 1,100 strikeouts. He became a four-time all-star, winning the pitching Triple Crown in 1940 when he posted 27 wins, a 2.61 earned run average, and 261 strikeouts, all season-best marks that year. He was a perennial Most Valuable Player candidate when he enlisted in the Navy just two days after the attack on Pearl Harbor. After serving most of the war aboard the battleship USS *Alabama*, Feller rejoined the Indians just ten days after the Japanese surrendered, in time for the final weeks of the 1945 season. Even with the three-year break, Feller instantly reclaimed his status as one of the game's elite. Two months into the 1946 season, his ascent continued, throwing the second no-hitter of his career. This time against the Yankees, retiring the great Joe DiMaggio to finish the game.

Will backed out of the box, forcing himself to slow his breathing.

Feller was already under his skin, and unless he cleared his head and regained his focus, the Cleveland pitcher was going to make mincemeat out of him. He faced Whiting again, prompting the third base coach to run through another series of signs. The man could have been calling in an artillery strike for all Will cared. He was simply using the ritual to buy himself a few precious seconds.

With his anger receding, Will set himself in the box, his bat circling the air as before. Feller began his delivery, rearing back just as Will squared again for the bunt. The pitch came barreling in, and then Will slowed it all down in his mind, processing the images flashing into view like a motion picture, frame by frame. Peripherally, he saw the third baseman charging toward home, anticipating the sacrifice in his direction. Indeed, the pitch was lower this time, streaking for the inside corner of the plate, all but guaranteeing a bunt on the left side of the infield.

And it was another fastball.

That son of a bitch Feller!

Will quickly pulled his bat back and watched the ball sail across the edge of the plate.

"STRIKE!"

The home plate umpire pumped his right fist in the air as he cried out the call, followed by the hometown crowd erupting in delight and Feller's mouth twitching in satisfaction. Buck Whiting pointed both palms to the sky, the time-honored coaching pantomime for questioning whether a batter had lost his mind. Bunting or swinging away, no hitter worth a nickel would take such a pitch.

Precisely why Will had held back. Feller was challenging him, daring to offer Will something the cocksure Indians pitcher was sure he would never catch up to.

The fans began stomping their feet, raucously demanding Feller's ninth strikeout of the day. The pitcher basked in the adoration, taking time to strut around the mound while bouncing the resin bag on his throwing hand. 38,000 Clevelanders saw a skilled master at work, methodically taking apart a rival, pitch by pitch. Will saw a grandstanding peacock, shamelessly preening for his worshipping fans.

With the crowd whipped into a near frenzy, Feller set himself again on the pitching rubber, sharing a hard stare with Will for several seconds. It was clear neither man cared much anymore about the score, the runners on base, or even the pitch count. They exchanged confident smiles, each knowing Will was done with the bunting nonsense, and both sure of their command of the moment. For Will, the pitch would be no mystery. Feller wasn't going to bother with anything off-speed or off the plate that Will might be tempted to lay off. He was going to come right after Will again with his best stuff.

The stadium was nearly shaking now from the decibel level. Will didn't step out of the batter's box this time, or even bother to look down at Buck Whiting. Slapping the plate with the end of his bat, he took a single check swing and loaded into position, holding the bat perfectly still this time. The runners eased into their leads, kicking up small clouds as their spikes swept across the dirt. With sweat dripping from his chin, Feller locked his eyes on his catcher, shaking off sign after sign, waiting for the only one he would accept. It came, and with a subtle nod, and then an arching leg kick, Feller hurled the ball toward the plate.

Before it even left Feller's hand, Will knew another fastball was on the way. He shifted his weight to his back leg and watched the pitch come in hard and low. With the practiced stare of a man who had seen thousands of such tosses before, Will eyed the oncoming ball hungrily.

His hips swiveled almost violently, his bat whipping around in a blur. He timed his swing perfectly, the bat connecting with the ball just as it kissed the outside corner of the plate. Will knew he had hit the ball true the second he felt wood slam leather. There was a tingling in his arms, the nirvana-like sensation of driving a ball that hitters had experienced dating back to the game's pre-Civil War founding. It was like splitting a log right down the center, or being in a perfect rhythm with a lover.

There was only a single flaw in Will's mechanics, but it was a costly one. The bat walloped the ball square, roughly an inch higher than Will intended. Rather than lifting the ball deep into the outfield gap, he instead hit a scorching line drive that whistled back toward Feller. The pitcher reached out with his glove a second too late, the ball rocketing past him as if shot from a cannon. There was almost no arc to the hit, the ball remaining waist high as it crossed the infield, finally curving downward as it neared second base, just to the right of the bag.

Dutch Meyer, the Indians' second baseman, was aware of Will's opposite field hitting and was positioned deep, skirting the outfield grass. He lunged to his right, fully extending himself in mid-air until his body was nearly parallel to the ground. The reach of his backhanded glove fell short however, and the ball careened off the glove tip, ricocheting into the outfield. By the time the center fielder pounced on it, Will had rounded the first base bag, the runners ahead of him each advancing a base. The ball was finally returned to Feller, who angrily snatched it out of the air.

Will trotted back to the bag, slapping his hands together in triumph as the crowd fell silent other than a scattering of boos. He knew he should have crushed the pitch to the fence, but happily looked past his near-miss. It was a clutch piece of hitting, the sort that came from the upper echelon of hitters, and it loaded the bases for Washington with no one out. Most gratifying, he had bested Bob Feller, the most celebrated pitcher in the game, who slammed the ball into his mitt in frustration.

Even with the intensity of the moment and the man's antics on the mound, Will felt a grudging respect for Feller. He knew the most accomplished players were also the most competitive, and despised losing more than anyone else.

The Senators lost to the Indians, 10-4, plating just one runner after loading the bases with no outs in that inning. It wasn't Feller's best outing, but it was enough to beat a Washington team that had struggled to score runs all season. After a brief surge in the standings, the Senators had stalled out, having lost their last four games.

An hour later, Will had showered and changed, and was departing the clubhouse for the team bus that would return the players to their hotel. On his way out, he knocked on the door of the small enclosed space behind the dugout that served as the visiting manager's office.

"Buck said you wanted to see me."

Longman was still in uniform, though his jersey was untucked and only buttoned halfway. He was hunched over a table, squinting through a pair of thick reading glasses at a spread of papers. Scouting reports, Will supposed. The manager peered over his glasses at Will.

"Night game tomorrow. Me and Lou are hitting the greens with Don Reading in the morning and we need a fourth. Want to join us?"

Reading was a base coach with the Indians, and Longman's former teammate from a thousand years ago.

"I hate golf, you know that."

"It's relaxing. Thought you could use the break."

"Nah, I'll pass."

Longman expected Will to say something more, but the catcher simply leaned on the door frame, waiting Longman out. The manager sighed in defeat, pulling off his glasses and gesturing for Will to come inside and close the door.

"Are we going to talk about it?"

"That bullshit bunt sign you gave me?"

"The bullshit bunt sign you ignored."

"Two on, nobody out, down by four runs. Who the hell calls for a bunt? So you can have two on, with one out, and Jake and Billy coming to bat? Jesus, Charlie, Jake hasn't hit the ball out of the infield in two weeks."

"That was Bob Feller out there."

"I don't care if it was Walter Johnson out there."

"Who's managing this team, Jamison?"

"You are. But come on, Charlie, give me a chance. You don't have anyone better with the bat when runners are on and you know it. You have to trust me again."

Longman was quiet for half a minute until he finally leaned back in his chair, tenting his hands across his belly. "Fine. I'll make you a deal. I bump you back into your old three slot, and don't give you anymore bullshit bunt signs. But whatever I give you in the future, you follow. You know, like every other player on this club. You got me?"

"I got you."

"Then get out of here."

Will smiled. "You really pissed at me?"

Longman frowned. "Pissed at who? The cocky bastard who ignored my signs and thought he could win this game all by himself? Are you kidding? That's the player I used to have. The player this team needs."

"Good, you're not pissed."

"Oh, I'm pissed," Longman said, putting his glasses back on and returning his attention to the array of papers. "That guy should have hit that pitch out of the park."

Chapter 24

A day later, the two teams were back at it on a mild evening in northern Ohio. It had been a scalding afternoon in the city, lacking even a wisp of a breeze off Lake Erie, and those in the dugouts and stands were briefly cheered by the fourth inning sight of the sun finally dipping below the horizon. With the falling mercury came a renewed energy among those on the field, slowly intensifying into a boiling point of its own. They slugged it out with one eye on the skies, willing the forecasted precipitation to strike elsewhere so they could finish a contest each side desperately wanted to win.

It was just the third night game ever at Cleveland Municipal Stadium. Light panels had been installed along the double-deck grandstands the previous spring, with only a single oversight by the electrical engineers. They hadn't considered the effect of the high-powered beams on the assorted species of aquatic insects breeding in the nearby lake. With the lights fully ablaze, thick swarms of mayflies buzzed around the massive fixtures by the thousands, like biblical swarms of locusts, producing a spectacle for players and fans alike.

The facility could hold more than 80,000 spectators, and though there was less than half that number this evening, they were a spirited and vocal bunch, anticipating a home sweep that would extend Washington's losing streak to five games. The Senators, however, were battling, and held a late, one-run lead. Washington starter Dick Holloway had pitched well, surrendering three runs on just five hits thus far, and Charlie Longman hoped to get him through one last inning. Every man on the roster was on edge, sensing the season and the team's hopes slipping through their fingers as Boston continued its winning ways, lengthening its lead over their American League rivals.

With Washington's struggles came at least one bright spot for Will. His leg was holding up well, even after resuming full-time catching duty. The game tonight was entering the bottom of the eighth inning, and the discomfort in his thigh was barely noticeable as he caught Holloway's warm-up tosses.

The umpire signaled for play to begin and the festive crowd settled back into their seats. Will lowered himself into position behind the plate, offering a wink to Smokey Abbott, Cleveland's acerbic third baseman, as he tramped into the batter's box. Smokey was a two-time all-star and a fiery competitor. Will had enjoyed sparring with him for years, beginning in AA ball nearly a decade ago.

Smokey dug his cleats into the dirt, swinging the bat back and rapping Will's shin guard as he spat a gob of spit in the direction of Holloway. Will smiled, knowing the bat tap and an occasional grunt were Smokey's idea of a warm greeting. He flashed a sign between his legs, shielding his fingers from Smokey's view as well as Cleveland's base coaches, notorious around the league for sign stealing. Even if he was tipped off about the pitch call, Will doubted it would help Smokey navigate the succession of Holloway's sliders coming his way. A pitch Will knew had eluded Smokey his entire career.

Just as Holloway began his wind up, a series of sharp popping sounds echoed through the stadium, followed by flashes of lights that flickered against the blackened sky. The noise came from high above the field, where the stadium lights were affixed to the overhang along the third base side of the grandstands. Two of the 12 bulbs embedded in the panel, each more than two feet in diameter, suddenly burst, sending showers of sparks into the air and shutting down the entire panel. The three other massive panels mounted high above the field simultaneously powered off, plunging every corner of the field and stands into pitch darkness.

There was complete silence at first, tens of thousands of onlookers stunned by the sudden blackout on a moonless night. The quiet was fleeting as a few hysterical screams emerged, followed by the sobs and cries of frightened young children clutching their parents. Panicked shouting broke out, and then it all became contagious, the clamor sweeping from box to box across the stadium, building into a crescendo.

Will rose to his feet, sliding the catcher's mask to the top of his head. Like those in the stands, he was regaled at first by the light bulbs bursting, as if part of an impromptu fireworks show. It all changed the moment the field became shrouded in darkness, sending a thousand-pound weight crashing into Will's chest, punching the air from his lungs. A lightheadedness took hold, blurring his vision and spinning his surroundings, nearly causing him to collapse to the ground.

Will fought to steady himself, until all at once, he was no longer in Cleveland.

The sounds came quickly, a rapid series of artillery explosions that grew louder as the Germans adjusted their aim. Will instinctively dropped to one knee, trying to see if the enemy was forming for another attack, but another layer of fog had rolled in, hindering their visibility once again. A machine gun chattered in the distance, the streaking tracer rounds emitting a bright glow that lit up the nighttime sky. He wanted to at least empty a clip in that direction, but he must have lost his rifle. Even his .45 was no longer holstered at his waist and Will cursed out loud, realizing he was completely unarmed.

"Jamison," said Smokey, his eyes still adjusting but able to make out Will kneeling in front of home plate. "You okay?"

Jesus, Janikowski, what do you think?

"They're coming," Will said, still looking toward the German lines.

"Who's coming?" said a voice Will did not hear.

He was focused on the incoming fire. The enemy gunners hadn't pinpointed the platoon's position yet, but their artillery was inching closer, the Germans determined to soften up the American defenses as they massed their armor for one final assault. The fog was like a solid wall, masking the German movement as their tanks rumbled closer to the American lines.

"Will!" Smokey's voice was louder now, but Will could not hear him. His eyes darted from side to side, droplets of sweat falling from his temples.

The catcher suddenly rose to his feet and grabbed Smokey roughly by the arm.

"We've got to get out of here, Delgado! Get your ass back to the half-tracks!"

"What the hell is he talking about?"

Smokey was dumbfounded, but answered the home plate umpire. "Beats me, blue. He's gone bananas."

"NOW, DELGADO!"

The shout startled the other two men, but it carried no further, the noise from the restless crowd drowning out everything.

"What the hell is going on down here?" It was Elwood Merritt, the third-base umpire and crew chief who had joined the trio.

His colleague spoke. "It's Jamison, Woody. Talking crazy to himself."

Merritt grabbed Will by the shoulders and shook him. "Jamison!"

Nothing. Will stared past the umpire, oblivious to those around him. Merritt was inches from Will's face and could see the glaze in the catcher's eyes and the sheen of perspiration drenching his face and jersey. The umpire suddenly reared back and swung an open palm, striking Will hard in the cheek, shocking the other two men looking on.

"Woody," his crewmate started, touching the chief's arm, but Merritt brushed the hand away.

It was too familiar to Merritt. He had fought in France nearly three decades ago, a 17-year-old machine gunner in the trenches, and had seen this before from his former squad mates. Cracking up, his former sergeant had called it. Others were less belittling. Merritt violently shook the catcher by the shoulders until Will finally came out of it, holding his reddened cheek.

"You okay, son?" Merritt's words were quiet and gentle as he gripped the catcher by the arm.

As Will's focus slowly returned, he studied the men around him. Merritt looked sympathetic, while Smokey and the home plate umpire hid nothing, their faces full of bewilderment. Will yanked his arm from Merritt's grasp and rushed to the Washington dugout, storming past his teammates and coaches without a word as he fled for the sanctuary of the clubhouse deep beneath the stands.

Thirty minutes later, maintenance personnel were close to restoring electrical power in the stadium. Circuits had been replaced and it was thought the two shattered bulbs would have little effect on the lighting in left field.

Inside the windowless clubhouse behind the Senators' dugout, a single overhead lamp provided a dim glow, powered by a small emergency generator. That is where Longman found Will, in uniform and cleats, his shin guards and chest protector still strapped to his body. He was seated on the cement floor with his back against a wall, his eyes staring off into nothing. Even with the poor lighting, Longman was struck by Will's blank expression.

With some effort, Longman lowered himself to the floor, next to his erstwhile star. He winced as he heard his bones creak, another cruelty of the aging process.

He looked at Will sideways. "You okay?"

After a few seconds, Will gave him a simple nod, saying nothing.

"They've about got them lights fixed. Switched out a fuse or two. Grounds crew had to get down on hands and knees down the left field line to look for broken glass. The umps will start the game as soon as the juice is back on. If you want, you can–"

"I'm not going back out there," Will said quietly.

Longman nodded, expecting that.

"Rookie's already suited up, getting Dick loosened again."

Longman was reluctant to continue, but he had little choice. Orders were orders.

"I spoke to Mr. Griffith by telephone. Had to tell him what happened."

"He have a good laugh?"

"No one's laughing, Will. For what it's worth, Woody, Bud Sanders, and Smokey are the only ones who saw it. Even Dick couldn't see that far. Woody told me what happened. I told the boys in the dugout you had the runs, some sort of stomach bug."

Longman waited again, expecting a rebuke, hoping for a wisecrack. But none came.

"Griffith is giving you ten days off. Wants that leg fully healed."

Will showed some life at last, looking at the manager quizzically. "My leg is fine."

"No, it ain't. It's slowing you up on the base paths. So you've got ten days, with pay. The overnight train to D.C. leaves the downtown station in ninety minutes."

"Charlie, my leg–"

"And I don't want to see you at Griffith Stadium. Don't need you tempted to get back on the field too early. Red-eye will have you home in the morning, then you'll see Doc Shapiro when you–"

"Shapiro? Are you kid–"

"Damn it, Jamison," barked Longman, startling Will. "Get this straight. I'm the manager, you're the player. You will go see the doc when you get home. You will then take ten days off, and when that's over, you'll see the doc again. When he clears you, you'll play. That understood?"

The two shared a look until Will finally spoke.

"The team. The boys aren't stupid, Charlie. Smokey will talk, and then everyone will know. You imagine what they'll think of me?"

"You mean the guys who didn't fight the Germans or the Japs? The guys who didn't spend a minute in combat, let alone get themselves wounded? Who cares?"

"I do."

Longman knew there was nothing more he could say. He put a hand on Will's shoulder and used it to push himself off the floor. He headed toward the door as the public address announcer called out Smokey's name, signaling the resumption of the game.

"Charlie?"

The manager stopped and turned back toward Will.

"I don't know if I can be that player again."

Longman sighed, taking a few steps toward his catcher. He crossed his arms, his voice soft and reflective.

"I'm a lucky man, Will. Managing a major league club, traveling across this great country in First Class train cars and five-star hotel rooms. Every day neck deep in a game I've loved since before I could tie my own shoes. I would trade it all, the job, the fame, every nickel I own, to spend just five minutes with my boy again. Just five minutes. Think I would care if he was playing baseball or not?"

His voice was breaking now, and Longman took a deep breath to collect himself. "Get yourself right, Will. And if you getting right means never playing this game again, I'll tear up your contract myself."

Chapter 25

ARLINGTON, VIRGINIA

Already stiff from the overnight train ride from Ohio, Will's sizable frame was pretzled into a metal folding chair along one wall of the austere waiting area in Arlington Hospital. Easily recognized and buttonholed in such settings, he was grateful to be the lone patient awaiting attention in the Orthopedics Department, in no mood to indulge anyone's long-winded commentary about whatever might be ailing the Senators. His day had already started awkwardly enough after a miscommunication with a Spanish-speaking flower vendor led him on an embarrassing side trip to the Obstetrics Department.

His solitude came with a price. With nothing to distract him, Will's thoughts were with his teammates, half a country away and likely already transiting to Chicago, where they would have the day off. Will had planned to visit his brother in Evanston, but instead found himself cooling his heels here, waiting to be poked and prodded by the same doctor who gave him a relative clean bill of health just weeks ago.

Will cracked his knuckles in exasperation. He could under-stand the concern with his on-field conduct of late, but whatever was touching off the outbursts, it sure as hell wasn't baseball. The timing was equally frustrating. His painstaking climb back was nearly complete, both his physical conditioning and powerful swing finally returning to prior form. In his absence, Cole Legler would surely slide back into the lineup, forcing Will to earn his starting position once again.

Still, he could not shake a cold truth. The loss of self-control he experienced in Cleveland had deeply unsettled him. As did the prospect of publicly humiliating himself again, without any ability to foresee or forestall whatever was ungluing him. He could not continue like this. Something had to change.

So here he was, with ten days off. He hadn't had that much time to himself during the summer months in more than a decade. He considered asking Kay to join him for a weekend at the beach, or even a few days in New York. A chance to rekindle happier times. It would at least provide a reason for Will to call on her. They hadn't spoken since she marched out of O'Malley's weeks ago, leaving Will with little idea where things stood. If she was still cross with him, Will could hardly blame her. She deserved an explanation, if not an apology. More than anything else, he owed her time.

He would have to first get through whatever medical examination awaited. The lobby remained barren this early in the morning, with the doctors' offices closed to the public for another hour. The Senators' team physician had a fully booked schedule but agreed to see Will before his regular hours. A comely receptionist in a pencil skirt and sleeveless top had arrived minutes ago and taken station behind a small desk. The young woman was coy at first, offering Will nothing more than a polite nod. Now he felt her eyes lingering on him, the woman having undoubtedly learned who he was. A few years ago, Will might have found the nerve to approach her. Instead, he looked away, the receptionist frowning at the disinterest she was understandably unused to.

Dr. Shapiro clumsily pushed through a swinging door, his bulk barely squeezing through the doorframe. Will learned years ago not to judge Eugene Shapiro by appearances, and as much as he abhorred being here, he couldn't help but grin when the doctor motioned him over. The man was an aberration in this city, reflected by the half-eaten, jumbo-sized donut in his hand.

He had served the Senators for better than a decade. A Pittsburgh native, Shapiro moved his practice to the Washington area so he could involve himself with a number of left-wing political organizations. He happened to be the attending physician at

Washington General when a sobbing, injured boy of about eight was brought in by his grandfather. The boy had fractured an arm falling from a treehouse, and as Shapiro was setting the arm in a cast, he learned the grandfather was none other than the owner of the Washington Senators. He and Griffith had almost nothing in common other than an affinity for baseball and their young grandsons, but quickly forged a lasting friendship. However the man carried himself, Will knew Shapiro wielded uncanny healing abilities, the doctor considered indispensable by virtually every man on the Washington roster.

Though Shapiro was paid handsomely by the club, his clothes were always in such rumpled condition Will wondered if the man slept in his office, or dressed himself in the dark. Even this early in the day the doctor's tie was askew, and the wrinkled white coat he wore already stained with coffee and grape jelly. His thick silver hair was tussled and, like his gray-speckled beard, in dire need of a trim. His ample belly spilled over the waist of his trousers, suggesting he might not have taken to heart the virtues of the healthy, vegetable-laden diet he was constantly preaching to the athletes under his charge.

He followed the doctor back to an examination room that smelled of medicinals and ammonia, hopping onto the metal table as Shapiro finished his last bite of the pastry. The doctor lowered himself onto a rolling stool as he reviewed the notes from Will's last physical, still not having offered a word of greeting.

"Well, well," Shapiro finally said, looking up at Will amiably. "The savior of the Senators."

Will made a face. "Who's calling me that?"

Shapiro grinned. "I am. You're our only hope this season."

"You may want to find a new savior. Charlie has me off the clock."

"So I heard."

Will began to unbutton his shirt but Shapiro held up a palm. "Leave it on. I don't need to examine you."

"You don't? Christ, Doc, what does Griffith pay you for anyway?"

Shapiro gestured with his pen. "How's the leg?"

"It's fine."

"How's the leg?" Shapiro repeated, narrowing his eyes.

"Right now, fine. After eight or nine innings, slightly less so."

"On a scale of one to ten–"

"A two," Will interjected. "By the time Charlie lets me rejoin the team, it'll probably be down to a one."

Shapiro nodded, satisfied with the answer, and jotted down a note in Will's file.

"About what we expected. Let's see where we are in a few months. We may be able to do something about the scar tissue when the season's over, alleviate whatever soreness you're still experiencing."

The doctor capped his fountain pen and placed it in his coat pocket.

Will wrinkled his nose. *That's it?* It couldn't be.

"Yes, we're finished with the exam," Shapiro said, anticipating the question.

"I was told I had to see you today." Will's voice was laced with irritation. "I rode a red-eye half-way across the country to get here. Why couldn't we have had this conversation on the phone?"

"We probably could have."

"So why the hell am I here?"

"Charlie called me last night, asked me to see you. In person. Told me what happened during the game."

Will threw up his arms. *Griffith. Shapiro. Did Charlie call the Washington Star, too?*

"He's concerned about you, Will."

"He shouldn't be. I haven't–"

"What about other symptoms?"

"Symptoms? Symptoms of what?"

"You tell me."

Will shook his head, either in refusal or defiance.

THE BATTER'S BOX 249

Shapiro sighed. He removed his glasses and crossed his arms. "Look, Will. I'm an orthopedist. A bone and joint guy. A field where there is generally one symptom—pain." He paused, weighing something in his mind before starting again, his tone lighter now. "Did you know I'm a card player?"

"No," Will replied testily, the conversation turning even more outlandish.

"We have a regular game here. Poker, after hours, in a storage room in the basement. We play high stakes, $10 and $20 blinds. Our game includes a couple buddies I went to med school with at Johns Hopkins. One is an oncologist, the other a podiatrist. Two of our department heads also play. We talk during the games. A lot. Mostly so we're not thinking about how much money we're losing to the foot doctor."

"Is there a point to–"

"It seems they're hearing about quite a few veterans like you that came back from the war with symptoms that are quite...unique."

"Unique?"

"Sleeping seems to be a common problem."

"Doc, I slept in a hole in the ground for three months straight. Usually in the rain. My bed here is paradise."

"No nightmares?"

Will was quiet again.

"What about triggers?"

"Triggers?"

"Something that causes a reaction on your part, like what happened in Cleveland. I remember Frank, the foot doctor, talking about the son of one of his patients who was a prisoner of war, taken to Burma by the Japanese after we lost the Philippines. The boy shared a small, lice-ridden barracks with 200 other prisoners. Now, whenever he's in a room with other people, even an elevator, and the doors close, he panics. Cold sweat, dizziness, sometimes just straight passes out. Frank believes the closing door is the trigger. It's what the boy's captives did every evening, penning the men in like cattle. So when a door closes now, the boy cracks. Finds himself back in that POW camp."

Shapiro leaned forward and looked at Will intently. "You ever experience anything like that? Something that has troubled or discomfited you? That you don't want to remember, but you suddenly do, reluctantly?"

Will didn't answer, focusing on the window and the small bird pacing nervously across the sill.

"Cleveland, Will. Charlie said it happened the second the lights went out." Shapiro softened his voice. "I'm asking as a friend, not a doctor."

There was more uncomfortable silence as Shapiro waited for Will to say something. Anything. But Will remained inexpressive, his arms folded across his chest like a hostile witness.

Shapiro shook his head in frustration. "So be it. Now I'm back to being a doctor. One who is not going to clear you to play until we talk about this."

"Come on, Doc, you can't–"

"Try me, Will. I'm taking this seriously, even if you won't."

Will squeezed his eyes closed for several moments, then exhaled a long breath. He reached into a pocket. "Mind if I smoke?"

"For Heaven's sake, son, this is a doctor's office."

Will started to put the pack away.

"Which means it would be impolite not to offer one to the doctor."

Will chuckled and held out the Lucky Strikes, then lit both their cigarettes with his Zippo.

"The stadium lights. I can't explain it, I just lost it when they went out. Nothing like that has ever happened before."

Shapiro reached for an empty coffee mug on the small desk and tapped his ash into it. "What exactly happened?"

"I don't know. It was dark, but I was seeing things, hearing things."

"Were they vivid? Do you remember what they were?"

"Some of it I recognized. It was at Noville. In Belgium. We were dug in on a roadblock, waiting for the Germans to attack. One of my men was there. He was going to get killed later on, and I knew that, but I didn't say anything about it. I don't know why. But damn, Doc, it was like I was back on that road, freezing my ass off all over again. I could feel the gravel under my feet. The cold air on the back of my neck. I saw and felt all of it, until the ump snapped me out of it."

Shapiro thought for several moments while stroking his beard. "I confess, Will, this is way out of my depth. You need a specialist, someone with a background in mental health."

Will flinched. "A head shrink? No way."

"We call them psychiatrists. And it would be completely discreet. No one would have to know."

"I would know. And there's nothing wrong with me. Or, at least nothing seriously wrong. Have you seen some of these vets around town? Missing arms and legs, blind, faces burned–"

"Do you believe that, Will?" Shapiro's tone had a harsher edge now as he jabbed his cigarette at Will. "That because you're physically fine, other than your leg, that there is nothing wrong with you? If you can look me in the eye and say that again, I'll drop this right here, right now. I'll clear you to play, and never speak another word of it."

Shapiro stubbed out his butt in the mug as he waited for Will to speak. Will remained silent, however, examining the cigarette in his fingers, his eyes drawn to the burning ember as he considered the doctor's words and the piercing truth behind them.

The doctor pulled out his pen again and scribbled on a pad. "Call this number. You'll speak to Greta, my secretary."

He tore the sheet off his pad and handed it to Will. "I'll find out who the best head shri—psychiatrist—we have here is. Greta will set it up for you."

The doctor held the sheet out and waited for Will to take it, but Will remained still.

"You want to ignore what's eating away at you, or fight this on your own, Will, that's your right. But whatever you're going through, you'll have to live with it for the rest of your life. Time, booze, girls—none of that will solve whatever is going on in your head. You think what happened in Cleveland is the end of things? It may be. What do I know? But it could also very well be the beginning."

Shapiro waved the paper in front of Will. "A simple conversation with a trained specialist. That's all I'm asking."

One conversation.

"It's the rest of your life, Will. What do you want to do?"

Chapter 26

Will never heard the gunshot, the report failing to register in each dream. He always knew when the gun fired, however, unable to miss the German officer's hand jerking back from the Luger's recoil. His first thought, every time, was that he might have lost his hearing. But then came the distinct thud of the bullet piercing the old woman's skull. The sound no longer made Will wince, having heard it so many times now, nor did his stomach turn at the sight of the red mist spraying from the back of the woman's head. Those were constants in the dream, and he had replayed the grisly scene so many times his senses had almost entirely dulled. The woman's death once shook Will from his slumber, sparing him from further horror during the night. No longer. Now, it was just the beginning.

He heard someone calling to him. It was Hector Delgado, next in line and still on his knees. He was pleading with the German to spare his life. Will frantically reached for his rifle, but it was not there, and so his arms flailed wildly through the air. It was too late anyhow. This time he heard the shot ring out, and saw the blood spurt from Delgado's shattered temple just before his lifeless corpse pitched forward to the sidewalk.

The German moved further down the line of civilians, his smoking gun held next to his ear and pointed toward the sky. His face remained expressionless, his motions robotic. He came to Monsieur Amand, the schoolmaster back in Noville, who was next to Philippe Dupard, his star pupil. The two were on their knees, laughing as Amand shared some private joke with the youngster. Will smiled, pleased the two were still together, but suddenly felt his body go cold. The shadowy shape of the German had eased behind the pair. The officer lowered his arm and pressed the barrel of the Luger against the back of Amand's head, but the schoolmaster had no reaction. He simply put a hand on Philippe's shoulder, as if comforting the boy.

"No!" Will cried out, reaching again for a weapon that was not there. "No!"

Will's eyes blinked open as the pounding on his front door reverberated across the small apartment.

After hours of fitful tossing, he had finally succumbed to a light slumber. He knew it would not last. No matter how tired he was, it was never enough to ward off the horrid images from Noville that overwhelmed his conscience the moment he closed his eyes. There was no remedy. He had taken up downing a drink or three in the late evenings, hoping to dull any remembrances, but the alcohol did little other than to exacerbate the emptiness of his bed. His hunger for Kay deepened each passing day, yet the possibility of her seeing him in this state, or witnessing the sort of episode that unfolded in Cleveland, was enough for Will to keep his distance. The risk of humiliation was too great, as was the prospect of his antics driving her away from him for good.

It wasn't just Kay weighing on him. He was far more ambivalent about returning to the diamond than he would have expected when he sulked his way out of Cleveland more than a week ago. Despite his qualms, the front office was urgently pushing to get him back in uniform, and with good cause. Lethargic and rudderless, the Senators had been middling for almost two weeks. They grinded through their schedule while Will was away, winning a few but also getting clobbered at times, even by the likes of the lowly White Sox and Browns. The *Washington Star* had conjured a story that Will's leg had been nursed to full strength, sparking an optimism around town about the team's prospects for chasing down the first place Red Sox and competing again for the American League pennant. Pure fantasy, Will knew.

More loud rapping erupted from the front door. Will sat upright, rubbing his eyes as he reached for his watch from the nightstand. He held it up to the glow of the streetlamp in his window, struggling to focus on the hands. 5:10am. He had been asleep for less than two hours.

Cursing out loud, Will swung his legs over the bedframe, gathering the requisite energy to club some manners into whatever idiot was stirring the entire block at this hour. He jammed his feet into a pair of slippers and stomped through the darkened apartment, clad only in his boxers and undershirt. Unchaining the front door, he swung it open and immediately stepped back, shading his eyes from the beaming overhead light in the outer hallway.

The recognition quickly set in, and Will's jaw fell.

"What the hell?" he mumbled, baffled by the sight before him.

Bob Feller offered a lopsided grin, as if greeting a long-lost chum. "I thought you might be up this early, Sergeant."

"You thought wrong."

Feller laughed. "My old bos'n on the *Alabama* used to that say quite a bit, Sergeant. Those exact words. He sure was a salty fellow."

"Knock off the sergeant crap," Will said crossly. "What are you doing here, Feller? Dressed like that?"

Not only did the Cleveland pitcher possess a blend of charisma and gaiety that chafed Will to no end, he could have stepped out of a recruiting poster for the Navy. Feller had a boyishly handsome face, with a dimpled chin, thick lips, and rows of perfect teeth that Will imagined had disarmed scores of young women over the years. He was wearing blue athletic shorts, a white t-shirt with *United States Navy* embroidered across the chest, and a pair of spotless white tennis shoes. Though he was a few inches shorter than Will, the man exuded physicality and athleticism, and the undersized shirt he was wearing accentuated every muscle in his upper body. Most infuriating to the bleary-eyed Will, the man still hadn't stopped grinning.

"Getting in some morning PT. Downside of being on a battleship for nearly three years, you're stuck running short laps on the dang quarterdeck. So now I run every chance I get. Thought you might want to tag along."

"Tag along?" Will was incredulous, and wondered if he might still be asleep. "We have a game against you guys in seven hours."

"Eight. Come on, Jamison, what do you say? I took a cab all the way down here so I could drag you along with me. I'm talking thirty minutes tops. Even a catcher can run that long."

Will frowned, in no mood for humor, and Feller read it immediately, holding up his palms in apology.

"Look, I'm not pulling your chain. I always run when we're on the road. Great way to see these cities. Beantown has always been my favorite, but Washington, well, any man that's ever put on a uniform is going to take a shine to all these great buildings and monuments. Know what I mean?"

Will was quiet, unable to disagree. He felt it too, every day.

"Don't tell our local scribes I said this, but downtown Cleveland and the Cuyahoga River ain't much to look at. But, hey, if you're not up for it, I understand. I know you've been rehabbing your leg, so if–"

"Give me five minutes," Will said, slamming the door and causing Feller to step back. The walls shuddered in response. He threw on a pair of shorts and his worn sneakers, then rummaged through his dresser until he found an old olive drab t-shirt to represent his former service. Leaving the apartment, he bounded down the stairs, two at a time, as he fought back a yawn. He found the Indians pitcher outside on the sidewalk, one leg perched on a fire plug as he leaned over to stretch a hamstring.

Without loosening a single limb or muscle, Will darted past a surprised Feller, turned the corner, and ran briskly down I Street, sparse of vehicles or any life this early in the morning. He was a blur passing from streetlight to streetlight, but Feller easily caught up to him within a few blocks. He trotted abreast of Will, noticing the big catcher stifling another yawn.

"Good gravy, Sergeant, you need some more beauty sleep?"

A milk truck motored by in the opposite direction, and Will considered shoving Feller in its path.

"You need a crack in the jaw? Where we going, wise guy?"

"You ever see the sun rise over the Lincoln Memorial?"

"Yeah. On a postcard."

Feller laughed even as he accelerated his pace. "We'll head for the Washington Monument, circle around, and hit the Memorial on the way back. I run a six minute mile. Can you keep up, old timer?"

Will matched his stride. "Are you trying to get me to take a swing at you, Feller?"

"No, I just thought–HEY!"

Will burst forward again, this time into a hard sprint. He ran the length of the street before turning sharply onto Virginia Avenue. The roads were still quiet, and he heard Feller's heavy footsteps in pursuit. Having proved his point, Will eased up, allowing Feller to fall in beside him again. The pair ran on, silently, their pace vigorous but measured, knowing they had at least three or four miles to go. It was still dark, even with the glow of sunrise on the horizon now, and the men weaved their way across streets and overpasses that were largely vacant.

They reached Constitution Avenue and ran along the National Mall, the dim lights of the Lincoln Memorial visible on their right. Rounding the Washington Monument, they returned to Constitution Avenue and ran back in the direction of the Memorial, both men pumping their legs for the final half-mile. With maybe a thousand feet left, Feller spat out a challenge between breaths to see which man would reach the top of the famous steps first. He dashed ahead, but Will did not follow, sparing his leg the needless strain. Feller lengthened his lead, the two men following the gravel path that lined each side of the reflecting pool fronting the Memorial. The familiar ache in Will's leg returned and he slowed his pace, knowing what would soon follow. He cursed in frustration.

Feller had stopped, frowning in disappointment as he trotted in place, waiting for Will to catch up. The two men were soon aside one another again, and began a slow canter up the 57 steps that led to the base of the Memorial. Will winced now with each stride but continued on, determined to finish this. They reached the top, each man thoroughly whipped, their cotton shirts soaked through with perspiration.

Catching their wind, they stood in front of the massive statue of Abraham Lincoln, made of white marble from, ironically enough, the deep South. The 16th President was perched on his chair, his face full of resolve and conviction, in one of America's iconic sculptures.

"Sun will come up in a few minutes," said Feller, bent over and still panting. "Right behind the Capitol dome. Mind waiting for it?"

Will nodded, unable to speak. He stood erect, hands on hips, his heart still pounding. He looked down the length of the Mall, following the gaze of the former President. From the Lincoln Memorial, the reflecting pool stretched nearly to the Washington Monument, followed by a strip of manicured grass as wide as a football field that carpeted the ground leading up to the Capitol. It was the most hallowed two miles of real estate in America, and perhaps the most majestic view, right up there with the observation deck of the Empire State Building and the photographs Will had seen of the new Mount Rushmore out in South Dakota.

"It's special, ain't it?"

He had forgotten that Feller was there. The man's voice was quieter now, more humble, and Will nodded in agreement.

"That it is."

"Mind if I ask you a question, Jamison?"

He turned to Feller. "Don't you want to see your sunrise?"

Feller shrugged. "Sun comes up every day, don't it? But you and I, we don't get to talk too often. You hardly said a word to me at the all-star game in '41."

Will gave him a sheepish smile. "Hardly said a word to anyone that day. I could barely keep my breakfast down."

He needed to rest his leg, so he sat on the top step, using the waist of his shirt to wipe the perspiration from his face. "What's on your mind?"

The pitcher chewed his lower lip as he sat next to Will. "I didn't see it. I was in the dugout, too far away. Smokey told me about it later that night."

Cleveland.

"Smokey's got a big mouth," Will flared. "And how many people have you told, Feller?"

"Jumpin' Jesus, man," Feller said, taken aback. "Let's calm down a bit. Smokey does have a big mouth, but he's also a stand-up guy, and neither of us has told a single other person. I promise you that. And stop calling me Feller. I'm Bob and you're Will, and we grew up within spittin' distance of each other."

They were both quiet for a full minute until Will looked at Feller again. "What did he say?"

Feller smiled tightly. "Smokey? I think you shook him up a bit. You know he didn't serve. So he was curious if I had been through anything like that."

"Have you?"

Feller rested his famous forearms on his knees and laced his fingers together. "Navy didn't have it easy, Will. The Japs were tough, every bit as tough as the Germans. Bet on it. They threw everything they had against us. Nothing was worse than those *Kamikaze* attacks. You know they gave their pilots only enough fuel for a one-way trip? How do you stop a man, a fanatic, who wants to kill himself, and take you with him? I was lucky, and my ship didn't really see much of it. We mostly did long-range barrages to soften up the beaches for the Marines. Or put up flak to protect the carriers. You know what I did?"

Will shook his head, surprised that he was genuinely interested. He had never really spoken to anyone who had fought in the Pacific. That included Jack, who, like Will, always seemed uncomfortable talking about his part in the war and steered conversations away from it.

"I was a Chief Petty Officer and a gun captain. My crew ran a

40-millimeter anti-aircraft gun battery. Four heavy guns, on one mount, with a range of more than four miles. Four miles, Will. I never saw the Jap pilots we were shooting at. Never pulled the trigger. Never saw a man die. Not once."

Feller stopped, and Will realized the man's bravado had completely vanished.

"I imagine all that don't seem like much to a man with a Silver Star."

"To hell with that, Bob. I bet it seemed like something to the men whose hides you saved by shooting those planes down."

"Still had it easier than most. Those *kamikazes*–"

"You think you missed out on something?"

Feller shrugged. "I volunteered, Will. Just like you. I wanted to be a fighter pilot, but couldn't pass the danged hearing test. I still fought the Japs, just did it from long distance. Some days I regret that. Other days I see those wounded vets in Cleveland, back home in Iowa, and everywhere else, and realize how lucky I was. What does that tell you?"

"That you still have your wits about you. What I saw—any man that wants to see those things, hear those things, can't be right in the head."

The two fell silent for a minute until Feller spoke again.

"We had a kid on our ship, a Marine, couldn't have been more than eighteen, nineteen years old. He was from Fort Dodge, about eighty miles from our farm. Nice kid, but damn, the boy didn't know when to shut up about the Cubs. The Cubs! I told him it would be a hundred years before those jokers won another World Series. Kid always wanted to bend my ear on the mess decks. Asking me what it was like to pitch to DiMaggio, Greenberg, Keller, and guys like that. Wanted to know how I thought I would do against Stan Hack and some other Cubbies I've never even heard of. This went on for better than a year. I learned to tune the kid out, but he was sort of growing on me. And he was a Marine, so he was pretty squared away. Actually thought about getting the kid a job with the team after the war. If he promised to shut up about the Cubs."

"Did he?"

Feller's face tightened. "It was late in the war. Our task force was steaming south, towards New Guinea, and we hit a nasty squall. Kid was caught topside, trying to get from his watch station to his bunk, and he got swept overboard by a 40-foot wave. Battleships don't exactly turn on a dime, so they radioed one of the trailing destroyers. But it was nighttime and the weather was about as hazardous as it can get for a small ship. They gave up after an hour and rejoined the fleet."

The Cleveland pitcher let out a long breath. "Japs surrendered three days later. Kid survives fourteen months in the Pacific, then gets taken out by a wave. A wave. And every day since then, I've asked myself, why him? Why not me?"

There was more silence.

Finally, Will cleared his throat. "Well, at least the kid wasn't around in October."

It was hardly a time for levity, but Will and Feller couldn't help giving each other a small smile. The Cubs had broken the hearts of their fans once again the previous fall, losing the seventh and deciding game to Detroit in the 1945 World Series.

Will realized at that moment how connected he was with this man. Something they shared that had nothing to do with balls and strikes.

Feller turned back to Will. "You regret enlisting?"

"Hell, no."

Will had to acknowledge the truth. "I don't know, maybe. It wasn't like I thought it would be. What the Germans were doing to our guys, the Jews, civilians, everyone else—I knew about it, but to see it close-up? I watched a Kraut officer walk down a line of villagers—old men, women and children—putting a bullet in the head of each one. What kind of man, what kind of human being, does that?" Will shook his head. "I know there were even worse things going on, but to see it happen, to have to watch it..."

Will had no idea why he was opening up to Feller, a man he barely knew. Feller had served, yes, but they were hardly friends. Yet Will felt no inhibitions, no shame. Not for his pleading tone, his inability to keep his voice from breaking, or even the tears suddenly forming in his eyes. Maybe it was because Feller was a stranger. Or perhaps they were cut from the same cloth, far more so than Will had initially thought.

"How the hell do I live with this?"

The question surprised him as much as it did Feller.

"With what you saw?"

Will nodded, giving it some thought before responding. "There was a man in my platoon, a boy really, who I was supposed to be looking out for. Got his head blown apart, right in front of me. Probably took a piece of shrapnel with my name on it." Will's voice was almost despondent. "When will the day come, one single day, when I don't think about that? About everything I saw, everything I did?"

Feller was quiet for a full minute. "It all kind of makes our game today seem pretty small, don't it?"

Will nodded. "I wake up some days thinking there's nothing more important than getting back to the all-star game. Like I've got something to prove to my old man, the fans, or even myself. Other times, it all seems so meaningless. That boy who got killed was a father. What am I? What have I done with my life?"

The two sat in silence for several minutes, watching the faint glow on the horizon brighten with each passing second, until the large orange ball began to emerge from behind the Capitol.

"I appreciate you coming out here to talk, Will. My friends, my teammates, even Ginny. I just can't share this stuff with them. None of them would understand."

"Seems like I did most of the talking here. But what about Pete Smalls? Or Willy Graber?"

Feller frowned. "They're great teammates, Will, but neither of those guys saw a day in theater. It was all exhibition games and USO tours for those two."

"It was for most of them."

"Except you."

"And you."

Feller shook his head, but he was smiling again. "A range of four miles, Will."

"You ever think that you can't live without playing? And at the same time, you wish you were done with it? So you could do something else with your life?"

"Like what?"

"I don't know. I met a man in Belgium, he was a school teacher. This was a tiny village. Couldn't have been more than twenty or twenty-five kids there. The man's whole life was those kids. And here I am, playing baseball. Baseball! And I just keep wondering if what I'm doing just doesn't mean a damn thing."

Feller turned to him. "Will, every teammate you and I have ever had, lived for this game. They ate, slept, and breathed it. It's what drives us, I guess, and makes us the very best on that field. It's why you and I make these ridiculous sums of money. But at the end of the day, it's just a field. Just a game."

"Meaning?"

"Meaning, take this for what it's worth, but you are either the dumbest son of a bitch I ever met, or the keenest."

They both smiled, but Will recognized the truth in Feller's words.

"Well, Sergeant, sounds like you have some things to work out."

"I guess I do."

"Would be a shame, not seeing you out there. You're probably the best catcher in this game. Don't tell our kid, Jimmy Hegan, I said that. I'll make you a deal, Will. Every time we're in town for a series, I'll wake you up at some godforsaken hour for a run. We'll come here, and if you're not sore at me for striking you out three or four times, we'll talk about things. Just you and me, and Mr. Lincoln there."

Will stood, offering a wry smile in return. "Deal. But we best keep him out of it. The man's from Illinois. Probably another Cubs fan."

Chapter 27

He raised the glass of ice water to his lips, grateful for even the smallest of diversions. Will was divided, unsure whether to use the seconds ticking away to invent a response to the man's question, or plot his escape from this prison of a conversation. His interrogator waited anxiously but without complaint, perhaps anticipating a breakthrough of sorts, and a few more revealing words. Something that might unveil hidden truths or vulnerabilities that once acknowledged, would coax his patient into opening up further, in the sort of deeply personal terms that had never been spoken aloud.

Better get comfortable, Doc.

The psychiatrist's office was both tastefully appointed and absurdly spacious. On the tenth floor of a nondescript building in downtown Washington, it was just blocks from Ford's Theater and the infamous balcony where Lincoln was slain. Considering his conversation with Bob Feller earlier that morning, it seemed Will was fated to spend the better part of his day in the former President's shadow.

Much of the office was wallpapered in framed degrees and certificates, all seemingly scripted in the indecipherable hand of a 16th century calligrapher. A credenza behind the desk held a number of small picture frames, photographs of what Will assumed were the man's children. The curtains were drawn to keep the morning sun from warming the room, and Will could hear the soft hum of the air conditioner gamely attempting to keep the expansive space cool. July was fast approaching, and Washington's trademark humidity had returned with a vengeance.

John Lindsey III, M.D., sat facing Will, his legs crossed at the knee. He was stoic and inscrutable as he tapped his pen on a notepad. They were seated in two upholstered armchairs opposite an ornate desk hand-carved from English walnut, Lindsey perhaps attempting to seem less authoritarian by sitting next to his reluctant patient rather than behind the stately desk.

He was in his mid-40s, handsome with energetic, coal-colored eyes and a lean, athletic build that suggested a rigorous exercise regimen. A squash player perhaps. Or maybe tennis, judging by the dark tint to his skin. It was the weekend, so Lindsey was dressed in casual slacks and a short-sleeved knit shirt, and Will thought the man resembled a dapper, suburban socialite far more than he did the Chief of Psychiatric Medicine at Washington General Hospital. Whatever his attire, Will assumed Lindsey was at the top of his profession. Shapiro wouldn't have recommended anyone otherwise.

Will appreciated the efforts of both medical men to keep the appointment confidential. There was irony that he was seeing a psychiatrist, considering the stress and anxiety from a simple visit to the man's office that morning had nearly turned Will into a basket case. He had even taken a municipal bus to the downtown address, donning a hat and sunglasses until he was safely on the elevator. It would be front-page news in Washington if a public figure such as Will Jamison was spotted here, and could even derail a career, given public misconceptions tying mental illness to violence and instability. Having battled such stigmas for years, Lindsey agreed to meet at his private office, rather than the hospital's psychiatric ward where he saw most patients. So here they were, on a Saturday morning in a mostly deserted downtown Washington, with the building almost entirely vacant.

Lindsey was warm and informal at first, and the discussion began easily enough. They explored Will's childhood, his family, and his early life experience. Will's playing career and enlistment in the Army were of less interest to Lindsey, and as the conversation stretched into its second hour, Will found a comfort level he hadn't expected, surprising himself with how forthcoming he was with the affable, soft-spoken psychiatrist.

His listener offered little commentary of his own. At times, Lindsey shifted the focus of his questions, occasionally asking Will to pause at points so he could jot down notes. For the most part, the doctor simply listened, pulling on occasional threads, entirely engrossed in everything Will had chronicled.

The questions eventually turned to Will's time in France and Belgium. He surprised himself, opening up to the doctor, his first time giving voice in a detailed manner to what he experienced. He spoke at length about the men he served with and those who were lost, capping his recollections with his return to civilian life and the Senators, each hardly as seamless as he hoped. His recalcitrance had been almost entirely forgotten, his words flowing without reluctance or reservation. Until now.

"Cleveland, Will." Lindsey had waited long enough.

Will nodded, giving in. For the moment. He placed the glass of ice water back on Lindsey's desk.

"It was a night game. Bottom of the eighth, we were in the field. Smokey Abbott was leading off for the Indians. Right as the inning started, a couple of fuses blew out, then every light in the stadium shut down. We were told later their circuitry got fried. The stadium got dark. Real dark. And I got dizzy, like my head was spinning. I couldn't breathe. Couldn't hear. Could barely see Smokey and the ump, and they were standing right next to me."

Will paused, rubbing the back of his neck.

"Go on," Lindsey prodded.

"That was just the first few seconds. I think everyone's eyes adjusted, but not mine. All I saw was fog."

Lindsey scrunched his forehead. "You were playing in fog?"

"No. But when the lights went off, all I saw was this blackness. And the fog."

Lindsey rubbed his chin. "The fog in Belgium?"

Will nodded. "In Noville. We spent two days in it. There were times you couldn't see your own two feet."

"Back to Cleveland. Tell me about what you felt when the lights went out. Describe everything you can remember."

"It was like a dream. Like I was back in Noville, and scared shitless all over again. I felt...I don't know...exposed. Surrounded by all these people watching me, wanting to kill me, but I couldn't see them. I felt helpless, paralyzed. I knew Delgado was going to get killed, but there was nothing I could do about it. I was just going to watch it happen all over again. That was it. I felt the ump smacking me in the face, knocking me out of it. I saw him, and Smokey, another ump, all gaping at me, like I had a third eye or something. I wanted to get the hell out of there, so I took off, ran into the clubhouse. I curled up on the floor like a little girl. The game started up again, but I couldn't move. Couldn't change out of my uniform. Couldn't even take off my catching gear."

"You know about triggers, Will?"

"Doc Shapiro mentioned them to me."

"It's a cue, something your mind processes that resembles some aspect of a trauma you've experienced. They can be the catalyst for some rather severe psychological distress."

"And you think the dark was a trigger."

"You don't?"

"I don't have a problem with the dark. I sleep in it every night."

"And how well do you sleep?"

Will was quiet.

"That, moreover, is a darkness you fully control. A light switch, yes? You can turn the lights on and off as you wish. But the stadium, your blindness, the notion of feeling surrounded and observed by others you could not see, that was all beyond your control. A close parallel to what you experienced in Belgium."

"Whatever it was, I can't go through that again. It was like I was someone else."

"For a brief time, Will, maybe you were. Not yourself, anyway. Tell me, did anything else happen in Belgium? Maybe something that you haven't spoken to anyone about?"

Will's heart skipped a beat. "What do you mean?"

"You were a combat soldier, Will. Involved in what I am told was the largest battle of the war. You told me you killed other men, as did most others in combat. I'm guessing you witnessed things that would horrify and traumatize any rational person. The brutality, the human carnage, all of it, would overwhelm any of us. You probably lost friends. Am I right?"

Will was quiet again, averting his eyes from Lindsey. How did he know all this? It didn't matter, Will had ventured far enough. He could only tell Lindsey, or anyone else, so much.

"Does anything stand out? Any particular episode or experience?"

Lindsey waited once again for a response, then finally lowered his pen.

"Will, you came here at your own volition. I assume because you recognize you have a problem, and you are seeking help in how to address it. That by itself, in my experience, is a rarity, and a step forward. You must trust me, Will. I assure you, whatever you disclose in our sessions will remain in this room. It will never be revealed or shared, at least not by me. I have sworn an oath to this."

Will fingered the seams of his trousers, wanting to leave.

And to stay. He needed help. He had fallen into a woeful abyss without any identifiable path out, topped off by downing just about any kind of drink these days to pacify the toxicity in his gut whenever his thoughts returned to Belgium.

Lindsey studied him, wordlessly, the internal conflict wrestling within Will's mind impossible to miss. There was more there, the doctor was sure of it. He had been in private practice for 16 years, and pure instinct told him when a patient was holding something back.

Will shifted in his seat. "We've been talking for a while, Doc. Have you figured out how to fix this?"

"I've known you for ninety minutes," Lindsey mused, as he finished penning a note to himself. "Before I give a diagnosis, I normally meet with a patient over a period of weeks, if not months. There is no more complicated organ than the brain, and there is nothing simple about understanding, predicting, or treating it. But I promise you, Will, we'll figure it out in due time."

"Come on, Doc. You must have some idea. I don't have due time. I have to fix this right now."

Lindsey was quiet for several moments before coming to a decision. He placed his notepad and pen on the desk.

"I can tell you what I think, which is far more than what I know. And I'll spare you the caveats. I think you are likely suffering from what we refer to as anxiety neurosis. Your conscience, Will, is burdened right now by persistent feelings of fear. Fear that bad fortune may strike, fear of some sort of calamity, even fear of death."

Lindsey leaned back in his chair and continued. "But I don't believe it is only your death you fear, Will. I've spoken to Gene Shapiro about you, about what kind of man you are. I've listened to you speak of your service, and despite your very admirable humility, certain aspects of your character come through quite clear. I heard it in your voice, as you spoke earlier of this Dorgado fellow. Throughout your life, you've always been a leader, and protective of those around you. The prospect of their deaths, I imagine, troubled you as much as the prospect of your own. And that may explain why Private Dorgado's death has been so unbearable."

Protective. Right.

"Delgado. Hector Delgado. He was a private first class. So I just need to get over this fear? To stop being so afraid?"

"It's not that easy, Will. This neurosis leads to attacks on your psyche, attacks that are triggered by some sort of stimuli that brings you back to the events that have traumatized your neural core."

"Panic attacks?"

"Of a sort. Not in the sense of anxiety, though. You're terrorized, plain and simple. And when we're terrorized, our bodies react accordingly. Shaking, sweating, weakness. And that causes us to avoid any stimuli that we would associate with the event."

Will struggled to sift through Lindsey's analysis. "So how do we fix this?"

Lindsey offered a sympathetic smile. "I wish I could tell you we have some sort of magic potion to make it all go away. We don't. You've heard the term combat fatigue, right? That's what the Army calls it. The name itself implies that all of this, whatever you are feeling and experiencing, will go away with a good night's rest. Or at least, as the months and years pass. It is utter nonsense, Will. Pure rubbish. What you are feeling will not go away on its own. We can't turn it on and off like...a light switch."

"So, what do I do?"

"There are options. Some have advocated for psychosurgeries to treat these conditions. Lobotomies to be precise, where the surgeon severs the frontal lobes of the brains to relieve any psychological distress. Others are using shock therapy, jolting the brain with electric currents to alleviate the trauma."

Will almost gasped. "You've got to be kidding me."

"I realize how barbaric it sounds, but these are innovative methods, Will, practiced by some of the most accomplished men in our field. I would advise you not to rule them out. I understand they've had some success with patients up at St. Elizabeths."

St. Elizabeths. The Civil War-era psychiatric hospital in Southeast Washington that until 30 years ago was named the *Government Hospital for the Insane.*

"There's no way in hell–"

Lindsey held up a palm. "I understand. I didn't expect you to be favorable to such options."

"Is there anything you can do?"

"I could prescribe some opioids."

"Drugs?"

"Yes. A pharmaceutical. There is a good chance that–"

"What's the downside?"

"There are side effects. Lethargy, drowsiness, confusion, even constipation."

Will made a face. "No, no drugs. I'd be a wreck on the field."

"That doesn't leave us with many options, Will. Regular counseling sessions would help. I don't see individual patients anymore, but I'd be willing–"

"Thanks, Doc. But even coming here today was a big risk. If word gets out, I'm done in this town, and the majors for that matter. I'll have to take my chances, stick this out."

"Stick this out?"

Will shrugged. "I've played through a lot. Strained ligaments down in Chattanooga. A sprained shoulder my rookie year here. Now a shrapnel wound in the leg. I can block things out, play through the pain. Not let myself get distracted."

Lindsey leaned over, elbows on his knees, his tone sharper now. "The brain is not a ligament, Will. If you think you can *block out* whatever is ailing you, you're fooling yourself." He paused. "You're not married."

"No."

"Girlfriend?"

Will was quiet for a beat. "No."

Lindsey stood and circled his desk, retrieving a business card from the top drawer. He returned to his seat across from Will and scribbled on the card with a fountain pen.

"You need someone to talk to, someone you can trust, you call me." He held the card out. "That has my home and office numbers, as well as my answering service. Call me day or night, whenever you need an ear."

Will looked at the card. "Thanks Doc, but I don't–"

Lindsey interrupted, his words sharp. "You internalize these issues and never speak of them, I guarantee at best, a life of suffering. At worst, you'll be hanging from the end of a rope. Take it."

Will accepted the card and gave the man a hard look. "You trying to scare me, Doc?"

The doctor sat back in his chair and steepled his fingers.

"My father was a world-class neurologist," he said, his voice gentler now. "He wanted me to follow in his footsteps, share a practice someday. It was tempting."

"Why didn't you?"

"Neurology is a tough discipline, Will. But identifying symptoms, say, for a head injury, there isn't much difficulty there. When the brain suffers physical trauma, the symptoms are fairly evident. We see it in the pupils, weakness or paralysis in the extremities, diminished reflexes. But when our psyches are traumatized, the symptoms are nearly invisible. At least, to most physicians. My sister had symptoms. Symptoms my father either never picked up on, or chose to ignore. Erratic behavior, mood swings, even violence. He took her to an asylum when I was fourteen, Will. Never let me visit her, not even once. She took her own life a year later."

They were both quiet. Lindsey's face was a mask, revealing little about his own painful experiences.

"We should have learned more after the first world war, but we haven't. Partly because the science and research hasn't progressed enough. Partly because so many in my profession refuse to resist conventional wisdom. But enough with the recriminations. I wish you luck, Will. You and men like you deserve so much more than this. You deserve peace, more than any of the rest of us. And I hope you find it someday."

There was nothing more to say, and both men stood. They shook hands once more, Will thanking the doctor profusely for both his time and discretion. Will was halfway through the door when Lindsey called for him from behind his desk.

"Yeah, Doc?" Will replied, turning back.

"Do you love her?"

"Who?"

"The girlfriend you don't have."

"You a mind reader, Doc?" Will asked, smiling.

Lindsey grinned back, the most expressive Will had seen the

man. "Actually, I guess I am, when you think about it. So do you?"

Will looked at him blankly, uncertain how to respond.

"My last word of advice, Will. And this one is on the house. If you love her, tell her more than you've told me. Tell her everything."

Chapter 28

It was late in the evening and another oppressive, humidity-filled day in the Nation's capital was coming to a close. An ominous patch of storm clouds hovered over the Capitol dome, and while most would have relished seeing a few lightning bolts strike Congress, the country would have no such luck.

Even in the steel-encased elevator, Will could hear the sharp crack of thunder outside. The midsummer gale had been raging for an hour now, pummeling the city with a torrent of wind and rain, and mercifully cooling off the triple-digit temperatures that had the region sweltering of late. Even the short scamper from his taxi to the hospital's main doors had given Will's slacks and golf shirt a soaking, a steady dribble of water continuing to fall from the brim of his Panama.

The elevator doors opened and Will stepped off, his eyes wincing from the incandescent overhead lights that reflected off the stark white walls and scrubbed linoleum floor. He took a few tentative paces to his left, following the directions he received in the main lobby, before weaving through several more hallways. A sober man would get lost in the vast labyrinth of corridors and wards that comprised the fourth floor of Sibley Memorial Hospital. And Will wasn't exactly sober.

He finally arrived at the surgical department, but not before drifting past a bevy of hospital personnel who eyed him queerly in passing, as much for his size as his inability to navigate a straight line.

The main reception desk was adjacent to a visitors lounge and mostly deserted this time of day. A handful of anxious family members were sprinkled among the chairs, their faces downcast as they awaited news of loved ones. A frowning, hawk-faced woman, her steel gray hair cinched back into a watertight bun, manned the reception desk, eying Will in his disheveled state with unconcealed distaste. The reception desk fronted a large nursing station, and

Will's eyes wandered past the scowling older woman to where a number of more human-looking doctors and nurses in starched white fabric milled about.

Kay stood out, naturally, like a Hollywood starlet among a gathering of monks. Her auburn tresses were fastened into a ponytail and pinned to a peaked cap, and her faultless contours were easily discernible even beneath the unflattering, one-piece uniform. She stood near a row of filing cabinets, coffee in hand, sharing a laugh with another nurse. Her colleague noticed Will watching and nodded in his direction, causing Kay to swivel her head. As their eyes met, a range of emotions crossed her face, including what might have been a trace of a smile. It quickly melted away as she excused herself from the conversation and briskly circled the reception desk. Crooking a finger, she led him out of earshot of the hawk-faced nurse and into the visitors lounge, her folded arms and narrowed eyes indicating just how joyful she was to see him.

"What are you doing here, Will?"

Her tone was demanding, but he was sure he heard a note of genuine curiosity in there, offering Will the faintest of hopes. It was an opening, and he straightened, fully prepared to deliver the compelling, heartfelt words he had ardently memorized hours earlier and rehearsed a thousand times since in his thoughts. But nothing came, a wave of panic seizing him as he faltered, unable to recall a single syllable.

"I came to apologize," he finally managed. "I wanted to tell you in person. I've missed you."

"Really? It's been weeks, Will."

He looked at his feet, trying to appear contrite. It was a struggle in his present condition, as enunciating each word was consuming all of his concentration.

"I know. I should have come sooner."

She stepped closer to him and studied his eyes. "Are you drunk?"

"No," he lied, trying not to sway.

"Jesus, Will, your breath smells like a fifth of gin. Eddie liked Gordon's. What's your brand?"

"Okay," he conceded, lifting his palms. "I've had a few. Nothing I can't handle."

"Eddie used to say the same thing."

"I'm not Eddie," Will snapped, raising his voice.

The older nurse shot them a reproachful glare, and Will put his hand on Kay's elbow, partly to lead her, partly to steady himself.

"Look, can we sit down?"

She nodded, reluctantly, and he guided her to a row of chairs against the far wall. Will removed his hat and pulled a pack of Luckies from his coat, placing one between his lips. He was about to strike a match when Kay snatched the cigarette out of his mouth and crumpled it in her hand.

"I can't smoke in here?" asked Will, genuinely surprised. He could see at least two of the doctors puffing away.

"I just want to see if you can talk to me without a beer in one hand and a cigarette in the other. Like you used to, once upon a time."

He waved a hand dismissively, despite knowing how desperately he wanted a beer and cigarette right now. He had once faced hordes of bloodthirsty Germans with nothing more than a knife in his hand and a stick of gum in his mouth, and now found himself cowering before a single, 120-pound woman.

"I've been here for three hours already, Will, and I'll be here for nine more. Can we wrap this up?"

He nodded, trying again to summon the words he had committed to memory, but it was so many drinks ago.

"I've been an ass," he started.

"Yes," she said, emphatic.

"You deserve better."

"Right again."

"You can stop agreeing with me anytime," he said irritably. Will closed his eyes and pinched the bridge of his nose in frustration. It was not how he wanted this to go. And he certainly hadn't expected the antagonism.

He tried looking her in the eyes. "Look Kay, I know you expected more from me when I came back."

"It's not about what I expected. It's about whether you have been honest with me."

"When?"

"Last month. Four years ago. The day we met at Siegel's."

"I don't understand."

She stood, the exasperation clear on her face. "No, Will, I don't think you do. Look, I have to work, and you're half in the bag. I'm off on Wednesday and you have an afternoon game. Why don't we meet for dinner?"

He stood as well, grasping the back of the chair to maintain his balance. "I'd like that."

"Only one condition."

"What's that?"

"No drinking. Before, during, or after."

He grinned. "There's going to be an after?"

She shook her head in exasperation. "We're past this, Will. Do you understand that?"

"Past what?"

"The word games. The innuendo. If there is going to be a you and me, we're going to have to be able to have a conversation. And there has to be a little trust. You can't shut down on me every time I ask...why are you smiling like a baboon?"

"You said there might be a you and a me."

She could not keep her lips from curling upward, but she would give him no more. His boyish grin and playful manner had been irresistible once, but no longer.

"I'll call you a cab, Will. You'll need to find your way back to the main lobby."

"Okay."

Kay turned on her heel and started for the nursing station.

"Wednesday. I'll stop by your place after the game," she said, over her shoulder.

"Good night, Kay," Will called after her.

"Good night, mister," she whispered to herself without turning around, her steely façade on the cusp of disintegrating.

The accordion door squeaked closed behind Kay and the bus lumbered away, coughing up a cloud of exhaust that quickly dissipated into the pre-dawn mist. Another thunderstorm had passed through while Kay was finishing her graveyard shift, leaving behind a rain-soaked city immersed once again in a dank humidity. Kay opted against her umbrella and donned only a headscarf against the drizzle, hoping the damp air might keep her awake during the short walk home.

It was nearly six in the morning, and in the twilight of the brightening horizon stood the commercial buildings and luxury hotels that lined Connecticut and Massachusetts Avenues, the two thoroughfares that connected downtown Washington to the city's more affluent residential neighborhoods. She was just a block from her flat on N Street in Dupont Circle, the stylish neighborhood named after a prominent Civil War naval admiral. Once home to the city's slaughterhouses, Dupont now flaunted some of the trendiest restaurants and priciest abodes in Washington.

Kay walked deliberately, bone-weary after finishing yet another 12-hour shift, almost all of it on her feet. She enjoyed her return to nursing, more than she had expected. It didn't quite compare to the exhilaration and rapture that came with performing on stage, but there was something to being a small part of the healing process, giving her a sense of self-worth that had eluded her since she was a child. It was all well worth the grueling overnight shifts, and even the occasional unwelcome advances and leering from physicians old enough to be her father.

Her home was in sight now. The flat was part of a 19th century brick Victorian that belonged to a wealthy Swiss expatriate. Kay was leasing the substructure, below street level, in what Herr Strauss referred to as an English Basement. Presumably to justify the absurd rent she paid for barely 600 square feet. It was clean and cozy though, and her only worry was heavy precipitation, when rainwater cascaded down the small, concrete stairwell and seeped under her front door. She could only imagine what was waiting for her now after the earlier storm. It would at least be comfortable. The below-ground living space had few redeeming qualities, but cooler air in the summertime at least made days like this bearable.

It was quite a departure from the lavish, 37th floor penthouse in Manhattan she once shared with her ex-husband. An existence she hadn't missed for a single minute. While Washington lacked the vibrancy and cosmopolitan feel of New York, Kay's emancipation had given her so much more. Her life here was a new beginning, and, for the first time, one to be led on her own terms, leaving her hardly fretting over her modest living conditions. She had money put away, enough to buy her own home in swanky enclaves like Georgetown and Woodley Park, but she was more than content with life in Dupont, and while things hadn't worked out quite as she imagined when she decided to leave Manhattan, she would not allow her newfound freedom to be subsumed by another man wallowing in a bottle and self-pity.

As she neared the Victorian, her eyes were drawn to the top of the front stoop, and the large figure leaning against the front door, a cigarette dangling from his lips. There was a growth of stubble on his face, his clothes bedraggled. The same clothes he had been wearing hours earlier when she had seen him last.

"Fancy meeting you here," Will said cheerfully, tossing the cigarette butt to the ground and twisting his heel on it.

Kay looked up at him from the sidewalk. "Have you been here all night?"

"I had a question for you."

"I thought we agreed to see each other on Wednesday."

"We did. But today is only Sunday. My question can't wait."

"Are you sober?"

"Mostly," Will said. A pause. "I think."

"Well, some refreshing honesty. What's your question, Will?"

He made his way down the steps and faced Kay on the sidewalk. "How did you know we have an afternoon game on Wednesday?"

"That's your question? That's why you presumably waited here all night for me?"

"Yes."

"You have a game almost every day."

"But you knew it was an afternoon game. And I'm betting you know what time our games are today and tomorrow."

A small smile. "One o'clock today, against Cleveland. Unless they make it a doubleheader, to get in last night's rain out. Then they'll probably move it to noon. Seven in the evening tomorrow."

"You know our schedule," Will said, both an observation and a question.

"I know more than that," she sighed. "I know the Senators are thirteen games behind the Red Sox right now. You were batting .294 before they benched you. Not your best, but up thirty points from the previous month. Your leg seems to be holding up well, better than some of those sportswriters thought it would. And you're getting into quite a few scuffles on the field. I also know what happened in Cleveland, with the lights going out—Dick Holloway told me about that—and I know I left messages with your doorman and the team. You ignored them all."

"But I'm here now."

"Yes, you are. Why?"

He gestured to a crumpled paper sack sitting at the top of the stoop.

"I brought us breakfast. Croissants and danishes. Thought you might be hungry."

"I'm famished. But that bag looks empty."

"I got a little hungry while I was waiting."

"Again," she persisted, determined to put an end to his stalling, "why are you here, Will?"

He let out a long breath. "I want to talk."

"What do you want to talk about? Us?"

"No, I can fix that, Kay. Eventually."

"Oh, can you. That's reassuring."

"At least, I think I can."

Will shuffled his feet and looked at his shoes for several moments before lifting his eyes again.

"Do you know why I enlisted?"

She shook her head. "I asked. You wouldn't tell me."

"I wouldn't tell anyone. The entire truth, that is. I want to tell you now." He paused. "I want to talk about the war."

"The war? I thought you might want to talk about what happened in Cleveland."

He nodded intently. "I do. I want to talk about both."

Kay considered that, and put the two together. "Will, I'm just a nurse with hardly any real experience. Have you considered speaking to a doctor or therapist? I can ask around if–"

"I tried speaking to a shrink. I want to speak to you."

"Why me?"

"You said I need to trust you. And you're right, Kay. You're the only person I trust. The only person I can talk to about...some things."

Kay bit her lip as he said the words. She tried to suppress the surge of elation, reminding herself how many times her hopes had been dashed before by this man.

"Okay then," she said, as indifferently as she could. "Let's go inside and talk."

Ten minutes later, they were seated at a small kitchen table in her basement flat. She had put Will to work, sponging up the rainwater that soaked her rugs near the front door. The showers had picked up again, and the soft drum roll of falling raindrops could be heard from a nearby open window that was only a few feet higher than the sidewalk above. Kay had set out cups and saucers, the cozy apartment quickly filling with the aroma of brewing coffee. She had changed out of her uniform, a thin cotton bath robe wrapping around her silk pajamas.

"I'm not sure I've ever seen you without makeup."

"Some say makeup is a girl's best friend."

"I say you should never wear makeup again."

The flattery was unplanned and off the cuff, and Will immediately regretted it, fearing it might push her further away.

"Sweet," she said quietly, surprising him. The suspicion in her voice from the prior evening seemed to have abated, at least for the moment.

"I know you're hungry," Will offered. "Do you want some breakfast first?"

"Breakfast can wait," Kay said, retrieving the coffee pot and filling their cups. "I want to hear what you have to say."

Will nodded, spooning sugar into his coffee. Kay placed the pot back on the stove top and returned to her chair, folding her hands and waiting for Will to begin.

As the standoff ensued, nervous knots began gnawing away at Will's stomach. How many times had he sat before her, just like this, resisting attempts to pry him open? To get him to lower his lifelong defenses, and reveal his innermost thoughts and feelings, no matter how baring or unpleasant they might be. The silence between the two stretched on, and he saw the frustration forming in her eyes, and the inevitable words crossing her mind.

Here we go again.

But as her eyes bored into him, something felt different to Will. The inclination to pull away from her, an inclination that previously had been almost reflexive, had morphed into something else. There was a notion now, wholly alien to him, not to pull away, but rather, an unmistakable urge to pull her close.

It would jeopardize whatever attachment she had to him, of course. Once she learned the truth about what kind of man he was, what he was capable of, everything could change. Kay was the one person he wanted, he needed, to be in his life now, but the risks were inescapable. Sharing the darkness about him might very well drive her away forever. A certainty remained, however. If he did not talk about it, and if he didn't open up to Kay, right here and right now, it would surely be the end of things for them.

No *after*. No *you and me*.

And nothing more than the lingering scent of lavender left behind in her wake.

Then he felt it. The warm touch of her smooth skin as she reached across the table and wrapped her fingers around his, giving his hand a firm squeeze. It was the simplest of gestures, but one that seemed to express so much. She was urging him on, no question. But with her touch, he felt her compassion, her acceptance, and yes, her uneasiness about his suffering. It also conveyed just two simple words.

It's okay.

He looked into her eyes, and at once, he knew that this woman would never judge or disparage whatever he was experiencing. More than that, he saw something else in those eyes, something more than the usual warmth and kindness he had first seen so many years ago at Siegel's.

There was a message there. A sentiment. One that could remain unspoken, because it was something each already knew, and had likely known for some time. There was a bond between the two of them. Lasting, unbreakable, and unlike anything he could ever share with another woman.

And then, as the realization took hold that he was hopelessly and eternally enamored with this woman, and the only risk was if he didn't give himself completely to her, the words began to pour out.

Chapter 29

DECEMBER 20, 1944
OUTSIDE BASTOGNE, BELGIUM

Will remained on one knee, breathless and shaking, the blood-drenched knife still clutched in his hand. His aim to finish off the two Germans in the shell crater without alerting others nearby had been botched, the errant rifle shot by one of his adversaries sounding like a cannon echoing across the German entrenchments. The noise hadn't yet drawn the squad of *Panzergrenadiers* Will expected, but that could change any second. He knew the American lines couldn't be more than a few hundred yards away, and though he was utterly exhausted, he thought he could manage one last race across a barren field with Philippe in tow.

But they had to move now. The surge of adrenaline from the struggle with the men in the crater was already fading, and Will could feel his ravaged body begging just to keel over and be done with things. He whispered as loud as he dared for Philippe, having left the boy safely outside the crater. There was no response, so Will quickly scaled the side wall. He froze in mid-stride, feeling a hard punch to the gut when he saw the small, limp hand dangling over the edge.

He scurried to the rim and found Philippe on his back, unmoving. Pressing a bloodied hand to the boy's neck, he felt a weakened pulse, and even in the dark Will could see how ashen his face was. He lifted Philippe into his arms, carrying him back into the crater and gently lowering him to the ground. Flicking Janikowski's lighter to life, Will held the flame to the boy's face, seeing his quivering lips and a thin rivulet of blood trickling from his nose. The boy's breaths were short and labored as he stared up at Will with pleading, tearful eyes.

Will lowered the flame to Philippe's torso. There was a black stain on the front of his woolen overcoat, and blood was welling between the boy's tiny fingers as he grasped his belly.

Philippe coughed heavily, causing him to convulse in pain. Will pushed away the boy's hands and ripped open the coat, using his bayonet to slice through Philippe's shirt and thick wool sweater. Thumbing the lighter again, he found the bullet wound, near the boy's abdomen. He reached for the first aid pouch on his cartridge belt, pulling out the sulfa powder and ripping the packet open with his teeth. Will sprinkled the powder over the wound, hoping to congeal the blood. Unwrapping a field dressing, he clamped it tightly over Philippe's belly and wrapped the long bandage ties around his thin waist.

"Hold on, kid," he whispered, tying off the dressing and squeezing the boy's hand. "I'll get us out of here."

Philippe began to cry again, tears streaming down his face as he shivered uncontrollably.

Will removed his cartridge belt and field jacket, covering Philippe with the heavy coat. The surviving German was stirring now, regaining consciousness after the vicious blow to his face from the butt of Will's pistol. Will chewed his lip as he weighed his options. They could not remain in the crater. He felt the dressing, already damp with blood.

There was only one option.

Will found his .45 and checked to see that the weapon was functional. Gripping the Colt with his right hand, he lifted Philippe and hefted him over his left shoulder. The boy didn't make a sound, perhaps in shock now. Out of time, Will took a deep breath and bounded over the side of the crater.

He made it only a few feet before loudly splashing through an ankle-deep stream. Warnings were shouted in German, and a volley of rifle shots rang out. Will looked to the horizon and even through the fog he could see Bastogne in the distance, several of its buildings on fire amid a spate of shelling. He ran as fast as his weary legs could carry him, certain they were on the verge of buckling. The German fire intensified but to little avail, the shots fired wildly into the darkness.

Not all of the shots though, as a bullet hissed by Will's ear, from the direction they were heading. He spotted the shapes ahead, near a clump of small willow trees. Two riflemen, on their knees, maybe 30 yards away, their Mauser rifles pointed in his direction. A forward observation post. He angled away from the two, slowing as he passed and emptying his .45 in their direction. His aim was badly off, but it was enough to make the Germans scramble for cover.

More bullets flew by, whizzing past the pair as they dashed through the night. Will tossed away the .45 and lowered Philippe from his shoulder, cradling the boy as he ran so he could shield Philippe's body from the German gunfire at their backs.

They were nearing a small rise, not unlike the ridges facing Noville, and Will was down to his final ounce of faith. He called on his depleted body once more, his determination driven by something unfamiliar, an optimism or hopefulness perhaps, that Will had forgotten existed after everything he had stomached these last two days. His legs propelled him forward as he began the ascent up the sloping hill, his lungs burning now as the Germans continued to fire at will. Machine guns and mortars had joined the fray, perhaps for sport.

And then it happened, faster than he ever would have imagined. There was an explosion behind him, at a spot he had run through just seconds ago. The blast was followed by a hard wallop to the back of his left thigh, knocking him off balance. He cried out, more in surprise than in pain, as he and the boy tumbled roughly to the ground.

Sprawled on his stomach, Will could see Philippe's contorted body a few feet in front of him. The boy was no longer quiet, wailing now from either the fall or his wounds. Will's hand moved to the back of his leg. He felt the shredded fabric, his hand coming away wet with blood. There was no time to dress the wound as bullets and mortar rounds continued to smack into the ground all around them. He raised himself to his feet and stumbled forward, crying out as a bolt of pain streaked up his leg. He gnashed his teeth as he lifted Philippe into his arms again and began hobbling up the slope, his thigh throbbing.

Over the explosions and gunfire, Will heard a sudden, distinct shout in English, followed by an outbreak of small arms fire that erupted in front of them.

The bullets passed over Will and the boy as the American troops poured covering fire into the German lines. The shooting behind them slackened and Will ran faster, buoyed by the realization of how close they were. It was still dark though, and he failed to see the large rock his boot clipped, sending the two crashing to the ground again.

His leg exploded in agony, and though Will was out of breath, he still managed to let forth a scathing string of curses. He was struggling to get to his knees when he spotted three GIs running downhill in their direction. A hulking figure with a single bar on his helmet plucked Philippe from the ground, the boy like a feather in the man's bulky arms. The other two men, wearing the same Screaming Eagle patch on their sleeves as their lieutenant, grabbed Will by each of his arms and lifted him to his feet. They followed the officer and boy, half-carrying Will to the top of the ridge line as bullets peppered the darkness. They all collapsed into a long slit trench, already brimming with paratroopers shooting at the Germans from the parapet. Though the pain in his leg was excruciating, relief and elation pulsed through Will's body as he gasped for air.

His rescuers resumed their firing positions alongside their squad mates. Will, still panting and wishing he could simply pass out, motioned for the newly arrived medic to check Philippe first. The aid man quickly looked the boy over and moved to Will, tearing away what was left of his pant leg and using a small penlight to examine the wound. He mumbled something about shrapnel and jabbed an amulet of morphine into Will's thigh, just as the Germans lobbed a round of mortar shells at the American position. Several exploded nearby, briefly throwing light on Will and those around him as the paratroopers instinctively ducked their heads. Too tired to move, Will managed to catch a glimpse of Philippe's face in that passing moment. His features were illuminated, and in that fraction of a second, Will saw how full of innocence he was. He also took in the boy's ghost-white skin tone, and felt a cold, merciless stab in his heart. Even in the fading light, he could see Philippe's lifeless eyes gazing up at the stars.

He wasn't crying anymore.

Chapter 30

The rain had tapered off, the cloudburst chased away by a rising sun just beginning to emerge from the layers of ash-colored clouds that filled the morning sky. Absent the steady tattoo of rain, the basement flat was hushed, save for the soft hum of a small electric fan and the rhythmic ticking of an antique mantle clock.

Kay hadn't said a word throughout Will's narrative, captivated as he recounted those breathtaking minutes in the sodden fields of the Ardennes. His recall was methodical, and of such precision and detail, it was as if the Belgian winter, the chaotic exchange of small-arms fire, and the frenzied shouts in German were alive in her small apartment.

Even if Kay had broken her silence at some point, Will would not have heard her. His own words had drawn him back to southern Belgium like a riptide, evoking dire memories of fallen comrades, unfathomable bloodshed and havoc, and the heart-rending loss of innocent lives. Their tepid coffee sat untouched, forgotten by each the moment he began.

There was little animation at first from Will. His tone was flat, and his words cautious and guarded. As he described the final sequence, she noticed the change in his cadence, the clipped words coming faster and with greater urgency. With the discovery of Philippe's death, Will seemed to deflate like a balloon, his body sagging heavily against the back of his chair. He stared out across the kitchen with despairing eyes, full of grief and guilt.

Will remained like that, quiet and unmoving, until he began absently rubbing his hands together. Hands he had once rabidly tried to wipe Philippe's blood from. It had taken three paratroopers to restrain Will, pinning him to the bottom of the trench until the morphine began to take effect, blunting his hysteria.

Kay was stunned by the extent of his suffering and anguish, and could only watch in fascination as he eased back into the present.

"I am so, so sorry, Will," she said, tender and soft. "I...I don't know what to say."

His face was blank. "What's there to say? He's dead, Kay. And it's my fault."

"Your fault? How can you say that?"

"If I had left him in that schoolhouse, he could have waited until the Germans left. He could have–"

"You don't know that, Will. They found the other villagers, didn't they? Wouldn't they have found him?"

No response.

"You were trying to save his life."

Still only silence from Will, his face remaining impassive, unmoved by her words. She covered his hand with hers.

"You're a good man, Will. It was the war. I'm sure you're not the only–"

"A good man."

"Yes," she nodded emphatically. "A good man."

His voice was full of self-loathing. "I got him killed, Kay. Don't you see?"

"No. I don't see. It was a tragedy, Will, but it was the Germans who pulled the trigger, not you. You can't punish yourself for what they did."

He stood suddenly, slamming both fists on the table.

"CHRIST, DON'T YOU GET IT?" he roared with sudden fury, gesturing wildly with his arms as both coffee cups tumbled to the linoleum floor, the porcelain shattering into pieces.

"Why am I here? Why am I alive? The men in my platoon, the schoolmaster, those villagers. That little boy. They're all dead! They're all dead, and I'm still here. Playing baseball. *Why?* WHY GODDAMN IT?"

She sat rigid in her chair, her eyes locked on the wall behind Will. She had braced herself for his fist, and though it had not come, she remained paralyzed, the vicious eruption too reminiscent of her ex-husband in his most malevolent extremes. It was more than just Will's raw words. It was the acidity behind them, and the stranger, a man she did not know, shouting her down with such venom and bitterness.

And then she saw it. He wasn't a stranger at all. This was, she now realized, a side of Will she had never known existed. One he never revealed to her or anyone else. And behind the invective and explosive rage, she saw now what others might not. A caring man, full of the deepest kind of hurt, fueled by nothing more than a singular compassion for others. For a child. The most endearing of human qualities, obscured by a crushing guilt that was devouring the man she loved.

She met his eyes, and spoke quietly, and calmly.

"Sit down, Will."

He swallowed hard, conscious now of what he had done. What he had said. To her, of all people, the least deserving person of his scorn.

"I should go. I never meant–"

"Sit down," she repeated, her voice firm.

Will nodded in acquiescence.

"I'm sorry, Kay," he said dejectedly, sitting down heavily. She had never seem him look so tired. "I don't know where–"

"Look at me, Will."

His eyes came up, meeting hers.

"Do you have any idea who I am?"

Will stared at her blankly.

"Do you know who I am?"

"I don't need any riddles right now, Kay."

"It's not a riddle, Will." She took a deep breath and exhaled it slowly. "Remember I told you that I had gone to a clinic, and learned I could never have children? I lied about that, Will."

"You what?"

She hesitated for several seconds, and when she finally spoke, it was her voice that was now fraught with emotion. "I didn't need to visit a clinic. I've known for years." She took a deep breath before continuing. "Back when I was dancing, I was with an ensemble in New York. It was one of the most prominent dance companies in the city, and there was a director. He was older and sophisticated. Made promises about my future. Promises in exchange for…favors. I was fifteen, Will, and my parents had spent outrageous sums on private lessons, academic tutors, and everything else a working-class girl from Brooklyn would need to compete against the girls from the Upper West Side, the ones with the fifty-dollar shoes and the private cars. I was suffocating under the pressure, Will. So I did what he asked. What he demanded. It went on for almost a year when I got pregnant."

Will sat back in his chair, floored by the revelation. "Did you tell your parents?"

Kay nodded, a derisive smile on her lips. "My mother. It went over real well. She was upset, to say the least. Upset, mind you, that I allowed myself to get pregnant, not that I had given up my virginity to a man more than twice my age. He could have put me on Broadway, after all. And after years of investing their lives in my dance career, Mother wasn't going to let—what did she call it?—a *development* like that interfere with their plans for the future. So she took me to a man calling himself a doctor in Queens, paid him in cash. Problem solved. Only it wasn't. There were complications, more than you want to hear. I ended up hospitalized for two months. All topped off by the notice I received from the company that I wasn't welcomed back. The director, of course, was worried about his reputation, so he blackballed me all over the city, spreading fabricated stories about my temperament and work ethic. That's a death sentence in the dance world. I was finished in New York."

"That's why you stopped dancing."

She nodded glumly.

They were both quiet until Will finally spoke, his voice betraying his disgust.

"I think your mother should meet my father."

She smiled, taking his hands in hers again. "Here is why I'm telling you this, Will. My life has to be about so much more than what happened to me all those years ago. Yes, I have my regrets, but I won't let that sorry episode, or the mistake I made in marrying Eddie to escape my parents, define my life. So here is who I am. My name is Katherine Ellen Maddux and I'm twenty-six years old. I love walking in the snow. I enjoy reading classical literature, as you know, but I also have a secret fetish for dime store detective novels. Keep that mum, please. I'm an abysmal cook, and you should never, ever let me near an oven. And do you know what my dream is? My life aspiration? You've never asked me, and I've never told anyone this, but I'll tell you anyway. It's a simple one. To one day have a man who loves me enough to take me out for a night of dinner and dancing. Even if he hates dancing. Especially if he hates dancing. Because that man would know I used to dance, and how much I loved it. The dinner would be nothing fancy, maybe someplace just like Siegel's Deli, where we could talk about everything in life that matters, and maybe some things that don't. I don't know everything about you, Will Jamison, but I know enough. And even though I know enough, I want to know more. I want to know everything. I know how hard it is for you to open up to me. But you need to understand, that knowing everything about who you are won't make me love you any less. It will, I believe, make me love you even more."

Will could not speak, overpowered by her words.

"I'm here," he finally whispered, not trusting his voice, "because you're all I have. All that matters. If I lose you, I have nothing."

She shook her head in bemusement. "You're not going to lose me. And what do you mean you have nothing? You have your brother, your father, your baseball career–"

"I have nothing," he repeated, more stiffly. "And fuck baseball."

Kay was quiet, the declaration a surprise. She had thought the game was everything to him. As it was to her ex-husband and every other ballplayer she had ever crossed paths with. But there was no mistaking the resolve and certainty in his voice. He wasn't just blurting out impulsive notions.

"You mean after this season?"

"I mean now. I'm done, Kay. I need to do something more with my life. Right now."

"Your contract–"

"I'll tear it up. Give Griffith his money back. Whatever I have to do. I'm finished playing. I have to do something else."

Kay nodded approvingly. "Okay, then. I was getting a little tired of following your life through box scores anyways." She cocked her head. "Do something else...like what?"

"I don't know. I need to figure that out."

"Maybe we can figure that out together."

"Maybe you need to walk away from me."

She shook her head, amused he still didn't see it.

"I want to share a secret with you, Will."

"Another one?"

"This seems to be the day for it," she admitted, rising from her chair and moving to his side of the table. She kneeled before him, placing her hands on his again. "*You*, are all *I* have. And want. You're going to marry me, Will Jamison. Marry, not date. I'm not girlfriend material, and I need to get this marriage thing right. You think I care whether you play baseball or not? I don't, I promise you. And I don't care where we live or what we do. I just know that we're going to be with each other for the rest of our lives."

It was his first smile in some time. "Are you proposing to me?"

Her eyes glimmered. "Maybe I am. I deserve it, Will. I deserve you. The real you. The one who's just like the rest of us humans. We've both lived through life's cruelties. We've suffered alone, and we've survived alone. But I want to be done with just surviving. I want to live again. I want to love again. And I want someone to love me."

Will sat back, marveling at Kay's passion. It was hardly the first time she had left dazed him like this, and he considered how uncommon she was. More thoughtful than any woman he had ever known, and, he now understood, possessed by the sort of inner strength he had always sought for himself. He felt the recurring pull of self-doubt, wondering how a woman of such caliber could possibly wish to tether herself to a man like him. But there wasn't even a trace of uncertainty in her voice. She wanted him. She loved him. And she was offering him what only a fortunate few had, and what so many others spent a lifetime searching for. And in that moment, Will knew. He would not become one of those others. He could not possibly let this woman go.

"Tell her everything," he said, eyes locked on hers and his face set in determination.

"Huh?"

"The shrink I saw. He said if I had a girl, one I loved, to tell her everything."

"I like this shrink. Do you have a girl you love?"

He looked at her, with as much purpose as he had ever felt in his life, and without the weight of a single chip on his shoulders.

"Very much so."

She squeezed his hands. "You know what that sounds like, Will?"

"What?"

"A you and a me. And an after."

Epilogue

It was past noon now and quiet again, the hum of the small tractor no longer carrying across the youth baseball fields. The groundskeeper had eased it into a storage shed on the far side of the complex, his work complete.

"Difficult to believe that was almost sixty years ago," Kay said softly, still adrift in distant memories as she stared off toward the cloud-filled horizon. She blinked her eyes, forcing herself back into the present, and smiled at her visitor.

"Well, Mr. Maloney, I hope that fills in some of the picture. Was it worth the long journey from Washington?"

Maloney shook his head. "Are you kidding? I would have flown to Tanzania to hear all that."

She laughed. "I'm impressed you found me out here in the Oregon wilderness. May I ask how?"

"It wasn't easy. Jimmy Hoffa would have been an easier find. We have people at the paper who do this sort of thing, much better at it than I am. Checked every database they could put their hands on. Financial records, Social Security, the VA. Hell, we even checked the criminal stuff, looking for arrests, DUIs, anything. Zilch. So I hit the family trees. The closest I came were your nieces, Will's brother's kids. They knew something, I was sure of it, but they wouldn't say a word. I have to admit, the more this became a dead end, the more intrigued I got. So I gumshoed it. Tracked down former teammates, men your husband fought with in Europe–"

"Any luck?"

"Tons. His old platoon leader passed away twenty years ago–"

"Ira Lucas."

"Yes, Ira Lucas. But I spoke at length with one of their squad leaders, Edward Janikowski. He's retired now, a former justice on the Illinois Supreme Court, if you can believe it. And Dick Holloway, of course. Heard the same story over and over again—your husband was a walking thesaurus of accolades. But no one, not a single soul, knew where he was."

"Case closed?"

"Yup, for Will Jamison," Maloney said, pausing. "For Will Maddux, different story."

He eyed her carefully when he said this, waiting for a denial, perhaps even feigned misunderstanding. He came prepared with photocopies of the legal documents from the Multnomah County Clerk's office, just in case. Documents that had been unsealed after the requisite fifty years. But Kay's reaction was mostly muted. If anything, there was a touch of approval in her eyes.

"Very good, Mr. Maloney. How did you unearth our little secret? And how did you trace me to Portland?"

"Through your first husband."

She furrowed her brow. "He's been dead for forty years."

"Yep. Died in 1963, early liver cancer. Apparently the man liked to drink."

"Apparently," she repeated, dryly.

"And with all that drinking, he had forgotten to change the beneficiary on a life insurance policy he had taken out when he was with the Yankees."

Kay raised her eyebrows, impressed, then suddenly frowned. "You know I didn't keep the money."

"Yes, I know. But his new wife in New York wasn't exactly delighted that your name was on that policy. Went to the local papers, made it sound like you were keeping food from her starving children."

Kay rolled her eyes. "That woman was the heiress to a family brokerage. No one was starving in that house. Still, I didn't want the money. I signed the check over and sent it to her."

"Which is exactly what the *New York Daily News* reported. And that the check was returned from Kay Maddux, of Portland, Oregon."

She clapped her hands together. "Ah, bravo, Mr. Maloney. And here you are."

"And here I am."

"That is some remarkable—what did you call it?—gumshoe work. My apologies for the subterfuge. My husband spent his entire life avoiding the press. We moved all the way out here, 2,800 miles from Washington, for that very purpose."

"Yet you agreed to meet me."

"I almost hung up on you. But you were the first one to call after all this time. I see you have no tape recorder, or even a pad of paper. No book, Mr. Maloney? Everyone is writing a book these days. Some say my husband's story might make an interesting tale."

"From what I've cobbled together so far, it would probably win a Pulitzer. No, Mrs. Maddux, this isn't anything I want to write about. I thought learning more about what your husband went through might answer a question or two I wish I could put to my father if he were here."

"Some of it we went through together." She took a deep breath before continuing. "He hit me, Mr. Maloney. Open-faced slaps, sometimes. The kind you can hear from a block away. Split my lip open once."

Maloney blinked, startled by the admission. "I'm sorry, truly sorry, to hear that. I didn't know." Maloney paused. "Did you ever consider leaving him? Will, that is."

"Leaving him?"

"Yes."

Kay sat back in her chair, folding her arms across her chest. "I had two husbands, Mr. Maloney. Both were baseball players, both had explosive tempers, and both struck me with their hands. But they could not have been two more contrasting men. There was a darkness to Eddie. He enjoyed violence, and sought it out. Will was the polar opposite. There was violence in him, but it was rooted in something very different, something I could never understand." She thought for a few moments. "We were two very broken people back then, Mr. Maloney. I consider it a miracle that our paths crossed. You've heard the term soul mate. Will and I were always soul mates. It just took some time, and a war, for us both to appreciate it. And after all that, do you really think I would have ever considered leaving him?"

Maloney smiled. "I did some checking here, locally, in the Portland area. Your husband was quite a figure in this community."

Her eyes sparkled, the pride evident. "What did you learn?"

"The man was a hell of a baseball coach. Maybe even a better coach than a player. Hired into the Portland school system as a physical education instructor when you first moved out here. Started coaching the freshman team at Madison High, then took over a varsity squad that hadn't won a game in nearly two years. Went on to win twenty-four city titles and four state championships, I believe. Retired in 1980. First ballot, Oregon High School Athletic Hall of Fame. And no one here, I presume, ever knew who he really was."

"Well done, Mr. Maloney. You don't miss a thing."

"Maybe," Maloney suggested, "he found some sort of peace or healing being with those kids."

"Maybe. Will was a fighter. Whatever was attacking his mind after he returned, he fought back as best he could. He gave up drinking when we got married, same with smoking. He saw therapists, and they tried, they really did. I think it helped for him to talk about things, things he wasn't always comfortable discussing with me. But they couldn't stop the nightmares, and they couldn't erase the memories of all he had seen, and done."

She leaned toward him. "But here is what I want you to know, Mr. Maloney, and why I was willing to meet with you this morning. Whatever his war experience did to Will's mind, know that my husband was incredibly good-hearted. He was full of gentleness and humor, and as brave a man as ever to wear a uniform. I know that all sounds like such a contradiction. He hit me after all, on occasion, and it hurt. But he was fighting demons that you and I couldn't possibly understand. And you know what, Mr. Maloney? I can take a hit."

Maloney smiled at her. "I bet you can." He swept his eyes across the sports complex. "You said on the phone this place was special to your husband. Why?"

Kay nodded. "Our house is right down the street. These fields opened in the spring of '48, and we started coming here almost every weekday afternoon in the summertime to watch the kids play. I sat here, on this very patch of grass, with my books, but Will, he watched every contest is if it was the deciding game of the World Series. It brought him such joy. Those kids grew up right in front of our eyes." She waited a few moments, another memory surfacing. "Do you know what else he did? About once a month, he would take me out for an evening of dancing at our local supper club."

Maloney raised an eyebrow. "Your husband liked to dance?"

Her smile was positively gleeful. "No, he hated it." Kay tapped him on the knee. "Does any of this help you, Mr. Maloney?"

"Very much so," he said, rising to his feet. "And I think you've told me more than enough. This is my first trip to Portland, and my flight isn't until morning. Maybe I'll catch up on my sightseeing."

"Make sure you visit Powell's Books downtown. And we have wonderful museums."

Maloney took one last look around. The groundskeeper had finished mowing for the day, pulling the shed door closed and fastening a padlock.

"Looks like they're closing up," Maloney said, gesturing toward the shed in the distance. "Are you staying? I can give you a lift home."

"I'll stay a bit longer. And these legs could use the exercise." She held out her hand. "I enjoyed meeting you, Mr. Maloney."

He squeezed it gently and smiled. "Thank you for sharing these things. It means a great deal to me."

"You're very welcome. I mean that. Whatever you're searching for, I sincerely hope you find it."

He gave a slight bow and began trekking back to the Taurus. He had his car door open and one foot inside when he looked back at Kay, still seated in her chair, thumbing through an open book. He groaned when he saw her husband's old chair, embarrassed he hadn't disassembled it before leaving. He was halfway back to the crest of the hill when he spotted the groundskeeper crossing the freshly trimmed outfield, directly toward where Kay was sitting.

More like plodding. The man's gait was short and deliberate. Maloney could see he was tall and thick-chested, but it was the ball cap, with white hair peeking out from underneath, that froze the reporter in place. The blue was mostly faded, but the white "W" stitched on the front stood out clear as day.

Maloney continued to the crest, and just as before, Kay turned in her seat.

"Mr. Maloney," she said, and this time there was alarm in her voice. "Did you forget something?"

"I came back to put away the chair. But maybe we should leave it out. That's a long walk for him."

"I don't understand," she said, casting a quick glance at the groundskeeper, who had reached the middle of the infield and was slowly drawing closer.

"I didn't put it together at first," Maloney said, gesturing to the aluminum cane hooked onto the backrest of her chair. "A walker and a cane. Who would use both?"

She could no longer hold back another merry smile. "He refuses to use the cane. I bring it anyway." She shook her head. "As I said, you don't miss a thing, Mr. Maloney. I'm sorry–"

Maloney gave her a dismissive wave. "No apologies, Mrs. Maddux. Your husband deserves his privacy. And his peace. But please let him know, I truly am an admirer."

They exchanged warm, appreciative smiles, and Maloney turned and started back for his car.

A few minutes later, the Ford Taurus had disappeared down the access road, and the groundskeeper lowered himself into his old chair with a sigh, wiping his moist temples with a handkerchief as he stretched out his long legs. He rubbed the usual tender spot on the back of the left one, unwilling as always to admit the obvious.

"That the newsman from Washington?"

"It was. A nice man. Seemed to know quite a lot about you."

"Reporters," Will grunted. "Couldn't find their peckers if they had a flashlight and a map."

He drank from the bottle of water she handed him. "I'm getting too old for this, Kay. They need someone else to cut the damn grass."

"You said that twenty years ago, mister."

"And now I'm twenty years older. Remember Joseph Redfeather?

"Is that a real name?"

"He played for me in '48 on the freshman team. Short, Indian kid with–"

"Yes, yes, I remember Joseph. He was your best pitcher back then."

Will grunted. "He was my only pitcher back then. I got an email from him on the Yahoo this morning."

Kay tried not to laugh. She loved it when he called it that.

"And how is Joseph Redfeather these days?"

"He's a great-grandfather, that's how he is. A great-grandfather!"

She smiled, enjoying the mock annoyance in Will's voice. He was always so sensitive about his age, and though Will was trying to frame his point in humor, she knew what weighed heavily on him. What weighed heavily on anyone their age. The idea that time, and life itself, was slipping away from them.

"Will, do you ever have any regrets about us?"

He looked at her curiously. "Like?"

"Children."

Will frowned. "Kay, I wasn't saying–"

"I know, sweetie, I know. But certainly you've wondered sometimes what it would be like–"

"Kay."

"–if I had been able to–"

"Kay, stop."

He covered her hand with his. "People our age, we could spend every hour of every day asking ourselves those 'what if' questions. I've thought about them. A lot. What if I hadn't enlisted after Pearl? What if I hadn't left the team back in '42, or '46? How long would I have played? Would the nightmares..."

His voice trailed off, and then he quickly recovered.

"And you, what if you hadn't quit dancing? Maybe there is some other existence out there, where I played baseball for another ten years, and you became a Rockette or something like that. What do you think the chances are I'd be sitting here, across from you, my bride of almost sixty years, still wondering after all this time how and why I got to be the luckiest fellow in the world?"

"Curse you, Will Jamison," she said, her eyes glistening. "For a man who could barely piece together a coherent sentence when we first met, you sure have learned how to charm a girl."

"Well, we've come a long way since that pot of coffee at Siegel's."

"Luckiest fellow. That's what has always awed me about you. That after everything you went through, that you're still so positive. About everything. And that you would consider yourself a lucky man. Do you really, Will? Consider yourself lucky?"

Her eyes were searching him intently, but that was hardly new. The question was though, and he considered his answer. She was right, as usual. The things he had seen, the things he had done, were more than any human should have to bear. What had come of men named Delgado, Meyer, and Amand. So many other names and faces he would never forget. Including a boy named Philippe Dupard, who never saw past age 12.

Will knew his history, so he thought of others too. The 24 million Russian soldiers and civilians who perished in the war. The two million Jews gassed at Auschwitz and Treblinka. Hiroshima and Nagasaki. The list was endless.

"Will?"

He turned to her, their eyes connecting just as they had that very first time at Siegel's, and every day they had been together since. And just like that, he wasn't thinking of untold deaths from a generation ago, or the horrifying memories and images he still could not escape half a century later.

She always brought him back, her presence a reminder of all that life had given him these last many decades. A reminder of not only those who had brought such joy and fulfillment to his existence, but also what he may have meant to others. A reminder, and a validation, that the path he chose so many years ago did indeed give his life purpose and meaning.

He reached out and laced his fingers with hers, then pulled the worn ball cap low over his eyes. Tilting his head back, he closed his eyes, ready for a bit of shut-eye, as he basked in the balminess of the late morning sun and the soothing touch of her even warmer skin.

"Luckier than most, Kay," he said, so faintly she could barely hear him. "Luckier than most."

ACKNOWLEDGMENTS

To my family—Stephanie, Maddie and Ben—I cannot express enough love and gratitude for your unwavering encouragement, support, and patience these last few years. These pages simply would not be possible without all of you in my corner, and I am so fortunate to be surrounded by such a spirited, fun-loving trio each and every day.

Where would I be without my three early readers? Retired Marine Neal Duckworth, whose insights and perspective were so invaluable, and without that magical Rolodex, I'm not sure what would have become of my final manuscript. Bernie Weisberger—veteran, scholar, mensch—who so generously shared his reflections on the World War II era and his personal experiences as a young soldier. May your beloved Cubs win one more for you. And Elizabeth Abrams, always ready and willing to offer reassurances and course corrections when they were needed most. Her contributions, as usual, strengthened this story immeasurably.

I am forever indebted to those I spoke to and those who have written about their personal experiences with post-traumatic stress. What I learned from each of you was instrumental in shaping the core of my protagonist, articulating his post-war struggles, and providing an authenticity that was imperative to the book. I have so much admiration and respect for your willingness to speak and write openly about what you have endured and lived with, so we can all better understand the challenges our returning servicemen and women face now and in the future.

To others, including Vic Weiss, Patrick Labella, and Kerin Colson, who lent me their expertise and other assistance as needed, thank you for coloring in small but critical pieces of this story.

A special thanks to Reg Jans, an extraordinary battlefield guide and trove of information who is a daily fixture in the Ardennes. Reg has dedicated himself not only to further educating World War II aficionados like myself about the Battle of the Bulge, but guiding the many veterans and their families who have made the journey to southern Belgium to retrace past footsteps and honor those who played their small part. Reg is an exceptional storyteller, and the day he introduced me to the mostly unheralded exploits of the 10th Armored Division was the day the final puzzle piece for this book fell into place.

And finally, my stellar publishing team, Dale and Julia Dye of Warriors Publishing Group. Dale will never know what it meant to hear his initial response to my manuscript. It is somewhat daunting and unnerving to attempt to write such things when you have never worn the uniform or been anywhere near the sights and sounds of a blood-soaked battlefield. The antidote to this, of course, is research, research, and more research. Still, it wasn't until I heard the validation from Dale that I finally exhaled, relieved to know I had managed to strike the right chords. Julia, a kindred Wisconsin spirit, spent so many weeks, days, and hours managing the editing and production process, and somehow still found time to answer my persistent questions and educate me on the virtues of the Oxford Comma. Endless gratitude to this pair.

While this story is a work of fiction, and I'm certainly no trained historian, my aim was to depict the events of December 1944 as accurately as possible. Most of the characters in this story are invented, but there are two noteworthy exceptions: William Desobry was indeed the 26-year-old officer who led the small American force in Noville. He survived his wounds and subsequent capture by the Germans and went on to a remarkable military career, including command of the famed 1st Armored Division ("Old Ironsides") and retirement as a lieutenant general. Baseball Hall of Famer Bob Feller will be a familiar name to many. He was one of the rare players from that era who not only volunteered for military service in the early days of the war, but served in an actual combat zone.

My family and closest friends are fully aware of the lifetime affection and admiration I hold for our World War II veterans. Those I had the privilege to spend time with in my early professional career provided the inspiration for everything I have achieved in my life. With every ounce of energy and emotion I poured into this story, my fingers were crossed that I was honoring those men rightfully, and doing justice to their experiences that were often far different than what has been portrayed in so much of our literature and popular films. They deserve no less.

Andy Kutler
March 2019

ABOUT THE AUTHOR

Andy Kutler is an award-winning author living in Arlington, Virginia. A native of Madison, Wisconsin and a graduate of Michigan State University (B.A.) and Georgetown University (M.A.), he has previously worked on the senior legislative staff of two United States Senators before serving as a senior policy officer with the U.S. Secret Service. He is serving today as a senior policy adviser and strategic communications consultant to the national security community.

The Other Side of Life was Andy's first published novel. It was awarded the **Bronze Medal** (Military & Wartime Fiction) from the 2016 Independent Publishers Book Awards, and **Honorable Mention** (War & Military Fiction) from Foreword Magazine's 2016 INDIEFAB Awards. Andy has also written extensively for the *Huffington Post* and the *Milwaukee Journal Sentinel*.

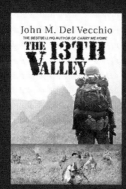

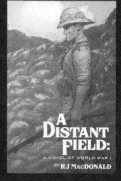

38789455R00179

Made in the USA
Middletown, DE
11 March 2019